M000275777

# THICKER THAN BLOOD

## BY DON BROBST

THICKER THAN BLOOD BY DON BROBST
Lamplighter Mysteries and Suspense is an imprint of LPC Books
a division of Iron Stream Media
100 Missionary Ridge, Birmingham, AL 35242

ISBN: 978-1-64526-256-5
Copyright © 2020 by Don Brobst
Cover design by Elaina Lee
Interior design by Karthick Srinivasan

Available in print from your local bookstore, online, or from the publisher at:
ShopLPC.com

For more information on this book and the author visit: www.donbrobst.com

Brought to you by the creative team at Lighthouse Publishing of the Carolinas
(LPCBooks.com): Eddie Jones, Ramona Richards, Shonda Savage;

Library of Congress Cataloging-in-Publication Data
Brobst, Don.
Thicker Than Blood / Don Brobst 1st ed.

Printed in the United States of America

# PRAISE FOR *THICKER THAN BLOOD*

"Don Brobst cuts a blazing swath from the Pyramids of Egypt to the Gold Coast of Chicago in this techno-thriller. His expertise in medicine, the Intelligence community, and data communications leads the reader to a surprise ending."

~ Joseph Courtemanche
Author of *Assault on Saint Agnes and Nicholas of Haiti*

*To my children, who never stopped believing in me.*
*And to my wife, who never wondered if I was on the right side.*

# ACKNOWLEDGMENTS

Special thanks to the dedicated men and women of the CIA and FBI who place their lives on the line every day. I will forever be in your debt.

# PROLOGUE

---

As the nearby mosque echoed the afternoon call to prayer, he stood, walked to the balcony doors and admired the hundreds of minarets between him and the Nile. The echoes of imams calling for prayer beckoned him, but he finally closed the doors. He'd pray later.

Returning to his laptop, he perused the possibilities through several pages until he'd finalized his selection—five-two, blond hair, blue eyes, cheerleader, American.

A smile coursed his lips, and his pulse quickened at the thought of it. There'd be no recourse. His action would be final. The funds withdrawn from his account.

He hit "Enter."

# CHAPTER ONE

D r. Bailey Pogue took a seat to the right of his friend Connor Banks as he'd been instructed. Connor's attorney placed two binders on the table in front of Pogue, then sat on Connor's left.

Across the table, two attorneys sat on either side of Mr. Wiggins, Connor's ex-business partner in his accounting firm. An unidentified man settled into a chair against the wall.

A court reporter connected her stenography machine to a laptop, while a videographer on the other end of the room adjusted his camera and double-checked microphones.

The mahogany shelves filled with books on case law lined the conference room of the Dirksen Federal Building in Chicago. Paintings of presiding judges reminded everyone this was hallowed ground.

The judge entered and everyone stood. He sat and motioned for them to take their seats.

"I'm Judge Maxwell, federal district court judge of Cook County. We've gathered today to hear arguments for allegations against Mr. Connor Banks from his former practice partner and the Securities and Exchange Commission. I remind everyone these allegations are serious, potentially resulting in jail time if Mr. Banks is found guilty. Mr. Wiggins also faces sanctions including suspension of his license and imprisonment if his actions are determined to fall outside trading regulations of the SEC. The gentleman to my right who will not testify today represents SEC interests."

Pogue wiped his sweaty palms on his thighs. He couldn't imagine being on the receiving end of such an intense legal battle. He'd only known Connor for two months, but somehow, they'd become more than racquetball buddies. Connor's sister, Ginger, worked in Pogue's building and had mentioned Pogue's unique abilities to memorize large quantities of information, and now he was helping his new friend in a way he'd never imagined.

Connor leaned toward Pogue and whispered, "You sure you got this?"

Pogue offered a faint smile. "I got it."

The night before over egg rolls and Kung Pao Chicken, Connor had voiced his concerns when Pogue told him he'd committed over four hundred pages of testimony and documents to memory—an ability he'd been born with. By quickly scanning written materials, he formed photographic/eidetic images in his mind that he could retrieve at will, enabling him to assimilate detailed data.

For the first two hours, Wiggins' attorneys questioned Connor on everything from his background and education to career choices in the stock exchange and glowing success as a high-end investor. Finally, they focused on who ordered the selling of a prominent client's portfolio.

When Mr. Wiggins had found himself in SEC crosshairs several months earlier, he'd quickly placed the blame on Connor and lawyered up. The plea bargain into which Wiggins entered included offering testimony against his former partner.

"Did you order anyone in your firm to trade DGB—Donner, Gwen and Branson stocks, Mr. Banks?" the lead attorney for Wiggins asked.

"Yes," Connor said.

"Did you have inside information that their stock may indeed drop due to the legal issues that were to be levied on January twenty-sixth of last year?"

"I did."

"So you acted on that information and told Mr. Wiggins, who knew nothing about your inside information, to sell those stocks before they plummeted the next day," the attorney accused.

"No, sir. I did no such thing," Connor said.

"You just told us that you took action."

"Not in that manner."

"So you didn't make your decision from that information?"

"That's correct. I did not. That would be considered insider trading, which is illegal."

The attorney leaned to his client, Mr. Wiggins, who whispered something to him. The attorney spoke. "Knowing that it would cost your client hundreds of thousands of dollars, you did nothing?"

"It would have cost him three-quarters of a million. That's correct. I did nothing at the time of which you are speaking," Connor said.

"Your former business partner says you ordered him to sell six thousand shares of DGB from your client's portfolio on January twenty-fifth, one day prior to the DGB scandal that caused its value plunge, which prevented your client a devastating blow."

Connor was silent.

"Well?" the attorney pressed.

"Well, what? I didn't hear a question, Counselor," Connor's attorney said.

"Did you or did you not tell Mr. Wiggins to sell that stock, Mr. Banks?"

"Excuse me," Pogue said. "I understand I've been given permission to speak."

"Remember you are under oath, Dr. Pogue," the attorney stated.

"Yes, sir. In Mr. Wiggins' deposition, he reported that Connor told him to sell all of their client's DGB stock."

"Thank you for making my argument even more specific, Doctor," he said smugly.

"The problem is that supporting documents from Mr. Wiggins' deposition taken on July seventh of this year don't correlate with what you're now saying."

"Would you care to enlighten us?"

"With His Honor's permission, I'd be happy to." Pogue turned to the judge.

"You may proceed, Doctor. Understand that you must be specific in your comments, and the material must be relevant. You're not here as a character witness."

"I understand. Thank you, Your Honor." Pogue turned to Wiggins' attorney and placed his hand on the binders in front of him without opening them. "If you wouldn't mind, review page two-oh-seven of your client's deposition." Pogue gave the attorneys time to leaf to the location. The judge did the same. "Mr. Wiggins refers to an email sent by Connor Banks ordering him to sell all DGB stocks in the client's portfolio on January twenty-fifth."

"As we just stated, Dr. Pogue. This is—"

"You'll find the item he referred to on page two-oh-seven, documented as Exhibit Forty-seven on page three ninety-eight." They leafed to the page. "If you'll examine Exhibit Forty-seven, it is indeed an email from Connor instructing Mr. Wiggins to sell those stocks, but on the electronic time-and-date stamp, the email was sent on January eighteenth, one week prior to the date you allege, and eight days prior to the earliest news of the breaking scandal. The lawsuit from DGB had not even been filed by January eighteenth, according to evidence submitted by you on Exhibit Sixty-six, page four seventeen."

"That's not correct," the attorney said.

"It's in your own records, sir," Pogue insisted. "Please refer to those pages."

"Let the record show that Dr. Pogue is correct," the judge said after reviewing the binders.

"Why would Banks order the sale prior to having knowledge of this impending lawsuit?" the attorney asked.

"A question for him, sir," Pogue responded.

"I had a hunch, as I often do," Connor responded. "If you'll examine my own portfolio, I held five hundred shares of DGB stocks, but I didn't sell my own. Would I not, if I was involved in insider trading?"

"Then why didn't you?" the attorney pressed. "Were you attempting to redirect attention from you toward Mr. Wiggins?"

"No," Connor said. "My client's portfolio's risk estimate documented by him on those funds was rated as low-to-medium. My own portfolio has been rated as high risk from day one. My choice. I rode the storm and lost—in this particular case. I couldn't take that chance with a low-to-medium-risk client. I had to sell when I first became concerned with market fluctuations."

Pogue pointed to the binders in front of the attorneys. "On page one hundred eighty-seven, Mr. Wiggins noted that he had no personal holdings at risk. *No dog in the fight*, in his words. But according to SEC documentation of Mr. Banks' firm's trading, your client sold two hundred personal shares of DGB stock on January twenty-fifth by brokering it through Mr. Banks' firm. But make no mistake. It was Mr. Wiggins' personal stock from a private LLC registered to him."

"You can't prove that." The attorney slammed the binder closed. The judge didn't.

"Exhibit Sixty-eight, page four nineteen is a fourteen-page SEC certified summary of stocks traded that day by The Banks Firm. They reveal the transaction took place at 2:37 p.m."

"I don't recall—" Wiggins' attorney began.

"Look it up, Counselor," Connor's attorney said. "We are done here—unless you have any more questions? Perhaps one or two more might bury your client deeper than you've already managed to do here today."

"I have one more for Dr. Pogue." The attorney slapped the binders with his hand and stood across the table from him. "You've implied that my client contradicted himself. You mentioned one or two items that I am certain could be explained away with a bit of due diligence and—"

"Sit down," the judge interrupted. "There will be no further aggression in my presence."

"Yes, Your Honor." The attorney sat.

Pogue turned to Connor's attorney. He nodded his approval for him to speak. "Your client contradicted himself seventeen times within the body of the deposition alone, counselor. In addition, there are five conflicting accounts between what he stated under oath in his deposition and what the attached exhibits reveal. Those may be found in chronological order with the first on page forty-seven, the second on page sixty-nine, the third on eighty-one, the fourth on ninety-eight, the fifth—"

"That's quite enough." Wiggins' counselor slammed his fist down.

"If anyone pounds on this table it will be me," the judge said. "Once more and I'll hold you in contempt. Do I make myself clear?"

"Yes, Your Honor."

The judge turned to Mr. Wiggins. "I will thoroughly evaluate the contradictions Dr. Pogue has outlined." He turned to Pogue. "Do you have them documented?"

Pogue nodded. "Yes, Your Honor. I've prepared them for you."

Connor's attorney walked to the judge and handed him the document. He offered one to Wiggins' attorney as well.

"Mark this as Exhibit One," the judge said to the court reporter, then turned to Wiggins. "If I find these contradictions to be accurate, you will be held accountable. All charges against you will be reinstated. No plea bargain."

The judge turned to Connor. "Mr. Banks, if these documents withstand my scrutiny, all charges against you will be dropped. Is that acceptable to the SEC?" He looked at the man to his right, who nodded.

The judge stood. "Very well. We are done here." He left the room.

# CHAPTER TWO

*Two years later*

The small rubber ball bounced off the polished glass with a *chirp* as Pogue's friend scrambled to return it. Connor, still not quite his equal on the courts, sent the projectile on a path beyond his reach—almost.

Pogue's deadly backswing rendered a satisfying *pock* that echoed inside the glass enclosure. Adrenaline burned in his veins as he watched the ball ricochet off the glass and whistle past Connor's head.

Connor grunted and shook it off, twirling his racquet in his hand. "Thought I had you that time. I can't believe you made that shot. Nice backhand." He took a crouched stance, preparing for the next serve. "Go."

Pogue served, and Connor drove it with a vengeance into the end wall.

Pogue dove—the tip of his racquet connecting with the ball as he landed on his side and slid across the floor, his sweaty skin squeaking like tennis shoes on a basketball court.

Connor raised his arms in victory as the wayward sphere bounced off the floor, inches short of the wall. "You okay down there, buddy?"

Pogue grimaced from his position on the floor. "I'm fine. Good game. The next one is mine."

"I've heard that before. For what it's worth, that was a valiant attempt." Connor reached for Pogue's hand, snatched him to his feet, and gave him a friendly punch on the shoulder.

The temperature in the enclosure seemed to have risen twenty degrees since they'd started. Pogue wiped his brow with his forearm and walked to his water bottle in the corner. When Connor's sister, Ginger, had introduced the men over two years earlier, not long before Connor's trial, she'd indicated her brother was a lonely bachelor without purpose outside of the stock market who loved racquetball as much as Pogue. But he quickly learned the truth about his friend. Bachelor, yes. *Lonely*—not even close. Connor's charismatic personality, combined with his wealth and handsome features, provided him a crowd wherever he went. And he seemed to know every influential businessman and politician in Chicago. Still, a vortex of mystery swirled about him.

"Janelle's fifteenth birthday is in two weeks." Pogue chugged his water and threw a towel around his neck.

"Fifteen? Seriously?"

Pogue shook his head, recalling the day he'd put her on the school bus for the first time. Seemed like weeks ago, not years. "Jenni and I would like you to come to a little party if you're free that night."

"I appreciate the invite." Connor practiced his backswing in the empty air. "I don't want to impose on your family time, though."

Pogue had always appreciated Connor's regard for family. It must have run deep in his life at some point—though neither he nor Ginger ever talked about it.

"You're family to us. And it was Jenni's suggestion."

"In that case, I'd be happy to come. Thank her for me and don't forget to text me the date and time so I can put it on my calendar."

"Have you considered starting your own family?" Ever since the trial almost two years ago, Pogue still only had snippets of his friend's backstory he'd pieced together. Connor came from serious money, was extremely successful, and played his cards close to the vest. But he seemed comfortable with kids—at least Pogue's kids.

"I've thought about settling down someday." Connor bounced the ball several times before tossing it into his bag. "But it's difficult to find someone who tolerates my habits."

"Habits?"

"Expensive and spoiled."

Pogue grinned. "Expensive, I knew. One of your suits costs more than my car, and your car costs more than my house."

"That's the tip of the 'berg. I like nice things. I've lived that way since I was a kid. Hence the *spoiled* part of my self-description."

Pogue glanced at the clock on the wall outside the glass enclosure. "Let's hit the showers and grab some lunch. I have patients this afternoon."

The men gathered their belongings before leaving the court and headed down the corridor toward the locker room. The cool air of the hallway made breathing easier.

"I don't want to be presumptuous"—Pogue dropped the empty water bottle into the recycle bin—"but how did you do with that investment you were excited about?"

"Really well." Connor grinned. "Couldn't be more pleased. My investors are happy, too. I wish you'd been one of them."

"So do I." Pogue gave a heavy sigh.

"How are you coming along with your ... you know ... finances?"

"I'm deeper than I've ever been." Pogue's stomach tied in a knot. He'd dreaded this conversation. "I'm even tight with what I owe you. But I'm pulling shifts in the ER and telling Jenni it's for our future—which it is. But I'm in a vise. That being said, I have a cashier's check with me today payable to you for the first installment of ten thousand."

Connor nodded. "I can't help but feel responsible. I got you into this with that stupid game I roped you into after the trial. And when you needed more money, I should have seen the warning signs and put the brakes on. I didn't realize gambling was an issue for you. If I'd kept my mouth shut you wouldn't be in this fix."

"I could have said no. But it was so easy to get back into the feel of it when we made as much as we did on that game." Pogue shook his head. "If Jenni found out I'd lost so much since then ... I went through our retirement fund."

"All of it?"

"Plus what I owe you. But like I said, paying you back is the first priority."

"Have you gotten your gambling under control?"

"I won't say it doesn't pull at me. I see what looks like a sure thing, and now I realize that doesn't exist. I haven't gambled in six months, and I installed a program on my laptop that keeps me from getting on those sites."

"That's a good step. We all make mistakes. What's your timeline for paying back what you owe me?"

"Ten thousand a month over the next fifteen months, starting today."

Connor waited for several club members to pass before speaking. "Listen. You pulled me from the jaws of hell almost two years ago. I haven't forgotten what you did in front of that judge. We'll get through this. I know you want to pay me back first. But you and Jenni have the kind of marriage other people dream of. Do not let her find out the money is gone, and don't let this mistake define the rest of your life. You're doing the right thing by working for your money instead of trying to win it back." He took a long drink. "Does she look at your bank statements?"

"She does. She asked about the missing money."

"What did you say?"

"I told her I invested it through you."

"She thinks I have it? That I'm earning interest for you?"

He nodded.

"God, Pogue. The first order of business is to keep this from her until you're able to put the funds back."

"I can't borrow that kind of money from the bank, or she'll know. I'm probably tapped out with them anyway."

"Does anyone else know?"

Pogue pushed open the locker room door. "Not a soul." He tossed his bag near the locker.

"Let's talk over lunch. I have something to run by you, too."

"You okay?" His curiosity piqued. Connor wasn't one to ask favors.

"I'm fine. Just something you might find interesting, especially considering what we're talking about."

"Now you definitely have my attention." Pogue checked the time again. "How about Giordano's?"

Showered and dressed, they headed north on Michigan Avenue toward the restaurant.

Normally, they might have chatted during their walk, but Connor had turned uncharacteristically quiet—eyes glued to the distance, deep in thought. *Something's eating at him.* Which seemed off, since generally, he spoke his mind.

Pogue returned to their earlier conversation. "You said you wanted to talk to me about something?"

"Yeah." Connor perked up. "You don't know much about my father, but because of his success, our family has had a private concierge physician since I was a kid—same one for twenty-seven years and friend of my dad's. He had a stroke a few weeks ago, and it doesn't look good for him working again."

"I'm sorry to hear that."

"Since I'll be taking charge of business operations of my father's organization over the next two years, I need to surround myself with people I trust. Finding the new doc is my responsibility."

Pogue slowed his pace to catch what Connor was saying.

"I'd like for you to consider being our family doctor—our concierge physician. There are things you'll need to know about our family other than we're wealthy, and we can cover all of that later, but would you at least consider it? I'm not asking you for an answer right now. But I know you. I can trust you, regardless of the fact that you've had a gambling issue in the past. It would also get you out of the financial hole you're in, and give you the money and lifestyle you want."

"I'd be happy just to be flush at this point."

"The world is yours for the taking."

"I'm a surgeon, not a general practitioner."

"Not an issue. You were an ER doc before you became a surgeon. That's more important to us than being a GP."

"I'm certainly intrigued."

Connor grinned. "Then I have your attention. I'll provide the details and give you time to look it over. But I'd like an answer as soon as possible." They stopped outside Giordano's door. "If you don't mind me asking, how much do you make now? Just a ballpark so I can get you thinking with the proper mind-set."

"After taxes and expenses, I clear about three hundred thousand. Maybe three fifty."

"As a surgeon? How many hours a week?"

"I'm on call every other weekend, and a regular workweek is about seventy hours between office hours, surgeries, and hospital rounds."

Connor's eyes opened wide. "You're operating on people, and that's all you make?"

"That's good money."

"For a plumber, not a surgeon. Triple that figure in the first year, with options for more on top of that—options we'll go into once the deal is done."

Pogue sized him up, but he didn't seem to be kidding. "You must have a big family."

"You wouldn't be on hospital call, just home visits now and then.

Most of the time, you just need to be available. I would still want you to keep your office running, but scaled down. We'd be your priority."

"I'm intrigued and flattered. When can I get more details?"

"Soon. If you do this, you can pay back what you owe to your retirement fund in no time and start actually investing in the market. It's a big decision. I wanted to make sure you were interested before pursuing it any further. You're my first and only choice for this position. You haven't met my father, and—like you said—you don't have all the details. We'll have to cover those issues before you decide."

Pogue offered a strong nod. "I'm very interested."

"Good. I'll have you meet my father later this week, and we can go from there if that works for you."

"That sounds great."

A police car sped by, catching Connor's attention. He seemed to refocus. "If you can make it on—" His cell phone buzzed, and he slid it from his jacket. After studying the screen, he said, "Pogue, I forgot I have an appointment. I'll have to take a rain check on lunch. Let me know what night is best to meet with my dad."

"You're joking. Seriously?" Pogue gestured toward the restaurant. "We're right here."

Connor flagged a cab. "Call me when you're done seeing patients." He stepped in and closed the door, and the car screeched into traffic.

*Connor has never acted this way before. I hope everything is—*

Another police car sped by with flashing blue lights and turned left at the intersection. Two marked cars and several ambulances followed. They blipped their sirens to move through the red light. Dread crawled through Pogue, and he flexed his fingers at the sensation. He quickened his pace along Michigan toward his office on Dearborn.

More sirens roared past. He rounded the corner where a sea of flashing red and blue lights accosted him—in front of his building. He checked his watch—forty-five minutes before the office reopened from lunch. Another siren blared to warn the gathering crowd that they were in the way. Some scurried—some didn't. His cell phone buzzed. Connor.

"Connor, something's wrong."

"I know. I have a text alert from the news reporting emergency vehicles on your street. I saw a few passing the cab after I left you. Is there anything going on?"

"It's my building—Ginger's building. I don't see smoke, and … Why is SWAT here?"

"I tried to call her cell. It goes to voice mail."

Pogue scanned the windows of her office on the first floor as officials pushed civilians back and hurried inside. "I can't see enough from here. Have to get closer." Pogue hung up and sprinted toward the lights and sirens.

SWAT teams darted past him, and news crews rushed to set up cameras as a swarm of gawkers lined the street.

"Excuse me! I have to get through!"

Nobody moved.

A heavyset man pushed Pogue aside. "Everybody wants to get closer, pal."

"I work in that building." Pogue grabbed the man's arm and shoved him. "Get out of my way."

When he reached the police barricade, he ducked under. Chaos surrounded him. Paramedics stood ready, waiting for the police to give them the "all clear." *There still might be danger.* His throat tightened. As the officer by the door let the emergency crews enter, Pogue rushed forward. The pit in his stomach gnawed at him. Sirens—too many and too loud. None of this made sense.

He studied the faces around him hoping to spot someone he knew when a man wearing a dark suit and standing near the entrance made eye contact with him, then scribbled on a notepad. Pogue turned as one of the policemen helped load a body bag into an ambulance.

*Body bag.* He couldn't look away. He'd seen more death in his lifetime than most, but the loss of life still gripped him.

Emergency workers wheeled out another victim. This one was alive. He spotted a yellow cloth around her neck. He'd seen that scarf earlier this morning when he dropped off a Starbucks.

Ginger.

# CHAPTER THREE

---

Paramedics hurried to the ambulance.

Pogue approached one of the officers. "I'm a doctor in this building." He pointed to Ginger. "I know her."

"We got it, Doc." The cop placed his hand on Pogue's chest to hold him back.

"Dr. Pogue!" someone shouted. "Over here!"

The man in scrubs pulled off his surgical mask. Pogue knew him. Doug Greenfield—a paramedic with the city for as long as Pogue could remember. Doug pushed Ginger's stretcher onto the ambulance with his free hand as a coworker helped.

Pogue hurried over. "That's Ginger Lucci." He was surprised at the weakness in his own voice. "She's a dentist in the building—a friend."

Doug held up the stat sheet. "She's been shot and we can't stop the bleeding. Pulse is one-sixty."

Pogue jumped inside the ambulance and pulled the door closed behind him. "I'm Dr. Bailey Pogue," he told the female paramedic as the vehicle pulled away. Then he gave Ginger his attention.

"How much blood loss, Doug?"

"Hard to say. What we saw at the scene wasn't all hers."

"What do you mean?"

"She wasn't the only victim. There was a dead guy next to her who looked like he'd bled out, and I counted at least three other bodies in the back of her office. Looked like a scene from *Fargo*. I'd estimate she lost two units—give or take—considering the puddle we found her in."

"Vitals?" Pogue checked her pulse—thready, weak, fast.

Doug held pressure against the bleeding wound on her chest. "BP ninety over sixty. Pulse one twenty. Oh-two Sat eighty-four percent.

Oxygen at two liters."

"Bump it to four."

"Copy that." Doug adjusted the oxygen.

"Check her pressure every 60 seconds."

"Copy. Checking now."

Pogue turned to the other paramedic. "Start a second IV, eighteen-gauge, normal saline, wide open."

She went to work immediately.

Pogue inspected the grazing mark and powder burns on Ginger's head, then the main problem—a gunshot wound to her chest. "Help me turn her. I need to see if it went through."

"It didn't, Doc. I looked when we put her on the stretcher. No exit."

"Then we have an arterial bleed close to her heart and a slug in her chest." Pogue checked her pulse again as the ambulance swayed through heavy traffic, rattling equipment on the walls. Still rapid—faint. He studied the monitor, then snatched Doug's stethoscope from around his neck and listened to her heart.

"Her pressure's dropping," the paramedic said.

"Tell me."

"Eighty over sixty."

Pogue wrapped the stethoscope around his neck and used his pocket light to check Ginger's pupils as he called to the driver, "We headed to Cook County? 'Cause we need to be."

"Yes, sir."

"ETA?"

"Ten to twelve."

"Doug, I need a one-and-a-half-inch, fourteen-gauge needle on a sixty-cc syringe, stat." He gave his attention to the other paramedic. "Patch me through to Cook County ER." He took the requested items from Doug.

With his index finger, Pogue prodded Ginger's ribs to find the exact location he required.

The paramedic held the phone in front of Pogue's face. "Dr. Taylor on speaker, Dr. Pogue. Go."

"Scott. It's Pogue headed your way with an unconscious, 34-year-old woman. GSW to her left mid-chest and one to her right temple. The head wound is superficial. The chest is our problem—no exit. Has a tension pneumo that can't wait. I'm going to relieve it now or she'll be DOA."

The speaker crackled. "Copy that. I'll stay on the line."

As Pogue pushed the needle between her ribs at the second intercostal space, a fine pink mist pushed out the plunger, filling the syringe barrel halfway. Pogue drew back the remainder as Ginger gasped an involuntary breath.

"Scott, oh-two Sat was only eighty-four percent, and now it's ninety. Anoxic—lips are blue. I reinflated her left lung and she took a breath, but she's still unresponsive. BP dropped to eighty over forty. Respirations are thirty-four since her lung reinflated." Pogue checked her neck and the monitor alarm sounded. "Scott, she has distended neck veins, and her pulse had dropped to ninety. It just jumped to one forty."

Taylor's voice came through the speaker: "Tamponade."

"You want me to deal with that here?"

"What's your ETA?"

"Four minutes," the driver shouted over his shoulder.

"Copy that. We'll take care of it in the ER," Taylor said. "I'll have a sterile room set up. Bring her straight back to Trauma Seven."

"See you in four minutes."

Attendants waited at the emergency entrance, gowned and ready for action. Pogue and Doug exited the ambulance as Dr. Taylor arrived.

"She's a strong woman, Scott. And she's a friend."

"You need to let us handle this. I'll come and talk to you as soon as I can."

Pogue stopped in the ER doorway and watched as Scott and Doug disappeared into the back with Ginger. His heart raced as his adrenaline struggled to find a place to go. Scanning the waiting room, he noticed only a few empty seats scattered about—par for the course. A small, vacant alcove overlooking the parking lot seemed the best place for privacy. A flat-screen television hung crookedly from the ceiling with water-stained tiles above it. There was no sound—only subtitles reporting the attack on his office: seven to ten dead. He stepped into the alcove and stared out the window. *This isn't real.*

The stale smell of death and disease hung in the air along with the faint odor of rubbing alcohol.

He needed a minute for his mind to slow down. Connor was probably beside himself, especially since this was on the news. Pogue started to pull up the number when someone touched his shoulder. He turned. A tall man in a dark suit held up a badge and ID.

"Dr. Pogue?"

"Yes?"

"I'm Detective Davis with the Chicago Police Department. You just came in with that patient?" He pointed toward the ambulance as it pulled into a parking space.

"That's right."

"She was injured in the shootings today?" he asked as he clipped the badge on his waistband between empty belt loops.

"I got there as they were loading her into the ambulance. What happened? Was this a terrorist act? The news is saying—"

"That was your building, correct?"

"I don't own it. I rent an office on the second floor. Hers is on the first. I don't think there's much I can tell you, Detective. I wasn't there at the time."

"Could we sit for a moment, Dr. Pogue?" Davis motioned to a couple of chairs in the alcove away from others in the waiting area. Pogue pulled up a chair.

Davis' worn-out badge, wrinkled suit, and scuffed black shoes gave him the appearance of a man who lived alone. When he crossed his legs, his pants, about two inches shorter than they should be, revealed no socks. He slid a pad and pencil from his inside pocket.

"Let's start with what you were doing in the ambulance," he said quietly.

Pogue clasped his hands in his lap. The crustiness of drying blood on his skin confirmed the reality of the day's events. His wet, bloody shirt clung to his arms and chest. A hint of nausea rose in his chest—that creeping, warm sensation—and he restricted the urge to be sick.

"The ambulance, Dr. Pogue?"

Pogue looked to the back of the ER where they had taken Ginger. "She's a dentist in my building and a friend. I returned from my lunch break, and the paramedics were carrying her to the ambulance on a stretcher, so I helped. I was about to call her brother when you interrupted me. So, if you'll excuse—"

"So you have no idea what happened?"

"I just told you. I walked into this. Tell me what you need so I can make that call." When he flexed his fingers, the dried blood crumbled in flecks to the floor. His mind clamored for calm.

"Your friend, Ginger Lucci, back there—guy shot her twice. I guess the slug to her chest may have done enough damage after all. She didn't look so good."

"We're finished here, Detective." Pogue stood.

"Take it easy, Doc. Just makin' a few notes." Davis flipped his pad to a different page and started reading, mumbling something Pogue couldn't understand.

He considered walking away, but Davis would probably follow him like a hungry dog. Pogue scanned the waiting room filled with sick and injured patients and took a deep breath to calm himself.

"You're trying to see how I'll respond to your comments. If you have a question, ask it."

"Fine. Did you know both of your office girls are dead?"

A hot wash of blood drained from his face.

"You didn't."

Pogue's legs weakened and he sat.

"My apologies. I actually thought you knew. Let me cut to the chase."

*Dead.* Terrible images chased through his mind, drowning out the sounds from the room.

"Where were you at lunchtime today, Dr. Pogue?"

*Lunchtime.*

*Focus.*

"Racquetball. I play racquetball two days a week—been doing that for years."

"Can anyone attest to that?"

"Her brother and the racquetball club. We sign in and out. It's a private club."

Davis nodded and jotted.

"I'm rarely in my office over lunchtime. My office girls aren't supposed to be either." *Why were they there today?*

"What do you mean they weren't supposed to be there?"

"I give them time to run errands, get their nails done, or meet friends for lunch. I encourage them to get away from the office so they can recharge. It makes for a better day—a better life."

"It certainly would have today."

"For God's sake …"

"Excuse me?"

"Does none of this matter to you? People died today, Detective. They came to work this morning and now they're dead. I'm covered in blood—my friend's blood. And you're looking for the shock factor of telling me my office girls are dead too? They have families—people who ..." A lump rose in Pogue's throat. He forced it down, bit his lip, and focused on a tree across the parking lot as his eyes began to water.

"Look. Being a detective sucks, but I do it *because* I care." Davis flipped his notebook shut and shoved it into his pocket.

Dr. Taylor pushed through the electronic doors, pulling off his surgical cap as he approached Pogue. "She's alive—for now. What you did in the ambulance bought us some time. Nice fieldwork. We drew a half-liter of blood from her pericardium."

"It was tamponade, then."

"It was. At least she has a chance."

Davis stretched out his hand to Taylor. "I'm Detective Davis from the CPD investigating the shootings." He pulled his jacket back to reveal the badge hanging loosely on his waistband.

Dr. Taylor shook Davis' hand but addressed Pogue. "She lost a lot of blood, so we won't know how she'll do for days. Whether it was enough to cause brain damage, we just don't know. I'm admitting her to ICU on a vent, so she'll be sedated."

"Sedated?" Davis said. "I need to talk to her."

"Are you not listening?" Taylor said. "She's unconscious from the trauma, and we need to keep her that way so she won't wake up with a tube down her throat breathing for her. We've paralyzed her with medications to keep her from fighting the ventilator. And we have to bring her back slowly—give her brain time to recover."

Davis nodded. "I'll check back tomorrow." He gave a side nod to Pogue. "Thank you for your time, Doctor. We'll talk soon." He walked through the automatic doors to the parking lot.

Taylor turned back to Pogue. "Have you called Jennifer?"

"She's visiting her folks in New Jersey."

"This is all over national news, you know?"

Pogue sighed. "No, I didn't." He pulled out his phone and dialed Jenni.

# CHAPTER FOUR

Nick Gambrel set his phone on the leather seat beside him but kept his hand on it, tapping his finger as he gazed out the window. The festive yachts in the harbor and brisk happy-hour antics mocked the darkness inside him. He'd rather be out there with his friends than in a limo with his father. Nick craved his dad's approval. Right now, he didn't have it. Ben Gambrel made failure unbearable.

"This was my fault," Nick finally said, breaking the silence.

"Was that the hospital on the phone?" his father asked, not disagreeing with the comment.

"No. Pogue. He's in the ICU with Ginger. I told him we're on our way." Nick wanted to be at the hospital earlier. Instead, his best friend, Pogue, who knew him as Connor Banks, took up the slack.

Ben poured a drink from the canister of the limo bar. "Contact Chief Denton. Tell him to provide extra security at the hospital."

"Already done."

Police Chief Denton was loyal to the Gambrels for reasons Nick was not privy. His father rolled down the window a few inches. That meant he was about to light a cigar. The coolness of the evening replaced the fading autumn heat. Winter was just around the corner. The cool breeze from Lake Michigan swirled through the partly open window. Ben closed it.

"Tell me again why she's in the hospital. You're in charge of her safety. You, the person I trusted with providing protection, fled the scene."

"I was never at the scene. I placed bodyguards in her office, she was armed, and another man guarded the lobby. There was nothing on the radar to indicate she was a target."

"You ran."

"I didn't run. I left Pogue standing on Michigan Avenue when I got a burn notice."

"Why didn't you tell me that before now?"

"There hasn't been a whole lot of time for explaining things, Dad."

"Who sent the burn?"

"The guard I stationed in the lobby of Ginger's building. Jackson."

Ben nodded. "Can you trust him?"

"Pretty sure I can. He's dead."

Ben took a cigar from his inner jacket pocket and inspected it. "Denton said they found Emily, Peggy, and Sherry in Ginger's lunchroom, all triple-tapped. They were experienced bodyguards. How did a hitman get the drop on all three of them?"

"They got sloppy. Those girls knew better than to be in the same place at the same time." Nick checked his phone when it buzzed a text. "I wish I could have seen the shooter's face when Ginger pulled a gun and blew his brains into the parking lot." Nick reached for his drink. "And why kill Pogue's office girls? What does that have to do with us?"

"They may have expected him to be there. Does he know anything yet? Have you talked to him?"

"Yes, but just the basics—literally moments before this happened."

"We need to look into Pogue's office girls. There must be a connection."

"From Pogue?"

"No. From someone wanting to see things up close and personal."

"Were these guys trying to get to us? Was Ginger collateral damage?" Nick needed to know what his father was thinking.

"No. They hit her when they couldn't get to us—to get our attention. The Families know she's not involved with the business. She's always made that clear." Ben lit his cigar and took a few puffs. Smoke filled the car. "You still should have checked to see if she was okay regardless of the burn."

"Maybe." Nick opened his window a crack. He hated cigars. "But how many times have you ignored a burn notice?"

Ben seemed to disregard the question. "Post a reward for information on who ordered the burn."

"How much?"

"A half-million. She's the first Gambrel burned in thirty years."

"Technically, she's a Lucci."

"She's a Gambrel. I don't care who she married. The Luccis aren't powerful enough to ripple our pond. Whoever tried to kill her did it because she's a Gambrel." Ben freshened his drink. Nick waited as his father puffed the cigar again. "Tell me you got this."

"Protection around the clock. US Marshals up close—our own men on the sidelines. We're sifting through the information as soon as the police receive it. We have to work our way around the FBI. They're all over this, but that's to be expected. I'll post the reward."

Ben rolled down his window again. The wind blew from Nick's side to Ben's, spritzing cigar ashes onto the old man's pant leg. He brushed them off.

"Do you have to smoke those?"

Ben ignored the question. "How's Pogue taking this?"

"Like one of us. Time to bring him inside. I've vetted him for two years. He's clean. And from what the ER doctor said, Pogue saved your daughter's life today. He needs to know that mattered."

Ben nodded. "But I don't know him."

"Trust me."

"Trusting you has nothing to do with it. Once you bring someone close to our family … you can't undo it."

"Pogue is a family man. He's a doctor living in society's upper crust, and is one of the smartest men I've ever met."

"That can be good and bad at the same time." Ben took another puff.

"Pogue's got his life together for the most part. Loves his wife and kids. But he wants more and needs more."

"What makes you so sure? Some guys are happy with less."

"The most important issue is that he's in debt up to his eyeballs from a past gambling issue."

"In debt to who?"

"To me, after going through his savings. I'm telling you, he wants the good life for his family."

"*You* lent him money?"

"I did, indeed." Nick grinned.

"Nice." Ben nodded slowly. Nick smirked. He recognized that sluggish nod. Ben looked like a man beginning to fall asleep on a train. In his father's case, it meant he was thinking seriously.

"I've made him a preliminary offer, Dad, conditional on meeting you, and on me coming clean about who I am."

"You were right about me meeting him before he gets all the way in."

Nick admired his dad. He'd worked his way up from the rough days of being a *wise guy* in the Chicago Outfit. Not an easy task, considering how many died before getting anywhere near the top. Just like Victor Santino from the New York syndicate, Ben was willing to do whatever it took.

"I told Pogue that Ginger's father would be coming and wanted to be alone with her tonight. He understood—just got a text from him. He's leaving the hospital so we can visit her privately. I know you'd prefer to meet him on your terms, and I don't want him confused about my alias and your last name. That needs to be a separate conversation."

"You're right, son."

"When would you like to meet him?"

"This week. Bring him to the mansion and we'll talk, then take the chopper to Harbor House and introduce him to the ruling class. Twenty minutes at the dinner table tells me a lot about a man."

"I'll arrange it." As the limo approached the hospital entrance, Nick spotted the squad cars out front. Chief Denton waited by the door.

"Sorry about Ginger," Nick said. "This never should have reached her."

Ben gave him a hard stare, then nodded without a word.

# CHAPTER FIVE

The quiet solace of the bedroom community beckoned Pogue. He needed the silence of his new home, more than ever before, to calm the fluttering within him and the endless questions for which he had no answers.

When he'd called his wife from the ER, she'd insisted on changing the flights for her and the kids. They'd be home tomorrow. He didn't argue.

When Pogue reached the outskirts of their community, the air seemed crisper, the grass more luminous, the sky no longer smothered. It was a good place to raise their family. His daughter Janelle had just started tenth grade. Landon came along much later. He'd entered second grade this year. Their youngest, Karen, loved school from the moment she met her kindergarten teacher. Although Jenni's hands were full with three busy kids, she made it look easy.

Pogue pulled into his driveway, parked in the garage, and shut off the engine. He pushed the remote to lower the door. For a moment he sat in the darkness. No noise. No people. No conflicts or questions. He thought of the girls in his office. They were young and happy when they'd arrived at work bright and early, excited about their plans to double date that evening. Now they were gone, and he was here, and that felt wrong.

He entered the house, walked through the living room, and opened the French doors leading to the patio. Along the back tree line, a shallow brook wove through the property. It calmed him as he approached it. Jenni wanted a gazebo with a swing so they could enjoy the serenity on summer evenings. The wood for its construction remained stacked neatly by the garage. Paying someone to do it would be easy, but he wanted to build it for her with his own hands.

The towering pines bordering the yard filtered a fading sunlight and cast long shadows across the newly laid sod. He closed his eyes and bathed in the silence interrupted only by the gently babbling stream. Tension from the day slipped from his body until the crunching of dried leaves behind jolted him. Pivoting toward the sound, he faced an imposing figure.

"Evening, Dr. Pogue." Dressed impeccably in a dark suit and blue tie, the gentleman stood tall, holding a brown leather satchel at his side. His sheer size spiked the intimidation factor. "I'm Special Agent Larson James with the United States Federal Bureau of Investigation." He handed his credentials to him.

Pogue studied the ID. Movement on the side street drew his attention. Two black SUVs came to a stop in the cul-de-sac.

"They're with me," James said.

"Why is the FBI at my house on the evening my office was targeted?"

"We need to talk."

"If this is about today, I told the police everything I know."

"I understand. We still need to talk."

Pogue pondered his options. An empty house with a man he didn't know was not his idea of a relaxing evening, but it didn't seem he had much choice. The chill in the air hurried his decision. "Come in." Pogue took the lead to the back door.

The men entered through the patio doors, and Pogue pulled them closed. He gestured to several chairs and a loveseat in the center of the spacious room facing a stone fireplace. A solid oak beam spanned the two-story ceiling. Worn cushions on the loveseat with a folded blanket draped over the back left little doubt this was a favorite cozy spot. He clicked on a lamp while James took a seat in one of the chairs, placing his satchel beside him on the floor.

"Dr. Pogue, you mentioned you spoke with the police."

"I did, but I don't know anything other than a dentist from my building was shot along with my two office girls and others. I don't know how many." He sat in the chair across from James—a round, glass coffee table between them.

James folded his hands in his lap. "I have the authority—and the obligation, for reasons that will be clear in a moment—to fill you in on a portion of what we know, but your confidence regarding this information is required."

Pogue's need to know what happened urged him on. "I can live with that."

Agent James took several folders and a thick envelope from his satchel and placed them unopened on the coffee table. He leaned forward and rested his elbows on his knees. "At one p.m. today, two armed men entered your building through the lobby. One went to Dr. Lucci's suite, the other took the stairs to yours."

He took a deep breath.

"The man who entered Lucci's office found three girls in the break room. He killed all of them—one shot to the head, two to the chest."

Pogue forced down a swallow.

"The gunman then searched the office until he found Dr. Lucci hiding in the janitor's closet. He fired one round into her chest, but she lunged at him. The office surveillance footage shows she forced him off balance, and he fell back into the hallway. In the scuffle, he fired one more shot that grazed her temple. Then Lucci pressed her own gun against his chin and pulled the trigger. She collapsed beside him."

*She had a gun?*

"We've identified her shooter." James leaned back in the chair. Pogue noticed the pistol in his shoulder holster. "Turned out to be a hitman who worked in the past for syndicate families in New York. He's been off-grid for years, but his prints are in the system. We don't yet know who sent him to Chicago. Interestingly, he was reported to have died in two thousand nine in Detroit after being identified by dental records. No prints were available since that body had burned in a car fire."

"They falsified dental records?"

"It would appear so."

"Why are you telling me all of this since it involves an ongoing investigation, and how am I connected?"

"Bear with me."

Pogue nodded. "What about the second man?"

"He walked in and shot your receptionist and nurse. Triple-tapped them, just like the others. You understand my terminology?"

"You mean they were shot once in the head and twice in the chest. I watch movies."

"I'm sorry. I meant no disrespect. What I need to discuss next is highly confidential," James said. "You can't mention it to anyone—including your wife."

*More secrets to keep from her.*

"You just told me I couldn't talk about it."

"We're about to take it up a notch. This is classified."

Pogue stood and walked to the fireplace where he turned on the gas logs. The immediate warmth was in stark contrast to his situation. "I don't want my family to be in danger."

"They may already be in danger. I need to tell you what's going on, but it must be in confidence."

"What do you mean they may be in danger?"

"I'll explain if you can maintain confidentiality."

*You can't commit to something like that.*

He adjusted the flames.

*Unless ... unless they really are in danger.*

"You have my attention, and my word, Agent James. What we talk about tonight I'll keep confidential from everyone—including my wife."

"I'll get straight to it then." James leafed through some pages in one of the folders and withdrew a photo. He slid it to Pogue as he returned to his seat. "This is your racquetball opponent? Your friend?"

He studied the photo. "That's right. Connor Banks. We play twice a week like we did today. He's an investor. Ginger Lucci, the one in the hospital, is his sister. Are you concerned he may be in danger too?"

"He's a person of interest. But his name isn't Connor Banks."

Pogue looked again, more carefully this time. "This is Connor." He tapped the photo with his finger. "I'm certain, Mr. James."

James drew the photo back to his side of the table and held it up. "The man in this picture is Nick Gambrel."

"Nick Gambrel—as in *the* Gambrels—the mafia Gambrels? You're mistaken. I've known Connor for two years. He runs a successful investment firm—a branch of his father's business. He's a friend of the whole family. I would know if this was Nick Gambrel."

"How? From the news?"

"That's one way, yes. His is a household name in Chicago."

"Have you seen his face on the news or in papers?"

"I ... can't recall it if I have. But several years ago I helped Connor in a legal proceeding involving the SEC and his former business partner, and the attorneys identified him as Connor Banks. They had documentation supporting the fact that he was, in fact, Connor Banks."

"I'm familiar with those proceedings. Nick Gambrel legally changed his name to Connor Banks when he was eighteen. But in reality, he *is* Nick Gambrel."

James laid another photo on the table of two men leaving a restaurant. "Do you know who these men are?"

Pogue picked up the photo. "This is Connor again and Ginger Lucci's husband. His name is Kurt."

James took the photo from Pogue. "This is an FBI surveillance still shot from video footage of Nick Gambrel and Kurt Lucci taken two months ago."

"Connor and Kurt are brothers-in-law. Ginger is Kurt's wife, so—"

"I'm telling you that this is Nick Gambrel." James handed him the photo. "Nick's father, Ben Gambrel, has operated the family business—the Chicago mafia—for twenty years. Nick is heir to the throne, scheduled to take over in the next two years."

Pogue's mind raced. His skin prickled and his stomach churned. That matched what Connor had told him earlier about taking over his father's dealings in the next two years. Should he say something? If he did, then—

James took the photo back. "I understand this is difficult to grasp."

"Are you here to warn me? And why give me all this information?"

"It's true that I came to warn you, but there's more to it."

"Why would Connor use an alias—go to the trouble of changing his name?"

"Would you have befriended him if you'd known he was Nick Gambrel? Or invited him into your home, or played racquetball twice a week? It's a clever ploy for him to maneuver about in society with a strong cover for years until he was ready to make his move. He has carefully maintained a low profile. You won't see him in the papers or the news or in magazines."

"Is Ginger involved? Is that why someone tried to kill her?"

James opened a new file on the table and removed another stack of photos. He carefully arranged them on the table in what appeared to be a specific order. Then he began by pointing at them one by one.

"Ginger Lucci's husband, Kurt, who you mentioned a moment ago is a member of another syndicate family operating out of New York. They're small compared to the Gambrels. They're not even newsworthy in Manhattan."

"I've never heard of Kurt's family in connection with organized crime."

"Like Nick, Kurt is in line to take over *his* family's business since his father, Albert Lucci, is reportedly in poor health. Kurt is your age and Nick's age. Albert still runs the New York business. Their reach hasn't extended beyond the Bronx—till now."

"Why now?"

"We don't know, unless it's Kurt's doing." James pulled a pair of reading glasses from a jacket pocket to glance at his notes. The half-framed cheaters made him no less imposing. "An alliance between the Gambrels and the Luccis gained FBI attention when Kurt's wife moved back to Chicago. She'd lived in New York with Kurt when they'd first married three years ago, but a year later she opened an office in your building, got an apartment in Chicago, and settled in—alone." He tossed the glasses on the open file. "Kurt and Nick have met on a regular basis since then."

"I remember when she started her practice." Pogue selected a photo. "Who's this?"

"Marc Santino."

"I thought he looked familiar. His face has been on the news, magazine articles, television—you name it. CNN did a piece on him about his charitable donations last year. Social media is a weapon to him."

"In sharp contrast to Nick, he loves the spotlight." James moved to another folder and handed it to him. "The Santinos have never operated in Chicago—but that may be about to change as well."

"Why do you suspect them?"

"Victor Santino, Marc's father, attempted to form an alliance with Ben Gambrel several times to no avail in the last four years, even though they've been friends for decades. There is every indication that the families are now close to merging on a common front, but not through Ben and Victor. There could be a new regime unfolding, operated by the next generation—Nick, Marc, and Kurt."

"Where does that leave me?"

"The attack in your office met specific goals. It appears they intended to execute Ginger and silence her office girls and yours, but the motive is unclear."

"You're saying Connor had those girls killed and tried to kill his sister?"

"Somebody did, but it would take extreme nerve for him to order a hit on his own flesh and blood, especially while his father still is at the helm of the organization. But we need to know what his involvement is and what's coming with this alliance." James gathered the photos from the table, stuffed them in the file, and closed it. "Did anything happen out of the ordinary with Nick between your racquetball game and the shootings today?"

*He talked about tripling my salary. Getting me out of the hole I've dug for myself. But I can't say that.*

"Connor, or Nick—whoever he is—received a text and left without an explanation other than to say he'd forgotten a meeting."

"Is that unusual?"

"He never forgets. And we always have lunch after our games."

"What time are we talking about?"

"Around one thirty. I checked my watch."

"Did you happen to get a look at his text?"

"Emergency vehicles flew past, his phone rang, he grabbed a cab, and left."

"It may have been a warning."

"He'd help his sister if he thought she was in trouble."

"Nick Gambrel is soon to be one of the most powerful men in Chicago. A direct hit on him would start a war."

"But killing his sister is fair game?"

"In a manner of speaking. But we need more information."

Pogue stood, walked to the French doors, and stared into the yard. This wasn't possible—to fool him for two years, gain his trust? For what?

"I need time to think, Mr. James."

"There's more." He handed a thick envelope to Pogue. "Read it. These files are permitted outside the FBI firewall only as hard copies. They leave with me."

"I don't want to read anything else. It's not just me in the middle of this. I have my wife and kids to think about."

"You may not want to read what I've handed you, but burying your head in the sand won't keep them safe. Please, read it."

"I'll just end my friendship with Connor—with Nick."

"You don't walk away from the Gambrels. You're in this up to your neck. It isn't your fault, but you're close to Nick, and it's too late to pull away."

Pogue reluctantly snapped the seal and removed the documents from the large envelope. The first section detailed infractions of Ben Gambrel, including lists of known associates who had disappeared since he took charge of the syndicate. Pogue skimmed through images of recovered bodies. Each photograph documented the consequences of resisting or betraying the Chicago Mob—the Gambrels.

After thirty minutes of poring over the documents, Pogue stood, stretched, and grabbed two bottles of water from the bar fridge. He handed one to James before sitting again and opening the next file. It included documentation regarding Nick's alleged association with drug cartels, in which no formal charges were filed.

Pogue closed the folders. "Mr. James, this isn't who Connor appears to be."

"He's an expert at making people see what he wants them to see and hiding the rest. Like it or not, you're in a position to make a difference."

"I can't believe he would be part of this."

"Read the documents."

"I just did."

"There are dozens of pages. Read them."

"I …" Pogue held up his hands. "I have a photographic memory. I read fast and retain everything."

"Everything?"

"Every word and image."

"Who else knows about this?"

"My memory? I don't know. My wife. A few colleagues over the years, I guess—maybe a med school professor or two. Ginger and Connor."

"I knew from your file that you speak several languages, including Italian and Arabic, but this information is not part of your profile."

"My profile?"

"You would be surprised, Dr. Pogue."

Agent James stood and slowly walked to the back windows, folding his hands behind his back. It was getting darker outside. "It's beautiful out here. I can see why you enjoy living in the burbs."

Pogue sighed. "You say I can't get away from Nick, so what am I supposed to do? What's your purpose of coming to me?"

James turned from the window to face him, his hands in his pockets and compassion on his face. "As of today, you're the man who saved the daughter of the reigning Chicago mafia boss, the sister of the upcoming boss, who also happens to be your best friend."

"That's not the way it is."

"It is. Ginger lied to you about her brother, and he played the part without a single slip. I'm not suggesting that he or she planned what happened today, but I guarantee Nick has been vetting you for a purpose."

"What could they possibly want from me?"

"The doctor who's been caring for the Gambrels for twenty-six years suffered a stroke last month. He's not expected to recover. The Gambrels haven't replaced him yet, but they will. They need someone they can trust."

Pogue closed his eyes and pinched the bridge of his nose. *This couldn't be.*

"Are you okay?" James asked.

"Just a headache. You were saying?"

"I believe they're going to ask you to fill the position to be their concierge doctor."

Pogue broke out in a cold sweat. He couldn't tell the FBI what Nick had offered. He didn't even know if it was real, or if any of what James said was true.

"You sure you're all right, Doctor? You look pale."

"I'm fine."

"There's another reason I'm here. You could help us."

Pogue cocked his head to the side. "Be an informant?"

"You could help us get on top of this."

"And die."

"If you take the offer to become their doctor, I believe you'll soon be invited into the inner circle. They've been grooming you—preparing you." James walked halfway back to the chairs and stopped. "We need you to get close to the family. You can find out what they have planned with the Lucci clan and where the Santinos fit. Something's coming together but we need an insider. I would like to share more of what we know, but—"

"Hold on." The reality of what James was saying reached a tipping point. His hope for getting out of debt and finding the solution to his financial problems were evaporating. Did they know about the money he'd borrowed from Nick? Something wasn't right. He needed more time to figure it out. And all that money—and debt …

"Dr. Pogue—"

"Stop." He faced James. "You know what I've been through today. My brain is on overload. I have to think of my family. I want no part of this."

"I'm trying to explain that you're already part of it. If I'm right and they've been preparing you—"

"The answer is no. I'm not spying on the mafia."

"What are you going to do when they approach you?"

"Turn them down." His head throbbed. He scratched the back of his neck.

Agent James walked to the table and gathered the files together, placing them carefully in his briefcase. "You're making a mistake. I'm trying to help you understand that if they want you, you can't walk away. You're underestimating their interest in you, their investment of time in you, and their resolve to acquire you." James handed him his card. "If you change your mind, call me."

He took the card and stared at it for a moment before slipping it in his pocket.

James walked to the back door. "Dr. Pogue, you need us as much as we need you. You can play this out in your head a dozen ways. But if I'm right, they won't let you out of this."

"I can't risk being a mole."

James faced him. "I've been doing this job for twenty-two years, and I'm telling you the Gambrels have dialed you down, vetted you for a position they will demand you take, or you'll die standing on your principles. The last thing I want is for your picture to be in this file." He pressed his hand against the satchel. "It may not feel like it, but I'm on your side." James pulled the door open, stepped out, and stopped. "Call if you need me."

Pogue closed the door. As James walked to the SUVs, Pogue's reflection in the glass accused him.

# CHAPTER SIX

When Pogue caught Jenni's eye in the baggage claim at O'Hare, she waved from across a sea of passengers. She tried to run, but with three children in a crowded room, it was impossible. She hurried, kids in tow.

"I missed you," Jenni said as she wrapped her arms around him.

Pogue held her tight. He let out a long sigh at the smell of her. "I missed you too."

"Are you okay?"

He heard the break in her voice and squeezed her soft cheek against his, already feeling the deception he harbored in his heart for what he knew—for not being honest about everything. He wanted to tell her about Agent James and what he'd said—about the trouble Pogue could be facing, about the money—but he couldn't.

*I'm not lying to her. I'm just not telling her everything.*

"I'm fine, Jenni. It's so good to have you home."

Landon tugged on his dad's coat. Pogue grinned. "Hey, bud." He gathered Landon and Karen in his arms, then winked at Janelle. She smiled and hugged him.

"I love you, Daddy."

"Love you too, little girl."

Even though she was older now, she'd never suggested he stop calling her "little girl." She kissed him on the cheek before letting go.

Arriving at the SUV, he arranged the bags in the back while Jennifer secured Landon and Karen in their car seats. Janelle buckled into the back. Once they'd pulled onto the Dan Ryan Expressway, Jenni asked Pogue, "How are you doing?"

His chest tightened, and he looked at his family in the rearview mirror.

Janelle was listening to music on her earbuds while the younger ones watched a movie on the DVD player. He turned up the volume just a little. "This has been rough, to say the least." He still spoke quietly so the kids wouldn't overhear. "We have our first funeral on Saturday—my nurse, Becky." He swallowed hard.

Jenni reached across the console and took his hand. "Maybe you need a little time off. You've been through a lot. You're not superman, Bailey Pogue. Well, to me you are, but not to the rest of the world."

A smile broke through. He needed that.

"Would you consider that? Taking some time, I mean?"

His cell phone buzzed in his pocket. Caller ID said "Connor." He hit cancel, set the phone on the console, and took her hand again.

"Why did you hang up on him? It might be important. It's okay to—"

"I'll call him back. I want to talk to you, not him right now."

"His sister was shot yesterday, and he probably needs to talk."

"I know she was shot, Jenni."

She pulled her hand away. "Bailey? I was just …"

His heart sank at his response. *That wasn't me. Why did I snap at her?*

"I'm sorry, Jenni. Really sorry."

"I can't imagine what you've been through—what you're going through. But I'm here."

"A thousand thoughts bounce around in my head, mixed with images of carnage I can't erase. This memory is sometimes a horrible burden."

"You see everything, don't you?"

"Every detail. I'm not sure what I need to do with it, but we can work through it. So thank you for insisting on coming home."

His eyes filled with tears as he slowly shook his head. He never should have let Connor close to his family—should have seen warning signs: the cars, the money, the mystery that always surrounded him. But why were those things wrong? What was so bad about having nice things and money in the bank? He'd worked hard as a physician and had nothing to show for it. That was mostly his fault for gambling, but taxes and malpractice insurance took a large chunk of what he earned. And what reason did he have for betraying Connor's confidence at this point? Was it where the money came from? He didn't even know how the Gambrels made their money. Was it necessarily something illegal?

"Hey, you. What about it?" Jenni said quietly, pulling him from his thoughts as she gently brushed a tear from his face with the back of her finger.

"Time off? The FBI is investigating the shootings, and I can't get into my office anyway. Probably for the best."

"The FBI? Why are they involved?"

Bile rose in his throat. *A simple question. I can answer that.* "They suspect it could have been a targeted attack, possibly terrorists."

"Terrorists? What about the police? Why aren't they involved?"

"They are. Spoke to a detective with the Chicago PD yesterday."

"Have you talked with the FBI?"

He looked back at the kids. No one was paying attention to them. "Met with them yesterday, too. They wanted to get my statement since I was one of the first on the scene." He reached for her hand and squeezed it. "To answer your question, I would love to take some time off."

She flashed him a smile. "It will be nice having you home. I do think you need to call Connor back though."

"I will as soon as we get to the house and settled." Pogue took a deep breath. "He sort of offered me a job as the concierge physician for their family."

"Where did that come from? Has he ever said anything about it before?"

"No. Their family doctor had a stroke, and they need a new one— soon. I'd still have my practice, but I would work fewer hours and make more."

"How much more?"

"I don't know. We were talking about it when all this happened. We'll have to get back to it."

She was quiet for a moment. "How is our retirement fund going?"

"Great. Connor knows how to make money grow."

"Having you home more would be wonderful, and extra money is nice. Would you enjoy that kind of practice?"

"I'm interested to see how much he's talking about paying, and I need to meet his dad at some point, so everything is on hold until then."

"Who is his dad?"

He swallowed hard. "I have no idea."

\*\*\*

"You know exactly what I'm saying, Nadir." Robert Savage's voice boomed over the phone like a five-star general addressing his troops. "Information harmful to US interests reached you in Egypt. Why in God's name would you act on it without my approval? I'm in the business of providing Intel for the Middle East, but not to be used against United States' interests."

Nadir leaned back in his chair. "And we appreciate it, Mr. Savage." Savage may have been a honcho in Washington, but to Nadir in Cairo, he was nothing more than a necessary evil.

"If you and I haven't already discussed it, Nadir, be assured I haven't signed off on it. This kind of mistake could be a deal killer."

"I thought you were the one who sent it since it came immediately after we last spoke."

"You were wrong."

"I should have been more suspicious due to the content. My apologies, Robert."

"Because you used that classified information, US citizens were killed on your soil. That's on both of us if this Intel leak gets out."

"What would you like me to do?" Nadir stood and walked to the window overlooking the city. He swept the curtains aside. The sky was clearer than usual.

"Since I didn't send the data, someone sold you information without my knowledge. I don't know if the problem is on my end or yours. Who did you pay for the information?"

"I will ask Philip."

"Do that. And no longer accept Intelligence unless it comes in the new package we spoke about last week and you and I have talked in advance to confirm. Future information will come to you only in that form. I'll communicate further by encrypted email on the new server system. For right now, we are on hold until the new method is finalized."

"Are you in a position to begin transmitting in such a manner yet?"

"Not quite. But I'm told we're progressing on course. It is the only way I'll communicate highly confidential information. And don't forget, I've made you very wealthy."

"I was wealthy long before our paths crossed, my friend." Nadir stroked his cat as it sunned on the windowsill. It bit him, so he swatted it and inspected his hand.

"That's not the point. We had a deal. I sell information that you provide to your people in Egypt and the rest of the Middle East. When your government acts on it, the world changes in your favor—and ours. Are you buying from someone else?"

"Not unless Philip has done something behind my back."

"If I go to prison I'm taking you with me. Do you understand?"

"Your threat? Yes, I understand threats. But I'm not doing the thing of which you speak. I will do my part to investigate on my end to look for a leak. You will do the same?"

"Count on it. We'll talk soon."

When Nadir hung up the phone, a pit formed in his stomach. He looked down at his cat rubbing its back gently against his leg. He scooted it away with his foot.

"I haven't forgiven you."

\*\*\*

Pogue poured a cup of coffee and admired his wife as she made lunch for the kids. She moved from the fridge to the counter to the island, then to the table. He couldn't take his eyes off her. She must have seen it on his face.

"You looking where you shouldn't be looking?"

"My eyes are exactly where they should be."

"Well, there are children in the room, so keep it G-rated." She pinched his cheek.

"Feels strange to be home on a Friday."

"It's nice. I like it."

He lingered on that thought until his cell phone buzzed. Caller ID indicated it was Scott Taylor from Cook County. He picked it up and walked to the back patio doors. "Hey, Scott. What's up?"

"Something happened last night to Ginger Lucci in the ICU," Taylor said.

"Hang on a sec." Pogue stepped onto the deck off the kitchen and closed the door behind him. "Talk to me."

"She's in a coma."

A gust of cool air twirled leaves in the yard at the bottom of the patio stairs. Pogue tucked his free hand in his pocket for warmth.

"I thought Dr. Harrison put her in a coma after you stabilized her, Scott."

"Not that kind of coma."

"What, then?"

"According to the toxicology report I pulled at five thirty a.m., somebody pushed meds into her IV—unauthorized meds. From the concentrations in the serum, it happened in the last twelve hours. Since the computer at the nurses' station showed her heart rate jumped to one fifty, Brenda, the charge nurse, came into Lucci's room to make sure the monitor wasn't malfunctioning. It had been steady at sixty-seventy. By the time she got in there, it was one eighty."

"Did they find out why?" Rain began pelting a few dried leaves on the deck, making a crackling sound. Pogue stepped under the overhang.

"Lucci woke up when Brenda walked in, so Harrison sedated her again. Now he can't wake her up."

"Hold on. I thought he wanted her in a coma."

"Since she woke up last night, he thought she might be able to handle consciousness. If so, he could remove the breathing tube. When she was unresponsive today, he second-guessed his dosages and asked me to look them over. I double-checked his calculations, and he was spot on for her weight and body mass."

"If someone gave her drugs to bring her out of her coma, that means she was in pain. She felt the respirator, the tube, her wounds—everything."

"To say nothing about being paralyzed by the curare and unable to move or talk. God, that would suck."

"Why is she still in a coma if Harrison didn't cause it, Scott?"

"That's the big question. It's why I did my own update on the toxicology titers."

"What'd it show?"

"Prolixin, Narcan, and Epinephrine—huge amounts. Someone did this deliberately. There's nothing in her chart for these drugs, obviously."

Pogue's conversation with Agent James the night before haunted him. Did this have to do with Nick? Kurt? Some mafia agenda? A rumble of thunder in the distance caused Pogue to peek in the window at Jenni. She was staring at him, then shrugged her shoulders.

"You still there, Pogue?"

"Yeah. Sorry. Whoever did this knew she was on a vent, so if they were trying to kill her, they had to find a way to do it while a machine breathed for her. If they turned off the vent, the alarm would sound."

"I've been thinking that exact thing, so here's a scenario. Picture this—the Narcan woke her up and the Epi made certain it did so in a brutal manner. Would that be enough to throw her into an unstable arrhythmia?"

"It would not only do that. The end result could be heart failure. You drained all that blood from around her heart yesterday. It wouldn't take much to push her over the cardiac failure cliff."

"They woke her for the pain?"

This was a sinister act—just like Agent James talked about. "Whoever did this wanted the combination of pain and heart failure to kill her in a way that appeared natural." He heard a commotion in the background. "What's going on, Scott?"

"The cops are wall-to-wall here. There's a guy from the FBI asking questions, and everybody is freaked. They're fingerprinting everyone who was here last night, including the janitor. I mean, seriously, it's including the janitor. Regardless of who attempted to kill Lucci in your office building, someone tried to finish the job last night in my hospital."

"The gunman who shot her is dead. The second killer is at large, according to Detective Davis."

"Davis is here too. Trying to avoid him. Kind of obnoxious." Scott lowered his voice. "How could anyone get past security to tamper with her IV?"

"The hospital has video surveillance everywhere." Pogue gathered his collar together with one hand, bracing against the coming storm. "Can't we check that?"

"Davis attempted to confiscate the footage. He was outranked by a Fed named Agent James."

A chill ran through him just hearing James' name. *You have to keep this from Scott too.* "So they're looking at the footage?"

"I think so. I just didn't want you coming down here to check on her and walk into this."

Pogue wanted to warn Scott, but he couldn't. He'd told James he wouldn't talk to anyone. But the road he'd chosen became muddier by the minute. "I appreciate that, Scott. How is she now?"

"There's very little brainwave activity. It's not flat but it's not good." He sighed. "Where do we go from here?"

"Is she under police protection?"

"Like the president. Detective Davis called in the US Marshals. They were already watching the hospital. But now they're stationed outside her cubicle in ICU."

"Thanks for the call, Scott. Keep me posted." Pogue ended the call and stepped into the house where Jenni met him with a towel.

"You're going to catch a cold out there."

Pogue brushed the stray drops from his hair and arms. "That was Scott. He was the ER doc when I arrived with Ginger. Somebody tried to kill her again last night."

"How could that happen in the hospital?"

"I don't know. She's under the protection of US Marshals until they can look at the surveillance tapes." He shook his head and sat at the kitchen table. "I need to call Connor and let him know."

Pogue began to pull up the number as Jennifer gently placed her hand on his wrist.

"Tell him I'm sorry about Ginger."

"I will."

She wrapped her arms around her husband. "And tell me I don't need to worry."

"You don't. The time I'm taking off will be good. It'll be over soon."

# CHAPTER SEVEN

The last person Pogue expected to see Saturday morning at his nurse's funeral was Connor—actually Nick Gambrel. He gave Pogue a bear hug, then reached out his arm and offered Jenni a squeeze. Uneasiness crept over Pogue. Nick Gambrel had no good reason to be there.

"What are you doing here, Connor? You didn't know my nurse, did you?"

"Never had the pleasure. I'm not here for her—no disrespect intended. I'm here for you." Connor turned to Jenni again but spoke to Pogue. "She knows, right?"

"Knows what?"

Connor spoke to Jenni. "Your husband saved my little sister this week. Did he tell you that?"

Jenni looked at Pogue. "He's a natural-born hero."

"He reinflated her lung while speeding through downtown Chicago in the back of an ambulance. If he hadn't, she'd have died before they reached the hospital, according to the doc in the ER."

Jennifer hooked her arm around Pogue's and pulled close.

"How's she doing?" Jenni asked.

Connor raised his palms. "The doctors aren't very forthcoming with information, especially since they don't know who tried to kill her in the ICU." He turned his attention back to Pogue. "Not to change the subject, but is there any way you could break free for a few hours this weekend? My father would like to thank you for saving his daughter, and we can cover some other opportunities and benefits at the same time."

Pogue stuffed his hands in his pockets and forced a smile. "I just don't believe I did anything any other doctor wouldn't have done."

"Well, Dad wants to thank you and meet you like we talked about anyway. You saved his daughter. He says it's time he met you."

Pogue glanced at Jenni. She smiled and looked at him as if he were her hero. He had to say no to the Gambrels. James' information made clear that the syndicate would own him if he got much closer.

"You should. Whenever it's convenient for Connor and his father." She turned to Connor. "I think it's very sweet."

"Thank you. I appreciate you letting me borrow him. I know you've only been home a couple of days. We need a few hours, if possible."

"Send me the address and the time. I'll be there."

"Nonsense. I'll send a car for you around seven tonight."

"Thank you. I'll be ready."

The service began, but Pogue's mind was elsewhere.

\*\*\*

Pogue sat at the nurse's station in the ICU next to Dr. Taylor and Brenda.

"Nice suit." Scott felt the fabric on Pogue's lapel.

"Just heading home from a funeral. My nurse."

"Oh. Sorry. My bad. I hate to bother you with this and pull you away from Jenni."

"She preferred to wait in the car. Your message said you needed a minute and that it was important. But you didn't say why."

"Brenda has something to show us."

Brenda had been the charge nurse of ICU for thirty years—decades before Pogue or Taylor had graduated from residency. Respected by everyone, including physicians, she was known as the rock of the unit—but not today.

"What is it?" Pogue gently urged her.

"She tried to communicate. Ginger Lucci—she tried." Brenda nervously adjusted her glasses.

Pogue continued to give her time to compose herself. "It's okay. You can talk to us."

"I think she tried to send a message." She swallowed hard. "Oh, God. I shouldn't do this."

Taylor placed his hand on her arm. "You mean when she woke up and looked at you the other night? Is that when you mean?"

"No. During the night last night."

Taylor placed his hand on her shoulder. "She's in a coma. Whatever you saw last night, I'm sure she—"

Brenda spread a torn piece of bedsheet on the desk, then covered her mouth with her hands.

Pogue and Taylor stared at the bloody letters.

"What's this?" Taylor scooted his chair closer and examined it without touching it.

"It's a square of her bedsheet," she whispered. "I found it by her left hand when I changed her linens this morning. It was under the covers, so no one saw it but me. I didn't know what to do so I cut out this piece with my bandage scissors and called you, Dr. Taylor. Other than you two, I don't know who to trust."

Pogue patted her arm. "You did the right thing." He tapped a few strokes on the computer keyboard, and Ginger's monitor readings appeared on the screen. "These show her current brainwave activity unchanged." He turned to Brenda. "Do we know about what time this happened?"

"Not really." Brenda leaned to peek at the guard, then spoke quietly again. "Somebody got past us—all of us. The marshals were questioning everyone about the attempt on her life the other night, and I didn't want to stir that up again. From what they asked, they seemed to believe it could be someone on the inside."

"An employee?" Taylor pulled up the log and studied Ginger's twenty-four-hour encephalogram on the monitor history. The EEG indicated a spike in brain activity from 4:12 a.m. to 4:30 a.m. "What? This was this morning."

"Oh, God." Brenda gripped the desk. "Am I in trouble?"

"You're not in trouble." Taylor moved the timeline to get a better look. "Has anyone seen what I'm looking at?"

"I don't think so."

Pogue pointed to the time stamp. "We'll need the footage from the cameras during that period. Can we do that?"

"The FBI took the footage from the other night. But we should have this morning's." Taylor studied the piece of cloth on the desk. "This is written in blood. I don't understand how she could do this with her brain function."

Brenda pulled up the electronic log. "There was no one else in her room but the guard, according to this." She turned to the men. "There's one more thing."

Both gave their attention.

"When I found this, her left index finger had blood on it. I checked. There was dried blood under her fingernail and on the tip."

Pogue nodded. "I had her fill out the forms in my office for the last marathon she ran since she needed her blood pressure documented by a physician—she's left-handed." He studied the bloodstained sheet as a single gruesome word stared back at him—KURT.

\*\*\*

The limo had arrived at 6:45 p.m. sharp. He hated leaving Jenni, but this had to happen, and putting it off seemed senseless. Now from the back of the limo, he took in the shocking opulence of the Gold Coast mansion district. He'd seen it before but not like this.

He caught Jacob, the driver, smiling at him in the rearview mirror.

"It's beautiful, isn't it, Dr. Pogue?"

Realizing his driver must have seen him gawking, Pogue offered a smile, despite the anxiety fluttering within him. *How does a man say "no" to Ben Gambrel?*

"It is. I've never met anyone who lived like this."

"It takes some getting used to, but there's no going back."

*I might never find my way back if I go down this path.* Pogue forced a chuckle. "How much farther are we going?"

"It's ahead on the left."

The three-story white mansion loomed over the surrounding neighborhood like the goddess of North State Street. Direct lighting enhanced the natural brightness of the quarry stone covering the expansive façade. Just across Lakeshore Drive, Lake Michigan awaited, poised for adventure.

Pogue was being treated as a member of the inside team, even though he wasn't a part of it—yet. The struggle inside him twisted his gut. Was there a way to be involved and stay clean?

"How long have you been a limo driver, Jacob?"

"Ten years. But I'm more than a driver, sir."

"What else do you do?"

"I'm a bodyguard—a martial arts expert, sir."

As they arrived at the estate, the limo passed through the first gate but stopped at the second while the gate closed behind them.

When the guard stared at Pogue, Jacob spoke harshly in Italian to the man.

Pogue wasn't supposed to recognize what he'd said. But he did. Jacob told the guard that Pogue was family and should be treated with respect.

*Family?*

The guard opened the inner gate and let them pass. As they did, Pogue noticed the emblem on the guard's jacket—an eagle grasping thirteen arrows in its left talon.

# CHAPTER EIGHT

Pogue stepped out of the limo while Jacob held the door. "Thank you, Jacob. It was good to meet you."

"You as well, sir. I'll be taking you home this evening, so I'll see you then."

Pogue made his way up the stone steps of the mansion. He stole a moment to admire the foreboding, two-story, double front doors. They opened.

"Pogue!" Connor shook his hand and pulled him inside. "Come in." He slapped Pogue's shoulder as they moved down the hallway toward an ornate staircase at the far end. Oil paintings adorned the walls, illuminated by chandeliers suspended from gold chains attached to the ceiling high above. Connor stopped halfway to the stairs.

"I appreciate you coming. I need to come clean about something first before you meet Dad." He gestured to a nearby door, and they entered what appeared to be a smoking room lined with cigar humidors. A small wet bar stood in the far corner. Leather easy chairs rested against the left wall with a small table between them.

*Come clean. Is he really going to do this?*

"This is my father's collection." He gestured toward the cigars. "Can I pour you a drink?"

"A small one. Thanks."

Connor poured, then handed one of the glasses to Pogue. Both men sat in the overstuffed chairs.

Connor sipped his drink, set the glass on the table, and leaned forward with his elbows on his knees. "What I have to say is difficult."

Pogue took a drink to have something to do.

"My name isn't Connor Banks."

Pogue's hand gripped the crystal glass. He'd tried to prepare for this, but—

"My name is Nick Gambrel."

Pogue tilted his head forward and stared under his brow as if looking over bifocals. "You're saying you have an alternate identity?" That sounded awkward—rehearsed.

"In a manner of speaking."

Pogue laughed briefly.

"I'm serious. My name isn't Connor Banks. It's Nick Gambrel."

Pogue swirled the whiskey in his glass and glanced around the room. "This is why you need a concierge doctor. For the Gambrel family?"

"That's right. My father is head of the family business, but I'll be taking over soon."

The room suddenly seemed small—the cigar smell overpowering.

"I'm the person you know as Connor Banks. Every part of that is true except the name—I'm really Nick Gambrel."

"Of the mafia Gambrels."

"Mafia. God. Yes—those Gambrels. But my father doesn't rule me. It's important you understand that."

Pogue stood, walked to the bar, and leaned against it as he turned toward Nick. "I'm supposed to be okay that the guy I know as Connor Banks is Nick Gambrel, son of the Chicago mafia boss."

"Mafia is a bad title. I wish you wouldn't—it's our family business. Unconventional, but a business just the same. I sincerely hope you'll be able to grasp that. I should have told you sooner. I wanted to and would have, but the timing never seemed right."

"It didn't seem right to tell me the truth?" Pogue surprised himself with his boldness.

"For my safety, I've kept my identity a secret since I was eighteen. My father thought it prudent. It has served me well. I'm still alive, I've established a successful career, I have the best friend I've ever known, and I'm about to take charge of a very large enterprise."

Pogue put his hands in his pockets, looked at the ceiling, then at Nick. "I would be a mob doc, then?"

"You have all the misconceptions that most people do about who we are and what we do. I despise the term mob doc because we're not the mob. Al Capone is no longer in charge."

"But you're in the syndicate, right? Would I be working for the mafia?" He was playing a part, but deep inside, he needed to know the truth. Could he do this or not? Was it right, or was it very wrong?

"I'm part of our family business, as I said. We're not *in* the syndicate. We *are* the syndicate. People who don't understand us call us the mafia. But we provide jobs with insurance and retirement benefits to our employees like any other large corporation. We have employees who have been with us for twenty and thirty years. They consider us family. We assure stability where others can't. 'Freedom and prosperity for everyone in the Gambrel family' is our motto. I hope that will include you."

One wrong comment could back him into a corner. If he helped James by getting close to these guys, he'd risk his life. If he didn't work for Nick, he couldn't pay his debt. Or, again, he could be killed.

"I don't know what you would expect of me if I did this. I was excited about being the concierge doctor for the wealthy Connor Banks family. But the Gambrels are a little frightening, to be honest."

"My name has to stay out of the news and off the Internet. I fly under the radar and I do it well." Nick stood and walked to Pogue. "Give this a chance. It could work." He extended his hand.

Pogue contemplated his next move. If he shook his hand, what did that mean? "There's more to it than that. I'm standing in the biggest mafia mansion in Chicago, owned by Ben Gambrel. That's a little scary. Have you ever killed anyone? Am I in danger just being here? I sound stupid. I'm sorry, I gotta—"

"You watched *The Godfather*, didn't you?"

"Everybody watched *The Godfather*."

"Drop the mafia tag. My dad hates it as much as I. What he built is an empire—a thriving business. We operate where no one else will, and we do it well."

"Ginger introduced you to me as Connor."

"She didn't want to. For my father's sake, she agreed. Ginger and Dad are close, even though she wants nothing to do with the business."

"What if I want to leave? Like right now. What if I said I'm going home?"

"Then Jacob will drive you. You're free to go if you want." Nick opened the door.

Pogue didn't move.

"If you do go, what you know about me has to remain confidential."
*What should I do?*

"But I would really appreciate it if you would meet my father first. He really does want to thank you."

Pogue walked to the door. "I didn't mean to insult your family. I'll do my best to call you Nick, but I don't know if I want to be on your payroll."

"Meet my father. That's all I ask." Nick put his open hand on Pogue's back and gestured toward the stairs. They began their trek up the spiraling white marble slabs to the second floor.

"I can't imagine how Jenni would respond if I told her about this. I mean—"

"Okay, that's what I'm talking about. You can't tell her or anybody else, regardless of whether you take the job or not. I keep my identity limited to close friends like you. Outsiders know me as Connor. As of tonight, you're not an outsider. In fact, there are more things I'd like to talk about that would be in your best interests. First, I need you to understand you are not to tell Jenni or anyone else who I am."

Pogue nodded. "Understood."

He and Nick turned left when they reached the second floor and approached the room directly in front of them.

"One last thing. Don't ask my father any probing questions. I'll explain anything you want to know in private."

Pogue nodded.

Nick gave a quick slap on his shoulder again, then opened the door.

A man who appeared to be a bodyguard stood near the centerpiece of the room—an enormous oak desk crowned with a sprawling granite slab. The shelves on the walls held mementos of better times. A vaulted ceiling boasted what appeared to be oil paintings reminiscent of the Sistine Chapel, while a cluster of aeronautical gadgets from a bygone era filled a display case near the entrance to the room.

Nick ushered Pogue toward the fireplace at the right end of the study where blazing logs crackled and popped. A man rested in an easy chair with his back to them.

"Father, I'd like you to meet our friend, Dr. Bailey Pogue."

The man stood and turned.

"Pogue, my father, Ben."

Ben firmly grasped his hand. "It's a pleasure to meet you in the flesh,

Dr. Pogue. I've heard many good things about you," his voice boomed.

"Thank you, sir. The pleasure is mine. And please call me Pogue."

"Very well."

Ben appeared to be in his early fifties at the most, in excellent health, and a little taller than Pogue. His graying temples streaked into thick, dark locks, which he swept behind his ears.

"It's an honor to meet the man who saved my daughter's life."

"It was the least I could do, sir."

Ben gestured toward the leather sofa near the fireplace, inviting him to sit. Warm room, cozy fire—why not?

Nick opened a hutch on the opposite side of the room and selected a bottle of Scotch while Ben took a seat across from Pogue.

"There's no way one can place monetary value on human life," Ben said. "I would never attempt to do so, especially for my only daughter. How might I express my gratitude for what you've done for our family?"

"I'm just glad I was there to help."

Ben stood and walked to where Nick finished pouring three glasses of whiskey. Taking two of them, he returned to Pogue and handed him one. He then retrieved a framed photo from the wall and set it on the coffee table facing Pogue before taking his seat again. The picture captured the image of a much younger Ben, a beautiful woman at his side, and two small children—a girl and a boy.

"That was taken after I'd bought that warehouse in the background. I was going to use it to work on an old military helicopter I'd planned to restore."

"You have a beautiful family."

"Had. We've done our best since my wife died, but ..." Ben picked up the photo and fondly studied the images as he spoke. "Do you know who I am?" The question hung in the air as Ben left his seat and returned the picture to the vacant spot, carefully straightening it to match the others. Dozens of family photos lined the wall. Most included the entire family on the beach, on a yacht, in front of a Christmas tree—happy and enjoying life. The last two rows were different. His wife was no longer there. Nor was the light in Ben's eyes.

"I do now, sir. All I know about you is what I've read in the papers and seen on the news or Internet. Until tonight I didn't know you were Ginger's or Nick's father." Pogue was surprised how easy it was to get the words out that weren't true.

Ben smiled. "If you ever need anything—anything at all—I want you to call me." He handed Pogue a business card that read *Ben* followed by a phone number. "This is my cell. Few people have it. If you're in desperate need, I want you to use it. If you would put the number in your phone and hand the card back, I'd appreciate it."

"I assure you, sir—there's no need to—"

"I'm afraid I insist, Pogue. There may come a time. I'm in your debt, and I always pay my debts."

*Am I taking Ben Gambrel's number?*

Pogue pulled out his phone and did as he was told. "Thank you, sir. I appreciate this." He mistyped the number into his contacts—nervous— then backspaced and reentered it. He handed the card to Ben when he was done.

"Our family is different." Ben gestured toward the opulent surroundings. "I'm a man of means—not just wealth and success. I can respond to problems and opportunities no one else can." He sipped his drink. "I'd like you to have dinner with us tonight."

"I don't want to impose, sir."

"I won't take no for an answer. Ask anyone who's crossed me." Ben laughed. Nick did as well.

*Dinner with the Gambrels? Just dinner.*

"I should probably get back to my family."

"It would mean a lot to me. It doesn't repay my debt, but I would very much enjoy spending a little time with the man who extended such kindness to my daughter."

Pogue couldn't force himself to say no. "It would be an honor. Thank you."

"Excellent." Ben motioned to the bodyguard. The man came to his side at once. "Have Charles fire up the chopper." He grinned at Pogue. "We'll go to my favorite place in Wisconsin—The Harbor House. The seafood is incredible. We'll be there in twenty minutes, and we'll be back quicker than if we ate at the Pump Room. Safer too."

Nick crossed the study and glanced out the window toward the chopper.

"I want you to feel welcome," Ben added. "I don't break bread with just anyone. We're kindred spirits, you and I. Whoever did this to Ginger did it to us both."

The resolve in Ben's eyes reminded Pogue of the conversation he'd had with Agent James. The pressure in his chest suffocated him.

Ben lifted his glass, finished the Scotch in two gulps as if it were water, and handed the empty crystal to Nick as he headed for the door. "Shall we?"

# CHAPTER NINE

P ogue attempted to relax and enjoy the décor and ambience of Harbor House. A modern grand dining room, filled with the extravagantly dressed upper crust of society, opened to an outdoor veranda overlooking Lake Michigan.

He sipped expensive wine while Ben, seeming genuinely interested, skillfully questioned him about his family and background, his education and upbringing, his medical practice, and goals for the future.

Charismatic and interesting, both Ben and Nick convinced him he was the most important person in the world. If he was in trouble, as James seemed certain, this evening certainly didn't feel like a well-spun web.

When Ben shared about his wife, losing her to cancer when Nick was a child, Pogue saw in his eyes the pain and loss as if it were fresh in his heart. It was not what he'd expected from the leader of Chicago's organized crime syndicate. He was so touched by this man's love for the wife he still mourned he barely noticed the buzzing of his phone. He checked the ID—Dr. Taylor.

"Sorry, gentlemen. It's the hospital. Would you excuse me for a moment?"

"Certainly," Ben said and pointed to the veranda. "I take calls out there. It's quiet and no one will disturb you."

"I'll make this quick." Pogue moved to the veranda and answered. "Scott. Tell me you're calling about something other than Ginger."

"Wish I could. I had a couple of surprises this evening. First, Detective Davis noticed me copying the toxicology report from Ginger's lab bank and called me out."

"Why did you do that?"

"I told you—I need answers. This happened in my hospital. Anyway, the conversation with Davis started rough but ended well. We worked out a few things—like him being a condescending jerk."

That made more sense to him than Scott realized.

"That's not the reason I called you, though. When I was leaving the ICU, Kurt Lucci strutted in."

A chill gripped him but it wasn't the night air. "He came to the hospital?"

"Says he knows you. Is that true?"

Pogue sighed. "Ginger's brother introduced us last Christmas. But that's the extent of it."

"Well, he's here and asking for you."

"Listen, Scott. He's from the Lucci family of New York." Pogue spoke as quietly as he could.

"As in the mafia? Why would you not tell me this before now?"

"I honestly didn't think about it. He lives in New York and hasn't seemed to care about her. I should have expected it, though. She *is* his wife."

"Yeah. A wife who wrote his name in her own blood on a bedsheet."

"We don't know what that meant. She could have been calling out to him for help."

"Whatever. He shows up in ICU unannounced with an entourage that looks like the cast from *Men in Black*. He wants to meet with you tonight."

Pogue's mind raced. "Tell him I'll be there later. It will be a few hours at best, though."

"I'll let him know."

"Did you give that piece of bedsheet to Detective Davis?"

"I was flustered when he caught me on the computer, so I forgot. Came prowling up like a cat."

"Well, do it. I have to go." He hung up and peered into the dining area as he slipped the phone into his jacket pocket. A man sat with Ben and Nick. Pogue eased his way around several tables to get back to them.

Ben stood and the unknown man did as well. "Pogue, I'd like you to meet a friend. His name is Arlo Ledger."

Pogue shook his hand. "Pleased."

"Same here." His broad grin put Pogue at ease—but not very.

As they sat, Arlo poured him more wine. "I've heard a lot about you, Dr. Pogue. You've become somewhat of a legend among our ranks. You saved Ginger, you haven't done anything to offend Ben yet, and Nick vouches for you a hundred percent. That never happens."

Ben winked at his son. "Never."

Pogue turned to Nick. He shrugged and grinned. "Whatever."

"Tell me a little about yourself. Something I don't know."

"What do you know?"

"That you're a man of principle—straightforward and honest. You have a beautiful family, a thriving medical practice, and you go to church—Calvary Baptist."

Pogue glanced at Ben—he was snipping the end off a cigar with a cutter he'd retrieved from his suit pocket. He didn't look up.

"Why are you asking me these questions?"

Ben cleared his throat and waved Arlo back. "Please excuse Mr. Ledger. He tends to dive in without checking the depth of the pool."

"Fair enough." Arlo chuckled as the waiter began placing food on the table.

Ben faced Pogue. "When I mentioned I'm a powerful man, that naturally means I have more enemies than most. Some of those enemies do their best to get close to this family—my family. Arlo is a trusted friend, and I wanted his opinion tonight."

"Opinion?"

"I invited him to meet you—not interrogate you. My apologies. Now, let's eat."

Nick stood. "Excuse me. I need to speak with my father for a moment in private."

Pogue's appetite disappeared. He'd be alone at the table with this guy.

Ben appeared surprised but didn't hesitate to follow his son. "Excuse us, gents."

\*\*\*

Nick leaned on the railing beside his father. The bright lights of Milwaukee's skyline reflected off Lake Michigan. "Did I exaggerate, Dad?"

"I'm pleased to say you did not." Ben lit the cigar he'd been preening and took a long draw. "He has charisma, talent, guts … everything we're looking for. I like him. Did you notice him around the waitress? He didn't give her a second glance. I gave her a hundred to show some cleavage and flirt a little. Your boy wouldn't bite. Didn't even peek as she walked away."

"But did you have to invite Arlo?"

"It's for the best. You're too close to this, son. Arlo can offer an objective point of view."

A brisk wind stirred the trees in the courtyard below the terrace. Nick welcomed the breeze clearing the smoke from the air. "Do you expect me to wait on Arlo? Because I've already asked Pogue to consider the position."

"What if Arlo turns up a problem and Pogue's already in? He'd be privy to information he shouldn't."

"I'll take the risk."

"You understand what it would mean if it went sideways?"

"I do." Nick pushed his hands in his pockets. "Won't happen."

Ben puffed his Cuban. "At some point in their lives, most men possess noble ideals. When they want something bad enough, they'll bend their world to fit."

"I'm counting on that."

"Everybody has a weak spot. Find it and use it."

"What do you see as his weak spot, other than his gambling debts?"

Ben grinned. "His family. He'd kill for his family."

\*\*\*

Pogue stepped down from the chopper as the blades finished one last turn. "Thank you for this evening, Mr. Gambrel." He shook his hand.

"Call me Ben."

"I enjoyed meeting you. I hope to see you again."

"Count on it, son."

Nick grabbed Pogue's arm. "I need to borrow you for a minute. Then Jacob will drive you home."

"It's getting kinda late, Nick. Can we do it another time?"

"This will only take a minute. It's important." Nick walked toward the house.

Pogue followed him in and down the hall to a ground-level library near the foot of the staircase. Nick poured a drink from a canister and looked at Pogue questioningly.

"I'm good."

The unmistakable aroma of cigar tobacco permeated the air in this room too, but there were no humidors in sight. Pogue had never seen Nick smoke, so he expected Ben must spend time in this inviting room. A winding oak staircase led to the second floor of the library's narrow balcony walkway that circled the room. He pictured himself sitting in an overstuffed leather chair, admiring books that had been carefully assembled on the shelves. But then he chided himself for the thought. He had to keep a clear head.

"Now that you've met my father and know who our family is, how do you feel about being our concierge physician? We need to move on it."

Pogue cleared his throat. "I'll take that drink after all." The tension in his voice surprised him.

Nick poured the drink. "I understand your concerns." He handed Pogue the glass. "Loyalty is powerful—*and* expensive. What you did for Ginger revealed your character, to me and to my father. Not everyone would have or could have done what you did. You're a gifted physician. For those and other reasons that we'll get to another time, I'd like you to consider coming closer to our family. My father agrees."

"I just met him tonight."

"We spoke on the veranda at the restaurant. We've discussed you many other times as well."

"I don't know."

"In less than a year you'll net seven digits if all goes as planned."

"Seven?" Pogue set the drink down and pushed his hands in his pockets to find a place for them. "What would a doctor have to do for that kind of money? I'm not trying to offend you. It's just that—"

"I'll be the first to admit there are gray zones to what we do, and therefore to what we need. Hence the seven-digit income. Discretion and loyalty are key. I'm inviting you to be part of what I'm doing—what this family is doing. Being our doctor is just one aspect. If you want more, there *is* more. This is your chance to live the dream."

Pogue rubbed his forehead. "What would be expected of me? I have no desire to live a life of crime, if that's what you're implying. Again, no offense."

"From the physician standpoint, we'd expect you to be on call twenty-four seven. There may be times when you'd be dealing with issues that require you to look the other way. But we'll prepare you for those and protect you. On one end of the spectrum, you'd provide care for runny noses and coughs. But with the opportunities that are coming, you would have considerable free time, travel the world, and you'd be untouchable by authorities—invisible. I'm being mysterious, but I need you fully on board before going into details. For everything we do, I would need you to be loyal and discreet."

"What do those words mean to you, Nick?"

"If someone has a problem they don't want reported to the police, we'd expect you to be discreet."

"You're serious."

"Dead serious."

"I'm not a trust-breaking kind of guy."

"Yes, you are. You've gambled away your life savings, and then some, and told your wife it's all safe."

Pogue shook his head. "That's not the same."

"I'm trying to make a point. The definition of being a trust-breaker, to use your words, is fluid. You broke your trust with Jenni by gambling because of the potential monetary gain. This is exactly the same. The risks are minimal and the rewards incredible. If you don't do this, you'll work for the rest of your life without making the kind of money that makes people drool. And just to be clear, we're in the business of providing information that helps people, not harms them. We offer services others can't. We don't deal drugs. We don't run liquor. We don't participate in prostitution. We provide services."

"What kind of services?"

"I can't go into that until you're committed."

"I need to give this some thought."

"I know you want a better life, to be out of debt, to have money to burn. I've seen it on your face."

"There may be some truth to that, but being involved with the syndicate scares me."

Nick folded his arms, looked at the floor for a moment, then back at Pogue. "This is your opportunity. You'll be able to give Jenni, Janelle, Landon, and Karen the best life has to offer. Do you want to walk away from the only chance you'll *ever* have to do that?"

The noose tightened. He could barely breathe and refused to break eye contact. He'd named his family members one by one for a reason.

"Besides, you should consider their safety."

There it was.

"The shooters in your office building may have been looking for you too. If you're part of our organization, I can protect you and your family."

Bile rose in Pogue's throat, and his heart pounded in his chest as the fight-or-flight response kicked in.

"I couldn't live with myself if anything happened to your family, Pogue."

Sweat trickled down the middle of his back. He knew too much already.

Nick calmly poured another glass and refilled Pogue's. "Here's my bottom line. You take this deal as our family doctor, and I'll give you your first-year retainer, replace the money you took from your retirement fund, with interest, and I'll forgive what you owe me. With a single handshake, you're out of debt and back on track. I'll introduce you to the other ventures we have going that you'd fit into perfectly, and the money will pour in."

"You're talking—"

"Over a million to start. Then we can add the other ventures as you choose—if you choose. If you decide this isn't for you, to be honest"— Nick paused and swirled the whiskey in his glass as if deciding if he should say what he did next—"I'll have to collect on what you owe me. I'm sorry, but I can't leave that standing out there for the next fifteen months."

As if concrete had been poured around his feet, Pogue stood but couldn't move—couldn't object. "You know I can't pay you back in full."

"You don't have to. Join us, get rich, work less, keep your family safe, and live a very happy life." He stressed the word *very*.

He had no choice. He couldn't pay Nick back even if he wanted to. He'd borrowed money from the mafia. He closed his eyes and took a deep breath. Then opened them and looked Nick directly in the eyes. "Okay. I'm in."

Nick handed him an envelope. "Your retainer, your retirement fund with interest, and consider your debt to me paid in full."

He took the envelope. "You knew I'd say yes?"

"How could you say no?"

*Dear God.*

# CHAPTER TEN

Jacob drove the limo to the emergency entrance at Cook County Hospital. "Would you like me to accompany you, sir?"

"No, thank you. I'll be fine. If you need to get back to the Gambrels, I can take a cab home."

"I wouldn't think of it, sir." He pointed toward the visitor's parking lot. "I'll be over there when you're done." He handed Pogue a card with his name and cell number. "Call me when you're ready. I'll pick you up."

"Thank you." Pogue took the card and left the limo. The brisk night air took him a little by surprise. He wrapped his jacket around him snuggly until he reached the hospital door, embracing the warmth as he stepped inside. His conversation with Nick weighed heavy on him, and his mind churned with thoughts of what he'd done. He'd get this meeting over with and go home to snuggle with his wife in front of the fireplace, although she'd probably be asleep by the time he got there.

Stepping onto the elevator, he pondered what he would say to Kurt. *What did that fragment of bedsheet with his name mean?* When he reached the third floor and turned the corner to the ICU entrance, his shoes seemed to weigh a hundred pounds. He punched the green button on the wall, and the doors opened.

Two men stood inside—one left, one right. As he walked through, they followed him with their eyes but stood their ground. As he approached Ginger's cubicle, another two stepped into his path. The US marshal was one of them.

"Evening, Marshal."

"I just need to search you, sir."

Pogue lifted his arms while the man did his job.

"You can go in now," he said, taking a step back to his post.

Pogue walked to the isolation room at the end of a limited-access hallway where they'd moved Ginger for security purposes. He entered and closed the glass door behind him.

Ginger's monitors beeped. Her pale face appeared thinner than the last time he'd seen her.

Kurt stood from the chair and met him halfway. "It's good to see you, Pogue." He shook his hand. "I wish it were under better circumstances. I appreciate you coming at such a late hour."

Pogue forced a smile. "It's the least I could do." He studied the slender man in front of him—his dark spiked hair and his tailored suit fitting perfectly. "I don't think I have anything new to offer though."

"No, no. I understand. I spoke with Dr. Taylor and Dr. Harrison, and they filled me in on what they knew. I wanted to thank you for saving my wife. Everyone knows what you did. If you hadn't been there …"

"I'm glad I was."

Kurt pulled up a second chair for Pogue. "I need to talk to you."

Both men sat facing each other.

"Nick called and said you'd decided to take the position he offered. We both think you're doing the right thing. You'll enjoy what's in the pipeline."

Pogue glanced at the glass door of the cubicle—the marshal and Kurt's men stood outside talking. "When did you talk to him?"

"Twenty minutes ago."

Pogue gathered his courage. "I must admit I still have a few reservations."

Kurt glanced at the monitors. "Keep in mind that Nick and I are experienced. We'd love for you to be a part of what we're doing."

Pogue changed the subject. "Will you be heading back to New York soon?"

"Actually, I'm looking for an apartment here in Chicago." Kurt stood and walked to the heart monitor, studying it as he spoke. "Manhattan is where we belong. But Ginger is determined to keep her practice here, so I think I'd better find a place closer. We've had a few issues. That's why I live most of the time in New York and travel here to visit. It's also why I'm only staying at her place until she's out of the hospital. Then I'll need my own apartment."

"I'm sorry to hear you two are separated."

"We're not. Not officially. To be honest, I just want her to recover so we can decide what it'll take to get us back on track."

"That's good news. I'm sure she'll like that."

"Do you think so?"

Pogue felt uneasy. "I do."

"I can't help but think she'd found someone here. She's beautiful. Why wouldn't she?"

"Probably because she loves you. I can tell you I never saw her with anyone else. She and I didn't talk a lot, but when we did, it was usually about her brother or trivial stuff. To be honest, I thought you two were divided by business between New York and here, that's all. Never thought much about it."

"That's going to change. *I'm* going to change."

He glanced at Ginger, then at Kurt. "I'd better head home. My wife will be worried."

"Thanks for coming by. Call me when you're free and Nick, you, and I—we'll get together."

"Sounds good."

Pogue left the room, skipped the elevator, and hurried down the stairs to the back ER entrance. He texted Jacob.

The limo pulled to the curb. "Everything okay, sir?"

"Yes. Time to go home to my wife."

"Right away, sir."

*** 

"It's late, Robert," Nick said, annoyed at the intrusion into his sleep. "Why are you calling at two thirty in the morning? What can't wait?"

"I found our leak."

Nick sat up in bed, suddenly alert. He reached for the nightstand and flipped on the lamp. "Who is it?"

"The information came directly from the office of Danielle Trent in the Pentagon. I had my suspicions about her because of her contacts, but I couldn't connect the dots."

"So it's on our end?"

"It is. Nadir is not to blame—at least not directly. Although he used the information, which means he paid someone for it knowing it wasn't us."

"Does Ms. Trent possess access to sensitive and top secret information?"

"Indirectly. She's been working with a federal prosecuting attorney."

Nick stood. "Oh, God. Don't say it."

"Sorry. It's Jason Franklin. Even though he's married into the Santino family, it's true."

"How do you know it's him?"

"Danielle Trent has worked with Jason in DC on a number of cases in the recent past and is currently assisting on three. She'd easily have access to what leaked to Nadir based on the fact that the data sent overseas came from several different departments and were more highly classified than what we've ever been comfortable divulging. That means someone would need access to all of those facilities and branches unless they had confidential access outside of the departments—as in the office of the special prosecuting attorney."

"Are you telling me she got our Cairo CIA agents killed?"

"That and significant collateral damage personnel in Egypt."

"Why would she have sensitive files outside the confines of the federal buildings?"

"Jason has top secret clearance. Danielle is required to as well."

"If we don't get a handle on this, you and I will be in prison or hell. I'm not sure which frightens me more."

"I'm on it, but I wanted you to know as soon as I confirmed it."

"You sure Jason isn't doing this behind our backs?"

"Nick, we're talking about Jason Franklin. He doesn't have the nerve or the ambition. I'm ninety-nine percent sure it was Danielle. But I'll find out one hundred percent. That, you can count on."

"I appreciate the call, Robert. Keep me posted."

\*\*\*

When Pogue arrived home at three in the morning, Jenni stretched out her arms from her snuggled position on the love seat. He was happy to dive in and feel her arms around him.

"I'm sorry I'm so late." Guilt clawed its way up his chest, sharper and more painful than before he'd left. "You okay, babe?"

"I'm fine," she said with sleepy eyes. "I just wanted to know how tonight went. I got cozy in front of the fireplace and fell asleep." She cuddled up with her head on his shoulder. "Tell me what happened.

Details. I want details." She glanced up at him briefly. The smile she gave him reminded him how lucky he was.

Telling her everything would lead to questions—questions he couldn't answer.

"I was coming back from dinner with Connor and his father when I—"

"No, no. Connor's dad. Where does he live? What's the house like? Dinner? Is he nice? Where did you go? Everything. I'm a woman. Remember?"

"I remember that vividly. Yes." He gave her a squeeze. "His father is a very wealthy, successful investor who lives in a mansion on the Gold Coast and really does own a chopper. We took it to Harbor House in Wisconsin for seafood."

"The Gold Coast? Are you serious? And you went to Wisconsin tonight? Harbor House?"

"We did."

She studied his eyes as if to see if he was joking. "I am so jealous right now you just don't know. You realize I love everything seafood."

"Yes, I do. I'll take you there myself soon. I promise."

"In a chopper?" She pulled herself against his arm. "Just kidding about that part."

"Well, it was a very nice restaurant, and Connor and his dad are amazing. They're both self-made men with more than their share of natural charm. I enjoyed meeting Connor's father, and we talked for hours."

"What's his name?"

"Whose?"

"Uh … Connor's dad?"

"Oh. Sorry. Ben."

"Ben Banks? Those names don't go together very well." She giggled.

"I think he goes by Benjamin—Benjamin Banks. That sounds better."

"Hmmm. Okay. I do like that better."

"Anyway, on the way home, I got a call from Scott telling me I needed to drop by the hospital to check on Ginger. She'd taken a turn for the worse."

"So is she? Worse, I mean."

"She seemed about the same to me. But I told them yesterday to call me if anything changed, so he thought it was worth notifying me that her brainwave function declined. Not surprised, though."

Jenni sighed. "This whole thing is really sad."

"I know. Connor's dad is a widower, and Ginger means the world to him. He showed me some pictures of his wife and family from when the kids were little. He clearly still loves her."

"When did she die?"

"He lost her to cancer when the kids were young. So about twenty-five years?"

"That makes all of this even worse. I don't want to ever lose you. Cancer scares me." She pulled her legs up beside her on the love seat and covered them with the blanket. "Did you talk about the concierge doctor stuff at all?"

Pogue's mouth turned to cotton. The fight inside him—*she's your wife.* Visions of his family in danger—horrible danger—haunted him.

"Bailey?"

"Sorry, baby. We did. We talked some about it but not all the details. I think Ben just wanted to make sure I was someone he liked. After all, he's the eldest and most likely to need medical care."

"Is he fragile?"

"Not in the least. He looks like he's in better shape than me."

She squeezed his bicep. "I doubt that." She grinned. "What do you think about it? Are you interested? You sound kind of upbeat, in a way."

"Do you have an opinion on me leaving my practice? I mean, it would mean a lot more money. More than twice what I make now." *More like three times, but don't say that.*

"What?" She sat up and looked him in the face. "You're serious. Holy cow, Bailey! I had no idea concierge medicine was that profitable."

"Neither did I. I think I may take the position." He remembered the check in his pocket. "Would you be okay with that?"

"I think so. Let's talk about it more tomorrow. I'm fading right now." She stood and looked back when he didn't get up. "Babe?"

"Sorry." Pogue stood, turned off the gas logs, and followed her down the hallway. Swallowing hard, he couldn't shake the feeling of being watched. Peeking out the back window into the darkness didn't help.

# CHAPTER ELEVEN

With the funds safely back in his retirement account, Pogue had been able to show his wife the deposit statement. Nick included a generous portion to indicate earned interest, as he'd promised, which pleased Jenni and put her at ease. Pogue had deposited the retainer check into a new account at a separate bank. He would find the right time to bring it up.

As he jogged through the woodland trail near his home, it seemed a dark cloud hovered above him. His pace was off, his breathing irregular, and he couldn't concentrate. Thick foliage and the rich scent of flowers along the trail normally distracted him from life's troubles, but today it wasn't working. The trees had dropped their brightly colored leaves, crunching under his shoes as he ran. Instead of being greeted by lilac blossoms, wilted, purple petals lay scattered about the trail.

He slowed after four miles and walked a cool-down pace before stopping, then slipped his phone from his pocket for the third time in less than twenty minutes. Staring at the blank screen wasn't going to change anything. He dialed the number, recalling it from the card.

"Hello, Agent James. This is Bailey Pogue."

"I was hoping you'd call, Dr. Pogue."

"I need to talk to you as soon as possible. Face to face would be best if you're available."

"Are you in danger?"

"Like I've never been before." Pogue continued to catch his breath from the run.

"Can you be here by eleven? The address is on my card."

"I remember. I'll see you then."

He stuffed the phone in his pocket and headed for the house.

\*\*\*

The man in the gray Cadillac parked across the street in Naperville, Illinois, watching as sixteen-year-old Amy King made her way toward her mom's parked SUV. She was still in her cheerleading outfit from tryouts. Yes, he had watched her, and she'd performed well. He positioned the camera so that the five-foot-two, blond-haired, blue-eyed beauty filled the frame perfectly. Quickly, he snapped the photos. Zoomed in as she neared her mother's car and snapped a few more.

And then she disappeared from view. He looked at the photos he'd taken, tucked the camera away, and drove off in the opposite direction.

\*\*\*

Pogue waited in the conference room alone. Floor-to-ceiling smoked windows on the hallway side afforded privacy but openness. A hardwood table nearly spanned the length of the room while beige carpeting complemented the dark paneling of the walls.

Agent James swung open the thick glass door and strode into the room, followed by another man carrying a laptop. Pogue stood and reached for his hand.

"Dr. Pogue, this is Agent Vaughn. He's here to assist me." James gestured toward the man, who took a seat on the opposite side of the table.

"Good to meet you," Vaughn said, stretching across the table to shake Pogue's hand.

"Same here." Pogue couldn't help but notice how large his hands were.

"He'll be documenting our conversation," James said as he pulled up a large executive chair and placed a file on the table, folding his hands on top of it.

Vaughn opened the laptop and nodded at James.

Pogue straightened in his chair. His raw nerves tingled from his scalp to his fingers. "I'm afraid you were correct in your assessment about Nick Gambrel and his plan to pull me in, Agent James."

Vaughn typed.

"I was invited by Nick to meet his father two nights ago. We flew in his chopper to a restaurant, Harbor House in Wisconsin, and met another man for dinner."

James pulled a document from the folder. "Arlo Ledger."

Pogue leaned forward. "How do you know that?"

Vaughn stopped typing and looked at Pogue as he spoke. "We've been watching them—the Gambrels. When you showed up, it was … unexpected."

James removed another page from the folder and handed it to Pogue. "Arlo is an attorney with some very dark connections including the Gambrel family and several others. He vets people. Very, very carefully, he explores their background in explicit detail. If there is anything in your past that would trigger a red flag, we need to know."

"There's nothing significant."

"What do you mean by significant? Is there anything at all?"

Pogue shifted in his chair. "I used to have a gambling problem. I'd bet on college games, and as a result, I pushed myself into debt. But Nick already knows about that."

"How would he?"

Pogue's gut cramped. James stood and retrieved a bottle of water from the credenza, sliding it across the table to him. Pogue sipped from the plastic bottle. The coolness of the water eased the burning in his chest.

"I had to borrow money from Nick to cover my debts after losing my retirement fund." Pogue shook his head. "It didn't work out the way I'd hoped."

"What happened at dinner the other night?" James asked.

"Dinner was fine. It was actually quite pleasant. But afterward, in Nick's mansion, he confronted me and I had to respond. That's why I called you today."

"I'm not following."

"I still owed him money. Nick—I owed him a lot of money. He used it as leverage so I'd take the job."

"As their physician?"

"Yes."

James stared at the blank legal pad in front of him, tapping his pen on it from the side. "When did you borrow the money?"

Vaughn typed.

"March of last year."

"Last year?" James' head tilted. "Why not go to the bank? You're a doctor. Surely they would have lent you—"

"I'd already extended myself and used my savings. I needed $150 thousand to pull me out of the hole. Nick offered to help and put no contingencies on it until now."

"You thought you were borrowing from your friend, Connor Banks, not the mafia," James said.

Pogue filled them in on the conversations he'd had with Nick and Ben, including his acceptance of the money.

Vaughn moved briefly to the calculator.

"Nick made sure you were locked in."

"He knew I couldn't pay him back. If my wife found out, it would kill her."

"Do you think they'd offer that kind of money if they only wanted you to be their doctor?"

"I ... don't know. I was cornered."

"I'm not here to judge." James leafed through several sheets in the file and slid one to Pogue. "The Gambrels paid their former doctor three hundred fifty thousand a year before taxes. Why are they paying you well over a million in cash?"

"Are you sure that's what they paid him?"

"Quite. It's on the document in front of you. I think I know the reason you're so valuable. You mentioned it to me when I was at your house. You have a photographic memory the level of which is quite uncommon."

"What can they possibly do with that?"

"We don't know, but they're clearly paying for much more than you being their doctor on call, especially if Arlo Ledger is involved in vetting you."

The conversations he'd had with Nick played over and over in his brain. What if this was the plan from the start—to trick him into gambling again so he'd get caught up in it and have to borrow from Nick? Why would they want him so much they'd force him into such a position and pay whatever it took to get him on board?

"He knew," Pogue mumbled.

"Excuse me?"

Pogue looked at James. "When I was in debt, he knew I had a problem with gambling. He fed it by providing the funds I needed to get deep in debt to him. How could I have not seen that?"

"Did he threaten you?" James asked.

"He implied that he couldn't protect my family unless I took the job. There's no doubt what he meant."

"You believe the threat was real?"

"It's real. His leverage is also real. His ability to destroy me if I'd turned him down was real." Pogue slid the pages back to James. "But there's something he's not telling me. He hints at a plan 'in the pipeline'—a new enterprise with Kurt Lucci and the promise of more money. He has refused to share details."

"I appreciate your honesty today and coming clean on these issues," James said. "The offer I made in your home still stands. The FBI needs information from the inside, which is where you are now."

"What will happen if they find out I'm spying on them?"

"I don't know how else to put this except to say that you're in danger no matter what you do at this point." James rested his elbows on the table. "I know you want to do the right thing." He slid the file to the side. "There's a way out—a noble way at that, if you care to consider it as such. And we can protect you if you're working with us."

"You want me to be an informant."

James rocked back in his chair and gripped the armrests. "When I was in your home, I never used the word *informant*. You did and then proceeded to shut the conversation down. I'm afraid it's much more complicated than being an informant."

"I don't follow."

"You'd be required to undergo training as an active participant in our investigation."

Beads of sweat erupted on his forehead. "An agent?"

"Whatever these families are doing is on a larger scale than we'd originally predicted, but we can't fit the pieces together. Like where Kurt Lucci fits in, for example."

"I met with Kurt at the hospital." Surprised at his weak voice, he cleared the lump in his throat. "Nick called him the moment I'd left his house the other night. Kurt indicated he'd like to meet up with Nick and me to talk about this *venture,* whatever it is."

"If you've been asked to join this enterprise by both Nick and Kurt, you're in a position of trust with both families. We haven't seen how Marc Santino fits in. Maybe he doesn't. But we'll need to know that as well."

The idea of working behind enemy lines chilled him to the bone. Nick wouldn't hesitate to put a bullet in his head if everything James had told him was true.

"You were at the edge of the circle when Nick was a friend named Connor. When he revealed his true identity, you went much deeper."

Pogue scratched the back of his head. "I want to help. I don't have a choice anyway. But I wouldn't know where to start or what to do."

"Quantico," Vaughn said.

"Beg your pardon?"

"Quantico, Virginia is where you start." James gave Vaughn a look. He was quiet after that. "It's intense, but you'll *need* intense. You're in good physical shape—that helps. According to your file, you speak several other languages, including Italian, French, and Arabic. From the documents I've read, you graduated from Harvard at the top of your class, and your IQ is one sixty-four."

"Where did you get that information?"

"We have files on every close associate of empowered organized crime."

Pogue rubbed his temples. "What does my IQ have to do with anything?"

James clipped his pen in his pocket. "Regardless of what we teach you, your intelligence remains your most valuable weapon."

"I don't know what that means." He swept his fingers through his hair and held them there for a moment. "How long would I be at Quantico?"

"Twelve weeks. The usual is sixteen. We can break up your training to meet the objectives. And you would have to keep it confidential, even from your wife."

He'd be away from Jenni and his kids. But the dangers wouldn't vanish—the bloodshed, loss of life, —and threat to his family.

"How could I possibly attend training without my family or Nick knowing? That's impossible."

"We'll provide cover and documents that show you're in advanced medical training and performing seminars in another state. You've done that in the past, correct? The courses you teach require travel for a week or more at a time?"

"Some do. Yes."

James studied the blank legal pad before him, then turned to Pogue. "The FBI won't let you back in your office for a week at the earliest. We can stretch that to four and keep your suite sealed until we finish."

"How long would I be undercover?"

James glanced at Vaughn. "I hope six to eight months. There's no way of telling till you're inside. We can't do that unless you're trained. You'll be gone for three weeks initially. Then we'll send you back regularly for six months while we help you integrate into your new job as the Gambrel's doctor."

"And my family?"

"The FBI will assign protection. Your wife won't know my men and women are nearby, but they will be—twenty-four/seven."

Pogue tapped his fingers on the arm of his chair. "You make it sound simple."

"It will never be simple. Doing this will cost you, but if you don't, it will cost even more. They want something from you—something you won't want to do. Working with us is your safest option, plus it's doing the right thing."

"When would training begin?"

"As soon as possible."

Pogue stood and offered his hand. "Let's get this done, Agent James."

James rose from his seat and shook his hand. He turned to Vaughn. "Let's get him sworn in before he changes his mind."

# CHAPTER TWELVE

Nick gripped the low railing of the yacht's helipad as the chopper approached. Lake Michigan's calm waters should make landing easy today. Even though the yacht was within eyesight of the mansion and a motorboat would suffice to reach it from the dock, his father had insisted on transporting Arlo by chopper from his home in the Chicago suburb of Wheaton. He fumed just thinking about Arlo's influence. That would change soon.

Once the chopper rested on the boat's helipad, Nick put on his best smile and greeted Arlo, escorting him to the lounge one level below.

"Did you have a good flight?" his father said over the thumping of helicopter blades winding down above. He stood and gave Arlo a hardy handshake.

Nick snatched a barstool, grabbed a bottle of Scotch, and poured himself a drink. This was a waste of time.

"I always enjoy flying in that beautiful bird," Arlo said as he settled into the plush armchair and placed his thin briefcase on the coffee table.

The fine leather sofa cushions squeaked as his father took a seat across from Arlo and reached for the cigar box on the table, retrieving a Davidoff—Dom Perignon Cuban. "What do you have for us so far?" Ben inspected the cigar.

Arlo removed a folder from the briefcase and slid it to Ben. "Other than the gambling problem that you already know about, he's clean—almost too clean—which made me think he might be scrubbed."

"Seriously, Arlo?" Nick's ears and face radiated heat. "God!"

His father cast him a look he'd seen a thousand times, then lit his cigar. He turned to Arlo. "A professional, you say?"

"That was my concern, so I searched his history for breaks or gaps, or anything that hinted of a manufactured backstory."

"How far did you go?" Ben drew a puff.

"Elementary school." He pointed to the file. "That's a hundred pages of *spotless*. There's nothing hidden—no skeletons, no landmines. But also nothing other than money issues you can use for leverage if you need it. He did go to FBI headquarters twice, but a friend of mine who works there said they probably questioned him about the shootings since his office was one of the targets. There doesn't appear to be anything else in his file, except the FBI was looking into his connections with you."

"Is that something we need to consider?"

Arlo shook his head. "I have a copy of the deposition they took from him. He didn't expose a thing. Makes him look even better."

Nick tossed back his second shot of Scotch and immediately poured another.

Smoke rings curled around Ben's head. He flicked a few stray ashes onto a silver tray beside him. "Any recommendations?"

"You wanted my assessment, and that's it, in a nutshell. Details are in the file. If you need motivation for him, we'll have to manufacture it. I know where to hit him."

"His family," Ben said.

"You got it."

Nick rested his elbow on the bar. "We'll take it from here. Thanks." He glared at Arlo.

Ben stood and opened the sliding glass door to the outside air and sunshine. "I appreciate the thorough work, Arlo. I agree with Nick, although not with his arrogance. We'll think on this one. I won't touch a man's family unless he leaves me no choice."

One corner of Nick's mouth turned up. He stared at the skyline and huffed.

\*\*\*

"I decided it might be a good time to attend that laser certification course." Pogue tried to swallow the lump in his throat, but it wouldn't move. He sat on the edge of the coffee table, facing his wife on the sofa. "After that, I could teach several training seminars like I did last summer. I'd be out of the office while the police finish their investigation, and I can start fresh with Connor's family when I get back."

Silence. The look on her face said it all.

"What's wrong, baby?" That was a stupid question. He grabbed the tissue box and gently placed it beside her. "Is it a bad idea?"

She shook her head and grabbed one from the box to dab the corner of her eyes. "I just thought you'd want to be with your family right now. This is hard on us."

Pogue had rehearsed an explanation but couldn't get it out.

Her eyes lit up a bit. "Do you want me to find someone to watch the kids? I could come with you to the seminar for a couple of days. We would at least have the evenings together."

This road he'd chosen was dark and filled with landmines. His stomach gnawed at his insides. But he couldn't live with himself if he did nothing and Jenni or the kids suffered. He had to play by the rules now—rules he didn't make or like.

"I'm not sure there's enough free time to make it worthwhile for you to be there." Pogue shifted from the coffee table and sat beside her. He wrapped his arm around her soft, warm shoulders.

She leaned in and rested her hand on his arm. "I've enjoyed having you to myself. But if you need to do this, it's fine. Really. You still have to take me to Harbor House. You're not getting out of that one."

Deception festered inside him. "I'm sorry. I'll be with you through Sunday. I leave for the conference on Monday."

She squeezed his arm until he looked at her. "We have the weekend then, right?" Her bright hazel eyes captivated him.

Pogue kissed her neck. "Yeah, we do. Harbor House isn't that far away."

*God, help me.*

\*\*\*

Pogue ascended the front steps of the Gambrel mansion. Before he knocked, a well-dressed gentleman, appearing to be a bodyguard with his superior muscular build and professional stance, opened the door.

"Afternoon, Dr. Pogue. Mr. Gambrel is expecting you."

"Mr. Gambrel?"

"Nick, sir."

"Of course. Thank you."

With heavy feet, he followed the man to the library. When Pogue entered the room, he returned Nick's nod as he appeared to finish a call. Nick slid the phone in his pocket and greeted him. The bodyguard stepped out and closed the door behind him.

"I appreciate you coming, Pogue."

Pogue cleared the frog in his throat. "I wanted to follow up on the conversation we had the other day."

"Good. Let's do that." Nick poured a drink for each of them.

"I have to leave town for a couple of seminars that I've had planned. I told you I'd take the position and tried to get out of these time wasters but couldn't." He took the drink from Nick and sipped it. The courage he'd come in with wilted. "I'll be able to get started as soon as I come back in a couple of weeks."

"That should be fine." Nick scratched his head. "I understand prior commitments. After all, I did just spring this on you."

"Where do we go from here?"

"When we spoke the other evening, I mentioned that once you were on board we would look at bringing you in on a business venture Kurt and I are putting together."

"What kind of venture?"

"We'll look at that when you're back from your seminars."

Pogue took another sip. The information regarding what Nick and Kurt were planning would have to wait.

*** 

Nick's limo stopped at Robert's office on State Street. He took the elevator to the eleventh floor. Meeting with Robert could never be considered a pleasure, but his downtown location at least made it easier to get there. When he reached Robert's floor, he stepped into the vestibule. The empty hallway reminded him that Robert's paranoia was alive and well.

"Come in, Nick," Robert called from a doorway down the hall.

Nick smiled at the camera in the corner, made his way to the suite, instinctively adjusted his tie, and stepped inside.

Robert held the door for him. "You sounded on the phone as if this couldn't wait."

"I'd prefer to deal with it head on."

The men sat in an alcove overlooking the city. The panoramic view as the sunset turned the sky from pink to orange set the proper mood.

"This office set you back a few coins, I'd imagine." Nick scanned the furnishings. "Quite a few."

Robert ignored the comment. "What's on your mind?"

"Have you spoken to C.J. Santino?"

"About?"

"Her husband, *Mr. US federal prosecuting attorney,* and his ties to Danielle Trent?"

Robert tapped the table beside him. "No, and I'm not going to. I don't want anyone to accuse me of tipping off a possible suspect in an ongoing investigation. This needs to have all the markings of an uncompromised pursuit of justice. If I don't do it per protocol, I'll be the one they investigate next."

"I don't like C.J. not being warned. She's going to blow."

"That's what we want. This has to go down like a normal investigation or it draws scrutiny. We don't need *scrutiny*. If C.J. would normally get royally pissed, she needs to act royally pissed when she finds out her husband is under investigation. It has to be real."

Nick stood and walked to the fridge. He uncapped a bottle of water. "So you want me to say nothing?"

"Not until she approaches you. Then tell her you'll get right on it. I'll tell you what you need to know at that point."

"And you're certain about this Danielle Trent woman?"

"The information Nadir received came from her office in the Pentagon." He handed Nick a manila envelope. "It makes sense."

"So you're investigating the man who's stealing government information on our behalf? But we need this guy *and* we need C.J."

"No. That's the beauty of this. I'm investigating the woman working for the man who's working for us. I'll clear Jason Franklin per due diligence protocols. But just like C.J. needs to show anger, her husband needs to exhibit genuine fear."

"You think Nadir knew?"

"If he didn't, how would money have changed hands? He'll hesitate before trying it again—for now. Cutting off the information supply until it's back under our control will force him to behave to get the Intel flowing again."

"I'm giving you some leeway, Robert. Don't take it for leniency."

"That sounds a little like a threat."

"Don't stretch this out. It has to be neat and clean. There's work to do, and I need C.J. *and* her husband in good condition." He stood to leave. "And if what I say sounds like a threat, it usually is."

# CHAPTER THIRTEEN

Pogue sat on his bed at Quantico and recalled the events of the past three weeks. As his plane had flown over Virginia that sunny Monday morning, his guilt clung to him. He'd lied to Jenni about where he was, about what he was doing, the seminars ... everything. To be certain Pogue wasn't followed, the FBI would monitor Nick, Kurt, and the rest of the involved families. They even provided a cell phone upgrade—the latest technology—that couldn't be tracked by anyone but the FBI. It would indicate that Pogue was in Colorado no matter where he was. He was officially off the radar to everyone except the government. Even his outbound calls appeared to come from somewhere else. And if Jenni tried to contact his hotel, it would reroute to his cell.

After he'd arrived at Ronald Reagan Washington National Airport in DC, a black Tahoe had picked him up at baggage claim and drove the forty miles south to Quantico Marine Base off Interstate 95.

Following a three-hour debriefing and lie detector test that lasted two, Pogue had spent the remainder of the first evening filling out forms. Within twenty-four hours he'd found himself in the thick of intense training.

An avid jogger and weightlifter since college, Pogue had expected his stamina to carry him through the difficult tasks and days at Quantico, but the rigorous training at the base was far beyond anything he'd imagined. The hours of sleep were so short and expectations so high he struggled with the best of them—most of them his junior by ten years.

Some courses began at four o'clock in the morning while others took place entirely during the night with exams scheduled for other classes or physical testing the next day. The point was clear—focus on the important, concentrate on what mattered, but never ignore what seemed to be insignificant background noise. Work under pressure, while fatigued and during sleep deprivation—your life might depend on it, and probably would at some point.

By the second week, the strange looks from other trainees and hard-to-explain questions about what he was doing there at the ripe old age of thirty-five transformed to encouragement as his reputation for being smart and his ability to fight with the rest of them gained the respect of his fellow recruits. They fondly referred to him as the "old man." Soon, they began to help him learn—to fight, to shoot, to know when he should run and when he should stand his ground. Most of all, he learned how and when to lie. He felt that somehow they knew without saying that this older guy needed their help, and if they didn't give it, he'd die out there.

Hand-to-hand combat had been the most difficult for him. Taking a life while protecting oneself was strangely different than killing an individual with your bare hands simply because he's so evil no one else should ever meet him. Not mastering these skills would threaten his survival.

Now he sat in his room alone—a room void of Jenni and her lotion on the nightstand and everything else familiar. All the training and combat withered from his mind as thoughts of his family bled through. He imagined Jenni snuggled up beside him in front of the fireplace and the kids playing on the floor around them. He lived for those moments—times when they had nothing calling them to action, no one pulling them from each other.

A knock on the door broke his trance. He stood and opened it, finding his commanding officer in the hallway.

"Pogue, I need a minute."

"Come in, Commander." Pogue stepped aside as he entered, then closed the door.

"I know you're going home this weekend for the first time since you got here. From experience, I can tell you this is going to be more difficult than you might imagine."

"Why would going home be difficult?"

"You're going to be seeing the people you love the most. The hardest thing you'll have to do is lie to them about everything. Think through your answers to potential questions ahead of time and rehearse responses."

"Like where I've been?"

"That and everything else. You'll have to make up stories about what you've been doing, why you have bruises on your arms and legs. Funny recollections of things you've done that you haven't actually done. Don't leave holes in your timeline, and don't give them a chance to ask questions. And whatever you do, *don't* contradict yourself. Remember your lies. It's rough enough for those of us with experience."

Pogue nodded.

"I give this advice a lot. But you ... you're a family man already—a physician. The rest of these recruits are single and in their twenties. To them, life with the Bureau was a choice, and it's still exciting and exhilarating. But you didn't choose this."

Pogue shook the man's hand. "I appreciate the heads-up, Commander."

He opened the door. "I'll see you back next week, Pogue. Best of luck to you."

"Thank you, sir."

As he closed the door, he glanced at his computer screen saver of Jenni and the kids. It was true. He would get to see them, and it would be a weekend of lies, but what the commander didn't know about him was that he was good at it. Lying to Jenni had become the norm for him. He lied about gambling, about losing their money, about borrowing from Nick and telling her who Nick was—everything.

As he drifted off to sleep, he heard the chime of an instant message from Jenni on his laptop.

*Bailey, I know you're busy, but I also know you love me and wish you were here. I wish you were here too. Can't wait to see you.*

He typed his reply. *I miss you too, but I won't miss the weather here in Colorado!*

He hit *Send*.

***

Agent James glanced up from his computer when the secretary walked into his office.

"Excuse me, sir. I wanted to let you know that a Mr. Arlo Ledger just checked into the Grand Peak Hotel in Colorado Springs."

"Good. Our information was correct, then."

"Yes, sir. He asked about his friend, Dr. Pogue, and the girl at the reservation desk refused to give out any information at first, just as you instructed."

"I know Arlo Ledger's reputation well enough to believe he didn't take 'no' for an answer."

"He asked to speak with the manager who reluctantly offered the information we instructed him to give. He explained that Mr. Ledger had just missed Dr. Pogue by one day and that he'd been there for three weeks."

"Very good. Did Mr. Ledger appear to believe it?"

"He was originally registered to stay for three days but didn't even spend the night. He went back to the airport and should be in Chicago on the red-eye in the morning."

James chuckled. "Now that's a vision that'll make you smile."

\*\*\*

The moment Pogue's plane touched down at O'Hare the night before, he'd turned off airplane mode and texted Jenni. He'd been so excited he could hardly contain himself, and there she was, waiting at the curb by baggage claim.

Now that they'd enjoyed a homemade breakfast on Saturday morning, he was ready to enjoy the moment fully—forget everything that had happened in the past three weeks and just be with his family.

Jenni dropped into the chair beside her husband. "What should we do today?"

Pogue didn't have to think long. "Let's take the kids to the zoo."

"If we go to Lincoln Park they'll get to be downtown. We could even grab lunch in the city. They'll love that."

"Let's get moving. I don't want to waste a minute." Pogue's cell phone rang. ID said Detective Davis. Pogue cringed. *No. Not now.* "Hello, Detective. What can I do for you?"

"Dr. Pogue, I know you've been out of town, but I believe we should meet at the hospital. I have information that may interest you."

Pogue stared at Jenni. She shrugged and gave him a smile. He whispered to her, "It's the detective from the Lucci case."

"Is this a bad time?" Davis must have heard him.

"Well, I just got home and need to spend time with my wife and kids."

"Dr. Pogue, I … if you meet me at Lucci's hospital room, I will take fifteen minutes. When we're done, you'll say it was worth the time. Then go be with your family."

Pogue faced the back door as he spoke. "You have my attention. What makes you think—"

"Fifteen minutes. It's a request. You name the time and I'll be there."

Pogue looked back at Jenni. "He's asking for fifteen minutes at Cook County."

She nodded her approval.

"Tell you what, Detective. I'm going to drop my kids and wife off at Lincoln Park Zoo, then meet you at the hospital around ..." He looked at his watch. "Noon. After that, I'm with them."

"Fair enough. I appreciate your time."

Pogue hung up the phone and looked at her. She winked at him.

"I stink as a father and a husband."

"No, you don't. You just made a deal with a guy you don't really want to see but know that you should, but you didn't bail on your family. Fifteen minutes is nothing."

"Thank you, baby. I promise I'll make it quick. It sounds important."

She kissed him on the lips. "I'll go get the kids."

"I'll meet you in the garage as soon as they're ready." Pogue pointed up. "Janelle was on her phone upstairs when I came down."

"I'll get her. We'll be there in a sec."

Pogue walked down the hall, through the living room, and stepped into the garage. Pulling the door closed behind him, he slipped his holster and pistol on under his jacket. Why on earth did Davis need to see him?

*  *  *

"Everything's in place, Philip. We've already begun screening for the right people. I promised you this." Nadir scanned the room instinctively. "You'll have the trade you've wanted for years, and we'll both be very wealthy."

Philip Ahmed grinned as he sat in The Megido, Nadir's favorite Cairo restaurant. "We've talked of this for quite some time, Nadir. The idea it could become reality is difficult to grasp—elusive, in fact."

"Are your people in place?"

"Of course. We've been ready and waiting for so long, some of our potential buyers have sought alternate suppliers, to no avail."

"They'll be back when they see that we offer what no one else possibly can." Nadir took a bite of koshary as he studied his friend. He leisurely cut into a piece of hamam mahshi. "It's a premium business, demanding a premium price. Anyone with means will pay for what we offer."

"But, what of your other endeavors?" Philip asked.

"Excuse me?" Nadir stopped eating and stared at him.

"You've been bartering information. It's no secret. I don't know the details, but there's been talk."

"Really?" Nadir placed his knife and fork on the table and folded his arms.

"At some level."

"I need to know who is talking. I need to know now."

Philip squirmed. "I don't have names, but several of my key contacts—"

"Contacts. I want their names."

"I would prefer not—"

"My other pursuits do not concern you, Philip. You are a middleman— my middleman. They are not the concern of your contacts either. At least they won't be once I deal with them."

"Your other activities do affect me when they interfere with supply and demand. My contacts are not pleased with delays and—"

"My other activities won't interfere with anything."

"How do I know this, Nadir?"

"Because I have said so. Now, prepare for your end of this business, and write me a list of your contacts' names. If you can't fulfill your obligation, I'll find someone who can."

Philip grunted under his breath. "Do not threaten me."

Nadir stood in the crowded restaurant, pulled a pistol from his jacket holster, and pressed it against Philip's forehead.

"Tell me, Philip. Do you see anyone in this establishment, my favorite restaurant, shocked at what I'm doing right now? Are they scurrying to your rescue? Are they attempting to contact authorities?"

Philip scanned the room the best he could with a gun barrel pressed against his skull. The patrons offered disinterested glances. Most turned away.

"No one cares about your concerns. There are a dozen men waiting to take the position I've given you, hoping to God you'll screw it up. These people not only don't care if I kill you—they pray to Allah I will. Tell me what to do, Philip. Should I squeeze the trigger?" He cocked the hammer.

Philip barely shook his head. "No."

As Nadir pulled the pistol from his head, Philip glanced around the room one more time. "I'm sorry, Nadir. It won't happen again."

Nadir sat, pulled his chair in, and clipped the gun securely into its holster. "No, it will not." He poured some coffee. "Would you pass the cream, please?"

# CHAPTER FOURTEEN

---

**P**ogue sat beside Ginger's bed while the US marshal stood outside the cubicle. Detective Davis entered the room and shook Pogue's hand.

"It's good to see you, Doctor. I appreciate you meeting me under such a vague premise, but I didn't feel right doing this any other way."

Pogue did little to hide his curiosity. "Well, you got me here."

Davis sat on the edge of Ginger's bed and pointed at her. "Ginger Lucci is a veggie whose life has been in jeopardy several times, which is why I wanted to meet you here."

"You lost me."

Davis reached into his suit pocket and pulled out an envelope with a government seal on the upper left corner.

"I just presented a copy of this to Dr. Harrison. It's a court order to keep Ms. Lucci on life support until we're done with our investigation."

"Why wouldn't she be kept on life support?"

"I'm glad you asked. According to the United States district court, a request to discontinue life support was filed yesterday. This document stays that request pending our investigation."

"By whom?"

"By whom what?"

"Who requested her to be removed from life support?"

"Her husband. Kurt Lucci." Davis emphasized his name and lifted his chin high as if mocking Kurt. "You weren't expecting that one, were you, Doc?"

*Kurt wants her gone. Out of the picture. Why?* "Detective, pulling the plug, to speak bluntly, is an action that would be highly inappropriate and illegal. She has shown signs of independent life since her injury. You know that from the piece of bedsheet Dr. Taylor turned over to you."

Davis cocked his head to the side. "We know that it's her blood. Other than that, we got nothing. Only she and God know what she meant."

"What about the surveillance footage?"

"It doesn't exist. The footage we need took place between four twelve and four thirty a couple of days after the initial attack, according to your friend, Dr. Taylor. He gave us the date and time. That surveillance appears to have disappeared, never existed, or has been erased."

"How can that be?"

Davis shook his head. "I need a higher authority, someone with more power to give me those answers." He grinned.

"Like?"

"Like you."

"Detective …" Pogue regrouped. "You've been on this case from the start. Are you a step ahead of who calls the shots, or are *you* the one calling them?"

Davis grinned. "I'm in charge of this case because I'm the specialist for particular criminal activities in my division. I've been tracking the movements of prominent organized crime figures. Ben and Nick Gambrel have been on my radar for years. *That* is what caused my path to cross yours."

"What are you saying?"

"I knew that your friend, Connor Banks, was not Connor Banks. I also thought you knew that long ago, but I subsequently learned that wasn't true. It seemed like you were involved."

"But now?"

Davis smirked. "I got a little too close to you and was summoned to the office of FBI Special Agent Larson James."

*He knows.* Pogue's poker face failed him.

Davis held up his hand. "It's okay, Doc. I know you're working for them, and I'm the only one in the department who does. It has to stay that way."

Pogue released the breath he'd been holding.

"That's the reason I wanted to meet with you and tell you what's going on. I appreciate what you're doing, but I have to warn you—you might be out of your league. These guys on the 'dark side' play for keeps. I've lost two partners in the last five years. The Gambrels, including your buddy

Nick, wouldn't give a second thought about making your wife a widow."

"That has occurred to me."

"Any chance of getting your hands on the surveillance footage we need from your fed buddies? Like I said, I need someone with more authority."

"I'll do my best."

Davis checked his watch. "Twelve minutes." He smiled, shook Pogue's hand, and walked to the door. "Go spend time with your family." He left the room.

Pogue pulled out his encrypted cell, punched in three numbers, and waited.

"Hello, this is Pal's Pizzeria. How may I help you?"

Pogue responded with, "Alpha, Delta, Foxtrot, Alpha, Romeo."

"Confirm."

"Tycoon."

Seconds later, James' voice came on the line. "What can I do for you, Pogue?"

"Tell me you talked to Detective Davis about me."

"Had to. He was nosing around where he shouldn't be. Guy's cut from a different mold, but he's a good cop. I trust him and told him. Why?"

"We need video surveillance footage from Lucci's room at the hospital for the date and time I'm texting you on the secure line. Your guys may have it but not realize to look at a particular time frame. Davis asked me to pull a string."

"Something of interest?"

"There's documentation that the CPD can't find. It's a time span during which Ginger Lucci may have written a note on a bedsheet on the morning in question."

"Send it. I'll run it up the pole."

*** 

Jamie Williams finished her dance class with barely enough time to get to her job at the popcorn shop on Michigan Avenue. Working part-time as a model for junior clothing at Aéropostale, she found her schedule constantly stretched. But her mother wanted her to gain experience in the "real world," as she'd put it. Apparently, that meant selling specialty popcorn.

She entered the shop and clocked in, beginning her work by mixing almonds with swirling caramel corn in an automated vat. That's when she noticed a young, handsome man entering the store behind a couple browsing through gift packages.

"May I help you?" She smiled at the couple, but her eyes were drawn to the man behind them. Dressed in a light suit and sporting Patrick Dempsey three-day stubble, he flashed a brief, bright smile before turning back to the shelf.

"Excuse me, miss?" The woman grunted. "Did you hear me?"

Jamie's face turned hot. "I'm sorry. Thinking about midterms."

The woman threw a disgusted look at the man by the door, then back at Jamie. "Do I have your attention now?"

"Yes, ma'am. What can I do for you?"

"As I just said, we would like the large gift package over there." She pointed to the display on the wall.

"Of course." Jamie rang up the amount on the register. "That will be one hundred forty-nine dollars and ninety-five cents."

"For popcorn?"

"For that particular assortment of gourmet popcorn. Yes, ma'am. That's twelve tins of quart-sized popcorn in assorted flavors, including Caramel, Almond, Buttered Toffee, Honey Glazed, CheeseCorn, Macadamia, CaramelCrisp, Pecan CaramelCrisp—"

"I don't think so."

"Pardon me?"

"I said, I don't think so. It's popcorn."

The young man stepped between the couple and faced the woman. "Excuse me, madam. There's no need for you to be a bore."

Jamie melted at his English accent.

The woman gasped. "How dare you?"

"May I suggest that perhaps you could buy some bulk popcorn from Walmart, place it in Ziploc baggies, and sprinkle flavoring over it before you ship it to your friends. That would be cheaper, and I'm certain they'll never know the difference."

"Of course they'll know the difference."

"My point precisely. If you want your friends to have the best, then pay for it. If you want to be a cheapskate, go to Walmart. No one's stopping you."

"Young man, you have no right—"

He handed the woman a pamphlet from the counter. "Decide what you want, then make your purchase. You can even do it online."

The woman huffed, turned, and stomped out with her silent husband trailing behind like a poodle on a leash.

"That was dreadful," the young man said, now speaking to Jamie.

She smiled. "Thank you for standing up for me."

"My pleasure. I apologize for asking such a cliché question, but haven't I seen you somewhere before?"

A cascade of warmth flooded her cheeks again. She hated that about herself—always turning beet red every time she was embarrassed. "I don't think we've met. I'd remember." Her skin prickled.

"Clearly, I've overstepped my bounds in the world of gourmet popcorn. I must make this up to you, and I believe you're obliged to allow me to do so, Jamie."

"Really? I'm obliged to let you make up for possibly getting me fired?"

"I'm pleased you understand."

"And how do you know my name?"

The young man pointed to her nametag. "So, Jamie … would you consider allowing me the pleasure of taking you out on a dinner cruise? The Chicago skyline from Lake Michigan is beautiful at night, and it is the least I can do."

He seemed almost … too charming. "I don't know."

"Tell me what I should do, then."

"Coffee first. Tonight after work at seven. Starbucks is on the corner."

"Good." His smile melted her.

"You know my name, but what's yours?"

"Lucas. My name is Lucas."

# CHAPTER FIFTEEN

Special Agent James reviewed the FBI files again. He'd been over this information a dozen times.

"Vaughn, would you come in here, please?"

When Vaughn entered, James pointed to the chair across the conference table. Vaughn took a seat.

James folded his hands on the table. "We need to get closer to the inside of the syndicate before Dr. Pogue is finished his training. How do we get ears to the ground before the window of opportunity closes?"

"We don't, sir."

James rolled his head back and stared at the ceiling.

"You misunderstand me, sir. No one gets in unless they're invited. It takes years for that to happen if it ever does, and you have to be someone special—you must have something significant to offer with a completely clear background. You know this."

James nodded in a discouraged way.

"Your question should be, sir, 'How do we get Dr. Pogue in position before he's finished training?'"

James shook his head. "He's not ready. I'd be sending him to his doom."

"Pogue has completed six weeks of training and rests comfortably at the top of his class."

James rubbed his forehead.

"Has he engaged with the Gambrels during that time?"

James opened a file. "Once. He met with Nick after the fourth week. He was also supposed to meet with Kurt Lucci, but he was in New York the week Pogue was in town. Anyway, they had dinner and caught up with Pogue's alleged seminars, but nothing of substance. I'm afraid we're going to lose our chance of getting him there in time."

"Waiting is a mistake, sir. The trail will grow cold. By the time he's finished, he may not be an insider—at least not as deep as we'd anticipated."

James struggled with turning a doctor into a mole. "I can't have his blood on my hands."

"Pogue has shown incredible aptitude. He outranks those in his class in age by an average of eleven years. His abilities have grown exponentially over the past six weeks. I'd suggest a soft landing with the Gambrels and send him off for training a week or two at a time over the next six months."

James scratched his forehead. "Fine. Get him in play. We can pick up training down the line."

"Very good." Vaughn stood to leave the room.

"Would you mind getting Quantico on the line, Vaughn? I need to speak with his commanding officer."

"Right away, sir."

As Vaughn left, James gathered the file together. "I hope you're as smart as everyone thinks you are, Pogue."

# CHAPTER SIXTEEN

Pogue walked into Nick's downtown office on the eighth floor of the Ballard Building. The sense of foreboding that hovered over him became easier to ignore. Now that he'd been summoned by Nick to talk over his new position, his chest tightened, but he could handle it. He'd barely taken a seat in the small, plush waiting room when the receptionist called him.

"Mr. Banks will see you now, Dr. Pogue."

Pogue stood. "Thank you."

She led him to a door down the hall and opened it for him to enter. Nick sat at the desk.

Pogue shook his hand as she closed the door.

"She called you Mr. Banks."

"She knows my real name, but she doesn't know you do."

Pogue nodded as he took a seat. "I'd like to follow up on the conversation we had on the phone yesterday. You'd like me to come on a trip with you?"

Nick moved behind the desk and sat. "Before we get into that, does Jenni know you work for me?"

"She knows I've taken a position as concierge doctor for the Banks family and that I can't discuss any of it with her because of privacy concerns."

"And that was okay with her?"

"She knows that, as a physician, there are many issues I can't discuss with her due to confidentiality. She'll be okay with it."

"Convince her that you're happy with this choice and it's a good thing. You can do that. You're the man. She's the woman."

Pogue's fists tightened. *I'd love to punch you in the throat.* He needed to change the subject. "What about that trip? Where are you going? What's it for?"

"We'll take my family's private jet to Cairo. No wasted time in airports and going through regular security. I'll spend three days introducing you to influential people you should meet regarding our international business interest."

"Who are the people I need to meet?"

"Our activities abroad border on areas that must remain secure. I need your commitment to discretion."

Pogue tilted his head back. "I thought I'd done that weeks ago."

"You did, but—"

"Yes—I'll be discreet."

"I know you don't enjoy lying to your wife. But, again—it's not like it's the first time. What you should focus on now is what this job is going to do for you and for your family."

Nick stood and poured them each a cup of coffee. He handed one to Pogue before sitting again.

Pogue set the cup on the desk. "After Cairo, what then?"

"I'll start the process of bringing you up to speed on current endeavors. The people you meet will be both influential and critical to our process. Then we'll head home. Five days start to finish."

"So this isn't a doctor thing but something to do with your business over there?"

"That's right. You'll see what your options are and how you can diversify to make more money. It will be you and Kurt, plus me on the way over. Marc Santino will fly back with us."

"Who?" Pogue's ears burned as his adrenaline returned with a vengeance. He did his best not to reveal he knew the name.

Nick grinned. "You'll like Marc."

This was the link James needed—the third family involved in this unholy enterprise. Pogue's head filled with questions. What about the details—what was in place—what might be coming? If he let his guard down, they'd run over him like a train.

"It'll be fun." Nick snapped him back. "It's a chance to travel while you and Marc get to know each other. The reason for it will be clear. I don't want to give away too much up front."

Pogue nodded. "I'll explain it to Jenni, in a benign way."

"Will she be upset you're leaving?"

"She knew when I took this position it would require some travel. She'll understand."

"You have a passport, right?"

"I have a passport."

"The next time you see my father, don't mention this. Remember, Kurt, Marc, and I are working on something, and we don't want to bring him into the loop until we're ready."

\*\*\*

Pogue climbed into the back seat of the Tahoe next to Agent James. He closed the door and the vehicle drove off.

"How are we doing, Doctor?"

Pogue grabbed a cold bottle of water from the cup holder, twisted off the top, and took a long drink. As he finished, he said, "I'm in deep."

James didn't attempt to conceal his enthusiasm. "What do they want you to do?"

"We leave for Egypt in three days to meet contacts there and return with another passenger."

"What?" The smile vanished. "Who?"

"Marc Santino."

"Santino? Are you sure?"

"That's what Nick said. It fits."

"I don't want you going to Cairo. You'll be there with no cover. I won't be able to protect you."

"I don't have a choice." Pogue gazed out the window. "The problem is I don't know what or who I'm looking for in Egypt."

"I had no intention of putting you in this kind of situation so soon." James gave a heavy sigh. "This isn't where I wanted you."

"Well, I'm there. You wanted deep—I'm deep."

James pushed a button and lowered the privacy screen separating them from the driver. "Let us out at the pier, please."

The driver nodded and pulled to the side of the road. James and Pogue slipped out the passenger side and made their way to a path by the waterfront next to Navy Pier.

"Every move you make they'll watch—your responses to situations, to threats, even pleasure."

"It's Jenni and the kids I worry about."

"We'll keep them under our wing."

"I have a hunch that Nick will be watching them too."

"Did he say that?"

"No, but if the FBI and mafia spot each other, we're screwed."

"I'll make certain we keep a safe distance."

Pogue gazed at the horizon of Lake Michigan. "I know what I'm doing is important. I'm coming to terms with the fact that it's the right thing."

"I don't like you going to Egypt. But you're right. We need answers." James checked his watch. "We'd better get you home. You have packing to do. One more thing—if anything goes wrong, use this." He handed him a small square of paper with a number scribbled on it.

"A phone number?"

"Not just a phone number—*the* phone number. For emergencies."

\*\*\*

The man pulled his low-profile bulletproof vest over his head and stretched the Velcro straps for a snug fit. Buttoning his freshly pressed shirt, he then formed a perfect knot in a matching tie to complete the look. After slipping on his shoulder holster, he completed his outfit with a dark sports jacket.

He checked the clip on his Sig Sauer 9mm, chambered a round, then fastened the pistol securely into the holster under his left arm.

Retrieving the police badge from the top drawer of his dresser, he buffed it on his sleeve before slipping it in his jacket pocket. After a quick check of his Benchmade switchblade, he closed it and clipped it to his boot. Three partial slits on the inner sidewall of the right rear tire would take seconds.

Lifting the cell phone from the dresser, he scrolled through the photos to find those he'd taken of Amy King.

# CHAPTER SEVENTEEN

The Falcon 7X luxury jet cruised at thirty-five thousand feet above the Atlantic. Pogue settled into the plush white leather seat as brilliant sunlight flooded the cabin. Swiveling his chair allowed him to gaze out the window or face fellow passengers. A flat-screen TV stood ready for viewing at each seat, though none of them were being used. Without the usual overhead storage bins, the higher ceiling allowed Pogue to move about without bumping his head.

Two young flight attendants prepared mixed drinks, but Pogue declined, sticking with Coke Zero.

"What's the problem, Pogue? Don't have the vintage you require?" Nick asked sarcastically.

"You know I drink very little."

"Too hedonistic?"

"I like to be the soberest man in the room—or in the jet, as the case may be."

Nick cocked his head. "An acceptable answer. That I understand."

Kurt exited the restroom and made his way to his seat. He leaned toward Pogue. "So what has Nick told you?"

"No specifics other than being the Gambrel's concierge physician," Pogue answered. "But I know you guys are excited about something on the horizon."

"That would be an understatement." Kurt sipped his drink. "It gives us the opportunity to declare our independence and branch into new territory with our family businesses for the first time in decades. Our fathers and grandfathers have done nothing more than maintain the status quo since the fifties."

"What's this new line of business?"

Nick jumped on the question. "Let's wait until we get our feet on the ground before talking specifics. I will tell you this: you'll be much more than the concierge doctor my dad expects. Medical duties will comprise a relatively small part of your income and responsibilities. Don't get me wrong, you'll need to be available on short notice when required for your medical expertise, but we'll ease you into our side of the business as an integral component. That's why you'll be earning seven digits in less than twelve months."

Kurt had the flight attendant refill his drink. "He's not exaggerating, Pogue. If anything, it's an understatement."

"The income we're talking about is not unreasonable for impeccable loyalty," Nick added. "That can make the difference between being rich or being dead."

"I don't want to be dead," Pogue said.

"Then be loyal and rich." Nick seemed to live by such a simple code, but that couldn't be true.

"What kind of danger are we talking about?" Pogue adjusted the window shade. "I have a family."

Nick held up one hand to stop Kurt from answering. "I won't pretend there isn't risk. But people who are not new to this environment will surround you. Kurt and I are your safety net, and I've already assured you I'll protect your family. For now, on this trip, I want you to meet key people involved with our new venture."

"Of all the doctors in Chicago, why me?"

Nick nursed his drink. "You're more than a doctor. You have talents and skills you've probably never considered valuable. But we'll get to those."

Kurt took a drink and looked for the attendant again. "You also have a unique skill set, Pogue."

"Skill set?"

Nick folded his hands. "Getting ahead of ourselves. The timing's perfect for you to be available with our doctor out of the picture." He leaned forward and rested his elbows on the armrests. "Kurt and I need someone who doesn't report to my father as our previous doctor did. Every family doctor is brought in under intense scrutiny. He stays with the family until he dies."

Pogue matched Nick's posture. "What if he doesn't want to?"

"He does." Nick rested back in his chair. "As I said, there's risk. But risk is mitigated by security, loyalty, and secrecy."

Pogue stroked his chin.

"Listen, Pogue, once we introduce you to some people and you have some answers, you'll feel better about all this."

Pogue poured more Coke and forced a grin.

*Better about what?*

\*\*\*

The hospital speakers sounded the announcement: "Code blue. Code blue ICU isolation room two."

Within seconds, doctors and nurses flooded the room, frantically checking monitors and pushing medications into her IV port. An array of machines and computer screens surrounded her bed. Lights flashed on each one.

The electrical shock gave a sickening thud as her body jolted. The thud repeated—then again—and again.

After a long fifteen minutes, everyone stood back. Ginger Lucci was gone.

\*\*\*

Amy King wondered what was keeping her father. She and her friend, Linda, sat on the wall in front of the school. He'd texted an hour ago saying he had a flat.

Amy let out a disappointed sigh. "He said he'd be here as soon as he could."

"It's okay." Linda patted her arm.

Amy offered her a brief smile as a black SUV pulled to the curb with blue lights flashing. The young man inside lowered the passenger window. "Is one of you Amy King? I'm with the Chicago PD." He showed them his badge. "I was sent to pick up Amy King, daughter of Foster King."

"I'm Amy. What's wrong?"

"Your father has been in an accident changing a tire on the freeway. I need to drive you to the hospital."

Amy glanced at Linda as her heart filled with panic. "Is he okay?" She fought back tears.

"All I know is we need to get you to Cook County Hospital."

"Oh, God. I need to call Mom."

"She's the one who sent me. Get in and call her on the way. We're wasting time."

"Go." Linda waved her on. "I'll be okay. I'll call somebody or … something. Go!"

Amy opened the door and jumped into the vehicle. The SUV drove off and turned right at the traffic light. Amy began to dial her mom's cell when the man grabbed it from her. He patted her arm. "It's going to be okay."

She looked at him and wanted to say something. But … she couldn't speak. She stared at the red, sticky button he'd placed on her arm. Then everything went black.

# CHAPTER EIGHTEEN

Detective Davis entered the ICU and was immediately accosted by Dr. Harrison.

"You have no right to keep us here till you decide to show up."

Davis flashed a smirk in the marshal's direction, the man who'd been guarding Ginger Lucci's room before her death. Davis turned back to Harrison. "Actually, I do. I appreciate you hanging around until I got here. It took me almost"—he checked his watch—"fifteen minutes."

"Fifteen minutes is precious time for a doctor."

"Time is precious for anyone, Dr. Harrison—especially Ginger Lucci, it would seem."

Harrison sat with a disgruntled huff.

"I'll be right with you. First I need to talk to the marshal over here."

"You can't keep me here. I'm a doctor. You can't ..." Harrison's voice trailed off over Davis' glare.

"I said, I'll be right with you, Doctor." Davis motioned to the marshal to head toward a counseling room. Once they were inside, he took a seat. "Tell me what happened today."

The marshal sat across from him. "I was at my station in Lucci's room when the nurse ran in, checked the monitors, and called a code. Everyone rushed in, including Dr. Harrison. They seemed to do their best to save her but couldn't."

"Anything out of place before, during, or after the code?"

"When Harrison came out, he headed straight for the nurses' station, picked up the phone, and placed a call. He seemed panicked."

Davis rested back in the chair. "Nothing fits. There has to be a connection that ties him into this."

"Harrison's nurse, Reid Beckman, was with him. She seemed skittish when I told everyone they needed to stay until you arrived. I had to stop her from leaving the floor. And she was trembling."

"I want to speak with everyone who attended the code. We'll meet in this room one at a time starting with Reid, then Harrison, then the charge nurse. The rest will be in no particular order. I'll take statements from everyone. You'll be last."

Davis opened the door to find the charge nurse standing with a tissue in her hand.

"I'm sorry to bother you, Detective. There's a Benjamin Banks on the phone. He says he's Dr. Lucci's father?"

Davis sighed. "I'll take it."

\*\*\*

Pogue followed Nick and Kurt into what they boasted to be their favorite Cairo restaurant, The Megido. A dozen men stationed inside the building entrance followed them with their eyes. To Pogue, the uninviting, dingy room seemed a great place for an ambush.

A stairwell on the right took them to the second floor. A thick cloud of cigarette and hookah smoke hung in the air by the landing.

A man stood before them at the entrance to a larger room. Nick stopped and gestured toward him. "Pogue, this is Nadir, our friend here in Egypt."

Nadir grabbed Pogue's hand and held it firmly as he glared. "Who's this you bring to my private establishment?"

Pogue allowed his "aggressive opponent" training at Quantico to kick in. He refused to back down.

"This is Dr. Pogue, the man we spoke about."

Nadir continued to stare and tilted his head. "I don't know you, but I shall."

Pogue gave a single nod. "I look forward to it."

A slow grin coursed Nadir's lips. "Please. Let us not waste a moment. Time to rest and enjoy the preparations."

Pogue's shirt clung to him from nervous sweat. "I'm honored."

Nadir turned to Nick and Kurt. "Come, my friends."

As they entered the room, Nadir clapped his hands, and several servant girls entered with drinks. Beams of light filtering through high windows illuminated thin lines of smoke in the air. Food on the table was impossible to identify, but everyone dug in. Pogue did the same.

Nick slapped him on the back. "Nadir seemed to like you. He doesn't like anyone."

Pogue offered a brief smile and sipped his mango juice.

Nadir stood with a glass in his hand. "My esteemed colleagues. It's an honor to welcome you and my new friend from America, Dr. Pogue." He raised it in a toast.

Pogue nodded, acknowledging the comment, and raised his mango juice.

"I'm excited to embark on this journey with my friends from the west. May we all prosper!"

Pogue smiled. *God, give me strength.*

# CHAPTER NINETEEN

---

ogue followed Kurt into the foyer of the luxury hotel suite. Nick approached one of the men at the entrance. "Is Robert Savage here?" The man checked his watch. "He'll be with you momentarily."

"Nicholas!" Robert Savage entered from a side room. "It's good to see you."

Nick shook his hand.

"And this must be Dr. Pogue, the man I've heard so much about?" Robert reached for Pogue's hand with his right and held an empty wine glass in his left.

Nick sighed. "Pogue, I'd like you to meet Robert Savage, Washington's envoy to the Middle East and Chairman of the Special Prosecutor Oversight Committee in Washington."

The man's name and title secured itself in Pogue's memory. He accepted Robert's handshake. "It's good to meet you."

"You as well, Doctor."

"Everyone calls me Pogue."

"As will I." Robert turned, and the men followed him down a hallway to a spacious, luxuriously decorated room. "Have a seat." The men settled into the overstuffed furniture. Robert sat in a more rigid chair. "Let me jump in and ask you a question, Doctor. What do you know about international politics?"

Pogue gave him a thoughtful look. "Since we're here in the Middle East, I know that Syrian refugees are a significant concern to the US as well as the rest of the world, along with refugees from any region disrupted by unstable regimes. Many governments, in addition to the United States, find themselves in the position of dealing with immigrants and refugees from a number of nations—a humanitarian crisis."

"Indeed. In fact, due to the current political environment, we're able to function as entrepreneurs as never before."

Pogue shifted in his seat. "I don't follow."

Nick leaned in. "Robert, I think—"

"Give me a moment." He poured more wine. "Allow me to pose a hypothetical situation, Doctor: If the Middle East is a breeding ground for war and terrorist organizations, where would the battleground be?"

Pogue raised his palms. "I would think here—Egypt and the surrounding Middle East areas. Refugees are infiltrating this country from the Sinai Peninsula through Port Said and occupying the area of Cairo known as the Sixth of October. I wouldn't be surprised if they're scattered throughout the Delta. There's evidence that militant factions have occupied regions along the Nile including the town of Minya in Upper Egypt. Where refugees go, ISIS, the Muslim Brotherhood, and other terrorists follow."

"Exactly." Savage held up his glass as a chalice. "So in your opinion, where would Intelligence be most lacking?"

"What do you mean by Intelligence?"

"Robert, please." Nick stood.

"Secrets. United States government secrets regarding the Middle East's enemy faction movements, plans, locations, America's strategies against them, et cetera. Would it not be helpful to understand the plans of other nations from the perspective of US operations in the Middle East? More importantly, if we supplied that intelligence, where would that information be of the greatest benefit?"

Nick placed his hand on Robert's shoulder. "I must ask you to—"

"Benefit to whom?" Pogue wasn't letting this go.

"Just benefit. Think of it as a commodity, not an ideal. Who would benefit most?"

Pogue spoke quickly to prevent Nick from objecting. "If Egypt is the battleground, they stand to lose the most if they know the least."

"That's where we come in. We offer the Intelligence they need to stay on top of things. They can't gather Intel as we can, but the US has everything these people need sitting on a shelf in some dark virtual warehouse gathering dust."

Pogue looked at Nick, then at Savage. "Would you excuse us for just a moment, Mr. Savage? I need to speak with Nick."

"Certainly." Savage turned to Kurt. "Would you care for a drink?"

Pogue moved to an adjoining room that appeared to be unoccupied. Nick followed.

Pogue turned to face him. "A few hours ago, we were talking about the medical profession and my retirement. Now we're discussing espionage in the Middle East. What's going on? What are you into? What are *we* into?"

"Money—having more money than God."

"Espionage sends people to prison. How do we get the information this guy is talking about, and what does it have to do with me?"

The voice Pogue heard behind him next was one he didn't recognize.

"The details of data collection will be clear in time, just like your role in our operations." The man folded his arms. "But you're asking a lot of questions for a newcomer."

Pogue found himself face to face with Marc Santino, the man he recognized from James' photos.

"My name is Marc." He extended his hand and shook Pogue's firmly. "I've heard a great deal about you, Dr. Pogue. Ideally, we would have brought you in a little at a time, but we wanted to be sure you could handle knowing the facts before we took this further. Our timeline has accelerated."

"What do I need to know?"

"I hope you understand we have to be cautious. To be honest, you already have more information than I wanted to give you. But Nick vouched for you and that's on him." Marc chose a seat in an alcove on the edge of the room. He motioned for Pogue to sit across from him. "Nick, would you mind grabbing us a bottle and three glasses? Then come back to talk."

Nick cocked his head indignantly. "There are servers here."

"I just need a second to poke Pogue's brain in private. Please."

Nick huffed. "Two minutes. I don't work for you." He walked to the next room.

Marc put his hand on Pogue's shoulder. "Do you know who I am?"

"Marcus Santino."

"Marc to you. I'm in charge of Intelligence operations over here through Robert Savage, the guy you met when you came in. I'm afraid liquor has loosened his diplomatic tongue. Nick works out the details with Nadir Mohmed and Philip Wassim."

"I didn't meet Philip, just Nadir."

"Philip is Nadir's man on the front lines in Egypt. I'm in charge of the Intel bartering over here. Is that clear?"

Pogue stroked his eyebrow with an index finger. "Yes. But I don't understand where I fit in. I have no connection to US Intelligence. I've never even served in the military." Any hope of getting out of this alive by simply turning over information to the FBI was down the drain. He'd better fit into this puzzle fast, or they'd ship him home in a box.

Marc reached for the bottle Nick brought into the room. "Where you fit in is simple—we need someone willing to travel without drawing suspicion while carrying Intel we'll provide. We can't send it electronically or it risks discovery or hacking. It can't be in written form or the individual caught with classified documents goes to prison for the rest of his or her life. What we're doing requires an individual who could travel regularly under the radar."

Pogue nodded once. "And you see me filling that role somehow?"

"A doctor teaching seminars would attract little attention, especially if he has been doing so for years. The visiting professor seminars at the medical school in Cairo are taught in English. There are several other organizations that can be used for guest lecturing in parts of the Middle East, and with US credentials like yours, getting you in is a sure thing."

Pogue glanced at Nick, then back at Marc. The last thing he wanted was to send up a red flag. He needed to play this well. "That doesn't solve the problem of how you'll smuggle the information."

"Unless that same individual had a photographic memory, like yours."

*James was spot on.*

"That is your role in a nutshell. It would be in addition to the physician duties you have with the Gambrels. I'm not involved with that."

Nick poured a drink for himself. "You'll receive documents from Mr. Savage in Chicago. He has access through a trusted source. You'll then memorize and deliver that information to Nadir and be paid handsomely for your efforts."

Pogue's muscles tightened to the point of cramping. *This isn't deep—it's trapped.* Agent James would have no way to protect him. *Say something.* "It sounds dangerous."

Marc shrugged a little. "That's true, but there are things in place to minimize the danger. You'll earn more in a year than you could in ten working as a surgeon."

"Ten? I was told three times my former salary."

"That was without your participation in our ... endeavors."

*If I push back, I'll never be heard from again.* "I'd like to go over the details to make sure I don't screw this up."

"Of course. We'll be traveling to the States together, at least as far as New York. We'll have a chance to talk on the plane." He held up his wineglass and seemed to be admiring its content. "This is my favorite Pinot Noir—eighteen hundred dollars a bottle and worth every penny." He poured another glass and offered it to Pogue. "Please."

Pogue took the glass and clinked it with Marc's.

*** 

Agent Vaughn stopped at James' doorway and cleared his throat.

"Yes?" James continued to type.

"You asked me to keep you informed, sir. Agent Pogue is connecting with individuals in Cairo, but it's more than what we expected. *Off-the-radar* more."

"Meaning?"

"We may need to contact Homeland, sir." Vaughn slid five photos across the desk to his boss.

He studied each. "Get them on the line."

# CHAPTER TWENTY

Their hotel elevator door closed with Pogue, Marc, Nick, and Kurt inside. As they began making plans to celebrate that evening, Pogue's cell phone buzzed in his pocket. Caller ID said it was Dr. Taylor.

"Scott. What's up? I'm in an elevator, so you're breaking up a little."

"Pogue, I've been trying to reach you."

"What's wrong?"

"Ginger Lucci died. She never spoke or responded to the doctors. She just died. They haven't been able to reach Connor or Kurt. Detective Davis did speak with her father Ben Banks though."

"God." Pogue turned from the other men. "I'll do it."

"I hate to mess up your conference, but I thought you'd want to know."

He glanced at the men staring at him. "Thanks. I'll call you back."

"Use my cell."

Pogue hung up and slowly tucked the phone in his pocket.

Kurt's grin vanished as he seemed to analyze Pogue's expression.

"That was Dr. Taylor from Cook County. He couldn't reach you, Kurt. Ginger passed away this afternoon."

Kurt looked at the floor. "I knew it. I felt it."

Pogue recalled the court order Kurt had tried to file to remove her life support. "She never regained consciousness."

Kurt looked at Nick. "Let's cancel that celebration tonight. Second thought, go ahead but count me out."

The elevator doors opened on their floor, but Kurt didn't step off with the other men. "I'm going down to the bar for a minute. I need to make some calls ... and drink."

Pogue took a step toward the elevator, but Kurt held up his hand. "I'd prefer to be alone. No offense."

"None taken."

The doors closed.

"I'm sorry, Nick." Pogue gave him a squeeze on his shoulder.

"It's going to hit Dad hard. Does he know?"

"He knows."

Nick took the phone from his pocket. "I had this turned off for the meeting. I'd better call him. Excuse me, guys." Nick went to his room.

Marc shook his head and stepped to the door of his room. "This sucks." He unlocked his door but stood there a moment. "Pogue, you understand the nature of what we're doing over here and your role in it, right? As it sinks in, don't let it mess with you. You can't back away at this point. Nick is your friend, so he may not be as blunt as I, but you are in this up to your neck. Do you understand that? There is only one exit plan."

Pogue pulled out the keycard for his room and turned to Marc. "I'm in. I don't want an exit plan. To be honest, I'm grateful. I don't know if Nick explained that I need the money, but I do."

"He did. But is that enough to motivate you to do what's required?"

"As I said, I'm grateful. You won't have any problems from me. I don't just want to be debt free. I want to live like you guys."

Marc walked into his room. "Good to hear. See you in the morning."

Pogue keyed into his own room and dialed Jenni's number. "Hey, baby. I had to hear your voice. I need to talk to you for a minute."

\*\*\*

Pogue tossed his bag into the limo's trunk while Nick tipped the valet and Kurt finalized preliminary arrangements on his cell for Ginger's funeral. He hung up and climbed into the car.

"You okay?" Pogue asked. "Is there anything I can do?"

Kurt nodded, then turned to Nick. "I know this affects you, too. I don't mean to be insensitive, you being her brother and all. But I need security for the funeral, and my mind is cluttered. Three prominent families will be gathered in one spot, and I don't want to place anyone in jeopardy. That location needs to be airtight."

Nick held up his hand. "I'll handle security. I appreciate having something to do."

"Would you consider saying a few words at the ceremony, too?"

"Absolutely."

The limo pulled onto the main road toward the airport.

Kurt looked up from texting. "How's your dad holding up?"

Nick shook his head. "He's seen death, but losing his only daughter hit hard."

Kurt turned to Pogue. "Ginger liked you. If you'd say a few words before I do and pray at the graveside, I'd appreciate it, knowing you're a man of faith."

"I'd be honored," Pogue said, wondering where that came from. "I need to let Jenni know."

Nick leaned in. "Pogue, I'm sorry. You can't bring her. She knows me as Connor, and we don't need to stir that pot. Everyone there will know me as Nick."

"That's okay. She'll understand."

*That isn't true and you know it.*

"By the way, Pogue, I'm getting off the plane in New York with Marc. Kurt will accompany you to Chicago, and I'll be there tomorrow afternoon."

His expression must have betrayed his surprise.

"There are some documents I need to gather from Kurt's apartment. He needs to get back to Chicago right away to organize everything for the funeral since Ginger will be buried in the family plot there."

"No problem."

*Why are you really going to New York?*

# CHAPTER TWENTY-ONE

Nick eased into the plush chair, smoothed the lapels of his sports jacket, and checked his reflection in the window. The familiar aroma of books drew his attention to the shelves nearly two stories high. Although similar to his father's library, this one bore no hint of cigar smoke and seemed a little smaller. Still, the Manhattan high-rise mansion boasted a number of first editions.

The woman seated next to him was a necessary evil. She had something he needed, and there were times one had to make concessions.

Carlee J. Franklin, known as C.J. to her friends, faced her father from across the desk. She crossed her legs slowly. The sister of Marc and daughter of Victor Santino, boss of the ruling family in New York City, she had gained the reputation as one of the most powerful and beautiful women in Manhattan.

Victor, revered for his aggressive tactics and peacefully maintaining family borders, arranged the marriage between his only daughter and Jason Franklin, a federal prosecuting attorney. She had balked at it, but her father must have made it worth her while.

She folded her hands and smiled. "You don't need to know every detail about it, Daddy. Marc, Kurt, Nick, and I are working together, and you should trust your daughter."

Victor didn't have a reputation for relinquishing control of anything when it came to the family business.

She stood and walked around the desk, leaning against it as she faced her father. "If you don't let us do this on our own, we have nothing to contribute. You just have to let go of this one little thing and trust us to do what will help the bottom line—for all of us."

"There's more to business than the bottom line, young lady."

She moved behind him and wrapped her arms around his neck for a tender hug. "I know, Daddy. And I want you to be proud of me, so you know we won't do anything to upset you. But I need control over this. Our goal is to provide information that will help people. The risk is low. I have ears on the inside—you know this." She let go, swiveled his chair to face her, and winked. An uncharacteristic smile crossed his lips. It didn't last.

"Information trading can mean anything from industrial espionage to stock manipulation to treason. I need to know where my family's reputation stands in all of this. And what is the long-term viability? Harmless vices are one thing. Treason, quite another."

"Don't be silly, Daddy. Would I do anything irresponsible?"

Nick uncrossed his legs and leaned on the arm of the chair with one elbow. "Mr. Santino, I assure you my father will be pleased once he understands what we're proposing. I wouldn't consider crossing paths with him."

"Nor should you with me." Victor stood and walked to the windows, appearing to admire the view—Central Park from the fifteenth floor across Fifth Avenue. It was one of the most coveted locations in the city. Owning the top three floors of an upscale Manhattan high-rise was a tribute to Victor's success.

He turned to them. "I'm going upstairs for a swim. It helps me think." He walked toward the study door. "Care to join me, Nick?"

"No, sir. Thank you. I've had a long flight, and I'm looking forward to getting home."

"You're avoiding the issue, Daddy." C.J. stood by her chair. "Do you trust me or not?"

Victor meandered back to his desk, rested his hands on the dark walnut slab, and looked at her. "It's not you I don't trust." He didn't attempt to disguise the glare he flashed at Nick.

Deep inside, Nick was punching the old relic in the face. Although he'd once been a great man, it was time to pasture this guy. How dare he? Nick smiled and accepted the rebuke without a flinch.

C.J. sighed. "You've made it clear you don't like Kurt and Nick, but we're the next generation. We understand each other and know the world as it exists with modern technology and social structure. It doesn't want the same things it used to." She scanned the shelves in the study and scanned the book spines. She finally appeared to find what she was searching for and rolled the ladder along its metal track to the spot. Once she'd ascended to the third shelf on the second level, she slid a tattered book from its resting place. She stepped down, walked to where her father stood, and held it in front of him. She blew a tiny dust cloud from the top, opened it near the middle, and plucked a black-and-white photo from its pages. She studied it briefly before laying it on the desk in front of him. "I want to be one of those guys."

Victor held it up to view in the light from the window. "Where did you get this?"

"I found it with Mom's things when I was little. I've looked at that picture quite a few times in the past twenty years."

He shook his head as he handed the photo back to her. "Those were different times, C.J."

"Were they? This is you and your best friends preparing to take on the world as young men. And you did it. You grabbed it by the tail and held on until it gave you what you wanted. You won, Daddy."

A sigh escaped his lips. "You're right. I did—but they didn't. I'm living the dream, but the other guys in that picture ... they've been dead for years."

"They're dead because they weren't Santinos."

"You're the sweet voice of reason, aren't you?" Victor stood straight and removed his hands from the desk. A hint of a smile returned, and this time, it stayed. He shook his head. "What assurance do I have that if I turn over control of this aspect of the business, you and Marcus will be calling the shots? With all due respect to Nick and his father, I'm not handing anything over to you unless I'm certain it's solid. I've worked hard to be where I am today."

C.J. calmed Nick with a single look. A slow grin formed on her lips, and she scooted onto the edge of the desk in front of her father. "I'll insist that we run the show."

Nick clenched his teeth. Agreeing to this ruse was hard enough without having to listen to it in front of the old codger. If anger produced smoke, he'd have a cloud circling his head.

Victor offered a nearly imperceptible nod. "If you're sure you're okay with things the way they're organized, I'll give my blessing once I see the final pro forma. What did you call this endeavor?"

Nick couldn't remain silent any longer. "Apollyon, sir." *God, C.J. Let him go swim.*

Victor kissed her cheek. "When do you go back to Chicago?"

"Nick and I fly back first thing in the morning. I'm attending Ginger's funeral."

"Yes. Sorry for your loss, Nick. Tell your father I'll call him."

"I will. Thank you."

"I'll be back in New York this weekend, Daddy. Jason is coming home from DC on Saturday."

"I look forward to seeing him. We'll go to Bond Forty-Five for dinner."

"He'll like that."

As Victor left the study, he called back without looking. "Love you, sweetheart. Bye, Nick. Have a safe trip."

Once the study door closed, Nick hurried to it, listened for a moment, then carefully turned the deadbolt as C.J. moved to the desk chair. She sat, pulled up the information on the computer, and printed out the documents. In a matter of minutes, she'd forged her father's name, stamped the papers with the notary insignia, and sealed the envelope with a wax signet as her father often did for important documents. She placed the papers in her purse.

Nick stood by the door. "You done?"

"Done."

"Let's get out of here before I explode."

\*\*\*

Since the flight arrived in Chicago early, Pogue texted Jennifer to pick him up at baggage claim instead of parking and coming inside. He hurried out to meet her and threw his bag in the back as it started to sprinkle, then climbed into the passenger seat. The moment he closed his door, the rain came in torrents.

"Hi, baby." He leaned over the console where they met for a brief kiss.

"I missed you." She eased the car onto the wet pavement. "I'm so glad you're home. It scares me when you fly in this kind of weather. They've been predicting storms since last night. At least it held off till you got home."

"How are the kiddos?"

"They hate it when you're gone. I think Janelle misses you as much as I do. She's changing so fast."

"That scares me more than flying in bad weather." Pogue shook his head. "She's becoming a young lady, and I'm not ready for it."

"We'll deal with that together." She squeezed his hand, then put both hands on the wheel. "After you called to tell me about Ginger, I wondered if you'd spoken to Connor and Kurt about funeral plans."

"Several times. Kurt wants me to speak at the eulogy and pray at the graveside."

"You guys that close?"

A hot flash prickled his skin. He'd almost slipped again. "I don't know. It's weird, but I couldn't say no. That would have felt … I don't know—rude? What's the word?"

"Sweet. That's the word—not for you—for him. It's an honor that he asked you to speak and pray. I think you should. You're a wonderful public speaker. A prayer for those families would be a good thing. How's Connor doing? Do you know?"

The wiper blades were barely making a dent in the storm.

"Do you have any bottled water?" His mouth was so dry he could hardly speak.

"Take mine." She pointed to the cup holder.

He took a sip. "Connor's fine. I think he was expecting it to happen. Either that or he's handling it really well."

"And what about you?"

He could tell the truth this time. "I'm sad that she never recovered. Her death was such a tragedy and left so many unanswered questions."

"When will the funeral be?"

That knot in his stomach returned. He sipped away the dryness again. "Saturday morning." He'd rehearsed this line a hundred times, but the knot twisted tighter just thinking about it. "There's one problem."

"Problem?"

"I'm invited but you aren't. It's for close family, and even they aren't bringing spouses." Pogue struggled to swallow. The water didn't help. He looked at her as she studied the slowing traffic on the flooded interstate.

"Really? Well, okay. I guess I'm not offended."

"One thing I've learned is that when someone says they *guess they're not* offended, they're *definitely* offended. To be honest, I wish you were going and I was staying home."

Jennifer cocked her head. "You don't mean that." She shrugged. "It's just hard to get this close to Connor and Ginger these past months and then not be invited to go to her funeral. That stinks."

"I know. I'm sorry. I wish they hadn't excluded you."

"If it's for close family, why are you invited?"

"Connor asked me to come since he considers me his best friend and still believes I helped Ginger more than anyone." *There—as rehearsed.*

"I've been very supportive through all of this." She adjusted the wipers and defroster. "Now to be excluded, it … hurts."

The sadness in her eyes brought tears to his. He batted them away, thankful she was concentrating on driving. "The reason you're not invited has nothing to do with you. It's not personal."

"It feels personal."

"There are reasons. Please let it go at that."

"What reasons?"

"It's something I can't talk about."

"I don't know what that means. I worry about you. I can't make myself stop. I have a bad feeling *all* the time, and I'm a nervous wreck."

"Everything will be okay."

Traffic moved at a snail's pace, now. Sheets of rain washed over the windshield as deafening hail pelted the car, making it impossible to be heard without shouting. He was thankful to have a minute to think. The hail soon stopped, and the rain turned to a drizzle.

"I found a tag on your luggage a few weeks ago. It was from when you were supposed to be in Colorado, but it was from Washington, DC."

*From silence to a bomb.*

"I said—"

"I heard you, Jenni. I … you need to trust me. This is—"

"Why are you carrying a gun?" Her jaw was fixed and her teeth were clenched.

A hot wash of blood flooded his face, and his eyes opened wide. Why hadn't he prepared for this? "Jenni—"

"I'm not ignorant. I know you've been carrying a gun. You lied to me about where you were. You've probably never been to Colorado."

A sting of conviction. "I've been to Colorado."

"If you're carrying a gun, I have a right to be worried. You're not a cop, so are you doing something illegal?"

*I have to tell her something.*

"I wish you would talk to me. I'm scared, Pogue." Her eyes filled with tears.

He softened his voice. "You have every reason to suspect that what I'm doing is wrong. I want to tell you everything but I can't. It's not about us, I promise you."

"It is. For you not to tell me what's going on when you've turned our lives upside down is *definitely* about us. Is what you're doing illegal?"

Focus. "If you knew what I was doing, you'd understand. You're right—I've been carrying a gun, and I've lied to you. I need you to trust me."

"I thought doing seminars was strange after all that had happened. But I went along with it. When you took the concierge job, I was for that too. But the traveling you're doing is a mystery. I don't know where you are most of the time."

"I'm sorry I can't tell you more."

Jenni blotted more tears. "Tell me you're on the right side of this thing."

"I promise you I am. I swear to you, Jenni." *Oh, God. I wouldn't believe me either.*

# CHAPTER TWENTY-TWO

Limos, Rolls-Royces, and Bentleys dominated the cemetery parking lot as hundreds of family members took seats near the graveside. Pogue sat next to Nick while the Lucci family congregated in white wooden chairs across from them. A gentle, pleasant breeze disrespectfully wafted through the few remaining colorful leaves on the trees.

Chicago police lined the roadways, blocking the exit and using wand-mirrors to search the undercarriage of each car before the vehicles were allowed to enter the grounds.

Kurt stared stone-faced at the coffin from fifteen feet away. An older woman held onto his arm. Pogue leaned toward Nick. "You okay?"

He gave a reassuring nod. "I'm fine. Dad wanted to be here, but … it's too risky. He'll be at the private ceremony later—the one they're having just for our family."

Pogue glanced over his shoulder at the swarm of people outside the fence. At least a dozen police cruisers blocked the cemetery entrance as four news trucks gathered, one of them parking on the manicured grass before the cops chased them off.

"TV networks? What's with that?"

"Vultures hoping for a glimpse," Nick said without looking. "The police are no better."

"You didn't hire them?"

"Only the ones checking cars coming in. The rest are recording license plates and snapping photos to see who's here. That's why Dad wouldn't come. He can't afford to be photographed. The last picture of him was taken almost twenty years ago."

"What about you? Aren't you concerned about being on the front page?"

"No one out there knows who I am, remember? And you don't see me looking back at the cameras, do you?"

Pogue took the advice and faced forward.

Nick broke the silence this time. "Still on for Wednesday?"

He gave a quick nod and straightened his posture as the priest began to speak. He spoke a few words and read Psalm 23, then introduced Nick. Nick stood, walked to the podium, and addressed the crowd.

"I'm Nicholas Gambrel—Ginger's big brother and Kurt's friend. Most of you know me as Nick. I can't believe I'm standing in front of Ginger's grave. She was a good wife, loving sister, and perfect daughter. One of her friends is someone she introduced me to two years ago—Dr. Bailey Pogue. I'd like to invite him as my friend, Kurt's friend, and Ginger's friend, to say a few words."

*That was faster than I'd expected.*

The moment Pogue stood, sadness and the sense of loss of his sweet friend brought unwanted tears. She was the one who should be alive, not this crowd of thugs. He made his way to the podium. Nick briefly embraced him and returned to his seat.

Pogue held the podium with both hands. The serene, solemn crowd before him contrasted sharply with the circus of police and news crews scurrying about the parking lot like cockroaches at a picnic. The wrought-iron-and-brick fence separating them offered little comfort.

He took a deep breath and let it out. "I don't have the right to be here. Kurt and Nick asked me to. So I stand for them and for Ginger. She was my friend. We met a little over two years ago when I accidentally bought two Starbucks for myself one morning. I handed her one of them, which she reluctantly accepted. So our friendship began."

After telling the crowd how Ginger had introduced him to her brother, Nick, and that they'd been friends and racquetball opponents for two years since, he said, "I don't understand the violence that could take the life of such a precious soul. Ginger didn't deserve to die. She not only deserved to live—she *earned* the *right* to live. Someone took that from her, and they had no right."

After he said it, regret and peace occupied the same place in his heart. Had he crossed a line somewhere? Maybe his friendship with Nick was stronger than he thought. Eyes focused on him—too many. He'd left the crowd on a cliffhanger. "I would like to ask Kurt to say a few words."

Kurt walked to the podium as Pogue made his way back to Nick. Kurt scanned the crowd. "I want you to know how much it means to me that you're here today—the Lucci family, the Santino family, the Gambrels, Dr. Pogue, and everyone." Kurt stared hard at the crowd of black-clothed, somber individuals before him. "I also know that whoever is responsible for killing my wife may be here. If that is so, I have a message: I'll find you, destroy your life, your family, and extract my vengeance. Thank you all for coming."

*** 

The room spun and drums beat in Amy's head. *Where am I?* Nauseated, she sat up in the bed and stared at the unfamiliar surroundings. Ornate drapes hung from the corners of the king-sized bed she rested on. Steel bars interrupted the sunlight filtering through two large windows on her right with curtains partially drawn. A bathroom, visible through an open door, boasted sterile white floors.

She swung her limp legs to the carpet. Moving slowly made her less dizzy, and her nausea was bearable. Outside the windows, beyond the sprawling lawn and flowering trees … Was that a lake? It looked like water, but her eyes were so dry she couldn't blink them into focus. Where was she? How did she get here? In the silence of the room, her heart pounded. She tried to swallow. Her throat felt like sandpaper. An itch on her left forearm. She rubbed and looked at the small circle of raised skin. Panic seized her as if a rope had been pulled tight around her neck. The officer at her school, something sticky on her arm … She had been in his car.

She stood. Her knees gave way, but she caught herself on the bedpost. Using a nearby chair as a crutch, she hobbled to the door. It was locked. She tried to shout, but her weak voice refused. Supporting herself against the wall, she took one step at a time toward the windows. They suddenly seemed so far away. She slowly forced her way to them.

The door opened behind her. When she turned, the dizziness came back, forcing her to grip the edge of the window with her hand. No more quick movements. Who was this in front of her?

"Oh, sweetie. You shouldn't be up." The young woman closed the door, pulled the chair close, and helped Amy sit. Her head still throbbed and now her fingers tingled.

"Looks like a storm may be brewing," the woman said.

"Who are you? And where am I?"

"My name is Deene. Don't be frightened. Everything will be clear soon. I'm not at liberty to give you the answers you want right now. But soon this will make sense." She sat on the edge of the bed and crossed her legs, her blond hair resting softly on her shoulders.

To Amy, she looked as if she couldn't be more than thirty years old. Her gentle manner helped slow Amy's pulse a little, and she finally took a deep breath. She forced herself to concentrate. "My father ... they told me he was in an accident."

"Your father is fine. There was no accident. The story that he'd been injured was to get you into the police cruiser." There wasn't a hint of remorse in her voice.

Amy's headache worsened as she tried to tie everything together in her head. "He was never in an accident?"

"No. I didn't want them to lie, but they insisted."

Amy gestured at the bars on the windows. "I'm a prisoner?"

Deene smiled. "Freedom exists in many forms. I'm here to help you."

"That's not an answer. Can I leave?"

"No, sweetie. You can't leave."

Bitter bile burned the back of her tongue. She pushed down the urge to vomit.

"It's not that bad, Amy. You're going to have the best the world has to offer from now on. Everything will be second nature in no time."

"What do you mean, everything?"

"The sex. It's part of the reason you're so valuable. It will be easy for a girl like you. Then all of the benefits will be yours to enjoy for a lifetime."

"You're ... what do you mean, the sex? I don't ... I've never ..."

Deene offered an insincere smile. "I see. Don't worry. We can help with that when the time comes."

Amy covered her mouth with her hand and sobbed.

"If you're hungry, push that button and talk." Deene pointed to the intercom. "The chef will prepare whatever you'd like. For now, I'll let you settle in. We'll be taking a trip to meet some new friends soon." Deene walked to the bathroom door. "I've placed some new clothes in the closet—all your size. Fresh towels are beside the shower."

Amy could no longer hold back the tears. "My father will look for me.

My mom must be scared to death."

Deene folded her hands in front of her as she approached Amy. "The sooner you accept this, the easier it will be." She brushed Amy's hair out of her face and softly stroked her cheek.

Her skin crawled at the touch of this woman.

Deene left the room. The deadbolt clunked.

\*\*\*

Pogue poured a cup of coffee. Jenni would be down in a minute, and they could spend the rest of the day together. His heartbeat quickened at the sound of her feet on the stairs. She stopped behind him and wrapped her arms around his chest. He turned to face her, and her eyes met his. He set the cup down.

She picked up his cup and took a sip. "Do you want to tell me about it?"

"Not much to tell. It was a longer ceremony than I expected."

"How did your speech go?"

"I think it was okay. Kurt sounded a bit …"

"Emotional?"

"More like irrational. But I have to give him credit for speaking at all. If I had to speak at your funeral, I don't know what I'd do." He hugged her tighter.

"Is there anything we can do for the Banks family or Kurt?"

"I don't think so. I'll be seeing Connor more than Kurt. I imagine once he's done with settling everything here in Chicago he'll move back to New York."

Jenni sighed. "I have to be honest with you, Bailey. The news reported the funeral of Dr. Ginger Lucci today. According to NBC, she was a local dentist and daughter in a prominent syndicate family."

Pogue took the cup back from her as lies flooded his thoughts. "Listen—"

"Did you know she was in the mob?"

"She wasn't. Her father is. I didn't know until recently, and I'm told she had nothing to do with the business."

"Is Connor part of it too? I thought they were brother and sister. Where does that put him?"

Pogue put his arm around her and walked to the kitchen table where he pulled a chair out for her. They sat. "I've been forced into something that prevents me from telling you more than I have. It's not what I want, but it's the way it has to be, and it has to do with why I'm carrying a gun."

"Are you involved with them? Are you involved with the mafia, Pogue?"

"If there was a fair way of answering that question, I would. But—"

"Just tell me."

"Yes."

Her eyes filled with tears as they studied his. "You said you were on the right side of this. I believe you. What can I do to get us through whatever is going on?"

"When it's safe to tell you, I will."

She wrapped her arms around him. "I'm scared. All kinds of things are going through my head. I love you and know you would never do anything to hurt us. But I'm afraid of losing you."

"I'm so sorry, Jenni." His tears trickled down his cheeks and onto her shoulder.

*You're breaking her heart, and all she can tell you is how much she loves and trusts you.*

"It's almost over."

*It's time to end this. One more meeting tomorrow and this is done.*

# CHAPTER TWENTY-THREE

P ogue sat quietly in the conference room at FBI headquarters. Across the table, Agent James reviewed a thick file. Vaughn sat at the end of the table, typing on a keypad even though no one spoke.

James finally closed the blue folder on the document in front of him, slipped his reading glasses into his top pocket, and crossed his arms. Pogue waited.

"We originally talked about you being undercover for a limited period of time." James' tone was clearly apologetic. "I no longer have that level of optimism."

"It's already been five months."

"While you were in Egypt, according to your report and our Intel on the ground, you met with some individuals who were off our radar. This cartel you're involved with comprises a millennial brand of evil we'd hoped would never materialize. We expected the families to expand, but this is different. They're deeply involved in sensitive political activities— selling secrets to foreign countries and adversaries as we discussed in your debriefing. Your information birthed a much clearer picture of what we're up against."

"How does this change the manner in which we proceed?" A thin film of sweat was already forming on Pogue's palms. *It means more lying to Nick. More and more until... This can't continue.*

"The situation is now partially out of FBI jurisdiction." James leaned back in his chair and gestured to Vaughn, who stood and left the room. "There's someone I'd like you to meet. And I need you to keep an open mind."

Vaughn reentered with a gentleman Pogue hadn't met. He stood to greet him.

James stood with both men. "Dr. Pogue, I'd like for you to meet—"

"The CIA." Pogue shook his head. "I should have seen this coming."

The gentleman who hadn't yet been introduced stared at him.

"Actually, Special Agent Jack Flannery," James said. "And yes, he's with the CIA. Flannery, this is Dr. Pogue."

Pogue shook his hand. "Pleased to meet you, sir."

"Are you?"

"Not really."

*Did this mean what he thought it meant?*

Flannery focused on Pogue. "Do you understand why the CIA is involved?"

"Considering the people I met in Egypt and the stakes of espionage, I was afraid it might come to this."

James motioned for the men to take their seats. "Mr. Flannery would like to explain what they've discovered."

Pogue let out a heavy sigh. "I'm no good at this. I'm not a career spy." His chest tightened at the thought of this continuing.

Flannery held up his hand. "Pogue, I understand you entered this process with the understanding it would be temporary. But in contrast to your own assessment of your abilities, you actually *are* quite good at it. From what we've been able to ascertain from information you gleaned over there along with our Intel, Apollyon is a syndicate being formed by the next generation of Luccis, Gambrels, and Santinos. It's a nightmare. Selling US Government secrets is treason."

"Like I said—"

"Give me a minute." Flannery folded his hands on the table. "In a manner of speaking, you're right. We *are* talking about spying. But we must use caution within our investigation to keep this new syndicate visible. If they feel like we're getting too close, they may stop what they're doing until the heat is off, and they'll look under every rock to find out what triggered our investigation. It won't take them long to discover your connection to the events causing their problems simply by examining the timeline."

Pogue straightened in his chair.

"The offense that engages CIA involvement is the selling of top secret information to Egypt and other areas of the Middle East by US Government agents to contacts abroad." Flannery opened James' file and removed several photos. "We have dozens of agents at risk like the ones you see here. This could upset the balance of power in regions that are increasingly volatile. We've been unable to make the connections between informants and their receivers until now, thanks to the relationships you've forged in Egypt."

Pogue's body remained tense with anticipation. It seemed they were setting the stage to request more from him. More, despite all the risks he'd assumed so far. "I got the information you were looking for."

"But we know what they want from you now." James tapped on the folder. "They can't pull this off without you. When you helped Nick in court a couple of years ago, that was a test—an audition. From that moment he was determined to get you on board as long as you vetted. You were the missing link in their plan—a way to carry the information. When the vetting was clean, Nick made sure he got you into debt to him by reintroducing you to gambling in the worst possible way—a sure thing that won you some instant cash."

"You've also been introduced to Robert Savage." Flannery handed him a page with the man's basic information. "He's the individual in the US responsible for selling information to enemy factions, but we've been unable to pin down how. We believe he's responsible for the recent deaths of a number of undercover CIA operatives in Cairo, Egypt. But he appears to be successfully pinning that on someone else. From your probing while you were over there, we now know he's brokering information through Nadir Mohmed via Philip Wassim."

Pogue rested his elbow on the table.

"Flannery is suggesting you work with them—the CIA." James dropped the bomb. "The FBI will help bring these men to justice and stop the transfer of sensitive information before it leads to the next Cold War."

"Or worse, all-out war and genocide in the Middle East." Flannery slid a map of the regions involved in front of Pogue.

Almost mechanically, Pogue turned to Flannery. "To whom would I report?"

Flannery glanced briefly at James, then back at Pogue. "To me, the CIA. We'll require some additional indoctrinational training at Langley. We need you inserted into the situation right away."

"I'm already *inserted*, Mr. Flannery." Pogue turned toward James. "You asked me to infiltrate the Gambrel family. I did that. That mission has now expanded to three families, all of whom will make sure I'm dead if this goes sideways, which it will at some point. When that happens, there will be no escape. I've turned over more information than you've gathered in years, and I can't keep doing that and living."

"Pogue—"

"I'm in the middle of a spy game that will get my family *and* me killed. These guys are playing for keeps. Where does this end?"

"I know you want to keep your family safe." Flannery laid his hands flat on the file. "This is how you do that."

Vaughn cleared his throat. "Excuse me, gentlemen. I feel compelled to point out several issues that may help clarify the situation for Dr. Pogue."

James nodded his approval. "Please."

"As you know, Mr. James, my IQ is one sixty. I say this not to boast since I had nothing to do with it. I note it to explain that I'm able to analyze information in an effective and efficient manner. I often think in terms of algorithms, various outcomes, and potential strategies and the percentages of each strategy in achieving a desired goal."

Flannery and James appeared confused.

But Pogue understood. "Go on."

"What you gentlemen may not be considering is that Dr. Pogue has an IQ of one sixty-four."

"What does my IQ have to do with anything?"

Vaughn held up an index finger. "What I have discovered is that you are in an incredibly sensitive but useful position of decoding the web of international espionage and protecting national security in a manner that is common to no other individual currently in the position of trust in which you find yourself."

Flannery may not have realized his mouth was hanging open.

James slapped his hand on the table. "What are you talking—"

Pogue held up his hand to silence him as he studied Vaughn's face. "You say that my IQ surpasses yours. Mine tells me my chance of survival under the circumstances in which I find myself is roughly one in fifty thousand."

"I concur. That is within my estimation. But … if you factor in a process of elevating your position of trust, undermining the current regime, and altering the expected course of events in a manner during which you maintain control, you shift the status quo in your favor—dramatically and covertly."

Pogue tapped his index finger on the desk. Flannery and James remained silent. "In other words, if I can infiltrate their plan and alter its course by, let's say, catastrophe or changing a set of variables or turning individuals against one another, I may be able to improve my chance of survival."

"Significantly. And your success as well—yes."

James made a *Time Out* motion with his hands. "You two make no sense. We're trying to destroy a cartel that already has a full head of steam."

"And Vaughn is talking about me staying alive while doing it." Pogue turned his attention to Vaughn again. "If what you say is true, by the time I'm burned, I'll be required to act quickly in order to gain the upper hand."

"Not only that, your survival will depend on it because the covert aspect will be limited." Vaughn leaned toward the center of the table with open hands. "You'll be operating entirely on your own if your cover is blown—if you're burned—which I expect for it to be at the flashpoint."

Flannery held out his hands. "I don't have any other options, Pogue. This is a matter of national and domestic security. You're in with the mafia, you're working with us, and there's no time to waste. I can't force you to do this. If I could, I would."

This was his new lot in life. It was foolishness to believe he had a choice. "Let's get this done."

\*\*\*

Amy focused on the door of her plush prison cell. After she'd had time to think and the cobwebs cleared, fear faded. She couldn't recall the last time she'd eaten and had no way of knowing how long she'd been unconscious. Food for strength was a priority. She wasn't going anywhere with anybody, no matter what Deene said. She looked in the mirror. *You can do this.*

Showered and dressed in the clothes Deene had left, Amy pressed the button on the intercom. A voice came over the speaker: "May I help you?"

"I'd like a hamburger, please."

"I'll fix it immediately."

"Thank you." She used the cheeriest tone she could muster and fought back her tears.

"Happy to oblige, miss."

Amy released the intercom button, moved to the stained glass window in the bathroom, and studied the borders of the frame. There didn't appear to be bars on that window from what she could see through the jigsaw pieces of colored glass. There might be a way ...

# CHAPTER TWENTY-FOUR

Jamie Williams tried on three outfits before deciding.

"Green skirt, white blouse, and your favorite heels." A sigh of relief. "That works." Her reflection in the mirror assured her. Her skirt brought out the green in her eyes.

Meeting Lucas for a dinner cruise would have to be a secret from her parents since they would never approve of such an extravagant date. Although she didn't have the best track record for the men she chose, spending time with Lucas in the coffee shop indicated they had chemistry. Tonight they would be in public the entire time—what could be safer?

She left the apartment before her parents came home and did her best not to make eye contact with the doorman. Waiting on the corner of the street, a check in her spirit—maybe guilt—began to drain her anticipation. Going against her parents' wishes didn't feel right. She considered ditching the plan, but a limo pulled to the curb. The back door opened and Lucas stepped out. He held it open for her.

"A limo?"

"Is there another type of car you'd prefer? Tell me and I'll get it."

"This is perfect and very sweet." She climbed into the spacious back seat of the Town Car, and Lucas slid in next to her, pulling the door closed behind him.

"You didn't have to rent a limousine, Lucas."

"You deserve the best."

He poured her a glass of champagne.

"I'm only eighteen."

"I won't tell anyone if you don't."

She hesitated, but not long. "Just a sip." She held the glass as he poured one for himself and lifted it in a toast.

"To our first official date. May there be many more." He tapped the rim of her glass with his and sipped the contents before placing it in the cupholder. "Thank you for joining me tonight." The limo pulled up to the pier. A red carpet marked the entrance to the yacht awaiting their arrival.

"You've been on one of these before?"

"I have a confession. My father owns a portion of this cruise line in Chicago. I was practically raised on these boats. I hope that doesn't spoil it."

"Not at all." The flowers lining the walkway smelled beautiful, even though the air was a little crisp.

On the short walk to the yacht, Jamie felt his hand gently caress the small of her back. She'd expected to wait in line to board, but there were no other passengers ahead of them.

She glanced around the pier. "Are we early?"

"We're right on time."

The yacht was long, white, and sleek, like something out of a movie. The bow of the graceful cruiser drifted forward to a sharp point, and lights shone to illuminate its elegant lines. Inside, tables in various locations surrounded an orchestra on the main level.

"Good evening, Mr. Montiel," the Maître D' greeted Lucas.

"Montiel? Your last name is Montiel?"

Lucas cast an accusing look at the maître d'.

"Sorry, sir."

"I didn't intend to let that cat out of the bag just yet." Lucas shrugged.

"Why? You should be proud. Your father is a great man. I'm sure you are too. And he doesn't own a portion of the cruise lines. He owns it all."

"How do you know so much about my father?"

"I read." She batted her eyes playfully.

The gentleman showed Lucas and Jamie to their table near the bow of the ship. It was the only one with a panoramic view. The Chicago backdrop was brilliant, and the sky filled with stars.

Jamie did her best to take it all in as she wrapped her shawl around her shoulders. She grabbed Lucas' arm when the yacht pulled away from the pier. "I didn't think we were ready to move yet. What about the others?"

"Others?"

"The people who are supposed to be sitting at the empty tables."

"We have the ship to ourselves tonight. Consider this your private yacht for the next three hours, because it is."

Jamie enjoyed the calming effect from the champagne and didn't protest when the waiter poured a glass of wine for each of them. The guilt faded, and warmth embraced her as if wrapped in a cozy blanket. So this was what alcohol felt like. She smiled at Lucas and drank the wine. God, he was handsome.

"Why do you keep your identity a secret?" Jamie held her glass to the side while the waiter refilled it.

"This may sound clichéd, but I like to know when someone cares about me and not my money."

"Well, you know that's true about me. I'll be honest. I just like your accent." She giggled and placed the newly filled wineglass on the table.

"That's good to know. And I haven't seen a thing about you I don't like. You're the one with the accent, by the way." They both laughed. "But seriously, I don't know much about you. You live in the city because I picked you up there, but where?"

"In the towers, and I love it. But I still live with my parents." She scrunched her nose.

"Nothing wrong with that. Tell me more."

"Let's see … I attend classes part-time, work in the popcorn shop. You know that part. And …" She bit her lip.

"And what?"

"I model. Hopefully, that will be my regular job someday." She struck a little pose with her hand on her chin.

"Do your parents support your dreams?"

"They aren't crazy about the modeling, but they get it. I'm not home much, so they worry about me—and predators." She clawed the air with her hands.

"I don't blame your parents. You're a beautiful girl in a city where many men are not trustworthy. They just sound smart."

"I guess so."

"Please, describe your normal schedule on a given day. Your life fascinates me."

"It would be easier to do it on a weekly basis since it varies."

"A given week, then."

"Mondays and Wednesdays I have dance class from one till four. The popcorn shop is Tuesdays and Saturdays noon to six. Thursdays and

Fridays are modeling days, and sometimes Sundays, depending on the shoot."

"It sounds exhausting."

"It is, but I love it." She smiled and sipped her wine. No more gulping. "What about you?"

"Compared to yours, my life is boring. I go to the office and figure out ways to build more business or cut expenses. That's it—until I meet someone like you." Lucas smiled when the orchestra played a slow song. "Would you like to dance?"

"I'd love to."

Lucas stood to help her with her chair. "You're a professional. Grant me mercy on the dance floor."

"I promise." Jamie held his arms as she stood—a little dizzy, but never better.

As they glided across the polished wooden floor with the city's skyline reflecting off the water, Lucas swept Jamie off her feet. Her arms around his neck, their bodies touching, the feel of his hand pulling her closer. Is this what love feels like?

***

Pogue followed as Vaughn led him into the conference room at seven a.m.

"Make yourself at home, Dr. Pogue. They'll be in shortly."

Vaughn left and Pogue helped himself to the coffee bar. This room had no windows to the outside, but a large glass wall lined the corridor partition, making the soundproof enclosure seem less like a holding cell, but not quite as private as the one he'd been in before. At the far end of the room, a large flat-screen TV occupied most of the wall. Agent James and Detective Davis entered, disrupting the uncomfortable quiet.

"Dr. Pogue." Davis grinned. "Good to see you. I hear you've been busy with your seminars recently." He used air quotes for the word *seminars*.

Pogue laughed only to overcome the seriousness of that statement.

"I'm sure it has been a challenge keeping all those balls in the air."

"That it has." Pogue set his cup on the table.

James opened a folder he'd carried into the room, reached for the remote, and pushed a button. The hallway windows turned smoky-opaque, preventing anyone from seeing inside.

"I appreciate you meeting with us at FBI headquarters, Detective, and you, Pogue, for making the time to come down. I know you head for Langley tomorrow. But we have a mutual interest in what I've finally received from the forensics lab." James clicked another button, activating the monitor. Twenty-one photos appeared in rapid sequence composed of three lines with seven images each.

James pointed at the screen. "These are 'still' shots of surveillance video footage from the night Dr. Lucci was almost murdered in her hospital room. Dr. Taylor alerted me to the time frames that would likely prove the most valuable, but there have been a number of conflicts in getting copies. What you see before you is the piecing together of several camera angles since some of the imaging is missing."

"Missing?" Davis interrupted.

"No one can find electronic records for the times in question. They were somehow destroyed. Several days ago, additional footage from early in the evening was made available by our own FBI forensics department after pulling them from a damaged hard drive. Someone wiped the main drive clean, but we found backup files on an alternate server that no one remembered existed because it was in an area known as a co-location. Vaughn explained that an automatic backup would be standard protocol in a hospital setting, so we dug in. After discovering a remodeling project took place two years ago, and the backup server was no longer accounted for, a maintenance man helped us find it—still operating. The photos to which I refer are the ones on the top row. Pay attention to the timestamps on each image. They're accurate. I've placed them in order as they occurred, left to right, top to bottom."

Davis pointed. "Who is that with Harrison? I've seen her before."

Pogue nodded. "Her name is Reid. Reid Beckman."

"That's right. I interviewed her the day Lucci croaked."

Pogue gave him a look.

"Sorry, I mean, passed away. Jesus."

"This is just the beginning." James pointed to one of the next photos. "You can see the guard in the corner doing something on his cell phone. To be fair, his job was to make sure no unauthorized persons came into the room, and he accomplished that. In the next image, Reid draws something into a syringe from a vial with her back to the guard. In the following photo, she hands it to Harrison, and in the next one, he injects it into Lucci's IV while Reid blocks the view from the guard. Thirty seconds between drawing up the solution and injecting it in the IV."

"That would be well within the norms, depending on what he gave her." Pogue turned to James. "I'm sure it's documented in her chart. Physicians are often the ones pushing IV meds in the ICU setting."

"An entire vial? Would that be within norms?" James showed Pogue the next photo. The vial was clearly empty of its former dark contents.

"Depending on the medicine, yes. For example, an entire vial of an antibiotic like Rocephin would be used at one time. There are others as well. This is not a smoking gun."

"They appeared to hide it from the guard." James backed up to that image.

"Appeared to hide it is different from hiding it. They may have been protecting patient privacy." Pogue studied the screen, a bit curious. "It seems unusual, but it's possible to require an entire vial of medication. But, again ... what's he giving her? What's in the chart?"

"Nothing."

Pogue turned to James. "There's no documentation?"

"Not a thing. It gets better. Look at the next two frames." James highlighted the images on the screen. "At first I thought these two were duplicates, but then I checked the timestamp. Harrison injected a second full vial here, then left the room with Reid. Again—nothing documented in the chart."

Pogue studied the photos as Davis spoke. "Where's the footage from four twelve to four thirty the morning we'd talked about?"

James glanced at both men. "Allow me to introduce the most recent evidence we have in this case."

A new image appeared on the screen. "This is Dr. Harrison entering Lucci's room at four fifteen a.m. You'll notice the US marshal leaves the room, possibly to use the restroom since Harrison is there and is trusted as her attending physician." James clicked to the next one. "This shows Dr. Harrison wearing blue gloves as he loosened Lucci's dressing on the right side." He moved to the next screen that showed a sequence of still photos. "Harrison stopped, reapplied it, and moved to her left. In this next frame, he places her left index finger in bloody drainage from the dressing, then writes on the bedsheet using the blood on her finger to write the name Kurt, which we've all seen." James advanced the screen to another series of stills. "Harrison throws the gloves in the trash, pulls up the sheet to cover the writing, and waits until the guard returns. Then he leaves."

Pogue stared in disbelief.

Davis huffed. "Well, I'll be. He probably thought they'd destroyed the footage with the drive wipe."

James stood and walked toward the screen. "Harrison wasn't counting on the FBI forensics lab finding these images since the existence of the server was unknown."

The three men stared at the pictures in silence.

Davis spoke first. "Motive?"

Pogue threw up his hands. "I have no idea. But why would a doctor of Harrison's status kill his patients, especially with his nurse at his side."

Davis nodded, then shook his head. "First off, patient. Singular. Second, Reid is more than his nurse. They've been shacking up together for a year. His marriage is on the skids, and Reid is pretty and single."

James clicked a button and turned off the display. "These photos give us probable cause for Harrison and his nurse to be involved. I'm going to question them. I still can't understand why Harrison would write Kurt's name on the sheets."

Pogue started to sip his coffee but put the cup down. "To divert attention." The men looked at him. "If Kurt were a prime suspect, we'd spend our time wondering about him instead of looking for someone else."

Davis stood and buttoned his sports jacket. "Let me know when you question them. I'd like to be there."

James took a seat across from Pogue as Davis left the room. "It's about to get ugly for Harrison. You know that, right?"

"If these guys are into his pockets, or somehow have him working for them, what will happen if you bring him in for questioning?"

James leaned back without answering. Pogue understood.

# CHAPTER TWENTY-FIVE

Robert Savage watched as Danielle Trent left her office at the Pentagon carrying a leather satchel and large purse. Typing with her thumbs on her cell phone, she didn't appear to notice him as she came closer. He stopped walking and waited near the elevators. When she finally looked up, she was only five feet away. She stopped. "Oh!"

"Ms. Trent. I'm Robert Savage, chairman of—"

"Yes," she said, startled. "I know who you are. I'm sorry. I wasn't paying attention."

"We have a meeting in a few minutes. Shall we?" He held out his hand, indicating the conference room down the hallway.

"Yes, of course. I was on my way there."

Slowly, they walked toward the room. Robert savored dragging out the anxiety, imagining every step must be driving her insane. Once they reached the room, they stepped inside. He had chosen this room specifically for its dull gray walls and dark, sterile furnishings. He'd even come in earlier and stood on a chair to loosen a bulb, making it a little dimmer. A man in uniform remained at ease by the door.

"Please, have a seat, Ms. Trent." Robert pointed to a chair by a metal desk.

They sat across from each other.

"Allow me to explain why I asked you to meet me today. As chairman of the federal prosecutor oversight committee, I have certain responsibilities."

"Did you want Mr. Franklin to be here? I can contact him and—"

"No, thank you." Robert gave her a condescending grin. "It has come to my attention that you have been involved in a number of sensitive cases that have subsequently resulted in the leeching of information to parties considered hostile toward the United States." He folded his hands and stared at her.

She shifted in her chair.

"I need a polygraph regarding your work with Jason Franklin. Today."

Danielle glanced at her phone. "I'm sorry. I thought this meeting would be brief. I'm tied up this afternoon. Perhaps tomorrow?"

"I've taken the liberty of clearing your schedule. For the next two hours, you're mine."

"You're overstepping—"

"Please, Ms. Trent. We're trying to clear up issues of national importance. I have the authority to do what's necessary to assure our nation's security."

"I ... I should call Mr. Franklin."

"Please don't."

She tilted her head.

"Shall we go?" Savage stood and held the door for her. She stood.

"Do I need an attorney?"

"Let's get this polygraph out of the way. That may resolve everything."

As they walked down the brightly lit hallway, his adrenaline rushed through his veins as if he'd spotted the perfect buck of the season in his crosshairs. Stepping onto the elevator, they traveled down six floors. Danielle straightened her skirt, pulled at her sleeves, and swept her hand over her hair. But she never made eye contact. When the doors opened, the hallway lighting was dimmer than it had been on the main floor. They turned left to interrogation room 716.

"Seven-sixteen? This is the bottom floor."

"For all intents and purposes." He opened the door for her. "Please, have a seat."

She stared at the chair but didn't budge.

"Ms. Trent, this is soft leather—not the electric chair. Please sit while the technician applies the sensors. Due to your sensitive position, you've undoubtedly been through this before."

Danielle settled into the chair. Within minutes, she was wired to a machine that held her future in its electronic hands. A clamp attached to her left index finger monitored her oxygen saturation and pulse, which coordinated information with the electric probes attached to her with sticky tabs in various locations of her body, including her forehead. She was sweating in a sixty-eight-degree room.

Savage removed his jacket, hung it on the back of the chair, and made himself comfortable as he opened a notebook. After the preliminary baseline questions covering her name, where she was from, and the high school she'd attended, he began the important questions.

"Ms. Trent, have you worked with special prosecuting attorney Jason Franklin on any of his cases?"

"Of course. I've worked on—"

"Just yes or no, please."

"Sorry. Yes."

"Do you have top secret clearance?"

"Yes. You know—"

"Please, Ms. Trent."

"Yes."

"Was that a requirement for your job?"

"Yes."

"Have you had top secret clearance for more than five years?"

"Yes."

"More than seven years?"

"No."

"Are you ever, or have you ever been, required to handle Top Secret US Government documents, which you are forbidden to share with anyone other than your boss, Jason Franklin, regardless of content?"

"Yes."

"Have you ever used your security clearance for personal gain or betrayed your country in any way?"

At first, she appeared unable to speak. "No." She mumbled a little.

"Pardon?"

"No."

"Ms. Trent, let me repeat the question. According to the polygraph, that response is inconsistent."

"Meaning?"

"It implies you're lying. Allow me to isolate your response. Since you've had top-secret security clearance, have you ever used that clearance for personal gain?"

She shook her head. "No. I've never ... No."

"Have you ever betrayed America's trust in you?"

"No, I—"

"Have you complied fully with the oath you took when beginning employment with the Pentagon?"

"Yes, but this isn't ... you're not asking the ..."

"Is that your answer? Are you saying you haven't personally prospered from your top secret clearance or betrayed the trust bestowed upon you?"

Danielle shook her head and seemed out of breath. "I'm going to need that attorney now."

"In matters of Homeland Security, you may not have that luxury." Savage looked at the notebook and flipped a few pages. "Have you ever used your top secret clearance in a manner that could potentially undermine United States security or place our forces at risk at home or abroad?"

"I refuse to answer on the grounds that—"

"Have you ever removed classified files in order to aid terrorist groups or other enemy factions sworn to harm the United States?"

Danielle tore the wires off her arms and the sensor from her finger. "We will reconvene after I have obtained legal counsel. Not before. I know my rights, Mr. Savage."

"I'm pleased that you know your rights since you've forfeited most of them with your responses in the last two minutes. You will *not* leave. You *will* be placed under arrest for conspiring against the United States of America until I get the answers to those questions. Since you opened the door to several of the questions I'm asking by answering related questions, you may not invoke your Fifth Amendment rights. I'm sure you'll have plenty of time to find an attorney in prison."

"Listen to me. These questions—"

He removed his phone from his pocket and punched two numbers. "Come in, please."

Two armed officers entered the room.

"Place Ms. Trent under arrest for conspiring to commit treason against the United States of America. Have her properly searched per female protocol and perform a detailed review of her handbags, office, car, apartment, etcetera. I'll have search warrants issued within the hour. Inform forensics I expect a full report on her personal and office computers by tomorrow morning."

"Yes, sir."

As one guard placed her in handcuffs, the other took her phone and began going through her satchel as instructed. "I have two thumb drives inside a key fob, sir."

"What?" She looked at the tiny black USB drives. "Those aren't mine."

"I'm sure they're not." Savage addressed the guards. "Upload those drives directly to me. Contact Jason Franklin and tell him I want to meet with him first thing in the morning, but don't say why."

***

Pogue's cell phone buzzed as he drove the Dan Ryan Expressway toward the hospital. Traffic was heavier than usual. Caller ID read Dr. Scott Taylor.

"Hey, Scott." Pogue switched the phone to hands-free mode. "What's up?"

"I'm in the ER, Bailey, and I have a mess on my hands."

"What's the problem?"

"Dr. Harrison's down here and he's in bad shape."

"Upset, angry, on a tirade? What?"

"He's been in a car wreck—a bad one."

"Is he stable?"

"No. I think he has internal bleeding. I've already sent him to surgery. That's not why I'm calling. Harrison grabbed my arm before they took him to the operating suite and told me *they* were trying to kill him."

"The surgeons?"

"I asked the same thing. He said it wasn't them, but he wouldn't say who. Just that *they* were trying to kill him. He was panicked, begging me to help him—begging me to call you. He said you'd know what to do. What does that mean, Pogue?"

"Do you have a number for his nurse, Reid Beckman? I need to find out what she knows—right now."

"It won't help. She was in the car with him, and she's down here too."

"Can she talk? I just need a second."

"She's dead, Pogue."

# CHAPTER TWENTY-SIX

Pogue was so engrossed in the FBI records regarding Harrison and Reid that he didn't notice Vaughn until he knocked on the doorframe of James' office.

"We've got chatter from New York, sir—regarding a female."

James looked up from the computer. "There's always New York chatter, Vaughn. What's different? That she's female?"

"No. Her name. It isn't Marc Santino this time, sir." Vaughn handed him a two-page document. "It's his sister, C.J."

"How encrypted was this?"

"Highly. The information regards a package being readied for transport."

"What package?" Pogue's curiosity piqued. "And who is C.J.?"

James typed on his keyboard, and the family tree of the cartel appeared on the screen. He turned the monitor to Pogue and pointed. "Your Apollyon buddies are about to make some sort of deal, apparently without informing you."

Vaughn pointed to C.J.'s image on the screen. "She has been on our POI sheets for years but never surfaced hard until this thread appeared, automatically triggering a computer-driven accountability profile. She's flown in and out of Chicago fifteen times in the past four months— sometimes for less than twenty-four hours—then flies back to New York."

"What's she doing when she's here?" Pogue cringed at the thought of another Santino in the mix.

"She visits the Gambrel mansion on every visit."

"She's staying there?"

Vaughn shook his head. "She always books a room at The Peninsula. After she checks in she visits the Gambrels, usually being picked up by their limo. On one occasion while she was in Chicago, a woman named Deene Manning rented a car using a credit card registered to C.J. Santino."

"Who's Deene?"

"She's not in our system."

"If C.J. used her own personal credit card accidently, Ms. Deene may be an alias for C.J.," James added. He rested his arms on the desk. "Why was there obtainable chatter in the first place? They've been meticulously cautious."

Vaughn opened his iPad. "According to Philip, our CIA asset in Egypt, the cartel's failure to provide merchandise on a timely basis forced him to find alternate suppliers for his clientele. He made a backdoor deal with someone else. If the Apollyon cartel rushed into production to capture the Intel market, it's possible a person in their system made a mistake before fully understanding encryption protocol. That's just a guess, but the halting of information bartering coincides with the time period Gambrel's doctor had a stroke, for whatever that's worth. If C.J. was exposed, someone covered the tracks after the fact. We only know about it because our software picked up the inconsistency."

"Who did you say your asset is?" Pogue checked the notes on his phone.

"Philip. Nadir's right-hand man."

"He's the guy I didn't get to meet when I was there, right?"

"He's a CIA informant they've allowed us to share." James scratched the back of his neck. "Business took him to Minya in Upper Egypt while you were in Cairo."

Vaughn set the iPad on the desk. "According to Philip, the cartel has assured him they are back in business. That means that they're preparing to use your expertise soon, Dr. Pogue."

"I guess I'd better be ready, then."

*Wish I knew how to do that*

\*\*\*

Robert Savage waited in Jason Franklin's reception room until he arrived. Franklin's receptionist greeted her boss. "Good morning, sir. This gentleman is Robert Savage. He would like to speak with you."

"I'm sorry to keep you waiting." Jason shook Robert's hand. "Did you have an appointment?"

"I apologize." Robert handed Franklin his card. "I was hoping to chat before you got into your day. Business brings me to the Pentagon often. As you can see on my card, I'm the special Washington Envoy to the Middle East and chairperson of the governing board of oversight for special prosecutors with the United States. I have a few questions."

"Did you say you were from oversight?"

"That's correct."

"Is there a problem?"

"I don't intend taking much of your time."

Jason turned to his secretary. "Would you contact Ms. Trent and have her meet us here?"

"Ms. Trent won't be joining us. She's currently detained."

"Detained?"

"That's correct. She won't be attending."

"What's this about, Mr. Savage?"

"It would be best if we spoke in private."

Jason Franklin entered his inner office. "Give me a moment. I'll be right with you." He closed the door.

Robert waited briefly, then opened the door and walked in.

Franklin quickly hung up the desk phone. "Mr. Savage, I said I'd be right with you. I was calling my wife as I do every morning when I get to work."

Robert closed the door, picked up the landline receiver, and dialed the switchboard. "This is Robert Savage, ID confirm as KW-85. A call was just made from this phone. I need to know to whom it was placed." Robert waited. "Thank you."

Franklin didn't move as Robert hung up.

"The call you made was to your personal attorney."

"You show up in my office unannounced with allegations of espionage. What do you expect?"

Robert sat. "I never mentioned espionage."

Franklin remained standing. "Do you know who I am?"

"Are you talking about being a federal prosecuting attorney or C.J. Santino's husband? Either way, I understand both."

Franklin stepped back. "What exactly is this about, Mr. Savage?"

"I need you to play ball. I'm not after you. I'm not your enemy, but we have a situation."

Franklin stared at him. "Do you think you can intimidate the organization you're about to assault?"

Robert sighed. "Do you believe you can survive the firestorm and publicity your family is about to endure on your behalf? I'm not the one you need to worry about. If you think the Santinos will come to your rescue, you're in for a rude awakening."

"You know what this family will do to me, right?"

"That's my point. I'm not blackmailing you. I need your cooperation."

"With what?"

"Danielle Trent. She apparently acted on her own and used her top secret clearance to obtain and sell information to enemy factions. I need your testimony against her."

Franklin took his seat and studied Savage. "You don't want to investigate my family—my in-laws?"

"No. I don't. I enjoy breathing."

Franklin leaned back in his chair. "What will happen to Danielle?"

"We'll discuss that. But will you cooperate? Will you testify?"

"Yes." Franklin pinched the bridge of his nose. "But if you believe I've been involved in espionage, why would you let me off the hook?"

"I'm not trying to end to the espionage. I understand your role in what has been going on, but Danielle went behind your back and almost ruined everything. I have to place the blame on her and make sure she takes the fall."

"You already know my wife, don't you?"

"Let's just say her reputation precedes her. I have not spoken with her about this. I need her legitimately angry that you're under investigation."

"But you said—"

"You'll be immediately cleared of all charges, but initially you have to be a suspect, or the judge will appoint additional oversight. We do not want that."

Franklin folded his hands on the desk. "You've done your homework, Mr. Savage."

"Just part of the job." He looked around the room. "You don't happen to have any coffee on hand, do you?"

\*\*\*

When Amy heard her bedroom door open, it surprised her, even though she'd been expecting dinner.

"Yes?" she called from the bathroom.

"I prepared some food for you, miss." The man's voice came from the bedroom.

"I'll be right out." She quickly climbed down from the stained glass window. She'd managed to remove almost half the molding using a piece of the shower curtain metal bracket she pulled loose from the wall. She washed her hands to remove the grit from the caulk on the window molding, then stepped out of the bathroom, hoping the window wasn't visible from where he stood. The door to her room stood open. A young, small man with the food tray placed it on the table in the corner of the room. A much larger man stood stiffly on the other side of the hallway with his hands folded in front of him.

"Let me know if I can prepare anything else for you, miss."

She forced a smile. "Thank you."

The man nodded and left, locking the door behind him.

Amy was so hungry she ate quickly, but she savored every bite. The food renewed her, and she could think clearly for the first time since being there. If her energy would hold out, her exit plan might actually work.

Tiptoeing to the bathroom, she surveyed the situation with fresh eyes. Removing her shoes offered her a better grip on the edge of the tub. From there she stepped up to the vanity, straddling the sink. Retrieving the metal bracket, she dug the sharpened metal into the window frame. From her new position, Amy reached to the top of the stained-glass window. She scratched at the molding, and large coils of caulk dropped in grotesque, graying curls to the windowsill and white marble floor. Each time she dug, more molding fell, more caulking crumbled, and the glass seemed to loosen from its moorings. She balanced herself on the vanity edge to reach the far side of the window, using her renewed energy to vigorously pull the seasoned plaster and caulking away. She could taste the dust as tiny fragments of old wood and paint hung in the air—the scent of freedom. She dug harder, pulling stronger. She was almost there. The molding on the left curve of the oval window suddenly broke free, and Amy placed her hand on the glass to keep it from falling.

A knock on the door of her room stopped her. If she left the window, it might fall. She couldn't tell how close it was to coming free.

"Yes?"

"I'm here for the food tray."

"I'm in the bathroom right now."

"I can come in and get it if you like. Is your bathroom door closed?"

"Give me a second." Amy held the glass window with one hand and stretched her left foot toward the door. Her toes barely grabbed the wooden frame, and she swung it closed. "It is now." Amy balanced on the vanity motionless, holding the window in place as she heard the door of her room open.

"I have the tray. Good night."

The door closed, and Amy turned her attention back to the window. She had one edge loose enough to pull away from the frame. Her heart raced with excitement. Slowly and carefully, she slipped the makeshift tool into the crevice to pry it free. When she did, the wooden frame splintered, and the metal shard stabbed her left wrist. She immediately dropped it as pain shot through her arm, causing her to release her grip on the window. She grabbed her wrist and slid to the vanity, then sat on the edge of the tub. Blood—so much blood. Direct pressure on the wound caused more pain, and the bleeding wouldn't stop. She gritted her teeth and pressed harder, but the blood forced its way between her fingers, forming a puddle on the floor as large droplets splattered between her feet. She found a washcloth, folded a knot into it, and pressed the fabric against her wrist. Tears ran down her cheeks from the pain. But the bleeding slowed.

Sitting on the side of the bathtub, she took a deep breath, held the washcloth in place, and tried not to move. *I have to stop the bleeding and clean up this mess. But how am I going to fix this cut? How will I ...*

Amy watched helplessly as the glass window slid from its frame in seemingly slow motion, shattering into a thousand pieces when it struck the marble floor. She lifted her feet as stained glass fragments sprayed across the bright white slab as if colored drops of water, stopping when they reached the wall at the far end of the room.

"Oh, God. Oh, God."

"What's going on in there?" The voice was different than that of the man who'd brought dinner.

"Nothing. I dropped a water glass. It's fine."

"I'm coming in."

"No! Don't. I'm undressed. I'll clean it up. Please!"

"Put some clothes on. I need to see what happened and clean it up. We can't have you cutting yourself on broken glass."

Amy's mind was getting foggy. "I promise it's okay." The warm sensation on her left leg caused her to look down. A stream of blood ran from her wrist and pooled at her feet. She pressed the knot harder into her delicate skin, wincing at the pain. She felt faint for the first time. Getting out of the room would be impossible with bare feet, considering the glass everywhere. She swung her legs over the edge of the tub and slid into it so she'd have a place to lie back, then leaned her head against the porcelain and closed her eyes. Spots in her vision told her she was in trouble. She couldn't hold the pressure against her wrist hard enough to stop the bleeding anymore. Her strength slowly evaporated.

"Miss?"

Was he in the bedroom? He sounded close. Her vision narrowed. Moments ago, she was on her way to escaping this prison. She now lay helpless in a white marble tub, quietly dying as she focused on the bright red pool circling the drain at her feet.

# CHAPTER TWENTY-SEVEN

ogue checked his pulse while he jogged a cool-down lap after a five-mile run through the woodland trail by his house. It was good to have the day off, but it could easily be consumed with *family business* errands. He hoped that wouldn't be the case, but his cell buzzed in his pocket. After checking the ID, he answered.

"Hello, Detective."

"Good morning, Dr. Pogue. I have some unpleasant news. Dr. Harrison died this morning—internal bleeding from a ruptured spleen. I believe I'm saying that right. There was apparently nothing they could do."

"With that level of trauma, it would take a miracle to pull through. I wasn't very hopeful, Detective Davis."

"There's more to this than I originally told you, Doc. Harrison's wounds were out of proportion to the car crash. I discussed that with Dr. Taylor and asked that he not call you until I could speak with you. Has he?"

"Called me? No. This is the first I'm hearing about it."

"Good. Another thing is that the injury to Reid was from a sharp object to her mid-chest, piercing her heart and causing her to arrive in the ER DOA. There should have been blood everywhere in that car, according to Taylor, and there wasn't. On top of that, Harrison's blunt trauma made no sense. Their car was T-boned from a semi-truck on the passenger side. The damage to Harrison was mostly on the left side of his body, and he was driving."

"It could have been seat belt trauma."

"The other injuries he sustained didn't fit that mechanism of injury, according to Dr. Taylor."

"You think he was hurt some other way?"

"Somebody beat him to death—or close to it—and put him behind the wheel, thinking he was already gone. Reid was killed at another location and placed in the car beside him before the accident. They strapped them both in, then plowed the car with a semitruck. I'm guessing they didn't count on Harrison waking up or living long enough to talk."

Pogue pressed two fingers against his right temple, fighting an oncoming headache.

"The icing on the cake is that the semi-truck driver was killed in a fight at a bar last night."

"I thought he was under arrest."

"Made bail."

"Thanks for the call, Detective." Pogue's call waiting line rang. "Looks like I've got another call. Talk to you soon."

"Watch your back."

Pogue hung up on Davis and picked up the second call.

"Pogue, this is Nick. Sorry to bother you, but I need your help."

"What's up?"

"We have a medical emergency at the mansion."

"Your dad?"

"No. Thank God. But I have a chopper on its way for you, and it has permission to land in your cul-de-sac."

*How is that possible?* "Okay, but Marc called early this morning and wants me to meet Robert Savage around noon downtown."

"I know. It won't take long at the mansion. I'll have my driver run you to where Marc needs you. After that, he can return you here and I'll fly you home."

"I'll need to shower. I'll be ready shortly."

"See you in a few."

Pogue ran to his house and entered the back door. Jenni stood in the kitchen. "I have to grab a shower and run out for a few hours."

She stopped pouring coffee and turned to face him. "You need any help in the shower?" She grinned.

"Woman? You trying to slow me down?"

"Is it working?"

"I ... "

"Go shower. When will you be home?"

"Early this afternoon. And I'll be leaving in a chopper that will be landing in the back cul-de-sac in a few minutes."

She looked at him and tilted her head.

"I know. It's just … I know." He hurried upstairs before she could ask more questions.

\*\*\*

Pogue's chopper landed on the helipad outside the Gambrel mansion. Nick waited by the doors and escorted him to the library on the first floor.

"Pogue, I mentioned to you that you'd be needed from time to time to perform discreet care on behalf of the family? This is one of those times. One of our employees has had an accident requiring medical attention. She's in our guesthouse. We'll take the back tunnel."

"Guesthouse? Tunnel?"

"I use that term loosely. It's really an enclosed, hidden underground hallway. We own all the property between the two houses. It made sense to build a tunnel for security purposes."

The men stepped out of the library, walked behind the winding staircase, and down one flight where Nick dialed a four-digit code on a keypad by a steel door at the end of a foyer. The door buzzed and swung open. Nick motioned with his hand, inviting Pogue through.

Chandeliers illuminated the passageway with patterned carpeting that spanned the entire length. Paintings and potted plants lined the expanse.

Once they stepped into a large foyer at the end of the hallway, Nick pulled the door closed behind them. The clunk of an electronic lock followed, and they crossed the room.

"You're about to meet a young lady, a girl I need you to tend to. She was using a kitchen knife and accidentally cut her wrist. I'm sure she'll need stitches since the workers reported a lot of bleeding."

"Why not take her to the ER?"

"Not an option. It's better if you don't know details."

Pogue nodded. "I didn't bring surgical supplies or instruments with me. I'm not prepared to suture a wound, especially if she hit an artery."

"You'll find our infirmary more than adequate. We've prepared for just about every contingency."

Pogue and Nick entered the guesthouse through a second door, much like the first made of steel. It required a code to open. Nick punched it in.

They walked down a short hallway and turned right, making their way another thirty feet to a room they entered on the left. Nick punched another key code on the pad and opened the door. Pogue noted that all of the codes carried the same tones.

"Remember, Pogue—just the basics. No chitchat. Like I said, it's sensitive."

"Understood."

When Pogue entered the exam room, white cabinets with glass doors lined the walls, and granite countertops bordered the room on three sides. A surgical light hung on a swinging arm above a stretcher in the center of the room where a beautiful blonde, teenage-appearing girl lay with a guard at her side holding pressure against a bloody bandage on her left wrist.

She appeared barely conscious as Pogue walked to the bedside. This was not the usual presentation of someone who had just accidentally cut herself with a kitchen knife. His warning flags waved frantically, but he acted the part as he was trained to do. He nodded at two girls standing by the cabinets, then turned his attention back to the girl on the bed.

"I'm a doctor, a surgeon, and I'm going to take care of you. Do you understand?"

The young girl didn't speak. She closed her eyes briefly as Pogue sat on a stool beside her bed. "Let's take a look at that cut."

As he tried to make eye contact, he carefully unwrapped the bloody towel from her wrist, which began to bleed profusely again through a jagged cut just distal to a butterfly tattoo. He rewrapped it and had the man beside her hold pressure again as Pogue stood and walked to the sink to wash his hands. "Are you allergic to any medicines?"

She didn't answer but not because she was unconscious. Her failure to respond seemed purposeful.

Pogue turned to Nick.

"She's not."

"I need vital signs, Nick—at least a blood pressure. You have a cuff?"

Nick motioned to one of the nurses, and they handed him a cuff and stethoscope. Pogue checked the girl's BP, and then looked at Nick.

"Her pressure is ninety over seventy, and her heart rate is one forty. She probably needs blood. I'd like to run a CBC. We need a lab."

"Or a CBC machine." Nick pointed to a Coulter counter nearby. "They've already primed it, calibrated it, and gotten it ready for you just in case."

*He has everything here.* Pogue gathered what he needed to run some labs. The results were available in minutes.

"Her hemoglobin and hematocrit are much lower than they should be."

"Would that be from the blood loss?"

"Most likely. With these levels, she needs a transfusion."

Nick motioned to one of the nurses, and she left the room.

"I mean right away. In order to type and crossmatch her, we have to take her to the hospital."

"We already have her blood type in our blood bank, and it has been crossmatched as of thirty minutes ago. Two units are at your disposal, and our nurse will bring it in shortly. I assumed you might need it."

Pogue gave him a crooked grin. "I've never known anyone to have a personal blood bank."

"As I said, we try to plan for every contingency. You want her to have one or two units?"

"Let's start with one and see how we're doing. We don't want any reactions even though it has been crossmatched." Pogue turned his attention to the girl again. "Can you move your fingers?"

Her eyes were closed most of the time, but she nodded as she wiggled her fingers.

"Good. Now this is important—did you try to kill yourself, or was this an accident?"

She shook her head, still with closed eyes.

"Not an answer, sweetie. Did you try to kill yourself? Tell me."

"Accident." Her soft voice quivered.

"With a kitchen knife?"

"No …" She suddenly opened her eyes and glanced at Nick, then turned back to Pogue. "Yes."

In that brief moment, Pogue saw the innocence reflected in the young girl's eyes. She was frightened for a reason, and it had nothing to do with the wound on her wrist.

"How old are you?"

"Six … eighteen."

"What's your name?"

"Amy—"

The man holding her wrist squeezed hard, and she winced and squinted her eyes closed. Pogue pretended to be too preoccupied to notice. He prepared the sterile field.

"Mary. My name is Mary."

Pogue didn't miss the slip but pretended to. "Mary, I'm going to numb this up, and we'll suture your wound. You'll be fine. You don't have any nerve damage or permanent problems. Numbing it will burn, but only for a few seconds. Grit your teeth, and it will be over by the time you count to fifteen. Normally ten would do, but this is a deep cut."

She nodded again and glanced at the guard who continued to hold her arm as a nurse skillfully started the IV for the transfusion on her left arm.

Pogue examined the blood they were about to give, the Lidocaine bottle, the suture materials, and instruments. Everything was presented in a sterile fashion as if he were in the ER. The truth was, he'd worked in ERs that were less prepared than this one. Carefully, he numbed the wound and explored it for deeper damage. He repaired the artery and deep tissues with absorbable suture material of small caliber—7–0 Vicryl. The final step involved placing external sutures and dressing the wound.

"There. You're going to be good as new very soon." Pogue gave her a smile.

Amy nodded with her eyes still closed. Pogue figured they'd instructed her not to make eye contact.

As he stood to leave, he noticed a bruise on her arm above the wound. "What's the bruise from?"

The guard answered. "I had to use my belt as a tourniquet. I pulled it pretty tight."

"Well, it worked. Good thinking. If it's not tight, the bleeding doesn't stop, so you didn't have much choice."

Nick opened the door. "You have an appointment in twenty minutes, Pogue."

He looked at his watch. "I didn't realize it was that late."

"Limo is waiting to take you. Let's go."

As the men left the building, Nick stopped and shook Pogue's hand. "Thanks. I appreciate you."

"No problem. See you back here after my meeting." He climbed into the back of the limo.

Nick waved. "The chopper will be waiting to take you home."

As the limo drove down Michigan Avenue toward Blanchard and Schmick, Pogue slipped his iPhone from his pocket and waited. When they arrived at the office building, he stepped out.

The moment the driver headed for the parking lot, Pogue selected the secured VPN on his phone, then swiped from the middle with both thumbs to opposite sides for access to the Secure/Encrypted line.

Once he received the clearance code, he texted Agent James. *"I need to look at some photos of girls who have been abducted in the Chicago area including the suburbs—long blonde hair, blue-eyed girls sixteen years old, pretty, first name Amy."*

James' text was almost immediate. *"What's going on?"*

Pogue typed, *"I just sutured up a young girl the Gambrels have at one of their locations. She was scared to death. Had a cut and a butterfly tattoo on her left wrist."*

James texted back, *"I'll get Vaughn on it right away."*

# CHAPTER TWENTY-EIGHT

Jamie Williams stepped from the cab and crossed the sidewalk to her dance class. Lucas surprised her when he approached from the side street. She ran and hugged him, then felt the heat of that embarrassing blush.

"I wasn't expecting to see you here, Lucas. Everything okay?"

"We don't have much time." He glanced in both directions. "I need you to come with me right now. Please."

She half-smiled, but the magic of the moment vanished when she saw his expression. "What's going on?"

"Trust me. We need to go."

"Go where?"

"I can't tell you. It's important—critical—that we disappear. I'll explain later."

"You're scaring me."

"I understand, but we have to leave."

He spoke to her as if something was coming for them. "Okay."

A van sped around the corner from behind them, and he grabbed her hand. "This way." Lucas dragged her down an alley to the right. She turned to see that the vehicle couldn't fit through the narrow passageway.

"Who is that?"

"I'll explain later."

They reached Cambridge and Lucas turned right. No van in sight. "Let's go."

"I can't." Jamie was out of breath.

"Just a little farther."

Once they reached the next intersection, Lucas stepped onto the curb, waving frantically as several cabs passed by. Finally, one stopped.

"Get in!" He opened the door and helped her. The van sped toward them two blocks behind. Lucas tapped the window to get the cabbie's attention. "Navy Pier as fast as you can. Please."

Jamie grabbed his arm. "What's happening?"

"They're trying to kidnap you. I was supposed to help them but couldn't. I'm in love with you, Jamie. I can't let them take you."

"You were supposed to kidnap me?"

"I got mixed up in this for money. I didn't expect to fall in love."

"Money? You're a Montiel."

"I'm *not* a Montiel. I lied about that too. I'm just a guy in love with you, and I can't let them take you."

In that moment, Jamie's heart shattered. "The fact that you fell in love with me is supposed to make you a good guy now? You're a jerk who gets paid to have girls kidnapped—"

The crash on the rear bumper caused the cab to skid sideways in the road and strike an abutment. The moment they stopped, Jamie jumped out and ran toward Navy Pier. She heard Lucas calling but she kept running. When she turned, the cab driver was shouting into his radio while Lucas ran toward her. The van was nowhere in sight.

She struggled for air and turned down a side street, stopping to catch her breath.

"Jamie, wait!"

Her heart pounded, and her legs ached as she forced her feet to keep moving. She turned right onto East Grand.

The van rounded the corner ahead and raced toward her with the left front bumper dragging and sparking on the street. She turned and ran in the opposite direction.

Lucas shouted from the side street, "Jamie, this way!"

Before she could respond, the van squealed to a stop beside her. Two men grabbed her and threw her into the van.

"No!" She heard Lucas scream from the sidewalk. "Stop! Somebody help!"

She kicked and fought, but her tired muscles were no match for these men. Someone from behind pulled a black cloth bag over her head. "Stop kicking!"

Struggling and cursing were mixed with the unmistakable sounds of someone punching Lucas until he stopped screaming for help. The door slammed shut and the van lurched forward, the bumper still grinding on the ground. Lucas' voice whispered, "Sorry" from somewhere inside the van. One more thud, and he was quiet.

"I'm ditching to the garage." It was a man's voice. "This dragging bumper is gonna get us pulled over."

She waited for the blow to her head that would end this, but it didn't come. She smelled something pungent pressed against her face. Then, nothing.

***

Pogue entered the office building of Blanchard and Schmick, took the elevator to the fifteenth floor, and stepped into a carpeted lobby.

A receptionist greeted him. "Mr. Savage is waiting to see you. This way, please."

He followed the young lady to the office at the end of the hall. Savage's office occupied the entire wing of the building with windows facing three directions—north, east, and south, offering an incredible view of the city and Lake Michigan.

"Dr. Pogue, we meet again."

Savage entered the room with his unmistakable gait—arrogant and forced.

"Good to see you, Mr. Savage. I understand Marc would like me to review some records for you."

Savage offered a single nod. "I have what you need right here." He removed a document from his desk with the embossed insignia *Central Intelligence Agency Top Secret—Classified* on the front.

"This is a forty-three-page document. How long will it take you to commit it to memory?"

Pogue flipped through the pages. "Give me forty minutes."

"Forty? To memorize a document with that level of detail?"

Pogue didn't answer. He walked to a nearby sofa, sat, and read.

"How is that possible?"

Pogue didn't stop reading. "A gift and a curse."

Forty minutes later, Pogue dropped the file onto the desk under Savage's nose. "Is that it?"

"Seriously?"

"Seriously."

Savage flipped halfway through the pages.

"Page twelve, the thirtieth line, five words in?"

Pogue closed his eyes. "Remainder."

Savage glanced at Pogue, clearly bewildered. "You didn't even have to think about that."

He opened his eyes. "What's next?"

"Page twenty, second paragraph from the bottom, second line states—"

He closed them again. "Anyone utilizing this document for any purpose other than to aid the United States in its war against terrorism—"

"Enough." Savage appeared rattled.

"Any more?" He stared at Savage with a grin.

"No. You leave for Cairo the day after tomorrow on Gambrel's private jet at eight a.m."

"Armed?"

"Yes."

"Alone?"

"Kurt Lucci and I will join you. We could also possibly have a guard and a passenger. You're not to engage the passenger at any time in any manner. You're free to do whatever else you'd like, but if there's a passenger, you'll maintain your isolation from him or her. I don't mean to be cryptic, but I don't know who it is. Is that understood?"

"Understood."

Savage handed him documentation that would permit him to enter the private tarmac at seven o'clock the morning of the flight. "The Gambrel limo will pick you up at six. Be ready."

Savage closed the folder and slipped it into his satchel. "Look, Pogue. This mission is critical. If anything goes wrong, we die—we all die."

Pogue nodded. *That's reassuring.*

\*\*\*

Larson James greeted Detective Davis as he took a seat across from him in the FBI conference room they'd met in before.

"What's this about, Mr. James? It's always a pleasure, but I'm kinda busy."

"Pogue told me he was called upon by Nick Gambrel to treat someone who might have gone missing recently—a sixteen-year-old blonde girl with a butterfly tattoo on her left wrist, blue eyes, and the first name of Amy, possibly. A search of the database gave us a single hit going back one month."

James put up the picture on the wall monitor.

Davis nodded. "That's Amy King. She was abducted a week ago from her school in Naperville. No ransom demands or contact from anyone. That's why she hasn't been on the news. The escape car was a stolen police squad, wiped clean of fingerprints like a professional job."

"I sent the photo to Pogue to confirm her identity but haven't heard back yet. If it's her, she's still in Chicago at one of the Gambrel mansions."

"What's she doing there?"

James shook his head. "I was hoping you could tell me. Was this on your radar for the Gambrels? Did we miss something?"

Davis stood and poured coffee from the carafe into a small Styrofoam cup. "This is odd."

"Which part?"

"I was there when Amy King's parents were questioned about their missing daughter. The father's car was sabotaged so someone could get to her."

"Anything strange about the family?"

"Not a thing. Then yesterday we had reports from witnesses who watched a young girl and guy being abducted in broad daylight near Michigan Avenue and thrown into a damaged van." Davis skimmed through images on his cell, then held one of them in front of James. "Her name is Jamie Williams. The information is incomplete, but we have traffic-cam footage of the van used in the abduction. It has no plates, but it does have front-end damage and a mark on the roof of which the owners may not be aware."

"A mark?"

Davis flipped through photos till he found it. "Here. Look right there where the paint is scraped off. It looks as if they tried to clear a low-hanging overpass, concrete beam in a parking garage, or something else that dragged across the roof. Images matching that *fingerprint* from other traffic cams show the van following an erratic path through that part of the city as if they couldn't decide where they were going. They ditched the van in a parking garage not far from where they picked up the girl. The lab is going through it for clues now. We're hopeful since the ditch wasn't planned that there may not have been time for them to wipe it clean."

"You said she was with a guy?"

"Our facial recognition on the garage cam identified the young man with her as Lucas Durham. He has a record, which is how we pulled him up so quickly. But nothing in his past indicated anything felonious—just scamming and conning. Nothing to put him in the same league with these guys."

"So we have potentially two girls abducted, one of whom is probably Amy King, the other, Jamie Williams."

"To answer your original question, this was *not* on our radar. I don't see how it fits anything we've been working on or Intel we've gathered."

"I need to call Flannery. If we're adding kidnappings to the mix, we've missed something. What if we rush in on a suspicion and the girls aren't there? The CIA loses the ability to get on top of their espionage case, and we're back at square one."

Davis sipped his coffee. "Changing the subject for a moment, I can finally give you a motive for Dr. Harrison's involvement in Lucci's death. Harrison's wife divorced him quietly last October. Mrs. Harrison currently has over five hundred thousand in her personal bank account, deposited at the time of the divorce, but it did not come from hubby."

"But why Harrison and Reid? What's their connection to the mob? And how does Ginger Lucci fit into it? All we have now is Harrison's motive for borrowing money from the mob—potentially, but no connection we know of."

"The syndicate invests in a physician who needs money with the hope that he'll be able to return the favor down the road. I doubt Harrison had any clue it would get this ugly."

The buzz from James' cell phone caused him to check the text. "It's Pogue. We have a positive ID on Amy King."

# CHAPTER TWENTY-NINE

reston Yeager, a seasoned CIA field agent known for his cool demeanor under pressure, stood with his hands in his pockets, shifting from one foot to the other while waiting for Flannery to finish what he keyed into the computer.

Yeager had earned his reputation. Nothing ruffled this guy's feathers—until now. Flannery noticed the difference. He would normally have invited him to have a seat, but Yeager was feeding him body language that was far out of character for him. Vaughn sat across from them, reading something.

"Agent Flannery?" Yeager stepped closer to the desk. "We've documented a clear and present danger, sir. Do you have a moment?"

Flannery stopped typing and sat back in his leather desk chair. He swiveled a little as he eyed Yeager. "Go ahead."

"Philip, our man in Egypt, is concerned about compromising his position with Nadir."

"Have a seat, Mr. Yeager."

Yeager sat in the chair next to Vaughn but offered him barely a glance. "Philip has provided reliable Intel indicating the transaction of information from US to Egyptian soil will take place in the next two days, potentially altering conflicts in the Middle East and exposing our NOC agents to discovery."

Flannery studied the closed folder on his desk. "They're classified as Non-Official Cover for a reason. They're extremely hard to find. That being said, we're about to hand over *verifiable* classified information that will place those operatives in harm's way unless we intervene in time. It's bait and Nadir has to believe it, so it must be real."

"I'd like permission to travel to Cairo to meet with Philip." Yeager rested his elbows on the arms of the chair. "I can walk him through this. If he panics, the attention he'd draw could hurt us. I'll keep him on point."

Flannery stroked his chin. "As soon as we upload the information, the package will be delivered. Go to Cairo. Keep Philip calm."

"Who will deliver the information?"

"He's one of ours, undercover." Flannery unlocked his desk drawer and retrieved a file. Pogue's name and picture appeared in the top left corner. "Once Nadir has vetted the Intel, we have a matter of hours to identify the players and stop them. This is a high-stakes game. Don't get in Pogue's way—just back him up."

"I can handle that. Thank you." Yeager left the room.

Flannery closed the door and picked up his cell phone.

"You lied to him." Vaughn appeared surprised. "Why did you tell him the Intel was real and verifiable?"

"I don't trust him. I have a feeling—a hunch. But I need him to believe the data is real. If he's up to something, he'll expose himself. If he's not, no harm no foul." Flannery dialed a number. "This is Flannery. I need tail coverage on Agent Yeager starting tonight. It requires travel. This is a level five priority."

"Would Agent Stecker be acceptable?" the woman on the other end asked.

"Lauren? She'd be perfect. I'll contact our asset in Cairo so they can coordinate. She's to remain out of sight. Yeager is experienced."

"Security level?" the woman said.

"Black, Sector Five."

"Confirm Level Black, Sector Five." The woman waited.

Flannery turned to Vaughn. "Confirmed."

\*\*\*

Nick walked slowly down the creaky stairs of the abandoned warehouse located three blocks from the docks. One of his favorite places to meet with his men years ago, he'd climbed enough ladders to have a downtown office now. Still, it felt right to be here for this. He made his way to the bar in the corner of the room he'd had built in those early days, unfolded a leather case on the counter, and removed a knife and honing stone.

Lucas sat on a wooden chair in the middle of the neglected room. It was unlikely he'd ever met the men standing in the shadows. Nick guessed he was probably trying to figure out who they were.

"Nick …"

He glanced at Lucas briefly and began honing the knife against the stone while leaning on the bar.

Lucas gripped the arms of the chair. "I'm sorry, Nick."

Nick held up his hand to stop him from speaking.

Lucas nodded.

Nick slowly walked to the smudged windows and studied the nearby buildings through the haze while twirling the knife in his right hand. It had been a while since anyone had cleaned these things. He turned back toward Lucas.

"Had a guy working for me years ago named Jimmy. Came from a family that didn't give him a second thought. Father was a thief, Mom a whore."

Lucas squirmed.

"He delivered pizzas for a living. His mom took the money to buy heroin every time he got paid, but he kept delivering those pizzas."

Nick walked to the bar, where one of his men poured him a drink. He picked up the glass and swirled the dark liquid. "One day, Jimmy came home and found his mom on the bathroom floor, cold and stiff, needle still in her arm." Nick shook his head as he gradually took strides toward Lucas. "Been dead for hours, but he called the ambulance, the police—nobody came. Sat on that filthy floor holding his mom's head in his lap for God knows how long."

Nick sat on the only barstool in sight and kept honing as he spoke. "I met Jimmy when he went back to delivering pizzas to pay for burying his mom. He brought one to my office by mistake. I'm not sure what I saw in the guy, but there was something. I offered him a job—a good job making good money, living in a nice place."

Nick walked around the room with the drink in one hand and the knife in the other, waving both as he spoke. "He worked his way up the ladder to the point where he met my sister, Ginger. She took a liking to him same as me, but my father didn't." Nick tilted his head and looked at Lucas. "Ginger … you never met her, right?"

Lucas shook his head.

"Anyway, she liked Jimmy because he seemed like a sweet guy. A little slow in the head, but sweet. It didn't matter what you told him to do, he'd get it done."

Lucas followed Nick with his eyes.

"One day, my dad noticed Jimmy staring at Ginger when she walked across the courtyard. He didn't like the way he *looked* at her, but she told my father it was okay. That Jimmy was harmless. Dad didn't care for her answer, and he instructed me to *deal* with it quietly."

Nick walked to Lucas and stood two feet from him. "He wanted me to send him back to his slum world to fend for himself because he looked at Ginger. God, Lucas. She was beautiful. Who wouldn't look at her *that way?*"

Lucas' eyes darted from side to side. The zip ties on his arms and legs held him to the chair, right where Nick wanted him.

"When I talked to Jimmy, he was upset and wanted to leave. If I'd just let him that would have been the end of it. Never would have seen him again." Nick walked to the bar once more, where one of his men grabbed the bottle, but Nick waved him off this time.

"Nick, I just—"

"Bottom line, I believed in him." He took a sip and stared at the floor. "My father asked if I'd taken care of Jimmy. I told him I had, but I'd just moved him where my dad wouldn't see him." Nick painstakingly dragged the edge of the blade over the honing stone as he spoke, causing it to make a high-pitched shrieking sound like fingers on a chalkboard. "One day I come home to find Ginger crying like I'd never seen her cry. I'm thinking a guy dumped her or some other lame girl drama. When I ask her what her problem is, she throws her arms around me and cries harder. She's squeezing me like I'm her lifeline and tells me Jimmy grabbed her and tore her dress. She hurt him and he ran, but not until he'd gone too far." Nick stopped sharpening, looked at the floor, and shook his head. He set the stone on a table.

"When my father called me to his office, it was my day of reckoning." He waved the knife as he talked as if it were a baton. "I'm the guy that's going to take over the family business one day, and my father calls me in to tell me my gut got my sister jumped."

Lucas physically trembled as Nick stared at him.

"Took me years to regain my father's trust. I was responsible because I believed in some worthless guy."

Nick examined the shimmering blade. He removed a cloth from his jacket pocket and drew the side of the knife carefully across it. "I swore that day I'd never let that happen again."

"I swear, Nick. I'll never—"

"I found you homeless, straight out of jail, no hope, no family, no money. I placed my trust in you, Lucas. I promised you wealth and a new life. Did I deliver?"

"Yes."

He slammed his fist on the table. "That's right. I did."

"I fell in love with Jamie."

"You even sound like him. Jimmy sat in a chair like the one you're in now."

"Please."

Nick blew on the edge of the freshly sharpened blade. It glimmered in the light from the windows. He shook his head, recalling the event with disgust.

Lucas dug his fingernails into the arms of the chair.

"When I drove this knife between Jimmy's ribs, he looked at me with these huge eyes. He couldn't believe I'd hurt him. You can't have people working for you if they betray your trust—not in this business."

"Oh, God …"

"I drove to the dockyard with him in the trunk, still alive." Nick shrugged. "I think he expected me to let him go."

"I made a mistake."

"Even with cinderblocks tied to his legs, he tried to swim, splashing around like a duck with a broken wing. When his face went under, he gasped for air but got water instead. That was that." He turned and focused on Lucas. "You're not the only one doing what I hired you to do. Those guys over there"—he gestured with his head to the young men on Lucas' left—"have the same job, the same perks, the same gift of freedom I gave you. I need them to appreciate what they've got instead of throwing it away."

Lucas sobbed.

"The next guy I pull from the gutter will know what happened here today. He'll know he's not the one in charge and never will be. These boys … they're going to remember this for the rest of their lives."

He looked at the two men standing behind Lucas and nodded. They held him down while he squirmed.

"I'm begging you, Nick."

He rubbed Lucas' hair as if he were a little boy, then drove the knife through his left hand into the armrest. Lucas screamed in agony as he stared at the shimmering blade piercing his hand—his body quivering in pain.

"God! Oh, God!"

Nick pulled the knife out and drove it through his right hand as the empty warehouse echoed screams of terror.

"I'm begging you!"

Nick shook his head in disgust. "That girl belongs to someone else. She will live with another man, bear his children, live for his pleasure, and satisfy his desires, for the rest of her life. After she stops hating you for what you did to her, she'll forget she even met you."

Nick pulled the knife out of Lucas' hand, then held the tip against his ribs. As Lucas screamed, Nick slowly pushed it in, dragging the blade across the bone. He snatched it out, wiped the blood on Lucas' shirt, then handed it to one of the men. Lucas stared at him, gasping for air, struggling for each breath. Nick wanted to take longer but he had work to do. Walking behind him, he pulled a clear plastic bag over Lucas' head, gripping it tight around his neck. Lucas gasped, but the bag sucked against his face with each attempt. Then finally, he stopped.

Nick faced the men in the shadows and took a few steps toward them, wiping his bloodstained hands on the cloth from his pocket. "You gentlemen have an important job. As you can see, I take that seriously. If anyone has something to say, now's the time."

The only noise in the room was the crinkle of plastic sheets as men wrapped Lucas' body.

# CHAPTER THIRTY

P ogue dressed as quietly as he could. The darkness at four o'clock in the morning reminded him it would be a long day, but he needed to be ready when the limo arrived. He wasn't looking forward to this trip. Talking on the plane for ten hours with Savage was not an inviting thought. At least Kurt would be there to buffer the conversation.

He carefully opened the door from the bathroom to the bedroom. Jenni stood with sleepy eyes and wrapped her arms around his neck. "I'm going to miss you. I'll be thinking of you every minute."

"I'll miss you, too." He kissed her and then pulled on his sports jacket and picked up his overnight bag. "See you soon, babe." He leaned in to kiss her again.

After he did, she said in almost a whisper, "Hey—I love you, Bailey. And I'm proud of you for whatever it is you're doing."

"Thank you, baby. I love you, too." He needed to hear that.

As he walked downstairs and into the garage, he opened his trunk, slipped on the bulletproof vest, pulled it snug, and buttoned his shirt over it. Then he strapped on his shoulder holster, pistol, and two extra clips. His jacket covered the ensemble, and he was ready to go. This was getting to be routine. Leaving through the side door of the garage, he climbed into the waiting limo parked in the horseshoe drive and looked back at his home. Their dreams when they'd built it, and how peaceful it once was now seemed no more than a distant memory. Those days were over.

\*\*\*

Amy left the Gambrel compound at 6:45 a.m. with a black bag over her head. It wasn't optional. Deene sat beside her.

"Are you certain you want Midway, ma'am?" the driver questioned.

172/ THICKER THAN BLOOD

"I'm sure. I don't want the scrutiny we get from O'Hare. I can't risk a
facial recognition scan."

Amy already felt the effects of the Valium Deene had made her take
before they'd left the house. She could barely think. Midway may be
where they were going, but where were they now?

After a relatively quiet trip, Deene finally pulled the hood off Amy's
head. As the limo drove up to a double gate at the airport's private jet
tarmac, she placed her hand on Amy's arm. "Keep quiet, or I make a call,
and your father gets an unpleasant visit. Got that?"

Amy nodded.

Deene smiled as she hit the button to lower her window and handed an
envelope to the guard, who broke the wax seal on the flap and examined
the contents.

He looked at Amy, then Deene. "This young lady is being transported
for medical care in France?"

"Yes. Victor Santino is sponsoring her treatment at a facility there. The
documents are in the envelope. It will give her a fighting chance if we can
get there in time."

"Yes, ma'am. Your jet is the maroon one right over there at apron
seventeen." The man pointed.

"Thank you so much." She took the papers from him and rolled up the
window as the limo approached the Gambrel jet.

"Almost there, Amy. Say goodbye to America."

Amy did her best to keep her head clear. Life as she knew it was over.
She'd soon be thrust into the black hole of human trafficking.

Deene put her fingers under Amy's chin and tilted her head to look at
her. "Even God can't help you now."

***

Pogue would never get used to this internal earpiece, but as his limo
approached the private tarmac gate, at least he knew he wasn't really alone.

"If you can hear me, tap your ear twice," Flannery said through the
com line.

He tapped twice.

"Good. We're on-site, and I see you at the gate directly in front of me.
Three vehicles and six men represent the FBI. I'm in the CIA task van five
aprons to the left of your jet with two other agents to help me keep an eye

on things. There's one limo ahead of you approaching the jet. Hold on till I see who's getting out."

Pogue spotted the CIA task vehicle as the limo driver signed in at the tarmac guard post. The van was marked as a food service vehicle. He couldn't identify the other FBI or CIA vehicles, but it was reassuring to know they were close by.

"Okay, Pogue." Flannery's voice in the earpiece took some getting used to. "The inhabitants of the first limo got out on the opposite side of the vehicle from us. I can't make out their faces. You'll have to tell me who they are once you're on board. Both are women, but that's all I can say. I may talk to you from time to time, but no one else can hear me."

*Women? Were they the passengers Savage said not to engage with?*

"Kurt's green Bentley and Savage's limo are directly behind you in that order," Flannery's voice came across.

"One of the women from that first limo just left the jet and is walking to the egress office," Flannery said. "Got a ninety-five percent match on facial recognition from our camera over there. It's Carlee Santino Franklin."

*So that's my mysterious guest? Great.*

Pogue's limo pulled up to the jet, leaving room for Kurt to park on his right and Savage's black limo on his left.

Pogue sent a secured text to Flannery before exiting his car: *"More company than I expected."*

Flannery responded. *"It's starting to look a little crowded if C.J. comes back on board. Let me know who the other woman is."*

Kurt, Savage, and Pogue stepped up to the jet and greeted each other.

"Shall we, gentlemen?" Kurt gestured toward the steps.

Savage boarded, then Pogue, followed by Kurt.

Pogue almost ran into Savage when he stopped abruptly in front of Pogue and turned around.

"What is this?" He fumed at Kurt, then shoved Pogue aside and stormed off the plane, yelling obscenities. Kurt hurried after him.

Pogue turned to see where Savage had been looking in the back of the plane. When his eyes met Amy's, the puzzle pieces connected. The arguing between Kurt and Savage got loud and snapped him back. He found a seat near the doorway to better listen but not be noticed by the two guards standing near the cockpit door.

Savage stood by the limo door he'd already opened. "Who is she, then?"

"She's part of the deal with Nadir. We've talked about this, Robert. She's the girl who we'll trade along with the Intelligence data. One girl. Our business is booming. Don't be an idiot."

"Then transport her in another aircraft, not with me. We talked about there being passengers, but never about this. What if someone tipped off the authorities and they were waiting for us in Paris or Cairo? I'd be arrested and ruined for human trafficking."

Pogue tried his best to indicate to the guards in the plane he didn't hear what was transpiring, fiddling with his cell phone as if checking emails.

"I had no choice."

That was Kurt's voice again.

"You did, but you made the wrong one."

Pogue peered out the porthole to see Savage getting into his car.

*"Can you hear this?"* Pogue typed to Flannery.

*"Yes."*

Kurt slowly re-boarded the plane and walked to one of the guards up front. "Where is C.J.?"

"She went to the terminal—the egress office." The man checked his watch. "Thought she'd be back by now."

Kurt settled into a chair across from Pogue. "I can't believe this. Did you hear any of that?"

"Hard not to. What's his problem?"

"He's not going. I was afraid he'd be spooked when he saw her." He gestured toward Amy. "I don't like it either. I mean … she's sitting right there. We can't even talk without her hearing what we say, even if she is drugged."

"She can see all of us. We're screwed if anything goes wrong."

Kurt looked at her again and shook his head.

"Who is she, Kurt? Why is she on this plane?"

"Pogue." Flannery's voice came across his earpiece. "If you're confirming Amy King is on board tap your earpiece twice."

He tapped.

"Why is she here, Kurt?"

Kurt turned and looked at her, then leaned toward Pogue. "Nick and I have another business that ties indirectly to your part. You deliver your package, and we deliver ours." He glanced at Amy again. "She doesn't involve you."

"She was kidnapped, Pogue." Flannery's voice came through the earpiece. "We didn't know she was tied into this."

"Why was Savage so upset, Kurt? Because you're trafficking minors and he wants no part of it?" It must have been Pogue's eyes that betrayed him.

"What is that supposed to mean?"

"It's a simple question."

"You act like you're a choirboy. But you're carrying military secrets in your head that will kill people by the thousands."

"If Robert won't fly, should I get off too? That's all I'm asking."

The pilot finished his preflight check and nodded to one of the guards to close the door as he fired up the engines.

Kurt stood. "Wait. Don't close the door. C.J. isn't here yet."

The pilot shouted to him before sealing the cockpit door. "She isn't coming. We've been instructed to leave. Take your seat."

Kurt shook his head. "No way. I'm not a babysitter." He shot a look toward Amy.

Flannery's voice spoke into Pogue's ear. "They're pulling the chocks from the wheels, and air traffic control just cleared your plane for takeoff. This is not the plan. We can't allow a US citizen to be kidnapped."

Every moment of training Pogue had received kicked in at once. As a man, all he could think of was stopping this. Instead, duty demanded he stand down and wait for orders. If that meant letting Amy King disappear into the void of human trafficking, he just couldn't let that happen. He placed his hand on his pistol.

Flannery's voice came through. "You're about to be boarded by the FBI. They approached from behind where they wouldn't be seen. They know who you are, but they'll rough you up like any hostile or your cover will be blown. Wait for my instructions but don't delay carrying them out. They're coming for her. If you're wearing your vest, tap your earpiece."

Pogue's heart raced. He tapped his ear.

As one of the guards attempted to pull up the steps and close the main hatch, two uniformed men grabbed the door's edge from outside and pulled it open. Gambrel's guards both fired their weapons at the agents trying to board. Their attempts were met with lethal force.

"Shut it down!" One of the FBI agents shouted as he and another agent rushed to the bulkhead.

"Shoot him, Pogue," Flannery instructed. "The first agent that boarded. Shoot him in his vest."

Pogue fired three rounds into the man's vest.

Kurt jumped to his feet, drew his pistol, and raised it to the second agent. The man took Kurt down with a single shot to his chest. The agent then shot Pogue in the vest twice. Pogue's body slammed against the bulkhead and slid to the floor, still clinging to his pistol. The agent he shot didn't move.

The third and fourth agents boarded and secured the aircraft.

"Stay low, Pogue." Flannery sounded urgent but calm.

Pogue crawled to Kurt, who struggled to breathe. Blood soaked his shirt in a growing circle.

Pogue's lungs burned, and his side felt like it had split open. "Kurt." He grabbed his arm. Kurt looked at him, wild-eyed.

"I forgot my vest." He leaned his head back. "I think I'm dying."

"Don't move!" The FBI agent behind Pogue held a gun to the back of his head. "Drop your weapon!"

"He's holding a gun against your head," Kurt said quietly. "Give it up."

Pogue dropped his weapon. The man grabbed the pistol and Pogue's hands from behind.

"Give me a second." Pogue moved his hands forward. The man stood behind him with his gun resting against the back of his neck.

"Open the doors!" Another agent aimed a rifle at the cockpit as the pilot and copilot released the door and exited. The agents quickly led the two men outside.

Pogue shook Kurt to keep him awake. "This isn't really it, is it? I just shot a federal agent and you're dying? That's how it ends?"

Kurt nodded. "Think so."

"Well, that sucks."

Kurt looked at him. "C.J. left us. She did this."

Pogue nodded. "You want to tell me anything?"

"Tell you what?"

Pogue shrugged. "I'm the only priest you're going to get. It's your call. I'm here for you."

Kurt shook his head. "No. Wait … yeah." He took a breath that seemed to hurt. "It doesn't matter anymore. I did it." A tear streaked down his face, followed by another. "I killed her."

Pogue waited.

"I tried to do it myself, then arranged for Harrison to handle it. But it was still me." His tears kept coming.

"Why?" Pogue didn't try to move.

"She knew too much. She threatened to tell you, then go to the authorities. Couldn't let that happen—everything would fall apart. Everything we'd worked for would be lost. Nick agreed she had to die. He hired the guys who hit your office."

Pogue held Kurt's arm until it turned lifeless.

"Kurt?"

The man behind Pogue reached forward and felt Kurt's neck for a pulse. "Sorry, sir. We thought he'd be wearing a vest."

Pogue nodded. "He was supposed to be."

The agent handed Pogue his weapon. "Your boss told me to shoot you. It wasn't my idea."

"I understand." Pogue made his way to the man he'd shot and checked his pulse. It was strong as the man opened his eyes.

"You okay, sir?" the man asked.

Pogue nodded. "I am. I thought I killed you."

"Yes, sir. They have to carry me out in a body bag. Any unfriendlies need to see dead FBI agents."

Pogue stood so he could get a glimpse of Amy. She shivered and sobbed in a fetal position in the back of the plane. He hurried to her and knelt, but she pushed him away.

"It's okay, Amy. I'm the doctor that took care of your wrist. I know who you are. You're Amy King, and you're going home to your family. It's over." Pogue turned to one of the agents. "Get her out of here."

Flannery came online again. "Pogue, we need to take you down fast. I assume someone is watching this. Get ready to follow instructions."

"I'm ready."

"You'll be shot, run to the second limo, then get out of here. Keys are in it and it's bulletproof. Hurry!"

One of the men picked up Amy and carried her out the door.

Another agent shot Pogue's vest. He slammed against the wall. Two more shots in succession from the lead agent to his chest made it difficult to breathe. He could barely get up as he fired a shot into the bulkhead and threw his gun on the floor. Diving out the door, he landed hard on the asphalt and hit his head on the edge of the stairs, then bolted for the second limo as blood ran down his face from a cut somewhere over his eye.

"Move, Pogue!" Flannery's voice was loud in his earpiece.

Pogue had almost reached the car when a bullet struck him in the back, forcing him against the hood. He shoved himself free and dove for the front door of the car. The moment he was inside, a hail of gunfire pelted the back of the vehicle and pitted the bulletproof glass on the passenger side.

"The CIA is stationed at the guardhouse gate," Flannery instructed through the com. "They'll shoot at the back doors and windows. Call Nick and let him know you're coming. Ditch the earpiece as soon as you're on the main road. We'll be dark after that."

"Understood." Pogue sped through the front gate where the gunfire pierced the vehicle's doors dozens of times and eventually shattered even the bulletproof back windows. Heading north on Cicero, Pogue threw his earpiece out the window and dialed Nick's number. He held the cell phone in his bloody hand. Was the blood his? Kurt's? He hurt in so many places it was impossible to tell.

"Pogue, what the—"

"Nick, we got ambushed."

"I know. C.J. called and said the plane was surrounded. She watched from the terminal. Was that you driving off?"

"I stole a limo."

"She said they shot up your car. You hit?"

"Yeah. I'm not sure how bad. I'm wearing a vest, but something got through."

"You sure?"

"I'm sure. They knew we were there, Nick. Somebody tipped off the feds. Was it C.J.? Did she burn us?"

"How do you know they were feds?"

"They were wearing flak jackets with FBI written in big yellow letters."

"Kurt won't answer and neither will the pilots."

"The pilots are detained. Kurt is dead."

"Dead? No. He can't be."

"He wasn't wearing his vest and got shot in the chest. Took him sixty seconds to die."

"What about Savage?"

"He and Kurt had an argument outside the plane. Savage left before the shooting started. I don't know why C.J. wasn't back on the plane when this went down."

"She said she would explain later. Was the girl still on board?"

"Mary?"

"Yes. Was she there?"

"She was on the floor in the back of the plane when the shooting started. I don't know what happened to her. I got out, but only after getting myself shot. I jumped in this car and haven't stopped. I shouldn't have left the girl, but bullets were flying, and when Kurt went down, I shot an FBI agent and ran."

"Where are you now?"

"Did you hear me? I shot a federal agent!"

"Focus, Pogue. Where are you?"

"North on Cicero, almost to I-fifty-five."

"Still in the limo?"

"Yes."

"Dump it. Have you passed West Forty-Fourth yet?"

"Coming up. Less than a block."

"Turn left onto it and stop somewhere. I'm talking to someone on the other line."

Pogue turned left at the light and pulled to the curb on a side street. The pain in his side was blinding, but he waited less than a minute.

"Okay, Pogue, pull into LeClaire Church on the corner of Forty-Fourth and Lawler straight ahead on the left, then drive behind the building and park by the green Dumpsters. I'll have the pastor come out to help you. We'll land in the parking lot and extract you. Take it easy. We're coming. Chopper's firing up as we speak."

"I'm almost at the intersection."

"Get behind that church."

"Pulling in now."

Before Pogue was fully stopped, two vehicles drove in behind him near the Dumpsters. As he struggled to open the car door, a tall, muscular black man yanked it open and helped him out. By the time he was at the back door of the church, the men from the other vehicles had covered the limo with tarps.

"I'm Pastor Clyde."

"Pogue."

"Have a seat and let's see what damage you've done."

"I need your restroom—bad. Please."

"Right here, son." Clyde opened a door off the main room.

Pogue used the restroom, supporting himself with his hand against the wall while the pastor stood in the doorway. Once Pogue zipped up, he stood for a moment, trying to collect his emotions, then vomited twice.

"I'm sorry, Pastor," he said as he flushed.

"Call me Clyde. And it's okay. You're shivering, son."

"I got blood on your wall."

"Don't sweat it." He turned to the hallway as he helped Pogue sit. "Emily!"

Clyde helped him pull off his torn, bloody shirt and removed the Velcro straps of the vest. Pain scorched his lungs with every breath. A young girl came into the room but didn't appear shocked at the scene.

"Yes, Daddy?"

"Get this man a blanket and fetch me my toolbox."

"Yes, sir." She hurried off.

Everything hurt as Pogue slipped the tattered vest over his head. Pain shot from his left abdomen to his chest. He couldn't stop shaking. It felt like twenty degrees in the room. He looked down at the bullet wound on his left abdomen.

"Do you have a mirror, Pastor?"

"Don't need one. It came out the side of your back right here."

Pogue arched his back involuntarily from the pain when Clyde touched it.

"Sorry. Bleeding is significant, but not arterial. Did you see any blood in your piss?"

Pogue shook his head.

"Vests are good, but they can't help you where you got shot. Too low of a hit. You had a slug bounce off the edge of your Kevlar and go on through your side. If it hit anything important, you'd be bleeding worse. Still hurts like the devil—that much I know." He examined Pogue's chest and back. "You got bruises everywhere … they meant to kill you, boy." Clyde walked around to face Pogue. "These aren't warning shots."

*They made it through the vest—something that wasn't supposed to happen.* "They killed a friend in front of me." The sound of an approaching chopper hovered overhead.

Pastor Clyde stood. "Let me see if they're our guys. I'd hate to think a police chopper followed you here."

"There were no police cars near me when I left, and I got here pretty quick."

"You never know." Clyde looked outside.

Emily ran into the room and covered him with a blanket. Pogue rested his head back and sighed. It warmed him to his bones. She set the toolbox on the floor next to him.

"Bandage him up, baby. I'll be right back." Clyde walked out.

"Yes, Daddy." She opened the toolbox, well stocked with bandages and dressing materials. "I'll do what I can, but you'll need some stitches, I'm thinkin'."

Whatever she applied to the wounds burned like acid, but he almost welcomed the added warmth. "Thank you. I appreciate your help. Don't worry, I'm not dangerous."

"If you were dangerous, Daddy would have killed you before you got out of the car."

Pogue smiled a little until he realized she wasn't joking.

Pastor Clyde reentered the room. "Your ride's here. Let's get you out before we gather a crowd. Luxury copters don't land in the parking lot often." He turned to Emily. "Clean everything with bleach, including the blood on the bathroom wall."

"Yes, Daddy."

Pogue walked quickly even though each movement brought new pain. He grew stiffer by the minute but followed Pastor Clyde to the helicopter.

"Thank you." Pogue went to shake his hand but thought better of it when he saw the blood.

"Glad to help. We'll take care of the car. Hope you weren't too attached to it." Clyde grinned.

Pogue noticed several men pulling it into an old garage.

"There will be no trace of it in two hours." Clyde tossed the damaged vest into the chopper. "Can't have that lying around here, just in case someone saw you heading this way."

Pogue nodded his appreciation and climbed into the aircraft. As it lifted away and carried him toward the Gambrel mansion, he pulled the blanket tight and analyzed his situation.

When he thought about them trafficking a sixteen-year-old girl, his nausea returned. How could the FBI not have suspected that with all of their resources and investigating? Did they know and not want to tell him?

He took as strong a breath as he could, but the pain gnawed deep inside. The Chicago skyline mocked him. The world was normal down there for so many people. He had no way to contact anyone. He'd never felt so alone.

# CHAPTER THIRTY-ONE

"How could this happen?" C.J. snapped at Nick as she stormed into the Gambrel library, slamming the door behind her. "That tarmac crawled with FBI agents. It was supposed to be clean." She postured as if he'd care. He didn't. "And how did Kurt get killed while your *buddy* Pogue walked?"

"Kurt was my friend too. And define *walked*."

"Excuse me?"

"I'll make this clear, C.J. He didn't *walk*. He barely escaped after being shot five times. How many times were you shot? You bailed on your friends and watched from a safe distance while the FBI dropped them one by one."

"Pogue was wearing a stupid—"

"Bulletproof vest? Yes, thank God. We should all be wearing them, but Kurt wasn't. Even so, one got through it—a military-grade, armor-piercing round. Does that sound like Pogue *walked* to you? This was not a drill—not a warning. We let our guard down and people died."

"Something's wrong with this picture, Nick."

"Let me narrow that down. Do you mean that Kurt's dead, two guards are dead, multiple FBI agents are dead, Amy King is *probably* dead, our information shipment is delayed, and Pogue's been shot? Is that what's wrong, or are you talking about why you abandoned the plane?"

"I had to check us out at the egress office. You know the routine."

"It has never taken me that long in egress."

"While I was inside, I noticed a man staring out a window in the direction of our jet. I watched and observed as our people arrived, including Pogue."

"You should have called Kurt and warned him."

"I tried. He'd already switched off his phone because it went straight to voice mail. When Savage sped off in his limo, the guy watching the tarmac spoke while holding his finger on an earpiece. That's when I knew it was real, so I phoned the pilot on his cell. I told him to close the door and go."

Nick pinched the bridge of his nose. "Nadir is upset and wants his Intel regardless of the girl. If we can supply a replacement, he wants us to."

"Another girl?" C.J. grabbed her hair with her fists. "Another girl. The only one we currently have vetted is completely different than what he ordered. Amy was handpicked for Nadir. Jamie's qualifications are perfect for the sheik, not him. We can't just hand Jamie over to keep him happy. She's worth half a million in Dubai."

"That's what you heard from what I just said? We're on the brink of losing it all. I don't care about the girls. I care about Apollyon."

"The pilot and copilot of the jet are in custody, correct?" C.J. walked with her hands on her hips. "Amy can potentially point authorities to us *if* she lives."

Nick sat on the edge of the desk. "The pilots both tell the same story. There was gunfire, shouting they couldn't understand, then federal agents boarded the aircraft. When the pilots exited the cockpit, blood was everywhere, including the walls and ceiling, an agent held a gun at the back of Pogue's head as he knelt in front of Kurt, body bags were being lined up on the tarmac, and the FBI took our pilots into custody."

"And Amy?"

"They saw the legs of someone lying on the floor in the back of the aircraft."

"Nick, I watched one of the agents carrying Amy to an ambulance."

"Cut to your point."

"Pogue dove out the door of an airplane and landed on his head. Think about it. He's a doctor, right? Then he's shooting FBI agents, diving out of airplanes, and making a clean getaway in a limo? How do you get away from the FBI in a stretch limo?"

"So he's got guts. And for your information, it was not a stretch limo, and it arrived at the church with more than two hundred armor-piercing rounds embedded in it. The only reason it was still rolling is that it had run-flat tires. Even the bulletproof glass was blown to shards."

"How did he get away from a trained FBI agent holding a gun to his head, with three other agents on the plane?"

"You don't know how many other agents—"

"I'm trying to make a point. Even if there was only one agent holding a gun at Pogue's head, how did he get out of there?"

"He saw a chance and took it. They shot him and missed or got him in the vest. He escaped with a bullet through his gut. Get over it, for God's sake."

"What do the pilots know about the charter?"

"Kurt leased the plane. Everything points to him. No one knows who you are except Amy—and she knows you as Deene. But she knew Pogue too."

"She was drugged."

"With Valium? Like that's going to keep her from remembering."

C.J. huffed.

Nick poured a drink from a bottle in the top drawer of the desk. "Get on a plane. Go back to New York. Let this simmer while I figure it out."

She walked to him and put her hand on his shoulder. "I know you vetted Pogue and he's your friend. He's smart, and valuable, and all that— but I don't trust him. Look deeper. Trained agents shot him repeatedly into a vest. When he didn't fall, they should have … would have taken him down with a headshot. But they didn't. Why?"

"They may have wanted him alive for questioning—to get to the top of whatever organization he was involved with."

She sighed. "Where is he now?"

"Upstairs in one of the suites. I took him to the infirmary in the guesthouse first. He assessed the damage to his abdomen, took some X-rays, numbed himself up, and stapled the wounds closed."

"How did he staple a wound on his back?"

"It wasn't his back. The bullet went in here under the rib cage and out the side. He reached around with a mirror, *John Wick* style, and stapled it. Stapled his forehead without numbing it. I told you—man's got nerves of steel, C.J. You don't give him enough credit."

She grabbed her handbag. "I'm going to check on Jamie, then I'm outta here."

# CHAPTER THIRTY-TWO

Pogue watched from the window of his room as the chopper landed on the helipad in the courtyard. Marc Santino stepped out. Pogue crossed to his bed and sat down, knowing he was about to be interviewed yet again.

After knocking on Pogue's door, Nick poked his head inside. "Hey. How're you feeling?"

"I'm okay."

"Marc just got here. You up for a quick debrief?"

"Sure."

He followed Nick to the elevator. The tension inside him mounted—something he'd keep to himself. They entered the library, where Marc greeted them.

"Pogue. You're looking good, all things considered."

"Doing my best."

Marc gave him a careful pat on the shoulder. "Have a seat." Marc motioned to a chair. Pogue eased into it while Marc sat across from him and handed him a glass of whiskey. "What happened to you guys at the airport was horrible, and I don't know how you got away from there." He looked directly at Pogue with piercing eyes. "How *did* you get away from there?"

Pogue took a sip and sighed, allowing his heart a chance to slow down. A strange calm came over him. "I told Nick earlier, but let me recap. The pilot started the engines, and Kurt asked why since C.J. wasn't back to the plane yet. The pilot told him she'd ordered him to leave. Kurt went on about not wanting to be a babysitter to the girl on the plane."

"What girl?"

"Mary is all I know her by."

"How do you know her name?"

"I sutured up a laceration on her wrist about a week ago at the infirmary in the guesthouse."

Marc glanced at Nick, then back at Pogue. "So you didn't speak to her on the plane?"

"I was one of the last ones to board and a little preoccupied. To be honest, she looked asleep or unconscious in the back."

"You say you were preoccupied?"

"Shortly after I boarded, Robert Savage stormed off the plane … almost knocked me over. Kurt followed him onto the tarmac. They argued about something and Savage left. When Kurt came back, he was furious."

"What then?"

Pogue stated how the bodyguards had attempted to close the hatch before two FBI agents forced it open. Then he recounted every movement and shot leading up to Kurt's death and his escape.

"Then you stole a limo?" Marc asked.

"I didn't have a lot of options. I got in and drove."

"How did you get off the plane with FBI agents holding you at gunpoint?"

"When Kurt died, I was on my knees facing him. The agent holding the gun behind me reached around to check Kurt's carotid pulse when he slumped over. I butted him with the back of my head. Felt the cartilage and bone crunch in his nose. I dove for the door and didn't look back. They shot a couple of times and didn't hit me, but then they did."

Marc nodded but didn't say anything.

"I'm sorry for leaving Kurt. But there was nothing I could do." Pogue set down his drink. "When we talked about the risks of this job, I didn't realize I'd be memorizing secret documents to smuggle out of the country. Having money doesn't help if I'm dead."

Nick picked up Pogue's drink and handed it back to him. "You cashed the check, right?"

Pogue took a sip. "I cashed the check."

Nick put his arm on Pogue's shoulder. "We need you to get back on an airplane and take that information to Egypt. Before you say anything, let me point out that none of us could have done any better than you did when that all came down today. Tell me your adrenaline didn't make you feel like you could fly!"

Pogue gave a faint nod. Then a smirk broke out. "A little." He had to sound convincing. "When do you want me to leave for Egypt?"

"Tomorrow. We have to get the Intel into our buyer's hands." Nick poured himself and Marc a drink. "Listen, Pogue—let's put this into perspective. This is why all of this was put into place, so you could deliver the Intel. And I'm glad Marc is here because what I have to say is something I wanted to tell you in person."

Every muscle in Pogue's body tensed.

Nick sat next to Pogue. "Once you boarded that plane, shot federal agents, and fled the scene of a felony murder, you crossed the line of being on the outside looking in, to being one of us."

Relief swept over him like a cool breeze. "I just reacted to what was happening. But is there something I should have done differently?"

Nick shook his head. "You did what I would have done. That's why you're alive. And you'll be on that plane at six o'clock in the morning."

Pogue took the last swallow and stood. "I'll be ready."

Marc got up and shook his hand. Pogue looked down at himself. "I need some clean clothes. I appreciate the ones you lent me, but they don't fit, and I'll be traveling."

"Preferences?"

"Something without blood."

Nick cupped his hand around the back of Pogue's neck. "I'm glad to see a sense of humor in the midst of this. It's a survival instinct. Leave your measurements with Carl, the attendant upstairs. He'll get whatever you need. And don't call anyone."

"No worries. Jenni thinks I'm in Colorado."

"Get some rest. Dinner will be at seven."

"Thanks, guys." Pogue left the room and headed up the stairs. He wished he could call Jenni. At least he was getting closer to ending this. But he had to admit that the adrenaline rush was not his norm. He didn't want to think that Nick was right. He felt for a minute like he could practically fly. The excitement of doing the right thing and helping a young girl mixed with violence and fear, death and dread. What if he enjoyed this? What if the simple life of being a doctor seemed boring after this? His own thoughts surprised him.

As soon as he gave his measurements to Carl, he searched for a way to contact Flannery. Cameras mounted in every corner of the suite made it clear they'd be watching every move. He was running *dark*.

\*\*\*

James walked into the isolation room at the military hospital. "Mr. and Mrs. King? I'm Agent James of the FBI."

Mr. King stood and shook James' hand. "Thank you for bringing my daughter home. Do you have any leads yet?"

Amy smiled faintly at James. "I'll tell you what I can. I got a peek out a broken window. I saw a beachfront. That could have been anywhere. But I heard the woman say we were going to Midway instead of O'Hare. That means that we were in Chicago."

"But you were drugged."

"I still remember them talking about the airport and some other things."

James sat beside her bed as Mrs. King stood on the opposite side. "You were kidnapped and held against your will, but were you harmed in any way?"

She shook her head. "They never got a chance, but they intended to sell me to someone in the Middle East, for … like a bride."

James exhaled. "You mean for sex."

Amy looked down and nodded.

"Did you see anyone else during your captivity?"

"A woman who called herself Deene, but someone referred to her as C.J. on the airplane. I remember what she looked like."

James pulled up a photo on his cell and showed it to Amy. "Is this her?"

"That's her. Who is she?"

"We spotted her by facial recognition on the tarmac cameras. Anyone else?"

"A man they called Robert, but I don't remember seeing him."

"I'll get more pictures for you to look at. What happened to your wrist?"

Amy shook her head and made a face. "I tried to escape and accidentally cut myself."

"You have stitches. Who did that?"

Amy looked at James without answering.

Her mother patted her other arm. "It's okay, Amy."

"He was there—the doctor who took care of me—on the airplane. He protected me. He knew my name and told me everything would be okay. The FBI men talked to him like he was one of them. He ordered another man wearing an FBI vest to carry me off the plane. I didn't see him again, but I heard more shooting after I was in the ambulance." She suddenly sobbed and turned to her mother. "When he sutured me, a man named Nick called him Poke, I think."

James looked at Mr. and Mrs. King, then at Amy. "His name isn't Poke. It's Pogue."

Mr. Foster leaned on the bed. "You know this man?"

"He's one of ours—a federal agent who is also a doctor."

Mr. King turned to Amy as his wife covered her mouth with her hands.

James pulled up a chair beside Amy's bed. "I need to talk to all of you about something very important. The people who abducted Amy know she can identify them. Until we put an end to this, I need to announce Amy died this evening."

"Oh, no." Mrs. King started to cry.

"If we don't, the people responsible for what happened may try to find you to shut you up. It's the safest way. We don't need long. A few days would give us time to find out who's responsible."

"You do what you have to do. Keep our daughter safe."

# CHAPTER THIRTY-THREE

After several hours of sleep, a knock on Pogue's door woke him. He gained his bearings as Carl, the attendant, entered with four large bags of merchandise. A second man followed close behind and unloaded additional items into the room.

"Let me know if you require further assistance." Carl arranged the items on the bed.

"Thank you for going to so much trouble."

"No trouble at all." He handed Pogue a single sports jacket bag. "I think you'll enjoy this one, sir."

"Thank you." Pogue took the bag and laid it on top of the other items on his bed.

"Make sure that one fits well." He left the room and closed the door.

Pogue pondered the comment. Since he didn't know anything about Carl and there were cameras everywhere, he didn't check right away.

He sorted through the articles one by one. Several pairs of shoes, underclothing, shirts, pants, and sports jackets all appeared to fit as if he'd ordered them personally tailored. One jacket remained—the one Carl had handed him last.

He slipped it on and walked into the bathroom. Examining the item in the mirror, he retrieved a note from the pocket. It said, *inspected by Flannery*. As he stared at his reflection, he noticed crosshatched markings on the buttons. He walked to the bedroom, cautiously slipped his cell phone into his pocket, and reentered the bathroom. He placed the phone on the counter. The screen displayed as if he'd hit the home button, but he hadn't. He placed a hand towel over it, then reached underneath to unlock the phone with his fingerprint. He lifted the towel briefly as if looking for something and noticed "Airdrop Secure" on the screen. He discreetly pushed the buttons on the jacket one by one until the screen read "Accessing Data." He waited for several seconds. It finally read "Data Transfer Complete." The home screen turned off.

Pogue tried on additional clothing items until he'd settled on those he desired to take to Egypt. They included a leather travel bag into which he packed the most important items. He took his second shower of the day, changed the dressings on his wounds, and slipped his cell into his pocket as he made his way to the toilet. After closing the door, he powered up the phone and scanned the tiny cubicle. No cameras were present to document his activities, but the scanner picked up a single listening device.

Pogue pulled up the data from the transfer. From the moment it appeared, a bar across the bottom of the screen indicated he'd have thirty seconds to read or memorize it before it self-deleted. The line began to move to the right, indicating the clock was running.

*Flannery here. Amy safe. Don't trust anyone.*

*Agency may need to contact you abroad. Your encrypted cell should work unless they block, but contact may be necessary if you're compromised. There's a passphrase if we need to communicate securely. When someone safe from our agency approaches you, they'll say,* "Have you been to the Nile?" *Your response will be,* "I've never traveled to Italy." *If they're not with the CIA, they'll be confused or ask again. If they're one of ours, they'll respond,* "I've never seen the Statue of Liberty."

*Intel indicates strong militant activity mobilizing in civilian-rich regions in the Middle East, including Upper Egypt and the Delta. We know some of the players but not all. Somebody is calling the shots, and we need to know who. Be ready. Watch your back.*

The screen went blank.

\*\*\*

Robert Savage finished deposing Danielle Trent, picked up his briefcase, and left the interrogation room. He stood in the hallway and savored the moment. This was what he lived for. As Danielle slowly lost her resolve, he would be there to push her over the edge. A few steps away, the observation room awaited him. He punched in his code and entered, placing his briefcase on the floor near Jason Franklin.

Franklin shook his head as he stared at Danielle through the two-way glass. "C.J. put you up to this, didn't she?"

"Yes. You've been part of an intricate plan to glean information from our government and deliver it to an outside buyer. That individual then sells the information where it is the most valuable."

"That's treason."

"It is. Everything was working smoothly until Danielle decided the profit margins were high enough for her to sell to an outside bidder without giving you the information to hand it off to the broker here in the States."

"What makes you say that?"

"She bypassed you and the broker. If the broker had seen the information, he'd never have passed it on. Neither would you. As a result of the information she sold, five men and four women died. The women had families. One of the men did as well. As a result of her actions, they were murdered on foreign soil."

He sighed and shook his head as he looked away from Danielle. "How do you know she bypassed the broker?"

"I'm the broker."

Franklin leaned against the wall. "Danielle really did go behind my back, then?"

"She did. I need you to continue to access information for me, and we'll pin the scandal on Danielle Trent."

"I can't believe she would do this."

"But she did. You and I are joined at the hip, Mr. Franklin. Your wife worked for it, it makes sense, and your career remains unblemished. I just need you to work directly with me from now on. In addition, I need you to testify against Trent in court."

"Is that really necessary?"

"I'm afraid so. This is a beneficial arrangement to all persons involved, and I prefer being on the good side of the Santino family. It's healthier."

"What happens to Danielle?"

"She did this to herself. It was not your mistake or greed. It was hers. For the time she serves, I'll keep her out of general population."

"Just make certain she's safe."

Robert smiled. "Of course."

# CHAPTER THIRTY-FOUR

Pogue's jet landed on time in Cairo and was immediately surrounded by armed guards the moment it parked on the tarmac.

"It's standard for them to do this." The flight attendant smiled. "They must believe you're important."

As the door opened and the steps folded out, that familiar rush of adrenaline prickled his skin. He welcomed it, but a sense of guilt nagged at him just the same. Was it a betrayal to embrace the danger? He'd been taught at Langley that survival depended on doing just that. Own it. Use it. The last time he'd left a plane like this he'd run down the stairs and was shot in the back. He brushed his fingers over the staples above his eye to remind him. He carried his backpack and overnight bag as he descended the stairs to two men waiting for him at the bottom, then followed them to the asphalt apron and entered an old Ford Bronco. He tossed his luggage in the back and climbed in. The vehicle made its way past the main terminal and delivered him to a private entrance of the airport.

He threw his backpack strap over his right shoulder and grabbed his overnight bag. When he arrived in the customs office, the guard took his documents to review.

"Why are you here?" The officer flipped through his passport.

"Volunteer medical care to the refugee camps. I'm a doctor."

"In a private jet? How much does it cost to fly from America?" The uniformed man continued to skim through the pages.

"The jet belongs to my benefactor."

"Where is the refugee camp?"

"The area called the Sixth of October in Giza." Nick had been specific about his cover. He remembered every word.

"Why not go elsewhere?"

"I go to other locations as well."

The man looked at Pogue as if studying every feature of his face, focusing for a moment on the staples in his forehead.

"Your travel visa will be twenty-five American dollars."

Pogue handed him the cash. The man placed a visa on one page and stamped it.

"Go over there." The man pointed.

Pogue walked a few feet toward the exit but remembered from the last time that there may be one more hurdle before he was on the outside. As he approached the final checkpoint, a man in uniform walked straight to him. Pogue showed his documents to the man, and the guard immediately pulled him aside to a room with no windows and a single door. They sat at a small desk across from each other.

"Who are you?" The man's English was nearly perfect.

"Dr. Bailey Pogue from Chicago, Illinois, in the United States."

"Dr. Pogue, you have many stamps in your passport."

"I teach medical seminars."

The man placed the passport on the metal desk and slowly slid it to Pogue as he sat back and folded his hands. "Have you been to the Nile?"

He was caught slightly off guard, but he quickly regained his composure. "I've never traveled to Italy." He continued to stare at the guard.

"Well, I've never seen the Statue of Liberty." The man had a faint, crooked grin.

A chill ran from Pogue's head to his feet as the man reached into the bottom drawer of his desk and removed a thin box the size of a large book. "Don't open this until you're alone. Place it in your backpack and keep it private."

He did as he was instructed. "Thank you."

Both men stood, and the man opened the door for him.

"Walk through the exit. Don't look back."

\*\*\*

Davis poured himself a cup of black coffee from the carafe on the sideboard, then took a seat at the conference table across from Flannery and James. They'd already filled him in on Pogue's escape from the plane and the news coverage of Amy's death being falsified. But by the look in their eyes, there was more.

"Pogue has uncovered information regarding the death of Ginger Lucci." Flannery crossed his arms. "Kurt, her estranged husband, confessed to having her killed with Nick's support and assistance."

"They burned a Gambrel? Nick killed his sister?"

"Kurt's excuse was that they—the mafia families—had invested a lot of time into Pogue. Ginger threatened to destroy it all."

Davis sipped the steaming black brew in his flimsy Styrofoam cup. "Why would Kurt confess this now?"

"He was dying. Pogue succeeded in getting him to talk in his last moments."

"Did they have to shoot the guy? It would have been nice to know what he knew."

"They returned his fire expecting he'd be wearing a vest, which is why they shot him in the chest. He wasn't."

Davis shook his head as he pulled out his little notebook but offered it only a cursory glance before slipping it back in his pocket. "We knew Kurt was a bad apple—to his own family and to New York City. He has a rap sheet a mile long, but we had nothing that would stick except petty, stupid stuff. Had to let him go time and again. His dad made sure he had the best attorneys, but to be honest, he was sick of Kurt too. He's a jerk, but I never imagined he'd have his wife whacked. If there's one thing that doesn't fit, it's that."

"You just said he was a lowlife who'd been in trouble with the law and his family," Flannery said.

"Yeah—but nothin' big or gutsy, if you know what I mean. Killing his wife would take serious *chutzpah*. Kurt Lucci ... did not have chutzpah. If you're asking me, he didn't kill his wife. Somebody else did."

James grabbed a bottled water. "Kurt confessed that he had Harrison do the deed after he'd tried and failed."

"There you go. I can see him having a part in it but not wanting to get sticky."

Flannery and James exchanged glances.

"What?" Davis couldn't read their expressions.

Flannery folded his arms on the table. "This is why we need your input. We know these guys. But we don't *know* these guys. You've been leading the mafia investigations for years, and that gives you the insight we're missing."

Davis looked intently at James and Flannery. "I appreciate that, and I'll do whatever I can to help. Now it's my turn to tell you what I know—something is happening at the Gambrel estate."

James put his water down. "More than trafficking?"

"Marc Santino and his sister, Carlee—she goes by C.J.—have been in and out of the compound numerous times in the past several days, especially since Ben is out of town."

"Why is he out of town?"

"Business deal in Wisconsin, from what we can determine. Nothing related to any of this. But something you need to know is that the hitman Ginger killed in her office worked for the Santinos but was paid by the Gambrels. The girls in Pogue's office who were killed—the Santinos placed them there."

"How do you know that?" Flannery asked.

"We pulled a couple of favors from our NYPD contacts and discovered that both girls worked for the Santino family in Manhattan for the past three years prior to coming to Chicago."

Flannery shook his head. "Have you found that second shooter? The one who killed Pogue's girls?"

"Twenty-four hours ago, CPD responded to a call about a guy locked in his car in a parking deck on Dearborn. Cops found him dead behind the wheel. One shot to the back of the head—blood from the floor to the ceiling and a hole in the windshield. A couple of hours ago the coroner identified him as Desmond Franco. He'd worked for the Santino family since 2001 in New York."

"How do you know he was the one in Pogue's office?"

"Facial recognition from cameras we thought were not working. They were turned on in the waiting room, not in the rest of the office. Ran the footage through our system and it turned him up. He's the guy."

Flannery brushed his fingers through his hair. "I don't like all the moving pieces right now. Pogue's in play. Where the Santino influence stops and the Gambrel power starts, I can't tell."

Davis stood and walked toward the door. "I don't know either. I can promise a power struggle between Nick and Marc at some point. Those two families are like water and oil. One spark and everything explodes."

Flannery rubbed his ear. "Oil and water don't explode. They just don't mix."

"Well, you know what I'm saying. We'd better pray nothing goes wrong, or Pogue is dead."

# CHAPTER THIRTY-FIVE

"**M**rs. Pogue? I'm calling from the school. I was just checking on Janelle since she didn't come in today and we haven't received a notice from you."

"There must be some mistake. I dropped her off at school this morning with Landon and Karen. She has soccer practice this afternoon, so she had her stuff with her. She should be there."

"Hold on, Mrs. Pogue. Let me get the principal Ms. Tanner on the line. I may have misunderstood."

Jenni waited briefly.

"Jenni, this is Ellen Tanner. Janelle never checked into homeroom this morning. I don't mean to alarm you, but she's not here."

Jenni took a deep breath, refusing to panic. "Ellen, Janelle does not play hooky. I need to call my husband. He's traveling so he may be hard to reach. I don't know—"

"Jenni, if you don't know where she is, I have to report this to the police. In situations like this—"

"I'm coming for my other kids. I'll leave right now. It will take me ten minutes. Can you have someone get them ready for me?"

"Of course. I'll see you shortly, Mrs. Pogue."

Jenni hung up and dialed Janelle's cell phone. It went directly to voice mail.

\*\*\*

When Jenni arrived at the school, she noticed two squad cars parked in the main drive. One of the officers was talking to Ellen Tanner on the sidewalk. She waved at Jenni, indicating she should drive around the police cars and park near the front of the school. She pulled up as an officer approached her.

"Mrs. Pogue," the trooper said, "I'm Officer Jess Blankenship. Principal Tanner has been filling us in on the situation. Sometimes young folks like to sneak off and do things they're not supposed to do. What do you think the chances are of your daughter being involved in something like that?"

"Zero."

He nodded. "That's what Mrs. Tanner said. What can you tell me about your daughter?"

"Her name is Janelle, she has blonde hair, blue eyes, slim build, and she's fifteen years old. Here is her picture." Jenni showed the officer a photo on her cell phone.

He handed her a business card with a number on it. "Would you mind texting her photo to the number on that card? I can post it right now as an alert to all our officers."

She typed in the information.

Officer Blankenship held his phone where he could see it. "I'm sure this is frightening, but we'll find her. Have you been able to reach your husband? Mrs. Tanner said he's traveling."

"He is, but I hope to hear from him soon." As she checked her watch, she heard Landon's voice. She turned to see him and Karen coming out of the school, led by one of the teachers. Jenni jumped out and hugged them.

Landon threw his backpack in the side door of the minivan. "Everything okay, Mom?"

"Sure, honey. We have to go home right now and wait for Janelle. She didn't go into the school today."

"Yes, she did. She walked us in like always."

"Did you see if she went to homeroom?"

"Not really."

"That's okay, Landon." Jenni shook Officer Blankenship's hand. "Thank you very much for taking this seriously."

"Certainly. I'll meet you at your house. We'll be setting up a little coverage for you. We'll find her. I've already sent her photo and description on the wire. She's labeled as missing, that's all."

"I thought you had to wait twenty-four hours to do that."

"Not in a case like this."

She took a deep breath. *A case like this?*

"It's okay, Mrs. Pogue. Standard protocol. In the meantime, your daughter is a missing child of a prominent ... she's ... I'll meet you at your house."

Jenni fought down the panic and got in the car.

\*\*\*

Pogue turned on his cell phone as he walked through the lobby of the Cairo International Airport terminal. Seven messages from Jenni popped up. Instead of taking the time to listen to each one, he called her. "Hey, baby. Everything okay? I just got—"

"No, everything is not okay. Janelle has been missing for hours. She never went to class even though I dropped her off as always. The police are here at the house. I picked up Landon and Karen from school, so they're here too. But Janelle is ... she's missing." Pogue heard the fear in her voice.

He stopped and waved off a half-dozen men offering him a cab ride to anywhere. "Jenni, is the officer in charge there?"

"Officer Blankenship with the State Police. He's been very helpful. But they're calling the FBI. The FBI!"

"Jenni, I need to make some calls. I want—"

"Make some calls? What can you possibly do from where you are? You need to be here."

"Jenni, let me do this, and I'll get back to you right away."

"Why can't you be here?"

"They did this while I was away on purpose."

"I don't understand. Where are you?"

"I'll call you right back."

"Fine." The pause on Jenni's end was anything but passive. "Hurry, Bailey—please."

"I will. I love you. I'll call you in a minute."

Dread crawled into his chest and squeezed him from the inside. He could barely move. Where did they take her? She must be scared to death. Panic washed over him as his rage boiled, threatening to take control. He stared at his phone and dialed the number he knew he needed to call.

"Pogue, what's wrong? Is my son okay?"

"As far as I know, Ben. My apologies, but my fifteen-year-old daughter is missing. She's a responsible child, and I fear she may have been abducted. My wife called to tell me she disappeared from school. I'm overseas working on a project involving Nick's business ventures. Can you help?"

"Where are you?"

"Cairo, Egypt, sir."

"What is my son doing in Egypt?"

"He's not with me. But my daughter back home is missing, and I couldn't imagine anyone with more power to make the right things happen than you, sir. All I'm—"

"I'll have my chopper at your house in thirty minutes with a security team. You understand me, son?"

"The FBI may be at the house as well, sir."

"I won't get in their way if they stay out of mine. We look after our own. Thirty minutes."

A wave of emotion mixed with appreciation passed over Pogue for the man he was supposed to despise. Ben was the only one who could help him right now. "Thank you, sir."

"Not at all. You did the right thing. Keep me posted and I'll do the same."

Pogue hung up and dialed Jenni. She answered immediately.

"The FBI is here, Bailey. They want to set up a command center in case there's a ransom demand or tips called in. It's on the news. Janelle is on the news as a missing child. There are TV crews showing up out front."

Pogue's heart ached for Jenni, for Janelle, and what he'd caused to happen.

"Let me talk to Officer Blankenship."

"Here he is."

"This is Officer Blankenship, Dr. Pogue. We're throwing all our manpower into this."

"I appreciate all you're doing, Officer. I have a request. Could you get the news crews out of there somehow? I have a chopper landing in the cul-de-sac behind the house on the side street, and I don't want them to film it."

"I'll see what I can do, sir. Is it FBI?"

"It's private."

"I'll take care of it. Here's your wife again."

"Bailey, what's going on?"

"Jenni … listen to me." His heart pounded and his breathing took effort. "I wanted to tell you this in person, but it can't wait. Connor's father is landing one of his choppers in the cul-de-sac behind the house in a few minutes. They have a security contingency that will help provide protection and look for Janelle."

"What does that mean?"

"It means they have armed private ground forces to guard the house, you and the kids, and to look for Janelle. They'll stay out of the way of the FBI. They're not part of any law enforcement agency."

"Pogue?"

"They're the Gambrels, Jenni. Connor's real name is Nick Gambrel. They're the Chicago mafia, and they're on our side."

"On our side? What are you talking about? Hold on while I go into the bathroom." He heard the door close, and Jenni spoke in a whisper. "When you told me you were involved with the mafia, I didn't think you were actually a part of them. What are you thinking? Why are we even—"

"Listen to me. I'm in a bad situation, and I'm calling in the cavalry to save my daughter and protect my family. To be honest, I don't care who these guys are as long as they bring her home. God help me, Jenni. I mean it."

"How deep are you into the mafia, Bailey?"

"Very."

"How could you?"

"You don't know everything."

"I know what I need to know."

"No, you don't. I'll explain everything when I see you."

"You're not in Colorado, are you?"

"No."

"How long would it take you to come home if you were already on a plane?"

Pogue threw his head back and looked at the sky as travelers scurried around him. *God help me.*

"How long, Bailey?"

"Twenty-three hours."

"Why are you doing this?"

"For our own safety."

"Tell that to Janelle." Jenni was silent for a moment. Then she hung up.

# CHAPTER THIRTY-SIX

P ogue slid his phone into his pocket as a vintage Land Rover with battered bumpers, a brush guard, and one headlight knocked out pulled to the curb in front of him. The driver reached across and rolled down the passenger window. "Pogue?"

"Yes."

"I'm your ride."

Pogue threw his luggage into the rear of the vehicle and climbed into the back seat beside another gentleman.

The man offered his hand. "Welcome to Cairo, Dr. Pogue. My name is Preston Yeager, and I work with the CIA through a private security firm whose interests are aligned with this transaction."

*What does that mean?*

"It will take us a few minutes to reach Nadir's building since traffic is heavy this time of day."

Pogue didn't know this guy. He didn't even offer the passphrase. Pogue's attention went back to the conversation he'd just had with Jenni. She must be horrified, not only by Janelle's disappearance but by what he'd told her. He needed to get home.

Yeager interrupted Pogue's thoughts. "I'm here to facilitate communications between you and Nadir and to make sure you have what you need. In addition, I'll provide protection. Nadir has offered an entire floor of his three-story luxury apartment overlooking the Nile for the duration of your stay."

Did Jenni believe what he'd said—that he was in a bad situation? She knew he was involved in the mafia already. They'd had that brief conversation. But she didn't know why he was involved and certainly not to the extent. He felt like he was buried alive, smothering.

"Have you been to Cairo before?"

Pogue turned to Yeager, wishing he would shut up so he could think. "Once." He turned and stared out the window. Calling Ben was the right thing to do. Asking the CIA or FBI to help would endanger Janelle, and it was a moot point anyway. They would be there without him asking. He would have made that call to Ben even if he'd had no ties to the CIA or FBI. He should hate Ben and all that he stood for, yet Ben was the first one to come to mind when trouble hit, and he put actions to his promises. Pogue regrouped and glanced at the driver, then back at Yeager. "What security firm did you say you work for, and what *transaction* do you mean?"

"DarkWater is the name of our firm. We provide security across the globe from the Nile to the Statue of Liberty. Our company is based in Italy."

Pogue's sigh of relief at the apparent use of the passphrase was short-lived. He had to confirm. "Have you ever been to the Nile?"

"Actually, I … I've seen it and crossed it on the bridge dozens of times, but I don't think I've been to it."

His statement was far from point. Yeager should have answered: *I've never traveled to Italy.*

"Forgive me, but have you been to the Nile?"

"No, as I just said I've only crossed it and seen it from a distance." Yeager seemed a bit annoyed that Pogue asked again.

This was wrong. Pogue forced himself not to let it show. *Flannery hadn't filled Yeager in on the passphrase. Why?*

"Don't worry about the driver," Yeager said. "I noticed you studying him. He has full clearance. By the way, how long have you been with the agency?"

Pogue cocked his head to the side. "Clearance from whom?"

Yeager offered a forced laugh. "Who do you think?"

Pogue tapped the driver on the shoulder. "What's your name?"

"Ahmed, sir."

"Do you have children?"

"Three, sir."

"I do as well. Tell me, do you have official security clearance?"

"Yes, sir. BlackWater vetted me."

"When?"

"Last November, sir."

"Thank you."

"Feel better?" Yeager's sarcastic remark came as he stared out the side window.

"He gave me a straight answer—like you should have."

\*\*\*

Ben perused the documents in front of him coordinating the forces he'd deployed to Pogue's house. Picking up the landline on his desk, he dialed a number. He hadn't had a reason to use it for quite some time.

"Victor here." The familiar voice on the other end of the line held a level of comfort.

"Vic, this is Ben. How are you in the Big Apple?"

"Fine. I'm sorry about Ginger, Ben. I was planning to give you some time and then call you."

"I appreciate that very much, Vic."

"Is there anything I can do?"

"Well, I just received a call from Dr. Pogue, the new physician we brought on to provide care for our family. His fifteen-year-old daughter went missing today, less than a month after he signed on with us. He's in Egypt per my son's bidding, carrying out some family business there. I know nothing about a northeast Africa or Middle East venture, and I don't appreciate being kept in the dark by my own boy. Now that Pogue's daughter is missing, it doesn't feel right."

"Are my kids involved with what Nick's doing? They've been less than candid when I question them about anything lately."

"Nick is involved with Marc and C.J., but I don't know the details. They've been cryptic with me as well. Whatever happened with Kurt Lucci in that Midway Airfield incident, my son and your daughter indicate they have no idea what went on. They blame everything on Kurt, who is conveniently unable to defend himself. But Dr. Pogue got hurt, I think. If he's the guy on the news that no one can seem to identify, he got his ass shot up pretty good. I was going to ask him on the phone, but it wasn't a secured line."

"I was interrogated by the FBI yesterday regarding the Midway situation," Victor said. "I haven't had the FBI on my doorstep for thirty years. My name, my signature, and my wax seal were on the documents presented at the guard gate of the private tarmac. They want to know how that's possible."

"You think it was Marc?"

"C.J."

"You sure, Vic?"

"She and Marc are in Chicago now, but she was here with Nick, and I left them alone in the study. Big mistake."

"You say she and Marc are in Chicago now?"

"I was under the impression they were with your boy. Is that not true?"

"I haven't seen any of them. But with Pogue's daughter's disappearance, I'm afraid I don't have control of my own affairs. That's unacceptable."

"What are they up to?"

"I don't put anything past Nick anymore. I've given him freedom he didn't deserve. He may be in over his head."

"Should I be concerned?"

"I don't want my kid destroying the legacy I've built. The FBI indicated Kurt was attempting to transport a kidnapped female minor from the private tarmac in a Gambrel jet in violation of half a dozen federal laws. Harmless vices are one thing. Kidnapping and human trafficking— quite another."

Victor gave a heavy sigh. "I love my children, but we have to find out what they're doing and get control of this. I hope it's not too late."

"I called to give you a heads-up."

"Be careful. My son is volatile and dangerous, but my daughter is … *lethal* is the best word I can come up with."

"I appreciate the warning."

"Ben, the FBI asked about you. Watch your back."

\*\*\*

Pogue scanned the neighborhoods as he and Yeager traveled down El Nasr Road from the airport. He needed to find a place they could pull over so he could talk to Flannery in private. High-rise buildings lined both sides of the beltway until they passed the International Convention Center. From there, Pogue knew from his last visit they'd soon enter Salah Salem Street and then cross the Nile. He had to make a move before they got too close to Nadir's apartment.

Pogue tapped on the driver's shoulder again. "Would you mind pulling over at the Starbucks there?"

"I thought you were in a hurry." Yeager folded his arms pompously as they pulled off the main road. "We'll be at Nadir's place in a few minutes."

"I need some good coffee. It was a long flight." Pogue hopped out, hurried inside, ordered coffee, and called Flannery on the secured line. He looked to the street. Yeager had no clear view. Pogue turned his back regardless and kept the street in his peripherals.

"Pogue. Where are you?" Flannery asked.

"I just arrived in Cairo. My wife called and told me Janelle is missing. If you can't assure me you'll protect my family, I swear I'll be on the next flight back. I've already contacted Ben Gambrel. Monitor Nick's actions. Find her."

"We're already on it, Pogue. Calm down."

"Her name is Janelle Allyson Pogue. She's fifteen. You have her date of birth on file, I'm sure."

"We got it. You understand what's happening here, right? You just forced three of the most powerful mafia families in the country to be concerned about your loyalty."

"Why do you say that?"

"You survived a firefight from the feds that no one else did and then escaped. They need you to deliver that information in your brain without a glitch, and they're watching you. Don't send up a flare by flying home and forgetting their investment. They expect you to care about family too. You called Ben for help instead of us. Perfect."

"I can't just sit here while she's missing."

"You're undercover."

"Hold on. Yeager's following me in here."

"You're CIA. Focus. We're on top of this. Get your head in the game and don't trust Yeager. Get off the phone before he sees you."

Pogue hung up, grabbed his coffee, and turned toward the door where Yeager stood.

"You good?"

"Yeah. Did you want some coffee? I didn't even ask. That was rude. Sorry."

"No, I'm good."

They walked to the Rover and climbed in.

"Before we get to Nadir's let me fill you in on a few things," Yeager said. "Recently, Nadir has been more demanding than usual. To give you the lay of the land, Philip Ahmed, who you will meet very soon, is my asset here in Cairo."

"A CIA asset?"

"He is."

"You said Nadir has been demanding?"

"He's hard to deal with on a good day, but he's been worse for the past week. Not sure why. Midway spooked him."

"Wasn't crazy about it myself."

"Understood. Be gracious but not a pushover." Yeager pointed to the building as they entered the multilevel garage. "We're here."

They pulled into one of the assigned spots for Nadir's apartment. "Nadir occupies the three top floors of this building—nine, ten, and eleven. We'll be staying on the tenth floor with a security detail."

Pogue grabbed his bag and backpack. "Let's do this."

The men walked through the echoing concrete garage to the elevator and stepped on. Pushing the penthouse button, Yeager typed a six-digit code into the keypad. Pogue stored the tone of each number in his head.

"We're about to enter the private residence of a man living at the top of the Egyptian food chain."

The doors opened, and two armed guards stepped forward and frisked them. One of the men reached for Pogue's bag.

Pogue held up his hand. "I don't think so, buddy."

Nadir strolled around the corner. "Gentlemen. Welcome to my humble home." He addressed the guards. "That's enough. These gentlemen are my trusted friends, as well as my guests. Dr. Pogue, Miguel will show you to your room. I'm sure you'd like to freshen up after such a long trip."

"Thank you very much." Pogue followed the man up a flight of stairs as Nadir called to him.

"By the way, Doctor, how would you prefer to download the information in your data banks?" Nadir pointed to his own head and grinned. "I've never seen it done. You don't have a USB port on the back of your head, I hope."

"If you have a laptop, I'll key it in the old-fashioned way."

"Excellent. We shall get to that in due time—tonight, perhaps. First, rest. Dinner in one hour?"

"That sounds good." Pogue turned to the guard who walked ahead as they reached the top of the stairs and continued down a corridor, turning left to a short hallway with two rooms. The man opened the door with a keycard, let Pogue in, and handed him the card.

"I'll be back for you in forty-five minutes."

Pogue entered the room, tossed his bags on the bed, and checked his phone for surveillance in the room. Two cameras—three microphones.

# CHAPTER THIRTY-SEVEN

Vaughn caught up to Flannery and James in the hallway. "We have a problem."

They stopped and gave him their attention.

"Three news outlets have reported Amy King is alive."

Flannery couldn't believe it. "From what source?"

"An unnamed relative tipped them off that she was in the hospital. CNN is speculating about an FBI cover-up."

"Of course they are." Flannery opened the door of a conference room near them. "Let's do this in here." They entered and he closed the door.

"There's more." Vaughn took a breath. "I've been working with the computer forensics team. We've come close to cracking the code on the web servers the syndicate is using. In fact, we have established a break point in their system."

Flannery held up a palm. "English."

"We're attempting to track the sources of the VPNs used by the cartel. There are many. We have a possible point of entry into the system that has a unique IP characteristic allowing it to identify the host, offering a brief glimpse at its origin. It requires only seconds to locate an active transmission site and traceable VPN or IP address. In other words, it talks to the data cloud and establishes the access point."

"Did you hear me say *English*?"

"Sorry, sir."

"Are you telling me you and your friend found the source of the VPNs?"

"Not the source—a way to find the source and possibly the physical locations. She discovered a bounce station where the cloud servers download information frequently, at precise times every day."

"In the US?"

"No. Cairo."

"Can your friend narrow down the location?" Flannery leaned forward, eager for the answer.

"It matches the location for the signal from Pogue's cell—the same apartment building. But that's not the worst of it. They're using advanced technology called TOR—The Onion Router."

"Why does that matter?"

"You put a message inside a virtual capsule and wrap it inside separate layers of code. Each layer has to be unwrapped by a specific server. The second server in line decodes, or *peels off* the next layer like an onion skin, and passes it to the next server in sequence, and so on. Until the message is fully unwrapped at the final site and released through an *exit gate*, no one gains access to what's hidden inside."

"What then?"

"The IP addresses change frequently and randomly, making it impossible to isolate the precise location. The best we can accomplish is to find the entrance and exit gates. That in itself will be tedious at best."

Flannery shook his head. "You're saying Pogue is on top of one of the cartel sites?"

"It appears so, but we won't know unless we implement a plan to give a brief but important window of opportunity to focus on the cities where our suspicions are strongest. It requires giving Pogue a task to perform."

Flannery sat on the edge of the table. "What does he need to do?"

Vaughn slipped his hands in his pockets. "He'll have to find the IT room—the tech room in Nadir's apartment—get past security, locate the access server, punch in a detailed code we'll provide, and get out before he's discovered."

Flannery rubbed his forehead. "I assume there are safeguards to this room?"

Vaughn sighed. "To it and inside it. Motion detectors, infrared sensors, heat monitors, and, of course, encrypted keypad access to the entrance that only two men have—Nadir and Philip. Can we trust Philip, sir?"

Flannery sighed. "I don't see where we have much choice. Pogue can't get into that room without someone turning off the safeguards."

"Killing the power will eliminate most of them, but not all. The keypad would still be operational, and possibly battery-driven devices like motion sensors and cameras. Philip's cooperation is essential to making this work."

"Okay." Flannery took a seat at the conference table. "What if we manage to overcome the safeguards?"

"Accessing the system requires Pogue to enter a data set to the gate. The lengthy sequence of code must be memorized because it has to be keyed in quickly or an input timer will lock him out. It prevents someone from reading it from a piece of paper and punching in the code keystroke by keystroke."

Flannery cupped his hands behind his head. "So, the system is designed to keep everyone out, unless they're Philip or Nadir."

"Yes, sir. I think Pogue has a chance if we can provide him access and give him the code in time."

"If he pulls it off, what then?"

"We have ninety seconds before the IP addresses change and we lose both gates."

"What if you *get* both gates?"

"That would identify the physical sites along with everyone involved in the espionage and trafficking cartel. Evidence of who the key individuals are—including the Gambrels and Santinos—would be irrefutable. Plus, there's the potential to uncover our government mole."

Flannery took a deep breath and looked directly at Vaughn. "How do we get Pogue into that room?"

"We cut the power. Not just to the apartment or they'd have it back on in seconds. I mean the whole building."

Flannery snapped his fingers. "Lauren."

James tilted his head. "Who?"

"I sent her to tail Yeager and keep an eye on him. She can team up with our asset Miriam on the ground there."

"They need to give him at least ten minutes to get in, plant the code, and get out."

"If we cut the power, won't the servers be down?" Flannery asked.

"They have battery backup that will supply power for fifteen minutes." Vaughn pulled up schematics on his iPad. "The battery backup is only to the servers—not to the safeguards. But we have another problem. Human guards. They'll be on top of Pogue before the power comes on."

"So we have to get him in and out." Flannery ran his finger across the schematics. "We have one shot at this. If they catch him in that room, he's dead."

***

Nick struck a pose in the study of the guesthouse as if he stood at the helm of a majestic ship. Soon it would be his to command.

"You know I'm right." Marc poured himself a drink. "I understand he's your friend and this has been in the works for a long time. But we've always agreed a business of this nature must be a well-oiled machine to remain below the radar. Right now it's a runaway train."

C.J. took her brother's drink from his hand. "There are too many coincidences. Too many conflicting stories, and now Savage and I are at risk if this spoiled Amy bitch is alive. And we have a problem we need to discuss." She glanced briefly at Marc, then Nick. "Pogue said Amy was on the plane when he dove for the tarmac, right?"

"What's your point?"

"She wasn't. I watched from the terminal. Amy had been extracted prior to his daring *escape*. There's no way he wouldn't remember that."

Nick walked to the bar to pour a drink. "Of course there is. To hear the pilot and copilot talk, the bedlam on that jet sounded like a war zone. Pogue remembered it wrong, or you do, and you weren't even in the jet."

"I remember it perfectly. The FBI lied to the world and said Amy was dead. There are only two reasons they'd do that. She knows too much, and they can't risk her being silenced. Spending my life running from this spoiled sixteen-year-old cheerleader, or living behind bars, are not options."

"That's a little dramatic, even for you." Nick inspected his drink, then sipped a little.

C.J. wasn't done. "On top of that, we'll never get Jamie out of the country with all the heightened security at the airports now. If Amy leads the FBI here, we're screwed for life."

Nick set his drink down. "That's why I had you meet me here. We need to move Jamie right away."

"Actually, we need to move both girls." Marc folded his arms, apparently to make a point.

"What do you mean, both girls, Marc?"

C.J. shook her head. "Even with what I just told you—the discrepancy in Pogue's story and all the coincidences and irregularities—I knew you wouldn't take any action on insurance."

Nick moved closer. "You didn't. Tell me you didn't."

"Janelle's upstairs." She smirked.

"What did you do?"

"Have you seen Janelle? She's beautiful—even prettier than Amy, with many of the same characteristics Nadir was looking for. She's a little younger, but only a year, and I think that's a plus, knowing his preferences."

Heat radiated from Nick's ears. "You've got to be kidding me. You're the one who kidnapped Pogue's daughter?"

She smiled as if she couldn't be more proud.

"Do you have any idea how many people are looking for her at this moment, C.J.?"

"I do, yeah. And since we need to make her go away, instead of killing her, we can relocate her."

"Kill her? Sell her? You want me to sell the daughter of one of my best friends."

"Yes, I do. Marc and I … we both do."

Nick circled the two of them, glaring at first, then studying the floor as he made one more pass.

Marc scratched his head. "Are you trying to wrap your head around this, or is it gonna be a problem?"

Nick stopped in front of them both. "This is the worst move either of you could have made. As a result of your actions we're compromised, and you two geniuses think you've bought us insurance by kidnapping Janelle and selling her to Nadir behind Pogue's back. Pogue and Nadir will have an ongoing relationship, and he just might notice if the daughter he's been looking for is tied up in one of Nadir's bedrooms. That's a problem."

"There are things to work out, but it's a good plan—"

"It's a catastrophically stupid plan. If you don't get that smirk off your face, I swear I'll put a bullet in your head right here, right now." He walked to her, almost touching her face with his. "We have to send Janelle home."

"And lose all that we've—" C.J. started.

"We're sending her home."

"We can't," Marc said. "She knows too much."

"When the time comes, we can drop her off somewhere neutral and tell the FBI where to find her. She can't possibly know enough to implicate us."

"She can implicate me." C.J. shrugged. "I talked with her when she first arrived."

"Then it's you who has a problem."

"We all have a problem." She suddenly had that cocky air about her. "I knew you wouldn't like this, so I took out a little insurance myself. She knows this is your house."

"How could she?"

"I told her. That's how we picked her up so easily from school. We told her Connor wanted her to come out and talk to her dad on the satellite phone because he had something important to tell her. She came, we bagged her, we left, all under the name of Connor Banks."

"You know what, C.J.? As pretty and smart as you are, you've gone against everything we set out to do."

She held up her hand. "Nick—"

"Stop talking, before I shove a gun in your mouth and pull the trigger."

For the first time he could recall, C.J. had nothing to say. But Marc did.

"You can't talk to us that way. We're Santinos."

"Who cares who you are? Does it look like I do? Here's what's going to happen—Janelle does not get sold, and she will go home when it's safe to send her. I'll explain it somehow to Pogue." He walked to the bar and poured himself another Scotch. After a sip, he turned to them. "Bringing the girls to the guesthouse was a bad idea. We're moving them to the warehouse."

"You think that's safe right now?"

"Do you want the FBI knocking on the door, Marc? If that happens, we're all in a sinking boat. We move them in the morning. The warehouse remodel is far enough along that we can maintain security there, and that's what we'll do. No discussion."

C.J. fumed. "My name and a drawing of my face could appear on the news at any moment. Savage's image won't be far behind. He checked onto the tarmac using an alias and fake passport. But facial recognition will pick him up if they access the registry. If Amy's alive, it's a matter of time."

"My concern is not with you or Savage being on the news. Anyone in our line of work who posts on social media deserves to go to prison. My concern is keeping this out of FBI jurisdiction. If worse comes to worst, we can move you to Dubai for a few years."

She shook her head slow and steady. "You suck, Nick. Do you know how angry my father was when he found out I used his seal to forge the papers to move Amy out of the country?"

"You shouldn't have done it in the first place. There must have been another way."

She turned to Marc. "Dad wants us home right away to discuss this."

Marc slapped his hand on the desk. "What did you expect, C.J.?"

"To not get caught. That's what I expected."

Marc slapped himself in the head and turned to Nick. "I'll fix this. It's time I took over the business anyway. Dad has gone soft. In the meantime, what about Pogue's daughter? You going to move her too?"

"I don't have a choice. I want Pogue to be back home when she's returned to her family."

Marc folded his arms. "In the grand scheme, she's collateral damage."

"No. She is not."

***

As Nadir paced back and forth behind him, Pogue sat in front of the laptop and typed out the data he'd memorized verbatim—twenty-three pages of classified documents. He sat back and read through the final product, searching for typos. There were none.

"There you have it, gentlemen—the most up-to-date method of transmitting sensitive data known to man. It cannot be printed. It must be read from the screen."

Nadir appeared surprised. "Why?"

Pogue rubbed his ear. "Firewalls."

"Firewalls?"

"That's not accurate. *Moat* is better." Pogue tapped a few keys.

"I'm ... what does that mean?"

"I've downloaded the information, but added moats after the fact, as you would with a server VPN. That way if the source code is missing, one would be unable to cross the moat and gain access to the data."

"Missing?"

"Dead." Pogue raised one palm.

"You're the source code. This was not part of the deal, Pogue. How do these safeguards work?"

"If they appear, blocking access from time to time, you will ask me the codes, and I'll provide them."

"Provide them now."

"I can't. I have to read the moat code in order to understand what that sequence is asking for."

"You built it. You know."

"I did, but it thinks for itself. At least it randomly sequences, which is similar to thinking for all intents and purposes."

"What is your reason for this?" Nadir's indignant attitude prevailed.

"Isn't it obvious? I die—the information you have is worthless. If I don't enter the access codes, the moats will begin to shut down the array."

Nadir sighed and admired the handiwork. "Very nice. I don't like it, but it's shrewd. Something I would do. The funds will be wired to the account arranged by Mr. Savage for Apollyon and yourself as soon as the data is authenticated. They are separate transactions. I insisted that you be compensated immediately upon downloading the information. I am well pleased."

"Thank you very much. Would you mind if I turned in for the evening or freshened up a bit? I'm exhausted."

"Not at all. I know it's late for you with the time change. Did you care to see some sights tomorrow or just have a leisurely morning?"

"We should probably be heading home."

"What about your safeguards on the system—the moats?"

"That can be done over the phone."

Nadir clasped his hands in front of him. "I'm afraid leaving is not possible. You must stay until we verify the data."

"How long?"

"Four to five days."

"I have obligations back home. This is not my only job."

"It should be."

"What do you mean?"

"Where could you make more money than you did today?"

"I must admit, I don't know exactly how much I made today."

Nadir put his arm around Pogue. "My friend, the information in this document will change the course of history for the Middle East. The battle against our enemies will be waged on our terms. Perhaps we will even upset the government's military and reach into Syria and Iraq in addition to forcing the hand of the United States to help us in specific areas. This is worth a great deal. You'll be paid personally one million American dollars."

Pogue smiled, doing his best to remain in character while his world back home unraveled. "Perhaps I can afford to stay and enjoy the sights after all." He was trapped. "I'll turn in, then. Good night."

# CHAPTER THIRTY-EIGHT

Jenni sat in her living room across from Agent James. He asked many of the same questions others had, then closed his iPad and placed it on the table.

"I know your husband, Mrs. Pogue."

She didn't expect that. "How?"

"He's a good man. Trust him."

She stiffened. "That's what he keeps saying. I do trust him, but why won't anyone give me answers?"

"We'll do all we can to find your daughter, but right now I want you to meet someone." Mr. James stood. "Her name is Raven Tyler, and she is more qualified to give you those answers."

A young woman, professionally dressed and wearing a sidearm, walked to Jenni's side. "I'm Agent Raven Tyler with the CIA."

James motioned for them to both sit. "Ms. Tyler will explain everything. You'll have to leave your home, but the FBI will remain here. A missing child that appears to have been kidnapped falls under our jurisdiction. We've set up a command center here in the event that whoever did this tries to make contact."

"Leave? What are you saying? Are my other children in danger?"

Raven placed her hand on James' arm. "Thank you, Agent James." She turned to Jenni. "Mrs. Pogue, may we speak in private?"

They stood and moved to the study. Jenni closed the French doors and joined Raven on the sofa.

"Your husband is working with the United States government, which has, we believe, placed him and your family at risk. We need to move you tonight as the FBI continues the search for Janelle."

"What do you mean, he works for the government?"

"I realize this is a lot to grasp, but it will be clear soon. Relocating you is a necessary precaution, Mrs. Pogue." She stood and opened the French doors. "Pack medications and important items, plus a few changes of clothes for you and the kids. We'll buy everything else. We need to leave as soon as possible."

Jennifer's tears forced their way down her cheeks. "I don't understand."

Raven placed a gentle hand on her shoulder. "We need to go. Let me know how I can help. Do you or the children require any medications regularly?"

Jennifer shook her head. "No."

"Where are we going, Mom?" Landon asked as he and Karen came into the room. Karen held her fuzzy, stuffed bunny and cried, probably because her mom was sobbing. Jenni noticed and knelt, gathering her children in her arms and putting down the tissue.

"Mommy's fine. And we're going on a little adventure. All of us."

"To see Janelle?" Landon asked.

"She'll meet us soon. Daddy too. Grab two stuffed animals you want to take and one game each. Don't forget your blankets."

The kids gathered the essentials, and Jenni packed them in a small suitcase. She walked to the entryway.

"We're ready."

Raven gave the kids a smile. "We're taking you kids to a fun place for a few days. Okay?"

Landon and Karen chuckled as if they were going to Chuck E. Cheese.

Raven led them out the front door to three SUVs in the horseshoe drive. She and Jenni moved Landon and Karen's car seats to the SUV in the middle. While buckling the kids in, another agent parked Jenni's minivan in the garage.

"Where is the safe house?" Jenni climbed in.

"Downtown Chicago. We can protect you there."

Jenni rode in silence for a moment, as her emotions boiled over, and silent tears flowed down her cheeks.

"I'm sorry. I don't know if my husband is okay. I don't know where my daughter is. I'm so afraid. I can't find peace. How did this start? We were a simple family enjoying life. Now look at us. Tell me my husband didn't do this to us."

Raven took Jenni's hand and squeezed it. "Listen to me. You're in this deep because your husband refused to turn his back on his country. He refused to let a girl your daughter's age be sold to slavery. I honestly don't know how it started. But my boss believes that what your husband is doing is defending our national security. At the same time, it has placed you in danger. That's why we're here. Capable men surround your husband. He's not alone, and neither are you. I'm here for you all the way. That's how this works."

Jenni took a moment to process what Raven had said. "I had no idea."

"Mrs. Pogue, I promise we'll do everything we can to get them back."

"He's in the mafia, Raven."

She smiled. "He told you."

***

"Nicholas! What are you doing here at the guesthouse?"

Nick's skin bristled. His father's interference was the last thing he needed.

"We're having a meeting. We didn't want to bother you, so we met here."

"You're here to avoid me." Ben turned to Marc and C.J. "Your father is furious. Whatever it is you've gotten yourself into, it's not what our families want."

"This is—"

"Stop, Nick. What were you thinking? You got three men killed at the airstrip, the FBI is breathing down Victor's neck, Kurt is dead, and we could be on the brink of war with the Santinos and Luccis. And for what— trafficking women? We don't do business that way."

"I beg your pardon, Mr. Gambrel, but—"

"Don't speak to me, Marc. Your father needs you to come home."

"I run the business now, Mr. Gambrel. My father is a relic, much like yourself." He glared at Ben.

"Don't talk to my father that way." Nick's anger festered. His hand instinctively rested on his pistol.

Marc refused to back down. "Pick a side, Nick. It's time we brought our families into the twenty-first century. The old generation likes it slow and steady as it's been for fifty years."

"My side is my side." Nick pulled his jacket to cover his weapon. "I've never made a secret of that. Don't cross me. And you need to show my father some respect."

"You don't have the steel to go against the Santinos," C.J. snapped at Nick. "You couldn't be stupid enough to—"

"I'm stupid enough to be in business with a bitch like you. So anything is possible."

If Ben's stare could kill, Marc would be dead by now. "Get out of my house. This is Gambrel property."

Marc tossed up his hands. "Fine. Don't forget what I said."

Ben had a Glock in his hand so fast Nick didn't see where it came from.

Marc laughed. "What are you doing? Put that away, old man."

"Get out," Ben insisted. He chambered a round as the incumbent slug clinked onto the floor. "What? You thought I was bluffing, you punk?"

"You won't shoot me or my father will kill everyone you've ever known—everyone you care about."

"Everyone I've ever cared about is dead."

Nick looked at his father.

"All of you get out." Ben stared them down.

Marc shook his head in defiance. "When I feel like going—"

"You're declaring war on this family?" Ben grinned. "You said you were in charge. Would you like to make that official? I'll start with you if you'd like."

"Dad, stop. Things got messed up. There's more to what we're doing than trafficking. And it's not really trafficking. We offer these girls a better life."

Ben continued to point the gun at Marc's head. Nick saw in his father's eyes something he hadn't seen in years.

"Take it down a notch, Dad."

"Where's Pogue's daughter?"

Nick flinched as a chill ran through his spine. "What do you mean?"

"She's missing as of this morning." Ben continued to aim the pistol at Marc.

"How do you know that?"

"He called me."

"Mr. Gambrel—"

"Shut up, Marc." Nick cut him off. "Ben Gambrel has a gun pointed at your head. He doesn't bluff."

# CHAPTER THIRTY-NINE

R obert Savage walked to the front of the room and placed a thin briefcase on the desk before taking his seat. He opened it, set a single file on the table, closed the case, and stood it on the floor beside him.

Danielle entered from the side door of the trial suite, wearing a black pantsuit Robert had sent for her to wear. He'd indicated in the package it was from Jason Franklin. Armed guards ushered her in and seated her beside her attorney, Mr. Wilson.

The judge entered.

The bailiff announced, "All rise!"

Both attorneys stood. Danielle followed their lead.

The judge took his seat. "As you were, everyone. This is not a formal trial, Ms. Trent. Rather a hearing for me to determine if there is sufficient merit for your case to move to trial. The charges are serious, but I have yet to hear the evidence. In lieu of opening statements, I would like to get to the point. I've read the briefs prepared by Mr. Savage and Mr. Wilson and would like Mr. Savage to summarize his intent as briefly as possible."

Robert stood. "Thank you, Your Honor. As chairman of the oversight body governing the United States special prosecutors, it came to my attention that certain classified US Intelligence documents found their way to hostile forces in the Middle East. The leaking of that information caused loss of life to CIA covert operatives."

"Over what period of time did this leaking of Intelligence take place?" The judge leafed through the documents.

"From February through the first week of June of this year, Your Honor."

"When and how did we sustain the loss of American lives as a result?"

"Eight weeks ago, Your Honor—all within a twelve-hour period. The killings were the result of unmasking CIA NOC operatives in that region."

"How many?"

"Nine, sir. Five men had their throats cut. Four women were raped and beheaded, all of which were videoed."

"Any collateral damage?" The judge continued to peruse the documents.

"Yes, sir. In addition to our own agents, seven assets and two innocents were killed as well, including a six-year-old boy from a stray bullet."

The judge appeared genuinely disturbed.

Robert's heart pounded. This was his stage.

"Go on, Mr. Savage."

"When we analyzed the data, the information pointed toward case studies under investigation by United States Prosecuting Attorney, Jason Franklin."

The judge looked directly at Savage. "Is he under the umbrella of this investigation?"

"Not any longer, Your Honor."

"Why not?"

"Our investigation initially targeted Mr. Franklin. Quite frankly, we were surprised when he fully cooperated with our efforts, which lead to the discovery of a single common thread in each confidential case—the involvement of Chief Prosecutor Franklin's first assistant, Ms. Danielle Trent."

Danielle started to stand, but her attorney stopped her and spoke. "Objection, Your Honor. Information allegedly pointed to Ms. Trent but was not proven."

"Allegedly, of course, Counselor." Savage continued to address the judge. "For each and every Intelligence leak, files were accessible to Ms. Trent."

"How do you know Chief Prosecutor Franklin didn't work with Ms. Trent or set her up?" the judge asked.

"The files were accessible to her, but she did not have the authority to remove any of them from the Pentagon or from the data center. According to forensics, a number of the documents that were leaked to the Middle East were found on Ms. Trent's home computer and on two thumb drives discovered on her person when she failed the polygraph test. She was on her way out of the building with the drives when we intercepted her for the polygraph."

"Mr. Savage, it would be difficult, if not impossible, to smuggle a thumb drive, let alone two thumb drives, from the Pentagon."

"That would normally be true, Your Honor. But the thumb drives were located inside a key fob that would be excluded from the scanners. That is suspicious in itself."

The judge nodded. "Do you have any other suspects or accomplices, Mr. Savage?"

"My investigation into Chief Prosecutor Franklin has completely exonerated him."

"Could he be complicit?"

"Not according to my investigation. No sir. He did not give Ms. Trent access to the files on several of these cases, particularly the Intelligence report that resulted in the deaths of the agents in Cairo, but she had that data on her personal laptop, which was in her home. Mr. Franklin had no confidential files on his computers or any other electronic media."

"Is he willing to give testimony against Ms. Trent?"

"He is, Your Honor."

Danielle turned abruptly to Robert. He ignored her glance but relished sensing it.

"You'll have your trial, Mr. Savage. Ms. Trent is hereby ordered to remain in custody until that time."

Mr. Wilson stood. "I object, Your Honor. I haven't had the opportunity to respond to these allegations."

"Do you have any information that would refute the information presented by Mr. Savage?"

"No, sir. But Ms. Trent is emphatic that her computer was sabotaged and that the thumb drives were not hers. She believes she is being framed."

"You will have your opportunity to defend Ms. Trent. I suggest you prepare diligently."

Danielle rose to her feet as the judge stood and left the room. The guards each took an arm and walked her through the side door.

*** 

Pogue arrived in his room and carried his backpack and suitcase to the closet floor. He removed the slim cardboard FedEx box the guard at the airport had given him, recalling the man's instructions to not open it until he was alone. Blocking the closet doorway with his body, he tore open the box and poured the contents into the suitcase—a nine-millimeter semiautomatic pistol along with a passport bearing the name Ethan White with Pogue's picture. The pages had several tourist visas and stamps showing travel to Italy and Egypt over the past several years. He stared at the document for a moment. Its inclusion in the package indicated that exiting the country might be as a fugitive. He memorized the stamps and dates.

Finally, he shook a shoulder holster and an encryption phone from the box and placed everything under his clothing in the suitcase. He carefully slipped the phone discreetly in his shirt pocket and exited the closet with his toiletries. Once inside the bathroom, he started the shower and turned on the cell. He allowed several seconds for it to scan the area. The report appeared on the screen: *Listening devices detected within twelve feet. Two active camera feeds at five feet and ten feet.* That confirmed what his own cell had told him when he'd entered the room. The bathroom was probably safe, but the toilet closet was clear for certain, according to the scan.

He sat on the toilet, closed the door, and texted via encryption: *"At Nadir's apartment. Package delivered. Unable to leave until data verified. Audio and visual surveillance in room. Transmitting from the toilet. Any word on Janelle?"*

He took a quick shower, then left the bathroom and dressed beside the bed. Once he had his jacket on, he slipped the phone and passport into his pocket and placed his suitcase on the stand in the closet doorway. He could block the view from the rest of the room that way. The phone buzzed in his pocket. He walked back to the bathroom, sat on the toilet, and closed the door again to the small water closet. He read the text on the screen from Flannery.

*"Amy alive revealed publicly. Your position compromised. Federal and state agents on the scene at your house but no news yet. Bounce server located in Nadir's IT room. Can you find it and send an encrypted message we'll provide?"*

Pogue stared at the message. He was no computer expert and never pretended to be. And how could there be no updates on Janelle? Where would they have taken her? The Gambrel mansion? He typed.

*"Is Jenni okay? And how am I supposed to infiltrate an IT room and*

*do something I've never heard of?"*

"Jenni and the little ones are under CIA protection," Flannery responded. *"We'll talk you through the server process."*

"I'll do my best. Need to get out of this tiny toilet closet. Staying at Nadir's apartment. Have an entire floor crawling with security. They want to take me sightseeing in the morning, but I have to get home."

Flannery responded immediately: *"Get out of the building if you can so we can talk. Don't trust anyone."*

He began to type again but a knock on the door of his room startled him. He slipped the cell into his pocket and opened the apartment door.

Yeager stood in the hallway. "You interested in going out for a drink? Well, a coffee, at least. Not much in the line of liquor in Cairo."

"Can we leave the building?"

"We can go wherever we want."

"That sounds good. Let's get some coffee."

The men walked to the elevator, but one of the guards stopped them. "I'm sorry, gentlemen. Mr. Nadir requested you remain indoors tonight. It isn't safe for Americans on the streets after dark."

"What do you mean? I always go out in the evenings when I'm here."

"Not tonight. Sorry, sir. I have orders."

Pogue gestured toward the patio. "Is there a place where we can have coffee?"

"Of course. Follow me. I'll have one of the men from the kitchen bring you your drinks. Is Turkish coffee what you desire?"

"That sounds great." Pogue walked to the doorway, and the two men stepped onto an expansive outdoor patio. A round, white marble table beckoned them.

"Someone will be right out, gentlemen."

"Thank you." Pogue pulled out his cell as if checking his email and scanned the area. No video. No audio listening devices near them.

"What are you doing?"

"Checking messages. Do you have any idea where the IT room might be?"

"Why?"

"The Wi-Fi signal will be stronger if we're close to it."

"What's going on, Pogue? Talk to me."

Since Yeager hadn't been able to give Pogue the passphrase earlier,

Pogue would trust his instincts until Flannery cleared him. And Flannery specifically said not to trust anyone. *Yeager seems skittish for a career man.*

"I've got a lot going on at home. It's a hard time to be traveling, but you gotta do what you gotta do." Pogue's phone buzzed with an encrypted message: *"Schematics attached for Nadir's building."*

Pogue memorized the diagram. The IT room had to be in one of two locations. One was on the ninth floor, and the other on the eleventh. Nadir lived on the eleventh. The conduits into the third-floor room were larger than the other floors. It may be to potentially carry more wiring. There were additional A/C units assigned to that area as well, possibly to keep the servers cool. The conduit was on the tenth floor not far from Pogue's room.

"What are you so engrossed in over there?"

Pogue shook his head, memorized the schematics, and deleted them. "Another email from my wife." He put the phone down and looked at Yeager. He needed to draw the attention away from this man's curiosity. "How do you do it? How do you balance a family and the kind of work we do?"

A man brought out two Turkish coffees.

"You're asking the wrong guy. I'm a confirmed bachelor. I play the field. I can't be tied down to one woman for the rest of my life, or even for a year. And kids? Forget it. I'll get a dog. If it dies, I'll get another one and give it the same name."

Pogue forced a laugh. "I need to remember to never let you babysit my kids." *I'd like to throw you off this balcony.* "Seriously, though—no thoughts of a family someday?"

Yeager lifted the cup to his lips as if he was stalling. He blew on the steaming, tiny espresso cup, but it still seemed too hot to sip.

"It's too late." His voice was quiet.

Pogue sipped his coffee. He could drink molten lava. "You're young. How can it be too late?"

Yeager set his cup down and rested back in the chair. "Not too late for my age. Just ... too late."

Yeager's eyes drifted toward the balcony as if being drawn there by a thought. "She was the reason I lived." He spoke without looking back. "The reason I got up every morning and came home every night. I wasn't always a bachelor." He focused on the cup and risked a tiny sip from the hot, murky liquid. "We were in Paris on vacation when a man walked up to our dinner table. I'd seen him before—met him on assignment with the company in Versailles three years earlier when a gunfight broke out."

A brisk wind whipped over the edge of the balcony, and the men covered their eyes from the dust for a moment. It passed.

"I killed his partner back then and thought I'd ended him as well." He looked directly at Pogue for the first time in minutes. "It was part of the job. I made an exchange, they double-crossed me, and I defended myself. Simple."

Pogue waited.

"This man in Paris—he looked at my wife and said, 'What a lovely woman.'" Yeager shook his head. "I reached for my gun but couldn't stop him. He shot me in the chest and her in the head. He knew I'd be wearing a vest. He wanted me to live—to suffer—to hurt."

"How long ago?"

"Five years. She and I were celebrating our three-year anniversary." He cleared his throat and his tone changed. "So no one gets close anymore. I won't be hurt like that again. I wish you the best, but ... I doubt you'll live a happily married life. Sorry for even saying that. Ignore me for the moment."

Pogue felt his phone buzz in his pocket. A new message.

"I'm sorry, Yeager. I didn't know."

"Not many people do. Sometimes it helps to talk. But what about you? How did you end up with the agency, and when?"

"That's a story for a non-jetlag moment."

"C'mon. I just bared my soul to you. Give me something. You owe me." He leaned on the table with his elbows. "Anything. Tell me about your family."

The non-sequitur moment made Pogue's skin prickle as his warning flags flapped in the wind.

"Another time. Right now, I just need to sleep."

"Have it your way. We'll have time to talk tomorrow."

They pushed away from the table and walked in silence toward the hallway and their rooms.

Finally, Yeager broke the silence. "So, sightseeing in the morning for a visit to the pyramids, right?"

"Sure thing. Eight o'clock?"

"Eight sharp. See you then." Yeager swiped his card and stepped into his room.

Pogue keyed into his room and moved to the bathroom as he processed the unexpected conversation. He removed the phone from his pocket. The secured message explained how to enter the server IP address encryption into the system. It also warned him not to access the room through the ventilation shaft. It was secured with motion sensors and battery backup systems.

He made his way to the small toilet closet that seemed to be the only place no one was watching. He read further.

*"The IT room confirmed on the top level of the complex. The power will be cut to the entire building at 10:15 p.m. You will have ten minutes. More to follow."*

A faint knock on Pogue's door grabbed his attention. He put his phone away and went to the apartment door, took a deep breath, and opened it.

Philip smiled politely. "Would you care to have a cup of coffee on the patio for a moment? Please." His eyes beckoned Pogue.

"Certainly."

"Let us go, then."

The men walked down one flight to a different patio, where Philip had prepared some traditional coffee. He poured one for each of them.

He spoke in a hushed voice. "I received word from your agency that you need my help getting into the IT room. This cannot be done. There is no way to access that room without being seen." He smiled at Pogue. "Nadir will kill me if I try. I'm sorry. I cannot." His continued smile made it clear that they may be on surveillance cameras, but apparently not audio.

"What happens if the power to the building is cut?" Pogue took Philip's lead and spoke quietly with a smile.

"The IT room has a redundant power supply that supports the servers."

"What about the safeguards? Would they be offline until the power came back?"

"Yes, but the power rarely goes down in this building."

"If it did, how much time would I have before someone checked the room?"

"Maybe three minutes. Several of the guards are assigned to report to that room in the event of a power failure. You will still require a code to open the door since it has its own battery backup."

"Can you give it to me?"

"They can trace the entry on the electronic log back to me."

"We'll have you out of the country by the time they find out." Pogue noticed Philip's hand trembling. "Who is watching us, Philip?"

Philip smiled. "I truly do not know. Perhaps no one. Some of the cameras don't even work, but others do. The footage for working video is kept indefinitely so Nadir can look over it whenever he desires."

"Stop trembling and smile more. We'll get this done."

"When do you expect to do this thing?"

"Ten fifteen tonight. And why didn't you speak with Yeager about this? Isn't he working with you?"

"I thought so, but he has been acting strangely the past few days—meeting with Nadir in private, excluding me. I'm very nervous. I don't want to die. I want to leave this country, and I don't trust anyone."

"This is going to happen tonight. If you want us all to live, what do I need to do when the building goes dark?"

"You must take the stairs beside the elevator. It is a narrow, metal, spiral staircase made as an internal fire escape. It is never used. You must make it to the eleventh floor and turn right when you enter the hallway there. The door has a small lens to look through to see if anyone is there. It is designed to reveal if there is fire or smoke before opening the door. The IT room will be on your left. Punch in the code, and do what you must do. But be out within three minutes." Philip shook his head. "This is madness. You will get us both killed."

Pogue checked his watch. "Give me the code."

"The code for the IT room is one-four-one-seven-star-seven."

"Okay. I'm expecting the sequence for the server from headquarters soon. This has to happen. I must get back to the States."

"Don't leave this spot on the patio until the power is out. The hallway and outdoor cameras are on a separate system and will reboot sooner. I don't want them to pick you up near the elevator if you come out too soon. I can explain why you were here with me having coffee. The camera footage will prove that, but you won't be still sitting after the reboot. And please … don't get caught. I won't be able to help you."

"Understood."

"I was serious when I said Nadir will kill me if he finds out I gave you the code for the room."

"I know. He'll kill us both."

# CHAPTER FORTY

First thing in the morning, Jennifer found something for the kids to watch on the TV in their bedroom, and then sat with CIA agent, Raven, in the living room. Tall windows covered one wall and overlooked the city. She poured coffee from a carafe on the table. A second agent stood by the front door.

Jenni's emotions got the better of her again. She'd cried so much during the night she thought she could hold it together. The tears came just the same.

Raven handed her a tissue. "I'm sorry for the turmoil."

Jenni sat on the sofa and stared at the carafe. "Could she be dead?"

Raven took her hand and made eye contact. "We have every reason to believe she's unharmed."

Jenni picked up the TV remote and held at it in her open hand.

"Watching the news might not be the best thing right now."

"I need to see what they're reporting." She turned the TV on. As she flipped through coverage of recent events, no one was able to explain what had happened at Midway, except that a major FBI sting had killed human traffickers in the act of transporting a young girl abroad. Officials withheld her name pending the ongoing investigation, but she was reported to be in critical condition.

One man remained at large following the shootout between the occupants of the plane and FBI SWAT teams. He was described as a male, approximately six foot two with brown hair, wearing black slacks and a dark gray sports jacket. A single photo showed him from behind. He had that jacket on the morning he left and hugged her in the bedroom.

Jennifer covered her mouth with her hand when they mentioned that he had been shot several times but escaped. The limo he had stolen remained missing. She handed Raven the remote.

\*\*\*

Miriam parked her car a block from Nadir's apartment building. She and Lauren stepped out of the vehicle quietly. Lauren threw a single strap of her backpack over her left shoulder as the women walked into the parking garage using the lower ramp.

\*\*\*

Pogue broke out in a nervous sweat as he sat on the patio in the cool night air, staring at his phone. No message to explain what he was supposed to do with the server. It was already 10:14 p.m. He'd have very little time to enter the sequence before the alarms cycled back on. Even a simple code would take time. Getting caught or killed would seal Janelle's fate. He had to make this work.

The lights suddenly went out. Pogue stood and hurried to the dimly lit patio door, went inside, and turned down the hallway as a few emergency lights flickered on. Fortunately, there was still plenty of darkness. He stood near the entrance to the elevators, but one of the guards maintained his post. Pogue pushed the panic aside as the clock ticked in his brain. A call came over the man's radio, and he disappeared down the hall.

Pogue entered the stairwell beside the elevator and ascended the metal walkway to the next floor. He carefully opened the door to the upper corridor and moved to the IT room. Punching the code into the keypad, he stepped in and pulled the door closed behind him.

Of the six servers, only one had a monitor and keyboard attached. He turned on the screen and typed a message on his encrypted cell line to Flannery. *"In the server room. What's the code? Not much time!"*

*"Vaughn here. Describe the server."*

Pogue typed in the description and the serial number.

*"Memorize the following code, but don't enter it till I tell you. We need to be ready."*

Pogue memorized the lengthy sequence in seconds. *"Hurry."*

*"Hold. Almost set to capture."*

He checked his watch, then heard voices in the hallway. They moved closer.

"I don't see anything," one man said. "But the guards will be here soon. The whole building is out—not just us."

Pogue's heart pounded so hard he was sure they would hear it. One minute forty-five seconds since the outage. He controlled his breathing—slow and steady.

"Let's go," the man said.

Pogue listened as their footsteps faded, then nothing. He stared at his phone.

*"Key the code and hit Enter,"* Vaughn instructed.

Pogue typed in the encryption, hit Enter, and shut down the monitor. According to his watch, it had been two minutes and thirty seconds. He opened the door, exited to the fire escape, and made it halfway down as the lights came on, trapping him in the stairwell. Voices in the hallway convinced him he had to find another way.

He walked down the spiral stairs to the ninth floor and peered through the peephole. Men carrying rifles were calling his name. It was time to do something unexpected—bold—change the status quo like he and Vaughn had discussed months earlier. He stepped onto the top of the elevator parked one level below on the eighth floor, opened the ceiling trapdoor, and lowered himself down. Closing the hatch behind him, he dropped to the floor. He pressed the button for the tenth floor, punched in the code Yeager had used—glad that he'd memorized it—then sat in the corner.

When the doors opened on the tenth floor, Nadir and Philip stood in the grand entryway.

"Dr. Pogue?" Nadir walked to the door and helped him to his feet.

"Well, you caught me." He brushed the dust from his pants. "I was trying to make it to the street but got stuck on the elevator. It was a little intense in there. It gets warm quick without the air conditioning. And I'm not crazy about closed spaces." He offered a weak laugh.

"Yes. We appear to have briefly lost power, but why did you want to get to the street?"

"I was looking for a bar. I really like my nightcap. You know, a drink at bedtime. Have one every night. Helps me sleep. And I knew the only way to get to the street was to sneak down since the guard stopped me before."

"He stopped you because it is not safe at this time of night, and there are no bars in this area anyway. I thought you knew that from being here before."

"I stayed in a hotel last time, and they had a bar in the lobby."

"Tell me what you would like, and I will have it sent to your room."

"Just a little vodka, maybe. Or a glass of red wine would be nice—if it's no trouble."

"No trouble at all. Please go back to your room, Doctor. I'm afraid of what may happen if the power goes out again. I cannot have you becoming injured or stuck on an elevator again. You are much too valuable."

"I appreciate that. Sorry to be a bother. I feel a bit foolish."

"Don't give it a second thought. I'll have it sent up immediately. And please stay in your room for the night."

"I'll do that. Evening, gentlemen."

As Pogue walked down the hallway and entered his room, he wondered if Nadir was putting the pieces together, or if he had no idea. Pogue entered the bathroom, sat on the toilet, and texted Flannery. *"Did it work?"*

*"It worked."*

Pogue typed back. *"Can you get me out of here?"*

*"Stay . . ."*

Pogue waited for a moment, then typed. *"Resend."*

*"Stay away from Yeager. Trust Miriam. She'll be . . ."*

Pogue stared at the screen. The message didn't finish. He checked his signal. His phone was blocked. Even though he was probably being watched on the room cameras, he walked to the closet and undressed, then took a quick shower. A knock on the door.

"Yes?"

"Your cap for the night, sir."

Pogue opened the door. "Nightcap. Thank you very much."

The man nodded and left as Pogue closed the door. He drank the contents in case he was being watched, then turned in for the night. As he lay in bed trying to figure out how to get home to his family and find Janelle, fatigue, alcohol, and jetlag caught up with him.

\*\*\*

"Sir, you need to see the results of the ping Pogue created with the static IP encryption message we had him program into the server."

Flannery looked at the laptop screen.

"We have both the entry and exit gates, sir."

Flannery pointed to a spot on the screen. "What's this?"

"That's one of a number of server locations. It's in Amsterdam. But over here is where Pogue is—the entrance gate. The next blip right there is in Kabul and is not immediately important." Vaughn pointed to a different location. "This is Mosul, Iraq." He moved his finger to another spot. "This location is what you need to see."

"That's here in Chicago."

"Lakeshore Drive, sir. It's the exit site for the TOR router."

Flannery squinted at the screen. "I know this address. It's Preston Yeager's building. Contact Miriam and give her the passphrase. Tell her to make contact with Pogue tomorrow. Hopefully, he got my message before they cut his phone off, but she can use the phrase and warn him about Yeager. Have her wait outside Nadir's apartment and tail them. Pogue mentioned sightseeing. It may be a way to reach him."

"Will do, sir. Lauren has nothing to report on Yeager's behavior. He hasn't met with anyone outside those we'd expected. In fact, he hasn't left Nadir's apartment."

"That's because Nadir *is* his contact. Tell her to get on the next flight home. I don't want him spotting her. First, call Miriam."

Vaughn dialed a number on a secured line, strolling with his lanky gait as he spoke. It reminded Flannery of an ostrich carrying a cell phone.

"Miriam, this is Brent Vaughn. Sorry for the late hour. I have specific instructions. Ready?"

\*\*\*

Ben hung up the phone, having just informed Vic of what had transpired with Nick, Marc, and C.J. at the guesthouse. Where were the girls they were trafficking?

He left the study and walked down the stairs to the security door. The underground walkway was on the other side. Jacob stood near the doorway, talking to another guard. They both turned to Ben.

"Jacob, I need to search the guesthouse—every room. But I don't know what we're walking into. You come with me." He checked his own weapon as he spoke to the other guard. "I need you to watch this end."

"Yes, sir." The man opened a cabinet and removed a snub 9 mm rifle.

Jacob removed an FN-5.7 pistol and checked the chamber. "You already have guards at the guesthouse, sir."

"Correction. *Nick* has guards there. We may face a hostile force at the other end of this tunnel. I don't put anything past him at this point."

"Would your own son resist you, sir?"

"To be honest, I'm not sure what to expect. Which means we should be prepared."

Jacob chambered a round and secured it in his shoulder holster. "On your six, Mr. Gambrel."

*** 

Nick answered his phone. "What's up, Robert?"

"Is this line secure?"

"Yes. Where do we stand with Jason Franklin?"

"His record is officially clean. More importantly, he understands our relationship now."

"And Ms. Trent?"

"I'm afraid she tragically hung herself in her cell this afternoon."

Nick smirked.

# CHAPTER FORTY-ONE

Pogue paused before climbing into the Land Rover. "Why don't we just hang around the apartment this morning, Yeager? I'm not really in the mood for sightseeing."

"Nadir wanted you to get out to see the pyramids and tombs. These people are very proud of their heritage."

"And well they should be. But cut the bull and tell me the truth."

"Nadir wants you gone so he can begin the confirmation process of your Intelligence data without you getting in his way."

That made sense considering Nadir's narcissistic personality. Pogue climbed into the passenger side of the back seat with one of Nadir's guards on his left as another man maneuvered the Land Rover into the chaotic traffic of Cairo. Yeager insisted on sitting in the front passenger seat. The drive took almost an hour from where they were staying on the Nile, east of the city. In the distance, the pyramids stood majestically silhouetted against the hazy blue morning sky of Giza.

"Impressed, Pogue?" Yeager called from the front.

"Who wouldn't be? They're amazing." He forced himself to sound enthusiastic when all he could think about was his daughter and wife.

Snaking their way through the streets toward the pyramids, he noticed Yeager texting but couldn't see to whom. Pogue had tried to get a signal earlier to no avail. He was still blocked somehow.

They approached the entrance gate to the pyramids, and after purchasing tickets and walking the steep incline to the only remaining fully standing structure of the Seven Wonders of the World, he was awestruck at the precision of the monument towering before him—enormous boulders placed into position thousands of years earlier had no mortar to secure them, but they fit together with precision like a giant puzzle.

As he snapped photos, doing his best to appear as a tourist, a young boy approached him selling postcards. The lad was insistent on gaining his attention even though Pogue tried to ignore him. Yeager had warned him not to pay attention to the children selling items, so he didn't, until—

"Mister, look. One dollar. The Statue of Liberty—and the Nile. It's from the lady. Please."

He looked down at the boy who held an envelope open. A cell phone inside got his attention. He glanced at Yeager fifty feet from him, talking on his phone with his back to Pogue while the guards who had accompanied them there sat in the air-conditioned comfort of the Land Rover.

"Who gave you this?"

"The pretty lady. It's for you. She said you would pay me ten dollars—American."

Pogue glanced again at Yeager, who remained on his phone. "Here's twenty." He handed the boy the cash and took the envelope, slipping it into his pocket.

"Thank you, mister."

"Put the money away. Don't let anyone see you, especially that guy. He'll take it. Go."

"Okay, mister." The boy stuffed the bill in his pocket and ran off.

He desperately needed to reach Flannery. Somehow he had to get home. He scanned the ruins and sighed. What was the phone about?

He felt the envelope buzz in his jacket pocket. Yeager, still on the phone, didn't seem to notice. The cell buzzed again. He pretended to gain a better vantage point of the pyramid before discreetly removing the phone and viewing the text. "Take the tour into the Great Pyramid."

He slipped the phone into his pocket and walked to Yeager. "I'd like to go inside the burial chamber of the Great Pyramid."

"You're welcome to slither through a tiny, dark shaft into a cold, abandoned, and ghoulish tomb. But you will do so without me."

"I'm here, so I think I'll go for it."

Yeager shrugged. "Very dead people—not my thing. I'll be right here."

Pogue ascended the stone stairs to the second-tier entrance, paid the fee, and stepped forward. He ducked into the shaft, inching down a long stone walkway angled at about forty degrees. It was so small he had to make the entire journey bent at the waist, moving slowly to avoid slipping or bumping his head on the tunnel's stone ceiling. The air became stale but cooler the farther he descended into the pyramid's depths. The silence of the tunnel reminded him he was alone. No voices, no footsteps except his own.

When he finally entered the grand chamber, a black, cold granite room ten meters square and ten high greeted him, illuminated in one corner by a single light. The sarcophagus stood empty in the middle with the heavy granite lid slid to the side as it had been for many years. Isolated from the outside by the long, narrow tunnel, he struggled to catch his breath in the stagnant air. Able to stand in the dimly lit chamber, he stretched his back. Movement in the corner to his right startled him. A woman remained in the shadows as if studying him, then stepped into the light.

"You are Pogue."

"And you are Miriam?"

"Have you seen the Nile?"

"I've never visited Italy."

"I've never seen the Statue of Liberty." She smiled. "That is not true, but now you know I am who you believe me to be."

He studied the cold, dank room. "The young boy was a smart move. Yeager didn't give him a second glance."

"He was happy to make a few dollars, and there are vendors everywhere. It was easy for him to blend in." Her smile quickly disappeared. "We don't have much time. Yeager will be waiting for you."

"Agent Flannery indicated not to trust him."

"Your superiors believe Yeager did something to your phone so they can't reach you. He has been compromised."

"How did you know he wouldn't follow me in here?"

"He's claustrophobic, something he has managed to keep out of his records for years. You are not. I've studied your files extensively. You appear to have no phobias—no fears. I must admit I fear a man who fears nothing."

"I fear losing my daughter. Does that count?"

"Here is what you need to know. We must get you out of the country—today."

"Do we know who the players of Apollyon are?"

"The computer program worked. That's how your boss knows Yeager is involved. Mr. Flannery felt Yeager was too eager to come to Egypt and had formed a closer relationship with Philip than he was supposed to without your agency's knowledge."

"Philip voiced concern about Yeager last night, but can I trust what he says?"

"Philip appears to be interested in one thing—getting free. He will be helpful to anyone who can get him out of the country."

"Yeager opened up to me last night about his murdered wife. He seemed very sincere and wanted to talk more. But I cut it short since I didn't know if I should trust him. He probably wanted me to spill information."

"Your CIA has identified Apollyon sources in three countries in addition to the US and Egypt from the program you initiated on the server. But it has become clear that Apollyon refers to one individual—the one at the top—the person in charge." Miriam peered up the tunnel and listened. She moved closer to him and spoke quietly. "I also have information from Agent Flannery regarding your daughter. He strongly suspects that Nadir will use her to force your cooperation. The agency wants you out of Egypt as soon as possible since the data you provided won't confirm when Nadir begins the process. This is today."

"How will me leaving the country help? If they think I'm back in the US, they may harm Janelle, or worse."

"They won't know you're back. They'll believe you have been kidnapped or compromised in Egypt."

"Why would they think that?"

"Because we're going to kidnap you."

"When?"

"As soon as you leave the pyramids and are on the main road there will be a small accident."

"Yeager will fight you, Miriam. He's a seasoned CIA operative."

"We'll do our best not to harm him. We have the ability to tase him if necessary. But that may look compromising since normally we would shoot a known adversary."

"I'll try not to get in your way, but being in an accident does not sound like a clear plan. A lot could go wrong."

"Flannery says you have been provided with a usable passport." Miriam seemed to ignore his comment.

"I have one. Yes."

"What name?"

"Ethan White."

"You'll need it today. You have it on you?"

"In my pocket."

"Where is your real passport?"

"Here." He handed it to her.

"You mustn't be caught with this one. I'll take care of it." She slid it into her pocket. "Are you armed?"

"I am. No one knows I obtained a pistol in your country."

"When you leave the pyramids, the accident will occur on the main road. When you exit your SUV, my men will abduct you. Resist, but don't use your weapon. Put up a fight, but I don't want my people killed by Yeager or his team, so we'll immobilize them first."

"Immobilize?"

"Disarm them. We don't know exactly how Yeager will respond. As I said, we don't want to harm him if possible."

"Understood."

"Keep in mind, Dr. Pogue, if the families have your daughter, they'll keep her safe as long as you're in play—kidnapped and alive. But the moment Nadir discovers you've betrayed him, he will order you both killed. The final decision would be with the family, but since they want to please Nadir and will know that you betrayed them, they'll approve. We must keep Nadir in the dark about your return to the States. If he believes forces opposing him in Egypt have abducted you, he'll focus on finding you so you can remain useful to him."

"What if he connects the dots?"

"He's pathologically paranoid. He'll believe someone is attacking you for the purpose of getting to him. Everything is about Nadir. That being said, the intersection we've chosen for the accident has working traffic cameras. I can guarantee he'll see the footage, so don't behave as if you're cooperating. Appear compromised, frightened, panicked—whatever he would expect—but not cooperative. We selected this location on purpose. We'll use it as a stage. If he believes you went willingly, you'll be collateral damage—someone he needs to eliminate or neutralize." Miriam looked toward the shaft leading to the outside. "Go back to him and do what I told you."

"I appreciate your help."

"I'm sorry my help became necessary."

He left the chamber and eased up the stone walkway to Yeager outside.

"Was it worth it?" he asked as Pogue exited the tunnel.

He looked back at the entrance. "It's a tomb without a body. But it's amazing that it's so old and seemingly impossible for someone to build it without modern equipment. Yet there it stands."

"Glad you liked it. Change of plans. Nadir wants us back at the apartment. There's apparently a problem with something he needs you to explain."

Pogue felt a swell of panic but kept calm. "With the data, the moats— what?"

"He didn't say. He just wants us back there. He said a phone call wouldn't cut it."

"Let's go then."

As they spoke, the SUV pulled up and they climbed in. Driving in silence along the smaller roads, Pogue tried not to appear apprehensive. They would be at the main road in—

The truck hit the driver's side of Pogue's vehicle so hard it forced the SUV onto its right side as sharp cubes of broken glass sprayed over the men. The Rover, grinding its metal doors across the pavement as it slid, threw sparks in all directions, including inside the vehicle. Pogue grabbed the handle above the window and held his body from being dragged across the concrete through the opening.

When they came to rest against a row of parked cars, he looked around him to gain his bearings. Yeager was moving in the front seat but didn't respond when he called his name. The man to Pogue's left was hanging sideways in the seat now above him, unconscious and dripping blood onto Pogue's shirt. Pogue unbuckled himself and pulled his body between the back seats to the rear of the vehicle. From there he kicked out the broken back window and stepped onto the street. A few people gathered on the fringes, most of them taking pictures but keeping their distance. He soon understood why.

Hooded men armed with automatic rifles surrounded the vehicle and grabbed Pogue. Yeager suddenly burst through the remainder of the splintered windshield, stumbling through the jagged opening, his face streaked with blood and his left arm limp at his side.

He staggered toward Pogue, scanning the armed contingency. "What the … Sorry, Pogue. Can't let them take you." Yeager pulled his pistol from its holster, aiming it at Pogue's head. He fired a single shot, but not before one man tackled Yeager and another lunged for Pogue, blocking the bullet's path with his body. Yeager fought the man off, shooting him and one other soldier before taking aim at Pogue again. The shot came from Pogue's left. Yeager's body dropped lifeless in the street—a pool of blood trailing toward the gutter.

He turned to the man who shot him. He wore a ski mask as he aimed his weapon at Pogue's head. "Drop your weapon and get in the van."

Pogue moved toward Yeager, but the man punched him in the gut, dropping him to his knees. Pogue fought back and rushed toward Yeager before a second man wrestled him to the ground. He removed Pogue's gun from its holster and zip tied Pogue's hands.

"Let's go." The man held his pistol at Pogue's head, gripping him by his tied hands. He kidney-punched Pogue and threw him into the van. The crowd grew but backed away. Once the door closed, the van sped away.

Miriam moved toward Pogue. She waited for him to catch his breath and recover from the punch to his back, then placed her hand on his shoulder. "You okay?"

"Just need to catch my breath." He gasped for air. "The man who blocked the bullet …"

"I'm fine, sir. Body armor. Dragon skin. It'll stop almost anything. "

"Thank you."

"No problem."

Miriam moved a little closer to Pogue. "It's important Nadir sees you didn't go willingly. It will feed his paranoia. He can see from the traffic cams that you were abducted, and our voices weren't recorded—only video."

"Are you sure?"

"I'm sure. And I'm sorry about Yeager."

Pogue rubbed his stomach. "Did you have to kill him?"

"He was trying to kill you. You saw that."

"But last night he told me about his wife being killed and now this. I don't understand."

"First, we had to leave before police arrived. Second, Yeager has never been married. Now that he's dead, Nadir will be obsessed with finding you."

"And if he does?"

"I want you in the air headed for Paris in an hour, then to Chicago passing through customs as Ethan White."

"Was Yeager one of the bad guys?"

"All I can say is that, in my estimation, he intended to kill you, and we stopped him. If you don't believe that, watch this guy over here digging the slug out of his dragon skin."

The man gave Pogue a grin as he pried the bullet out with a pocketknife. It landed on the floor near Pogue's feet.

"A souvenir." The man slipped the knife into an ankle holster.

Pogue picked up the round and examined it. "Now I have one job. I need to find my daughter."

"You need to find her, but you need to also stay alive while remaining … well, dead."

The van wove through traffic as they made their way through the city toward the airport.

"You have an advantage over your enemies. Whoever took your daughter will believe that they may have lost you to kidnappers who want the information you possess. As long as they don't know you're in the United States, they'll believe you're compromised compromised or kidnapped. They'll hold onto your daughter, their only bargaining chip, to keep you from giving information to anyone else."

"I have to find Janelle before they discover I'm in the US?"

"It won't be easy."

He nodded as the van pulled onto the airport tarmac. When he exited the vehicle, he turned to her. "Will I see you again?"

"If all goes well—no."

"Then thank you. For everything."

"Find your daughter. Let me see it on the news."

Pogue boarded the chartered jet.

# CHAPTER FORTY-TWO

P ogue settled into his seat as the Learjet left the runway. Nadir and Philip in Egypt, as well as Nick, Marc, C.J., and even Ben in the States thought him to be captured or killed in Cairo. He hadn't been able to contact his wife or Flannery, but Miriam promised to handle that.

A half hour into the flight, one of the attendants approached him.

"Mr. White, you have a call, sir." She handed him a cordless phone and walked toward the front of the airplane.

He held the phone to his ear. "Ethan White, here."

"Pogue, it's Flannery. Miriam gave us a heads-up. Thank God you're on that plane. Nadir is already searching for you under every possible rock. We still don't know for certain where Janelle is, and we're running out of time. If they discover you're home …"

"That's a very heavy pause."

"We need to contain the situation. You can't contact your wife or anyone else. We have almost all the identification we need on those involved. You did it. Now we have to round them up, and we have to keep you in play for another twenty-four hours."

"Can you let Jenni know I'm okay?"

"When it's safe. We can't take chances right now. If I'm right and Nick has Janelle, it's critical he doesn't find out you're alive in the States until we're ready to move on him. If he sees her as a liability, which she will be, it's possible he would want to get rid of the evidence."

Pogue didn't want to hear those words. He needed reassurance. The lump in his throat would not allow him to speak until he collected himself. "I can't let her die. I won't."

"We're going to find her."

"You know Yeager is dead?"

"Miriam told me. He was at the top of this monster, but the one called Apollyon is over him. We have what we need from Yeager's servers, but not the ID on Apollyon. We didn't realize it was a person until now. We thought it was their organization."

"Are you certain?"

"Yeager was a double agent, but he wasn't Apollyon."

Pogue drew from power he didn't know he possessed. "Where do we go from here?"

"When you land, Vaughn will meet you at the tarmac and escort you through customs as Mr. White. For now, you're a ghost to everyone, including your family. That's the way it has to be."

"Understood. See you then." Pogue hung up the phone and focused on the sky stretching out before him as the sun shone through a blanket of billowing white clouds. He rested his head against the seat. How could the world appear so beautiful and be so evil at the same time? Somewhere along the way he'd missed who Apollyon was, but he would make this happen. One way or another, he would find Janelle, even if it meant doing it alone.

***

Pogue's plane landed and taxied to a designated location on the tarmac.

The flight attendant approached him. "Mr. White, your driver is waiting."

He looked out the porthole as she opened the front door and lowered the steps. Vaughn stood beside a black SUV. What a welcome sight.

Pogue hurried down the steps toward Vaughn and shook his hand.

"Welcome home, Mr. White. I'm afraid this is not the way you expected to return to your homeland, but at least you're safe ... and dead at the same time." Vaughn laughed awkwardly. He opened the back door for Pogue then entered on the opposite side.

Flannery turned to Pogue from the front seat as the driver pulled away and headed toward the access road.

"I didn't know you'd be meeting me, too." Pogue reached to shake Flannery's hand.

"Wasn't planning on it, but I needed to speak with you due to significant developments since we spoke. A lot can happen in ten hours. First off, incredible job in Egypt. No one—and I mean, no one—could have done better. Which brings us to today. We're moving on targets in five countries. We've learned from one of the servers that the government of Syria would like very much to find out who is involved with the Intelligence the Egyptians are actively seeking—the information they believe you were to deliver. If you'd carried the original, correct information that Mr. Savage provided, Syrians would have the upper hand in Egypt *and* Sinai. That would be a game-changer for them and the entire Middle East. Yeager wasn't just making money—he was betraying Nadir and altering Middle East history for a fee."

The SUV waited its turn behind another vehicle at the gate to exit the tarmac.

Pogue rubbed his temples. "Savage provided me with a series of instructions—names and coordinates. It was supposedly intended to help Egypt. I realize it's not the one I delivered, but it's the one he wanted me to hand off to Nadir."

"Savage's list was comprised of undercover operatives actively working in Iraq, Syria, Turkey, Jordan, the Sinai Peninsula, and Northeast Africa—primarily Egypt. The numbers you memorized were coded latitude and longitude values for every safe house and operations center in each of those countries. Do you recall how many there were?"

"Forty-seven."

"Correct. That corresponds to more than two hundred US citizens and another hundred and fifty civilians in positions of trust from the respective regions who would have been placed in jeopardy, and that's just until war breaks out."

The truck in front of them pulled forward through the gate as their SUV stopped at the booth. The driver opened the window to hand the man some documents.

"Nadir thinks the Syrians kidnapped me?"

"We believe so." Flannery removed his credentials from his pocket to show the guard.

Pogue tilted his head. "Yeager wasn't loyal to Nadir?"

"We didn't even know of the connection until you sent that encrypted software message that gave us access to his server. It was the other way around. Nadir was loyal to Yeager. Nadir had no idea what Yeager was doing behind the scenes with the cartel, which includes Robert Savage. And Philip was an innocent pawn—a CIA asset stuck between Yeager and

Nadir. He didn't know who to believe since neither could be trusted."

The SUV pulled through onto the road leading to the terminal as the driver closed the window. Pogue glanced at the customs entrance.

"Who has my daughter?"

"We located where we believe they're holding her. Amy King gave us important details along with what you told us about your visit to the guesthouse and the infirmary when you first met her. We're reasonably certain Janelle is in the Gambrel guesthouse where Amy was held, just north of the main house."

"But they've had time to change the plan—to move her. That's what I would have done."

The SUV pulled into a parking spot and stopped. When no one got out, a guard from the entrance approached the vehicle.

"It's the best we have. If she's not there, we may get a lead to help us find her." Flannery opened his window. "There is one man inside the Gambrel mansion that we've used as an informant over the past year. He's the one who delivered the *special* jacket to you that synced with your cell phone."

"Carl."

"Correct." Flannery showed the guard his credentials. "He informed us that Nick and the Santinos have been busy in the compound of the guesthouse for the past few days. We need to move on them this morning."

"When I went there to suture Amy, we entered through an underground tunnel that connects the main house with the guesthouse. There's a steel security door that opens by a digital code. The hallway is monitored by surveillance cameras from each end."

Flannery and Vaughn glanced at each other.

Pogue continued. "The guesthouse is huge and secure. It's not going to be easy to break in. What's your plan?"

"We're going through the front door with a search warrant."

"You'll never get past the main gate before she's dead."

"Nick isn't there. Only Ben."

"Let me talk to him. If you don't, Janelle will be nothing more than—"

"The FBI will take the lead on this. We can't risk warning the Gambrels that the CIA is involved. Kidnapping or missing children cases are not our jurisdiction, so it would tip off Ben that we're looking at something bigger. He'll let the FBI in."

Pogue nodded, took a deep breath, and blew it out.

"I've arranged for you to be in the command van watching the operation with Agent James. You've been inside the mansion, and you know Ben, so you can advise James. But that's all. You can't let anyone see you."

Vaughn interrupted the conversation. "The news is reporting that a United States citizen was kidnapped in Cairo yesterday."

"Did they give his name?" Flannery reached for the phone.

Vaughn turned to Pogue. "Your name and photo are the Internet front news story."

"I need to call Jenni."

"Your family is safe as long as this holds." Flannery turned his attention to Vaughn. "Let Raven know so she can fill Mrs. Pogue in. She needs to stay put and know that her husband is okay. No leaving the safe house."

"Yes, sir."

Flannery dialed a number on his own cell. "Agent James. We have Pogue and we're headed to the Gambrel location. Let me know when you're ready to breach." Flannery hung up his phone and turned back to Pogue. "Let's get you through passport control. I hope you got some sleep on that flight. This is going to be a long day."

***

Nadir tossed the TV remote on the coffee table as the silent flat-screen continued broadcasting photos of the latest news—the murder of a US CIA operative in broad daylight, the kidnapping of a prominent American physician, witnesses, phone calls, and now his own government wanted to know what Yeager and Pogue were doing in Nadir's personal SUV. The worst part of all—his clients circled like vultures looking for the data he'd promised.

He focused his attention on the automated report from the surveillance system detailing who accessed secured areas during the blackout. Philip's code was used to enter the server room while the lights were out, but the cameras showed him with Nadir during that time. When the power came back on, why was Pogue on the elevator? Did Pogue punch in the apartment code, or did the elevator return to the floor automatically after the power reboot?

He picked up his phone and dialed his lead man. "Have you found

Philip?"

"No sign of him since last night, sir. His apartment wasn't touched, and his bed doesn't appear to have been slept in."

"Stay there and wait. He can't disappear into thin air." Nadir hung up and sipped his Turkish coffee. The chessboard on the coffee table showed his king lying flat. He cursed and slung it against the wall.

# CHAPTER FORTY-THREE

Pogue leaned forward, resting his elbows on the armrests of his swivel chair. He was thankful they'd allowed him this close to the action. Being inside the FBI van was considered the front line. He adjusted his headphones and studied the monitors—one for SWAT and three for the FBI ground teams. Agent James, seated to his right, explained the sequence of events while Pogue listened to the surface teams on his headset.

"They're approaching the front door with a warrant to search the premises. Dressed in plain clothes, our hope is that they'll cause less tension. But we have the SWAT team ready if it comes to that."

Pogue knew there was no perfect scenario for searching the building. He prayed Janelle would be nothing more than frightened when he found her. As the men approached, the door opened. Pogue watched, shocked at the lack of resistance.

"That's him." Pogue pointed to the image on the monitor. "That's Ben Gambrel. He never answers the door personally. What's he doing?"

"He knew we were coming." James sighed and keyed his mic. "Be on your guard, gentlemen. They're informed."

Pogue wiped his sweaty palms on his thighs. "He doesn't know about the cartel's plans. Nick has been very clear—don't let his dad know anything about Apollyon."

"He knows something or he wouldn't answer the door. Listen so we can hear what they say."

"We have a search warrant to inspect your property, Mr. Gambrel."

"You don't need a warrant, son. Come in, all of you men. My house is open to you." He took the paper from the lead agent and glanced at it briefly as he held the door open for them.

All six men entered and the door closed. Pogue could hear their voices and see the video from the lead agent's body cam.

Pogue stared at the monitor. "You need more men." He turned to James. "You need more men."

James pressed the monitor button. "This could be an ambush. Send in the second team." Both men studied the monitors.

Pogue shook his head. "Send another team to the guesthouse and push the first guys through the tunnel."

James hesitated.

"Do it now, James. Something isn't right."

James pushed the button and spoke. "Team three, approach the guesthouse immediately. Enter and hold for team one. Team one, go to the tunnel …" He looked at Pogue.

Pogue took the cue. "It's behind the main staircase, down a single flight."

"Behind the main staircase and down one flight," James repeated.

As the men moved to the staircase, Ben's demeanor abruptly changed to anger, and several of the guards in the hallway took an aggressive posture.

"Tell your men to stop and face him."

James did as Pogue suggested.

"Ben's men are getting ready for something."

James keyed the mic. "Hold your position, team leader, and have Gambrel's men stand down."

"Mr. Gambrel, your men appear to be taking an aggressive posture. This is concerning. Please have them stand down."

"I told you that you're welcome to inspect this house. That doesn't mean you can march wherever you please."

The lead man responded. "It does, sir." He drew his weapon along with the other men as team two entered the front door, locked and loaded. The team leader repeated the order. "We have served you a warrant. Tell your men to stand down. Please, sir."

Ben motioned to his men. They stood at ease.

Team one made their way down the stairs to the steel door. "What's the code, Mr. Gambrel?"

Ben walked to the keypad and punched in numbers time and again, but nothing happened.

Pogue grabbed James' arm. "The code is five-six-three-six-five-two-seven."

James keyed the microphone and repeated the sequence.

The man pushed Gambrel aside and punched in the code. The door opened and the men went through.

"The code is the same on the other end." Pogue's heart pounded. He felt short of breath.

"Use the same code at the guesthouse," James echoed.

"Copy that, sir."

James released the button and pointed to a second screen. His men approached the front door of the guesthouse. No one answered the doorbell. Pogue turned his attention back to the first screen as Ben placed a call. He could hear Ben speaking to someone from the team leader's microphone. "Finish up in that room!" Ben said.

Pogue stood. "Team three needs to get in there. Something's going down in the guesthouse."

James ordered them. "Team three, forceful entry now!"

The man kicked the front door, but it didn't open. He tried again, but it was too strong.

James pushed the button. "Ram it."

SWAT appeared in seconds as Pogue watched Ben remove the phone from his pocket again.

"Punch that door down!" James pounded his fist on the counter.

"Copy that, sir." SWAT rammed the door, splintering wood across the foyer.

Ben stormed up the guesthouse stairs from the tunnel and into view. "Why are you kicking in my door?"

"We have our orders, Mr. Gambrel."

"I can see that. I would like to speak with the agent in charge. I presume he's listening?"

"We'll have him come as soon as we've secured the premises."

"I'd like to speak with him first, if I may."

"He's stalling. Search the house now!" James ordered. "Tell Mr. Gambrel I will be there shortly." He took his finger off the button and spoke to Pogue. "What am I getting into?"

Pogue cleared his throat. "I'll listen and talk you through it."

"You okay?"

"I'm all right."

*I'm not all right. I need to be in there.*

James took off the headset and placed a wireless earpiece in his right ear. "Whatever we find in there, you need to tough it out."

"I'll be fine. Go." He focused on the monitors.

James left the truck, walked through the front gate, and entered the house without interruption. Pogue heard him speak.

"Mr. Gambrel. I'm Larson James, FBI agent in charge. We have reason to believe two missing girls are in this house."

Pogue heard clearly and saw what was happening on the lead agent's lapel cam as they entered the second floor. The first thing he noticed through the camera was carpeting rolled up in the hallway. New carpeting was already installed in the room the agents entered, but the window was boarded up in the bathroom.

Pogue's skin bristled as he pushed the button. "Unroll that carpet in the hallway. Get James up there." *It's not her. Oh, God . . . don't let it be her.*

As the men moved back to the hallway, Pogue saw James stepping onto the second floor from the stairwell. The agents unrolled the carpet. It appeared to be new and unblemished with nothing wrapped into it. But as they neared the end of the roll, dark stains of dried blood had pooled along the final four feet in stark contrast to the white fabric.

*I have to get in there. I have to find her.*

James turned to Ben. "That's a lot of blood, Mr. Gambrel." He turned to the group leader. "Type and DNA that immediately. I want the results as soon as humanly possible." James took the camera from the lapel of the agent and clipped it on his own jacket as he walked into the bedroom. He made his way to the bathroom, and even though the floor and tub were clean, dark stains in the grout were spotty and irregular. "Scrape out this grout and test it. Tell me it's not blood."

James faced Ben again. "Mr. Gambrel, you are under arrest for obstruction of justice, evidence tampering, kidnapping, human trafficking, and interfering with a federal investigation. You have the right to remain silent. Anything you say can and will be used against you in a court of law. You have the right to have an attorney present during questioning—"

"Mr. James, I know my rights. Don't waste your time."

James continued reading Ben his rights regardless, then had the agents cuff him to take him to headquarters.

James waited until they'd escorted Ben from the floor. "You okay, Pogue?"

He could hardly breathe. His chest tightened, and the air wouldn't come. "Have you checked all rooms?"

"The men are done with the main building, and we're almost finished here. We have one more door to open."

James moved across the hallway to where the men were unlocking the door.

As they stepped in, Pogue sat and stared at the monitor.

*Please don't be dead. Baby, please be okay.*

He spotted something on James' body cam. "Her backpack."

"Where?"

"To your right, behind the chair."

James picked it up and unzipped the top. "Her name is inside the flap. But she's not here, Pogue."

Everything began to tilt in that moment. Pogue stood. His hand went to the wall to steady himself. *Not here ...*

"We'll finish up and see what else Ben knows. And stay put, for God's sake. Understood? Pogue, are you listening? Pogue?"

He took off the headset, set it on the counter, and left the truck quietly.

\*\*\*

Morning came early for Ben. He rolled onto his side and looked at his watch. His luxurious bed probably helped him forget yesterday's troubles. Out on bail before midnight was easy for a man with his money and influence. He suddenly sat up and squinted at the door of his bedroom.

"Good morning, Ben."

Ben turned to the voice on his right. His eyes grew large as if he'd just realized his situation.

Pogue took several steps closer, holding his pistol at his side. "I hope you slept well, sir, even if it is only six a.m."

They were alone—just the two of them. Pogue stepped out of the enormous closet.

"Pogue? I thought you were ..."

"Kidnapped? Dead? Not yet. Are you armed, sir?"

Ben looked at the bedside table. Then back at Pogue. "No."

Pogue walked closer, slid his hand under Ben's pillow, then looked in the drawer of the nightstand. No weapons. He slid the pistol into his shoulder holster, and pulled up a chair beside the bed and sat.

"Mr. Gambrel. I need to speak with you on a matter of urgency. I regret the intrusion, but this regards my daughter."

Ben pushed himself into a sitting position. "How did you get in here?"

"Yesterday, while the FBI arrested you in the guesthouse, I walked in the front door of the main house, up the stairs to your bedroom, and waited in your closet."

"No one stopped you?"

"Your men were occupied with you. I took a chance."

"You stayed in my closet all day?"

"All day and night. Yes, sir. It's a big closet. I used your bathroom once before you came home."

Ben scratched the back of his neck. "I'll be damned."

"I needed to talk, and there was no other way to get you alone."

"If you're here to kill me, you won't get—"

"No, sir. I'm looking for my little girl. I have no fight with you, Mr. Gambrel. Never have. When I needed help, you were there for me, exactly as you promised. You have never wronged me."

Ben glanced around the room.

"If you cry out, the room will be flooded with your guards, and I'll be as good as dead. I'm asking you not to. I'm not threatening you. Give me just a moment, and I'll be gone."

"What do you want? What did you say about your daughter? You haven't found her?"

"No, sir. I'm sure she's quite frightened by now."

"Good God." Ben studied Pogue and reached for his glasses from the nightstand. "Have you talked to Nick?"

"Unfortunately, I have reason to believe he may be involved."

"Is that why you contacted me instead?"

"Not really. I've come to suspect Nick since that time."

"But you trust me? He's my son. I'm not going to sign his death warrant."

"I know that Nick is probably not the originator of the plan. The Santinos don't have the same code you do, Mr. Gambrel—at least not the Santino children."

"Marc needs someone to straighten him out. He dragged Nick into this and now look where we are—kidnapping girls."

"I think you may have an idea where my daughter could be without realizing it."

"What makes you think so?"

"Before the FBI ever arrived you found blood in that room in the guesthouse that you knew nothing about. Now your limos are missing. They have been since yesterday, *before* the FBI arrived. I'm certain they have GPS and LOJACK devices. Nick doesn't know you'll be looking for him, so he's probably not hiding the cars from you."

Ben stuffed a pillow behind him and propped himself against it. "Well, you're wrong about that. Once I realized the limos were missing, I contacted the company that handles our security, and they found the cars just like you said. Nick has since disconnected the GPS and LOJACK systems, but not before we found where they'd been for several hours." Ben pushed himself up in the bed. "I'm not naïve. I know that if Nick got himself involved in this he's not without blame." Ben cocked his head to the side. "How did you get away from your kidnappers?"

"How do you know about that?"

"The news. You're the headline."

"I'll explain another time."

Ben swung his legs to the side of the bed but didn't stand. "If I tell you where your daughter may be, what happens then? You kill my son?"

"I find my daughter. She's all I want. Your son is still my friend."

Ben opened the drawer to his nightstand, removed a pen and pad, and scribbled something on it. "I've done things—things I've regretted and things I've had to. But I've never taken a man's daughter. The fact that it was part of what they charged me with last night meant they had reason to suspect she was here."

He tore off the sheet of paper. "I understand making money and have never been timid about getting my hands dirty. You know very well I'm no saint. When people got in my way, I eliminated them one way or another. But this is different. This time, Nick is the problem. Marc and C.J. took him down the wrong path, but that won't matter if he's done what I suspect."

Ben handed Pogue the paper. "This is the address of a warehouse I own but haven't visited for years. At one time I put an old military chopper in it that I'd planned to restore. You saw the photo of it the day

I met you." He paused. "When I lost my wife to cancer nineteen years ago, my aspirations and passions died with her. I don't know why I still own it, but I do. Can't seem to let go. Anyway, that's where the tracking devices located the limos before they were disconnected. Both vehicles were there after leaving the guesthouse yesterday morning. At noon the signals disappeared." Ben shook his head. "I didn't know about the blood in that room until yesterday. I'm sorry if—"

"It isn't my daughter's blood. It's from another girl."

"How do you know?"

Pogue sighed. "I don't. I have to believe I'm not too late." He studied the address. "Why give me this knowing I'll go there?"

"It's only a matter of time before the FBI searches public records and shows up at the warehouse. That property isn't hidden. My name is on the deed. Never had a reason for it not to be. They'll have no mercy on Nick if they find him first."

"What makes you think I will?"

"He's your friend. More importantly, I'm your friend. I've survived because I'm an excellent judge of character. You have a conscience, you care, you show mercy. For God's sake, you've been in my closet all night. You could have done this when I first got home at midnight. Instead, you let me sleep." Ben shook his head. "You're a great son to someone—a good man. It's your weakness and your strength. Taking a man's daughter is worthy of death. I hope you'll not find yourself in that position."

"If I do?"

"You will do as you must, Pogue. Then I will be the man I've always been and do what I must as well."

Pogue nodded. "Would you walk me out, please, sir? I'll never make it to the front door without you now that your men are back in position."

Ben stood and threw on a robe that he'd draped across the end of the bed, then the men walked to the front door of the house. He faced Pogue.

"May the end of this day find your daughter safe, and my son as well."

In that moment Pogue saw a man—a father and friend—humble, yet wielding great power. The crime boss of Chicago shook his hand warmly. Was he sorry for what he'd done, or for what he would have to do?

# CHAPTER FORTY-FOUR

Nick arrived at the warehouse office at seven a.m. and punched his access code into the keypad. Once he heard the electronic lock release, he pushed open the heavy steel door and stepped in.

The guard behind the desk stood. "Good morning, Mr. Gambrel. Everything's quiet."

Nick took a moment to admire what he'd accomplished.

A steel wire cage with a digitally locking door stood isolated in the center of the warehouse where an array of computers displayed everything inside the building and even the parking lot. Forty feet above, metal crossbeams interrupted by skylights every fifteen feet spanned the ceiling of the twenty-thousand-square-foot structure. A large helicopter, deteriorated by years of neglect, stood abandoned near hangar doors at one end of the building. Accommodations for the girls occupied fifteen hundred square feet at the opposite end. Branching off the guarded hub of that section, two hallways housed ten dormitory rooms, each with a private bath.

Nick checked the monitors. The two girls appeared to be sleeping as guards stood outside each of their rooms. He turned to the man seated by the desk. "You can go. I have a meeting in a few minutes. I'll see you this evening."

"Very good, sir."

Once the guard stepped out, Nick focused on the parking lot monitor as the man drove off. Moments later, a Lotus arrived and pulled in next to his Bentley. Nick opened the door for his visitors.

Marc entered first and gazed at the structure. "This is a big warehouse."

C.J. followed Marc in.

Nick pointed. "My father was going to rebuild that chopper over there, but he lost interest when my mother died. I don't think he's been here in twenty years."

Marc stepped into the cage and scanned the monitors. He turned to Nick with a look of concern. "So, Yeager was our man with the CIA, and he's dead. Pogue is missing, probably in enemy hands. What if he turns on us to save his own skin?"

"He won't. He's not like you or me—or her." Nick gestured toward C.J.

She glared. "You think so much of him you're blind to what's real."

"What's real? You mean you kidnapping his daughter for insurance? Nice move. It would have been helpful to let me in on that before she showed up in my guesthouse."

"She's more than insurance." C.J. sat on the edge of the counter. "Janelle's worth a fortune. She looks so much like Amy, it's shocking. We can use her to keep Nadir quiet while preparing to deliver Jamie. We can't afford for these girls to be found on American soil."

Nick slid his hands into his pockets. "This whole sordid thing was conjured up by you two. Pogue was playing by the rules, and you decided to kidnap his daughter? Now you want to sell her because she's pretty?"

"She's nearly Amy's match. She meets our needs, and she's collateral damage."

Nick tossed his phone on the chair. "You just want her because she's his daughter."

Her guilty expression betrayed her.

"No, C.J. If I can find Pogue and bring him back, I'll reunite him with his daughter."

Marc pulled up a chair next to the monitors. "We're the council—or we soon will be. We'll bring others in as we see fit. We can make this work. Jamie is still a viable commodity, but I agree with C.J. We need to move her soon. If we add Janelle to the mix for Nadir, that seems like a plus to me."

"I told you, you can't sell Janelle."

Marc stood and postured. "Who are you to make the call? You don't run everything."

"I run this."

C.J. slapped her hand on the counter and pointed at the monitors. "You both need to be concerned about getting those girls out of here. And if that

Amy brat is still alive, we have to shut her up."

Marc leaned on the counter and studied the monitors. "We can make this work if we stay calm and move Jamie overseas."

Nick walked to the doorway of the cage. "Agreed. We need to send her to Dubai as soon as possible. I'll deal with Janelle."

"You're going to muck this up," C.J. snapped. "Don't drag *our* family into this."

Nick tugged at his ear. "Like it or not, your family is as deep as anyone into this. You forged your father's name and used his seal on Amy's documents. Now he's not only incriminated, but he knows what we're doing and that it went sideways, just like my father knows. He'll find out the girls were in the guesthouse any time now. You and Marc insisted on the early timeline for kick-starting this operation even though the warehouse wasn't ready. Bringing Janelle into the mix is on you."

"Both of you calm down." Marc glanced at C.J. "We're all in this for the long haul."

Nick walked past Marc to the desk and tapped his fingers on the surface while staring at the computer screen.

Marc sat in a chair by the door and rested his elbows on his knees. "First we establish the new council this afternoon in my office downtown at two o'clock, just like we'd planned. We'll outline the new working order to take over the Gambrel and Santino family businesses under Apollyon."

Nick turned and leaned back against the counter. "After we convene the new council we'll determine the best approach to take control. Our fathers will have to recognize our authority."

C.J. huffed. "What if they don't? Our dad is going to explode."

Nick reached for the keyboard and changed the camera on the third monitor to gain a better viewpoint. "The takeover is far from a done deal. Although I'm pushing my father into retirement, I respect what we're doing, and I still respect him. We can't stop this. We have to sell Jamie or bury her. What makes more sense? And I have to get Janelle out of FBI crosshairs before they come snooping around."

"I still think—"

"I know what you think, C.J., and it's not going to happen." He turned to Marc. "Touch base with Savage and Nadir. See what's going on. I'll see what I can find out about Pogue."

"Are you inviting Savage and my husband to the council meeting?"

Nick shrugged. "The way I see it they belong there. Jason and Savage have a new understanding of each other's roles. I think it would be good."

"This is a big day, C.J." Marc stood and took a few steps toward the door. "The best-case scenario happens if we have enough support from Savage and your husband for the old regime to come to terms with us. Let's get going. We have work to do. See you at my office, Nick."

Nick focused on the parking lot monitor as they left the building and got into their car. "Yeah. See you then."

\*\*\*

By ten o'clock in the morning, Nick appeared to be putting the final touches on the proposal for the council. His phone buzzed. He glanced at the screen but put it down without answering. A noise from outside the wire cage startled him. He turned. For a moment, he couldn't move.

"Pogue?"

"Hello, Nick."

"What the … How long have you been here?"

"Long enough to know what you're planning with Marc and C.J."

"What *we're* planning. You're a huge part of this. Oh my God. How did you get away? This is a miracle! And how did you make it back to the US? Did customs stop you? Passport control? You're on the news, man. Everybody's looking for you."

"Call your father."

"What? Why?"

"Just call him and put him on speaker."

Nick picked up his phone and glanced at the screen. "I've missed seven calls from him." He hit the callback button.

Ben answered right away. "Nick?"

"What's going on, Dad?"

"Pogue is in Chicago."

"He's here with me. He told me to call you. You're on—"

"I've been trying to reach you for hours."

"I was in a meeting and silenced my phone. I know we need to talk about what happened yesterday. Marc is an idiot. I never intended—"

"The FBI showed up after you left." Nick looked at Pogue as Ben spoke. "They raided our home and found a bloody room in the guesthouse. They even took samples from the grout stains around the tub. Once they finish testing it, who will I go to jail for? I was arrested and spent the evening trying to explain something I know nothing about."

"That never should have happened. Those men were paid to clean that room up by now."

"It looked like someone was murdered in there. Were they?"

"No. There was an accident."

"If you're with Pogue, you must be at the warehouse. Are you there, Pogue?"

"I'm here, sir."

"Nick, give Pogue his daughter. Whatever else you've done, I know you didn't take her. Did Marc? Do you know where she is?"

"It was Marc and C.J. But, Dad, listen—"

"Help him. We'll sort the rest out when you get home. He's one of us. We're supposed to protect our own."

Pogue stepped forward toward the door of the cage—toward Nick.

"Stop." Nick raised a pistol.

"Why are you pointing a gun at me? You just said you were glad to see me."

"Nicholas, what's going on?"

"Just … stop for a minute while I explain the situation." Nick held the phone with his free hand.

"You know where she is, son?"

"Dad, I'll call you back." He hung up on his father and tossed the phone on the desk.

Pogue slid his hands into his pockets.

"Put your hands where I can see them."

Pogue didn't budge.

"Please, Pogue. Just … get your hands up."

He slowly removed his hands from his pockets and held them at shoulder level. "She's here, isn't she?"

Nick glanced at the monitors, then back at Pogue. "Marc and C.J. wanted leverage. It wasn't my idea."

"Now they want more."

"That was never my intent. Whether you believe it or not, I had no idea what they were planning, and I'm really glad you're okay."

"You could have stopped them."

"I care about your family, but I'm not the only one calling the shots.

And I kept them from harming her."

"Said the man pointing a gun at my chest."

Nick put the gun in his holster. "Put your hands down. Just keep them where I can see them." He shook his head. "C.J. had access to the guesthouse, and I didn't know Janelle was there until it came time to move the other girl last night. Nobody has laid a hand on her. But things can't go back to normal just because you're back."

"You promised me that you would take care of my family. Giving her to me would be taking care of my family."

"Nobody gets out, Pogue. No one walks away. You know too much. Besides, we need you. Nadir has been calling every hour asking if I can still deliver since the server moats are shutting him out. With you here, we can fix that."

Dread crawled up Pogue's spine as he realized that Nadir would still be a problem, and so would Nick, once they found out the Intel was false. The only way to keep things moving for the cartel would be for Pogue to deliver the true information from Savage, which he could never do.

"I'll call Nadir and let him know he can relax."

"Let her go first."

"Not until I clear things with the new council we're forming and make sure there isn't a family war. Like it or not, I have partners. I hate them, but they're still partners."

Pogue looked at the monitors on the desk where Nick had been sitting when he came in. His daughter was on one of the screens. He walked to it. "My God."

"Yes, she's here. I'll take you to her, but you can't leave with her yet."

Pogue took a step toward Nick.

Nick pulled out his pistol again and chambered a round. "Don't do this."

Pogue stopped. "You remember she's fifteen, right?"

"Give Nadir what he needs to unlock the data, and I'll keep Janelle comfortable until we work this out and the Intel verifies."

"Let her go and keep me prisoner." *That will at least buy some time.*

"The new council will decide."

"It has taken control, then?"

"The old council is no longer in touch with reality."

"You're overthrowing your father?"

"He and Victor Santino aren't capable of leading this organization any longer. I don't expect you to understand."

"He could die if there's a war. Any of us could." Pogue took another step. "Have you thought about that?"

"You're my friend, Pogue. But you're not leaving me many options. Why can't you go with this? Be a part of it. I still want that."

Pogue shook his head. If he unlocked the data he'd given Nadir, they'd know it was fake. He needed to divert the conversation. "I know you helped Kurt kill Ginger."

"What?" Nick appeared stunned. He lowered his weapon. "Why would you say that?"

"Kurt told me. Just before he died. You know I'm telling the truth. There would be no way of me knowing if Kurt hadn't told me that you guys got Dr. Harrison to finish what you started. He was the only one who knew, other than you."

"Who have you told?"

"Why would you do that to your own sister?"

"It's complicated."

"I know killing Ginger was Kurt's idea, but you could have stopped him."

"You've crossed the line into family business." Nick shook his head without breaking eye contact. "Ginger never understood. She was going to tell you everything, then go to the FBI. It was business—nothing personal."

"What's Janelle?"

"She was insurance. And now that you know everything about Ginger, I have an anvil hanging over my head that you can drop whenever you want. I do what I have to. Sometimes it hurts—like killing Ginger. I wanted this to work."

"But it's not like that anymore, Nick."

"No, it isn't."

Pogue looked at the computer screen. "Oh, God."

*** 

Nick turned for only a second. When he looked back, Pogue had a bright laser spot on his chest. Nick spun to see where it came from. No one was visible.

The blast into Pogue's chest threw him against the computer cage wall. He slumped lifeless to the floor.

"God!" Nick shouted. Before he could tell where the shot came from another bullet from above whistled past his ear. He dove for the cage door as several more blasted small craters in the concrete, scattering painful chunks in the air. He glanced at Pogue, slouched against the wall. "Pogue!"

More gunfire erupted, forcing Nick to take cover behind a stack of crates outside the cage. The shots continued but Pogue didn't move. Nick fired into the ceiling beams. A barrage of lead pelted the floor, pinning him down.

"Pogue!" He called again, but there was no response. He tried to move closer, but the bullets peppered the concrete, preventing him from getting near.

Gunfire erupted from two men who approached from the back of the warehouse and shot into the metal beams above. In seconds they lay silent on the ground. Nick bolted out the door as fresh rounds ricocheted off the cinderblock wall.

# CHAPTER FORTY-FIVE

---

P ogue sat upright from his slouched position on the floor and pulled the cell phone from his pocket. Ben had hung up, but hopefully, he'd heard enough. He tucked it away.

The CIA snipers rappelled from the metal ceiling beams to the floor. The lead man approached Pogue. "He's gone. We made sure we didn't hit him. Should we pursue?"

"Were you able to get the tracker on his vehicle?"

"Absolutely."

"Let him go but have the chopper follow." Pogue jumped to his feet and headed to the back of the warehouse to find Janelle.

"Understood." The team leader stopped him. "Hold on, Doc. We shot two of the guards back there. But there's a third, according to our infrared readings while we were in the rafters. We need to neutralize him before you get closer.

Pogue said, "I heard his conversation with the Santinos." He grabbed his vest where he'd been shot. "They're having a meeting and I know where he's going, but they may change the location. We have to hurry." Pogue scanned the monitors. Only one girl was on the screen now.

"Give my men a second. It looks like you were right. Nick was seriously thinking about shooting you. I'm glad you thought about having us shoot first."

"I didn't want him putting a bullet in my head." Pogue pointed to the monitors. "I don't see her. I can't wait here." He pushed past the man and ran to the rooms in the back of the warehouse. Two agents stood in the hallway with a young girl that wasn't Janelle.

"She was here, Dr. Pogue." An agent exited the dorm room to his right. "In this room."

Pogue burst in and scanned the small bedroom where his daughter had been earlier—the faint scent of her perfume. His heart sank as the adrenaline slowly left his body and reality took its place. He turned to the commander. "Where is she?"

The commander turned to one of his men. "Bring up the outside footage."

The man ran back to the monitors in the cage. Moments later, he returned with the video loaded onto an iPad. He handed it to his boss. "Looks like Gambrel got in his car and drove to the corner of the building where he stopped. There was a scuffle with someone, a door opened, then closed, and they drove off."

"Can you play that slower?" Pogue asked.

"Yes, sir."

The slowed video showed the images at one-fifth speed. When Nick's car reached the corner of the building, Pogue recognized who he believed to be Jacob, Nick's bodyguard. He'd pushed Janelle into the car and jumped in after her. It sped away.

The commander closed the iPad. "You sure we shouldn't pursue, Doc?"

"I don't want him to panic and get my daughter killed."

"All clear in the dorm, Commander." One of the men came from the back of the structure. "One hostage, zero hostiles."

The commander reopened the iPad and showed Pogue another image. "Here's where the car is right now. Looks like they're heading downtown to this area."

"They've changed the meeting location to a different building. That's Nick's place—Connor Banks' financial offices. Why would they take her there, unless they had nowhere else to go?" Pogue said out loud. "They have to decide what to do with my daughter, and I know Marc and C.J. want her out of the country or dead." He turned to the commander. "I need to get to that meeting."

"We can arrange that."

"Just get me close, and I'll walk the last block."

One of the men checked Jamie's blood pressure as she sat on a chair in the hallway. She appeared exhausted, but alert. His heart went out to her. He addressed the commander. "Who is she?"

"Her name is Jamie. We've been looking for her."

Pogue walked over and knelt in front of her as the man finished checking her vital signs.

Jamie offered him a nervous smile. "You're him, aren't you? Janelle's dad."

"I am. Is she okay?"

"She said you'd come." Jamie looked around. "Where is she?"

He swallowed the lump in his throat. "It looks like your guards abandoned you, but hers didn't. They took her."

"Why?"

"They're afraid of me."

She hugged him and sobbed. "It looks like they should be." She leaned back from him and stared into his eyes. "They almost never let us talk, but one of the men—Jacob—did now and then. Your daughter kept me going. Find her."

Pogue stood and turned to the commander. "You heard the lady."

\*\*\*

Pogue walked through the lobby of Nick's building as if he owned it. Direct confrontation was the only way to get inside without risking a bullet through the skull. Nothing covert. Just straight through the front door, unarmed. The uniformed guard at the desk stared at him as he approached. The closer Pogue got, the more concerned the man seemed.

"I'm here for the council meeting with Nick Gambrel. It's in Connor Banks' conference room."

"You're ... I remember you. You've been on the news."

"That's right."

"Mr. Banks isn't—"

"Nick Gambrel is. Make the call."

"I don't believe—"

"Call."

The man dialed a number and spoke. "Dr. Pogue is in the lobby. He says he's here to see Mr. Gambrel."

Pogue tapped his fingers on the counter. He could hear someone speaking on the other end and men approaching from behind.

"Stand in front of that yellow tape so they can see you on the camera." The man pointed to the spot. Pogue moved to his right about a foot.

Within seconds, two men he'd heard reached him. One of them frisked him while the other kept his hand on Pogue's shoulder.

"He's clean," the man said as he finished his search. He turned his attention to the gentleman at the desk, hanging up the phone.

"They want you to bring him up. Both of you."

The men glanced at each other. "Let's go, Dr. Pogue. You should have disappeared when you had the chance."

Each man took one of Pogue's arms and escorted him to the elevators, waiting in silence for the doors to open. They stepped on, and one man slipped a keycard into a reader, punched a four-digit code on the keypad, and pressed the button for the top floor.

The glib elevator music sounded strangely out of place. The doors finally opened to a lobby with an unattended reception area directly across from the elevators. The men ushered him down the corridor to the right, stopping at a room with double doors.

They opened from the inside, exposing a spacious conference room. A semicircular granite table, close to thirty feet long, dominated the room. An oak front, mounted below the granite, appeared to be solid wood. Windows from floor to ceiling bordered the enclosure on two sides, offering a generous view of Chicago's skyline with Lake Michigan in the background.

Pogue stepped in and the doors closed behind him. A guard remained on each side. He scanned his surroundings. Nick, Marc, and C.J. were seated in the center of the room at the top of the curved table. A man shuffling documents perched to the left of C.J. He appeared nervous and avoided eye contact. Robert Savage arrogantly leaned back, rocked in his leather chair to Marc's right, and smirked at Pogue. Another man in a three-piece suit sat next to Savage and solemnly folded his hands in front of him, focusing on a stack of binders on the table.

"God, Pogue." Nick slowly stood. His mouth hung open for a moment. "I thought you were dead. How did you get out of there?"

"Dr. Pogue appears to be back among the living." Marc folded his arms on the table. "Short-lived as it may be. Although I'd wager Mr. Yeager is still quite dead."

"I didn't kill him."

"But he's dead, right?"

"Yeah. He's dead."

Nick set down the folder in his hands. "You didn't answer my question.

How did you get away from those guys at the warehouse?"

"That really doesn't matter."

"Kill him right now or I will." Marc sat straight and placed a hand on his holster.

Pogue turned to Marc and C.J. "This never would have happened if you hadn't kidnapped my daughter. That was a *Santino* move if I'm not mistaken."

Marc stood from twenty feet away and drew his pistol, pointing it at Pogue's head.

Pogue shouted. "Breach!" He dove to the left behind the granite desk as a resounding crash through the doors behind him drew everyone's attention.

When Pogue hit the floor, he heard Nick cursing. He turned to see him duck behind the conference table to avoid the onslaught of firepower that had entered the room. CIA and FBI agents shot both guards near the doors. A man near Pogue fired at the agents and abruptly landed limp next to Pogue. Pogue grabbed the semi-auto pistol from his hand. Several shots from somewhere on the other side of the room brushed past his head.

Savage stood and fired at the agents before taking one to his forehead. He fell hard to the floor.

The man in the three-piece suit huddled at the foot of the table, hugging his knees with his head down. He didn't appear to have a gun—or the desire to be involved.

More bullets whizzed past Pogue. They came from where C.J. and Marc had been. The roar of gunfire deafened him. He peered over the table edge as shards of granite pelted him from bullets striking the tabletop. Blood dripped into his eye from somewhere on his head. He brushed it away.

By the time he spotted C.J., she already had her pistol trained on him. She fired before he could. The bullet grazed his scalp as he shot at her once, causing her to drop behind the cover of granite and oak.

She huddled on the floor, reloading her pistol. When Agent James stood, she turned and fired a single shot at him. James fired back. C.J. slammed against the window and slid slowly onto her right side as a bloody smear formed on the glass behind her.

Pogue spotted Nick trying to pull Savage's body away from a hidden door that appeared to be a panel in the wall behind the conference table. Pogue fired into the door, but Marc took the opportunity to stand and shoot at Pogue, then Flannery. One slug hit Pogue in the side below his vest. Flannery grabbed his arm and took cover.

Pogue winced at the pain in his abdomen while bullets struck the walls around him. He fired into Marc's chest.

Marc fell against the window, clutching the wound and cursing. As he attempted to raise his weapon, Pogue aimed and fired again. Marc's head snapped back. Pink mist appeared behind Marc's head as his limp body fell to the floor.

A searing pain entered Pogue's right chest. He gasped as he turned to see Nick squeezing through the opening behind the desk with a gun in his hand. He disappeared through the door panel. Pogue scrambled over the conference table and with a rush of adrenaline threw Savage's lifeless body out of the way. He pulled the door open. With his pistol in his hand, he hurried toward a light in a room near the end of the dark, narrow corridor. His lungs burned and he felt weak.

He turned the corner into the room and stopped. Nick stood with his back to the windows, his left arm hooked around Janelle's neck, his right hand holding a gun to her temple.

"No!"

"This can't happen, Pogue."

Pogue looked at his daughter. "Janelle."

"Daddy?"

"It's okay, baby. You're going to be fine."

"She's not—you're not. And ... I'm not."

"Let her go. You have me."

"I can't go to jail, Pogue."

"I'll help you. I'll tell them you cooperated."

"I'm Apollyon."

"I know."

Nick shook his head. "When you have nothing to lose, you're capable of anything. You of all people should know that."

Something warm and wet ran down Pogue's skin where he'd been shot. Voices in the corridor near the conference room drew his attention. "Don't come down here!" It was all he could do to shout. The pain—the lack of air. "Stay back."

"You okay, Pogue?" Flannery yelled from the doorway of the hidden corridor.

"He has her." Pogue looked toward Flannery.

When Pogue turned back to Nick, he no longer had the gun pointed at Janelle. It was aimed at Pogue's head.

"I'm sorry, Pogue."

The shot stunned Pogue. The glass behind Nick exploded as blood and brain matter splattered the wall. The gun slipped from Nick's hand. He slid to the floor, a pool of blood forming around him. Pogue grabbed Janelle and pulled her against his chest, holding her tight as Flannery entered the room with his gun still trained on Nick.

"Don't look, Janelle. Keep your eyes closed for me. Okay, sweetie?"

Janelle nodded and sobbed uncontrollably.

Flannery checked Nick's pulse, then holstered his gun and moved to Pogue. "We need to get her out of here, Pogue."

"Give me a minute." He felt Janelle's sobs as her body shook. Taking a deep breath became harder for him every second. Pain gripped him—and weakness.

"You've been hit. Are you aware of that?" Flannery held pressure on the bleeding.

"I'm wearing a vest."

"It went through or around it, and you're losing blood. A lot." Flannery turned to one of the agents. "Tell the chopper to land on the roof. Now!"

Pogue let go of Janelle, knelt, and looked into her tear-filled eyes. "I know someone who is waiting to talk to you." He looked at Flannery, who handed him his phone. Pogue dialed Jenni's number with his blood-soaked hands and handed it back to him.

"Mrs. Pogue? This is Agent Flannery with the CIA. There's someone who wants to talk to you." He handed the phone to Janelle.

When she heard her mother's voice, she began to sob uncontrollably again.

A wave of nausea passed over Pogue. His strength left, his chest burned—but he'd done it. He'd have to pay for this, but he'd done it. Ben would know. Pogue was responsible for what happened today—all of it.

*Is this really it? It's not so bad.*

"The chopper is here."

Pogue heard Flannery's voice, but he couldn't take his eyes off Janelle. Then everything went dark.

# CHAPTER FORTY-SIX

Jenni sat in the waiting room of the ICU. Agent Flannery, Agent James, and Detective Davis were with her.

"I don't know what to say to you men. If it weren't for you, my husband would be dead." She dried her eyes. "But once the syndicate puts everything together they'll come after him and kill him. Won't they?"

"I wanted to talk to you about witness protection. We can relocate you, and no one will find you."

"How would that work?"

"You'd have new identities, and we'd move you to a new location. In this case, perhaps a new country."

"What about the kids' friends and education? What about Bailey's medical practice and our family that lives here in Chicago?"

"That would be the most difficult. Your husband would not be a practicing physician. We'll provide jobs for you. And you'd be alive."

"What would our families be told?"

"We would stage an incident. An accident. That's usually the most effective as far as making an entire family disappear."

Jenni couldn't fathom putting her family through such trauma. "Does Bailey know what you're proposing?"

"He does." Flannery nodded.

"What did he say?"

Flannery clasped his hands. "He refuses to put his family into witness protection. I wanted to appeal to you for that reason."

"Behind his back?"

"No. I told him I would speak with you and share his intentions and my opinion."

"And what are his intentions?"

"Pogue plans to give himself up for his family."

"What? No. No! I can't live with that. There must be another way."

"Witness protection is the best answer."

"But they'd still come after us, wouldn't they?"

"I don't … I honestly don't know. Unfortunately, Ben Gambrel knows the most intimate details of the final event since he got his information from C.J.'s husband, Mr. Franklin, who hid under the table the entire time. He saw the shooting, heard everyone talking, and put the pieces together."

Jenni couldn't think. She forced herself to breathe. "I need to talk to my husband."

Flannery sighed. "That would be a good idea."

Jenni walked to the nurse's station and gained permission to go to Pogue's room. When she walked past the federal marshal and entered the cubicle, he had the news pulled up, listening to a replay of the reunion between Jamie Williams and her family.

"That's what gives all of this meaning, Jenni. Without family we have nothing." He took her hand and looked into her eyes. "We're not doing it. We're not going into witness protection. It won't work anyway. They'll find me. It's what they do. No matter what story the federal marshals come up with, Ben and the Santinos will find me."

She controlled her emotions. She had so many conflicting feelings. And she didn't want to lose the man she loved.

"They're going to kill you, Bailey. You killed their children—an entire generation of cartel children from three families."

Pogue nodded. "If I die then so be it. Think of the girls and military personnel and cops and … everyone that won't die because these so-called *children* are dead. My family survives. It has to be this way."

"Bailey—"

"I believe that Ben Gambrel has a heart. I've seen it. I've felt it. There may be a way through this fire, and I have to try."

"If you're wrong, you die. Let's do the witness protection. We'll make it work somehow. Please … don't do this."

"I have to do the best I can for my family. Talking to Ben *is* the best I can do. If I run, he'll chase me. We'd be looking over our shoulders for the rest of our lives."

She dabbed her eyes with a tissue again. "I pray that God would make a way. If you feel that this is what we should do, then I'm with you. But I don't want to live my life without you. I can't imagine waking up knowing you aren't there anymore."

"And I hope to God we'll grow old together. I have so much to make up for, and I'd love nothing more than a life spent doing just that. I'm so sorry for all I put you and Janelle through. I love you so much, Jenni."

She held him tight. "And I love you."

# CHAPTER FORTY-SEVEN

Jacob pulled up to Navy Pier. Pogue stood from the bench, tossed his empty Starbucks cup into the trashcan, and walked to the car.

"Hello, Jacob."

"Dr. Pogue. Good to see you." He opened the door for him.

Pogue stepped in and rode in silence to the Gambrel mansion. The sun shone brightly off Lake Michigan as a pleasant, brisk breeze reminded him of his love for the city. Jacob pulled through the mansion gates and stopped at the front entrance. He stepped out, opened the door for Pogue, and accompanied him up the marble stairs. They entered the spacious foyer and walked down the long hallway together.

"I'll take you to Mr. Gambrel. He's upstairs in his study."

Pogue followed Jacob up the winding marble staircase. The stark reality he'd probably leave this place alive but die on the streets of Chicago in a day or two had played over and over in his mind for days, but it was for the best—to try—for his family. Jacob stopped outside the study.

"I want you to know that I'm sorry, Dr. Pogue. I helped Nick and shouldn't have. I knew better, but—"

"It's okay, Jacob. Really."

"Thank you, sir."

Jacob opened the door and Pogue entered the study. Ben stood at his desk, facing him when he walked in.

"Come in, Pogue. Please. Take a seat." He motioned to the chairs by the fireplace and walked to meet him. Jacob poured drinks for both men, and Pogue took his as Ben did. When Jacob left the room, he closed the double doors behind him.

Pogue spoke first. "Ben, I know this is not easy for you. I also know it's necessary. Your son—"

Ben held up his hand while looking at the fire in the fireplace. Pogue stopped speaking. Ben sipped his brandy and continued staring at the embers. He finally spoke. "That day … it was a difficult day." His usual booming voice seemed dampened by emotion. Pogue waited.

"I've never been more disappointed in my son. But he was still my son and didn't deserve to die. Even though he"—Ben paused as if carefully choosing his words—"was responsible for the death of his sister, my only daughter—the only person on earth who reminded me of her sweet mother." Ben cleared his throat.

Pogue remained silent.

"I couldn't believe my ears when you placed me on speaker without Nick knowing, and he said what he did about Ginger, along with his plans for the future to destroy me and everything I'd built for our family."

"It was never my intent to—"

"Let me finish."

"Yes, sir."

"I blame Marc and C.J. for putting those thoughts in Nick's head. I'm glad they're dead. Nick didn't devise that plan—at least that's what I choose to believe." Ben took another sip. "To be honest, he didn't have it in him."

The long silence forced Pogue to say something. "I'm very—"

"I loved Nick. I loved Ginger. They both loved you and I understand why. You've touched my heart in a special way. I want you to know that …" He paused and tried to control his emotions. "I wish you were my son."

The lump in Pogue's throat made it difficult to speak. "Thank you, sir."

"I must avenge my son's death. It's the code and everyone knows it, including you. His life, his death, must be avenged."

Pogue lowered his head and swallowed hard. "I do understand. My request is that you spare my family. It is my only request, Mr. Gambrel."

Ben looked at Pogue for the first time since they began talking. "What do you mean?"

"I know that Nick's life must be avenged. I'm responsible for your son's death."

"Yes, it must be avenged, and it's true that you were there. When you placed your phone on speaker in your pocket, I listened to every word—

every word *he* spoke, and every word *you* spoke. You did your best to help him—to save him. Yes, you were there, but you didn't kill him. He did that himself. You could have, and many would have. But you didn't. You tried to save him. You were his friend. I listened while someone else shot you and Nick ran. You could have killed him when you had the chance in the warehouse. I heard him tell you how much you meant to him. And I know he kidnapped your daughter, or at least was party to it. If I had my daughter's kidnapper in front of me and a pistol in my hand, there is no doubt what I would do."

"I don't know what to say."

Ben shook his head and looked him in the eye. "It wasn't your fault."

"I'm so sorry for all of this."

Ben stood. "My life has rarely been spared, but it was recently by a man who had the drop on me in my own bedroom. I respect life. I love life." He walked to the window and looked down at his chopper on the pad. "The same man tried to save my daughter's life. Circumstances beyond his control and mine took her from me. That same man tried to save my son, but he wouldn't have it. He insisted on dying. I don't know why, but I heard him condemn himself with my own ears. Someone must pay, but it won't be you." He turned back to Pogue. "I'll have to live with this for the rest of my life. I drove Nick to his fate. I'm the one who had the power to do so and the ability to stop it."

Ben walked to Pogue. "I'm told that all charges against me were dropped on the recommendations of the CIA and FBI, with whom I have *apparently* cooperated fully from the beginning." Ben tilted his head. "You wouldn't know anything about that, would you, son?"

Before Pogue could respond, Ben continued. "I faced life in prison if any of the trafficking or espionage charges stuck. But you told the FBI and CIA that I had no knowledge of any such dealings even though they occurred on my property." Ben stared at him. "Why would you do that?"

"Because it was true. I knew from Nick that you were kept in the dark intentionally. He and Marc, and especially C.J., insisted on it. I told the authorities the truth."

Ben smiled faintly. "You told them and they believed you—even Detective Davis dropping the obstruction charges? No inquiry? No inquest?"

Pogue sighed. "You know who I am. I won't insult your intelligence.

The fact is, you didn't know about Apollyon and their dealings or of my daughter's kidnapping. I told them the absolute truth."

Ben shook his head slowly.

"You weren't guilty of any of this, Ben."

Ben offered Pogue his hand. "Tell your family I'm sorry for inconveniencing them by taking your time today. Please—keep in touch. I mean that. And if you decide you'd still consider being our concierge doctor, the offer is open."

Pogue placed his glass on the table. "I appreciate that very much. Thank you."

"And may I call on you from time to time, as a friend?"

"It would be an honor, sir."

Ben smiled. "You'll always be welcome in my home. If you need anything, anything at all, just call that number."

"Regarding the Santinos—"

"As far as they are concerned, Victor Santino knows that the CIA took his son and daughter down for crimes against the state."

"Victor doesn't know?"

"Victor will never know. You did what I wanted to do. What I couldn't do. It will never fall on you. I give you my word."

"Thank you again, Ben."

The men shook hands.

As Pogue left, he stood on the stairs of the Gambrel mansion, admiring the beauty surrounding him. The brisk air from Lake Michigan chilled his skin, and blue skies spanned the horizon. He had more time, another day—many more days with his family. He'd be grateful for the rest of his life. Right now, it was time to go home. He had a gazebo to build.

### THE END